Simon Seeker

A Novel

FRANK WALLACE

SIMON SEEKER
A NOVEL

iUniverse books may be ordered through booksellers or by contacting:

iUniverse
1663 Liberty Drive
Bloomington, IN 47403
www.iuniverse.com
1-800-Authors (1-800-288-4677)

Because of the dynamic nature of the Internet, any web addresses or links contained in this book may have changed since publication and may no longer be valid. The views expressed in this work are solely those of the author and do not necessarily reflect the views of the publisher, and the publisher hereby disclaims any responsibility for them.

Any people depicted in stock imagery provided by Getty Images are models, and such images are being used for illustrative purposes only.
Certain stock imagery © Getty Images.

ISBN: 978-1-5320-7204-8 (sc)
ISBN: 978-1-5320-7205-5 (hc)
ISBN: 978-1-5320-7206-2 (e)

Library of Congress Control Number: 2019903559

Print information available on the last page.

iUniverse rev. date: 05/08/2019

The NATURALIST is a civilized hunter. He goes alone into a field or woodland and closes his mind to everything but that time and place, so that life around him presses in on all the senses and small details grow in significance... His mind becomes unfocused, it focuses on everything, no longer directed toward any ordinary task or social pleasantry. He measures the antic darting of midges in a conical mating swarm, the slant of sunlight by which they are best seen, the precise molding of mosses and lichens on the tree trunk on which they spasmodically alight. His eye travels up the trunk to the first branch and out to a spray of twigs and leaves and back, searching for some irregularity of shape or movement of a few millimeters that might betray an animal in hiding. He listens for any sound that breaks the lengthy spells of silence. The hunter-in-naturalist knows that he does not know what is going to happen.

Edward O. Wilson

Chapter 1

Simon

He had done as instructed: start the fire in the basement, open all of the windows and prop the cellar door with a kitchen chair. Then he had gone a last time to his father's room and stood by the bed. A suggestion of a smile shaped the man's lips. Simon knelt by the side of the bed and laid his head in the crook of his father's arm. Then he stood, one hand on his father's chest. He looked down. Smoke was flowing quietly around his feet. He pulled the covers up over his father's head and walked into the hall.

His backpack sat upon the kitchen table. Alongside it, the list he had composed over the past weeks. More had been crossed out than remained. A pair of socks, underwear, a pair of jeans, a light rain jacket, a comb and toothbrush, a bottle of water, a half dozen eggs he had collected and boiled the night before. He lifted his pack, opened the door, and stepped into the forgiving freshness of early morning.

Not everything would be gone when he returned, if he returned. There was his baleout; one of his father's word tricks. Simon had built it in the barn's loft with bales of hay. It was a place where he went sometimes to be alone. In it his books, his black and white decipherings of nature's coded surfaces; the shed antlers of deer and moose, grotesqueries of cankered tree limbs, artist's fungus upon which he had carved landscapes, nests and chrysalises, insects and small mammals preserved and carefully labeled in glass jars. Over the past months he had spent more and more time there, not only to avoid watching his father's losing battle with cancer, but to prepare for a future, adding things from his bedroom and the house: clothing, pictures, books, things weighted with almost twelve years of memories.

He opened the pens. The sheep, pigs, and goats paid little attention. Empress and Bucephalus, Belgian workhorses, his closest four-legged friends, snuffled and nuzzled as he led them out. He had told them what was going to happen and believed that in some way they understood. The telling had helped him as well, giving shape and space to what had raced so mercilessly to its end.

He walked past the apple trees in blossom, the vegetable garden green with promise, and took the steep path to the hillside aerie where he sometimes slept. It was a moonless night, but Simon had learned to find his way in the dark, parsing shadow from substance. He lay back, his head on his pack, and looked up at the stars. Orion, his chosen guardian, ascendant, bright-belted, his sword drawn, watched.

He sat up. There was a glow now from the windows in the kitchen, and as he watched it became a glitter. Reds and yellows, the first lick of flame up the back of the house in a teasing and insistent embrace. Up to this point he had done as his father had instructed. But now he would make his own decisions. He would not stay and wait for the forest service. He would not call Roger who was now his guardian. He would not go to live at the Wind Lake School as his father and Roger had many years earlier. The people he knew were in books, many of them on their own, making their way among strangers as now he must. Boys forever trapped between covers. He felt their restlessness. He wanted to be out in the real world with real people. And maybe he could find his grandparents. Somewhere called Boston where Edward Wilson and the Red Sox lived.

Telling his father of his plan would have upset him. Simon wasn't sure what happened to worries when a person died. You could deal with troubles over time. He had learned that. But what if there wasn't time? Where did the troubles go?

Now flames had enveloped entire walls of the house and lit the night with conflagration. Except for an incongruously friendly crackle it was a silent spectacle, unseen by anyone but Simon, hushed by night. Only the flames moved, now reaching the eaves, making the night suddenly chill. Simon watched as the roof, bursting like a pod of milkweed, flung red seeds into the night, one of them a soul.

With the farm as his teacher he knew a good deal about the impermanence of things. He had seen life and death in the seasons and among the animals for which he cared. His father had added to this natural instruction a context of meaning, a simple transcendentalism as perfect as a hen's egg, as invisible as stardust and as vast as the night sky. Simon heard the *chop chop* of a helicopter in the distance. He shouldered his pack and walked into the woods.

He took the trail he had often used in search of wild mushrooms. One day he had found Barker, their golden retriever, his neck torn open by a hunter's trap, his body rigid and cold. Simon had felt it was an omen. There were such things, like the sounds the wind made sometimes at night, the shape of a root vegetable, or the fear he saw in the eyes of animals. He had buried Barker and marked the grave with a circle of stones. Now he knelt by them, removing the mat of twigs and leaves. Something would grow here in time, he thought. Something of Barker would carry on. He looked again at the stars, intermittent now among the branches of trees, and took a bearing.

There had been lots of sudden advice these last weeks on how to get along in the outside world. *Feed people's egos and they will fill your stomach*, his father had instructed. *Let them make you up and you will make out well. People love to talk about themselves.*

Simon had traveled with Ulysses, Alexander, and Huckleberry Finn. He knew somewhat the habits of the human heart. His cosmology was a hodge-podge of Heraclitus, Planck, and Pullman. He believed absolutely in parallel universes. He had grown up in one.

The forest between the farm and the road was as densely spun as a chrysalis. The pine beetle and the spruce budworm had woven this web with their cyclic devastations, littering the forest floor with a tangle of spidered roots and ancient trunks. Where sunlight penetrated, a tumult of seedlings competed for the space. Simon made his way slowly, reaching the highway at 4:15am. Kneeling briefly he re-tied a shoelace, adjusted his pack, and set off down the road.

Chapter 2

Tom

By the time Tom Bewick arrived at Spruce Valley Farm things were under control. The Forest Service helicopter sat heavily in an adjacent field. A tanker was parked in the drive, its intake hose extended down to the pond. A pungent mist shrouded the morning sun. Nothing remained of the farmhouse but a pile of smoldering timbers. Goats grazed along the ditch. A muscular Belgian workhorse approached as Tom walked up the drive. He stopped, the habit of a farm boy. The stallion muzzled his neck. He saw the fire warden talking with a couple of the firefighters and recognized her. It was Ellen Dawson, the ranger at Long Lake. She had given a talk on forest management to his senior high school class. Jody, her daughter, had been his classmate.

"Mrs. Dawson?"

She turned, smiled, finished her conversation with the two men and approached.

"I'm Tom Bewick," he said, extending his hand. "From Jody's class."

"Paul and Marnie's son. You were in the senior play."

"Not my best thing."

"You were very good," Jody said. "You were thinking about a career." She stepped back and looked at him more carefully. He was about five foot six, she guessed. Quite handsome with black hair and brows, casually but cleanly dressed in jeans and a blue short-sleeved shirt with a loon on the pocket. "Are you a lover of loons?"

He looked puzzled. She pointed to his shirt. He laughed. "Right. My father gave it to me. Yes, we had loons on a pond near our house. I loved them. He bought me this shirt when I was in high school."

"I love 'em too. They can sing you to sleep." She was quiet for a moment and then back to business. "So what happened to the acting career?"

"Yeah, well. My parents thought it was a dumb idea. You know, starving actors and all that."

"Hey, you don't need to make a decision for a while. Let's see, you'd be a senior in college now. You're at Orono, right?"

"Right, but I'm taking a year off. I'll be a senior next fall. I'm working at *The Washington County Star*."

"Well, I guess that can be a good thing."

"I hope it will be. So here I am. Can I ask you a few questions?"

"Sure thing."

Tom took out his note pad and removed the cap from his Pilot pen. "So what's the story here?"

"Fire started about four this morning, probably in the basement. Windows must've been open. Roof seems to have just blown off. It's all over the place."

"Anybody inside?"

"We won't know that for a while for sure, but most probably the owner, Larin Seeker. Nobody knows much about him. A recluse. Didn't like visitors. Moved here about thirteen years ago. Lived alone. His car is over in the shed by the barn. Old Land Rover."

"I saw the signs as I drove in. KEEP OUT. PRIVATE LAND. VISITORS NOT WELCOME. NO SOLICITING. Pretty weird."

"I came here once," Dawson said. "It was hurricane Bob. When was that? Nine or ten years ago? I was trying to get word to the outlying farms."

"You turned around?"

"I did. Seemed to me he'd sooner put up with a hurricane than a fire warden."

"Seeker." Tom repeated the name. "Don't think I've ever run into that name before. Doesn't fit very well, does it?"

"Fit?"

"Well, you know. A recluse. Not the kind of guy to seek people out."

"There you go! You can put that in your story." She smiled.

"So you assume he was inside the house."

"Seems likely. Jerry spotted the blaze from the fire tower and the chopper got here in about fifteen minutes, but even by then it was all over."

Several chickens wandered around their feet as they talked, scratching for grubs, indifferent to the devastation.

"What's going to happen to the animals?" he asked.

"I guess they'll just have to forage for a few days until someone figures out who owns this place."

"Who's gonna do that?"

"I suppose Elias will call in the State Troopers. It's not the kind of thing a game warden deals with very often. I don't think Elias would know where to start."

"Any idea how the fire started?"

"Could have been anything. Oily rags in the cellar. Mouse gnawing an electric cord."

"He had electricity? I didn't see any wires coming in."

"Generator. Out in the shed."

It appeared to be a pretty uninteresting story. Still, there wasn't that much else going on in the county. He might get his byline on page one. "I suppose it could have been arson," he suggested.

"What gives you that notion?" she asked.

"Well, it would make a better story," Tom said, grinning.

Mrs. Dawson laughed. "OK, draw me a picture."

"There's this hermit living up on this farm. Nobody knows anything about him, so there are all these stories. Like he's a miser and he has money hidden all over the house. Some pulp cutter gets thinking about it and decides to check things out. He shows up and threatens the guy. He puts up a fight. The pulp cutter kills him. He didn't mean to. And he gets mad because he can't find the money so he starts throwing things around and tearing the place apart. He searches the out-buildings, letting all the animals out..."

"You're wasting your talent on the newspaper, Tom. You should be writing thrillers. So he burns the house down in order to hide the crime. Right?"

"Right."

"Well, you've got a couple of problems. First, nothing has been disturbed in any of the outbuildings. They're all neat as a pin. Second, the animals. It's standard practice to let them out when buildings are adjacent to a fire site, just in case it spreads. I expect Bob did that when he landed the chopper. Sorry to ruin your story, but—" Ellen's two-way radiophone crackled. She picked it up and pressed the button. "Dawson. Right...yeah, we're about ready to close up. We need to get someone out here to keep an eye on things for a while. Maybe Martin."

Tom tapped her on the shoulder. "Mrs. Dawson?"

She turned to him. "Me," he said. "I'll stay. I'd like to look around. I've got a sleeping bag in my truck."

"Hold on a minute," she said, lowering the phone. "You sure about that?"

"Yeah. I'd like to. I can work on my story."

She raised the phone and pushed the button again. "Never mind about that. I've got someone here...right...right...OK. In about an hour." Ellen hooked the phone back onto her belt. "Well, you are a serious reporter, Tom," she said with an approving nod. She smiled. "I'm impressed. And by the way, you can call me Ellen."

"Thanks. So how's Jody? I haven't seen her since graduation."

"She's fine. In her senior year at Bates. Majoring in natural science. I guess that's what they call it. She wants to be an environmentalist."

"Good for her."

"Yes, she seems pretty focused. That's good." Ellen thought for a moment, then looked up and smiled. "Like her friend Tom. I'll tell her about our conversation."

"Thanks. I hope to see her again before too long."

"Great." Ellen turned and looked at the devastation once again. Then she unclipped the radiophone from her belt and handed it to Tom.

"Here, you keep this. Just in case. I've got another one in the truck."

"I've got my cell."

"Won't do you any good out here."

"Right." Tom examined the device. "I've never used one of these."

"Just push that button on the side there and say, 'Hey Ellen, turn off the TV.'"

"All I know is 10-4. That comes at the end, right?"

"Right. Nothing much to worry about. There's nothing left to burn. Still you never know what's down in a cellar. If you see a flare-up, give me a call. Just don't wake me if a bear nuzzles your toes in the middle of the night." Ellen smiled and turned to the men who were packing up the truck. Tom walked to the barn.

Ellen had certainly been right about the owner. The barn was neat as a pin. The animal stalls had been recently cleaned and bedded with fresh shavings, the floor swept. The tack room was arranged like a small museum. On one side a dispensary, stocked with salves, ointments, and various animal nostrums. A toolbox sat on the windowsill. There were two saddles resting on sawhorses. Nice but not elegant. Even more interesting than the saddles were the boots that sat beneath them. Two pair. He picked one up and examined it. Small. A woman's, perhaps. *A woman unknown to the world. The dark lady.* Things were looking up.

The story wouldn't be in the fire. Ellen was probably right about that. Not in the history of the place either, unless maybe a follow-up. No, it would be the man, the recluse, the seeker who wasn't one, and his lady-friend. He'd have to go into Machias tomorrow. See Mary Potter at the town office. Find out about Mr. Seeker. Just because you're a recluse doesn't mean you don't have to pay taxes.

He put the boot back against the wall precisely where he had found it. You couldn't think of it as a crime scene, but still it was better not to disturb things. At least not until after the State Police had had their look around.

The helicopter lifted from the field. He looked up. The pilot waved. Tom waved back. The chopper tipped and turned up the valley.

Tom explored the remaining buildings. The chicken coop looked as though it might have been prepared for a photo shoot. The roosts had been scraped clean, the floor swept and strewn with sawdust. Even the windows had been washed.

He walked back to his truck, took a yellow pad out from behind the driver's seat and returned to the barn. Pulling a bale of hay out into the sun, he sat down and began to write.

"At approximately 4:00 a.m. on June 17, the fire warden at Long Lake received an alert from the watchtower on Moose Mountain. Smoke was rising in Spruce Valley. Twenty minutes later, Ranger Ellen Dawson and helicopter pilot Ronnie Thibodeau were at the scene of the blaze. The 200-year-old farmhouse…" *Two hundred? NOTE: check age of house at town office* "…at Spruce Valley was ablaze. They were able to contain the fire until the pump truck arrived 20 minutes later to extinguish it. It is unlikely that the farm's reclusive owner…"

Tom took out his note pad to check the first name. Larin.

"…Larin Seeker, survived the fire, the cause of which has not yet been determined. His vehicle was found in the shed." *Add something about the history of the farm. Maybe a sidebar about modern day fire-fighting.* The helicopter. He'd read something recently about fatalities in fire-fighting, how the forest service gets the old planes and how often they crash. That would take some back-grounding. He made a note. "Check high-risk lines of work. Mention the dark lady or not?" *Better not. Not yet anyway.* Still, that's where the story would be. The recluse and his lady friend. What he needed now was more about Larin Seeker and the history of the farm. He walked back to his truck and tossed the note pad onto the passenger seat. There had to be records of some sort at the town office.

Chapter 3

Ben

Once you cross into Maine at Calais, the fastest route between St. Stephen and Boston is Route 9, which runs west through Washington County. It was always a sentimental journey for Ben Pyle. He had been born here, ridden his bicycle on this same road as a child. Until his parents died in an automobile accident. It was just before his tenth birthday. They had gone into town to get his present. He had never found out what it was. Then Social Services had taken him away.

Now he was bound for Boston, driving a refrigerated 16-wheeler loaded with mussels from Prince Edward Island. He made the trip once a week. Up on a Thursday, back to Boston, leaving pre-dawn on Friday.

Ben enjoyed the solitude of an untraveled road. It was a good time to think and to plan. You had to plan. Good things didn't just happen. You had to make a spot for them, open yourself to new experience. Most of the people he knew—not including Rosie—thought they had the world all figured out. Their opinions were like their tattoos: they'd made up their minds and then they were stuck with them. The cabs of their trucks were all the world they wanted. Ben wanted more.

He marked off the miles between St. Stephen and Bangor with a few familiar landmarks—nothing that most drivers would notice, but things that he recognized for the difference they made in the forest landscape. Curtis Bog, for example, a sudden clearing where nothing grew except a few stunted tamaracks. Everything in miniature, a slight mist, no signs of life; not even birds, like it was somehow off-limits. It was the kind of place extra-terrestrials might choose to land. Ben had seen that movie with Richard Dreyfus. Dreyfus was just a Joe, nobody special. But he had an open mind. He was ready for something to happen and it did.

One morning Ben had seen lights out on the bog. Very faint. He'd stopped his rig, got down, and crossed the road. The lights seemed to brighten and dim. Or perhaps it was just the mist. He could not have said what it was about Curtis Bog that revived the stunted hopefulness of his youth. It was caught in time, a scattering of trees no larger than children, standing in a field, expectant, quiet. Empty, yet filled with unaccountable promise.

This is where the visitors would arrive, here in this remote and silent openness. It had been intended that he should drive this route. One day they would make themselves known, acknowledge him. When he was deserving, if that was the word. They would know; they would have watched for years. He would see it in their eyes. Such immediate and deep understanding. Then he would understand, too: who he was, what he was meant to do. It was not something he could have explained.

The stop had now become a ritual, a break in the long drive from Charlottetown to Bangor, where he would pause to have breakfast at Hauler's Truck Stop. Now he drove the rig onto the breakdown lane, turned off the headlights and sat there for a moment as the engine idled patiently. Then he got down and crossed the road. Even without a moon he could see the bog clearly, the little trees soaking up the starlight.

He reached for the pack of cigarettes in his breast pocket and stopped. They were as stale as last week's news. He hadn't smoked for over a month. A shortness of breath one morning, his fiftieth birthday. No accident. A warning. He carried the pack as a reminder and a test of his resolution.

You couldn't be casual about things like that. You had to stay sharp. You had to look temptation right in the eye and smile. He had bought a book on being all that you can be. It wasn't just an opportunity; it was an obligation. He thought of how few friends he had, how no one he knew would have stood here, being alone with himself. How loud the world was. How loud people were.

He heard a sound and turned.

A small boy stood several feet away from him, his attention, as Ben's had been a second before, focused on Curtis Bog. A young boy, too young to be out here on his own at this time of day. And he wore a backpack.

Ben opened his mouth to speak but didn't. He looked back at the bog. *Possible, but not probable.* The expression came to him like a fragrance from the still grasses. He hadn't thought of it in years. His father had taken him to a movie in Machias about a flying saucer landing in a city. It was his first encounter with an alien, a man with a robot who stopped time. *Could this really happen?* he had asked his father as they left the theater. *Possible but not probable*, his father had replied. Ben had thought about that for months. Possible but not probable. It was the only movie they had seen together and one of only two things he remembered his father having said to him alone. Possible but not at all probable that a boy should be standing not ten feet away from him in the middle of nowhere before sunrise. But then… He cleared his throat.

"Pretty amazing," he said.

The boy turned. He couldn't have been more than ten. A Red Sox baseball cap topped his red hair. They exchanged smiles. Ben nodded towards the bog. "It's like out of a story. Everything in miniature. Amazing."

The boy nodded. "Do you know why the trees are so small?"

"No," Ben replied. "I've wondered about that."

"It's because of the moss. It's too thick. It uses up all the nutrients and there's nothing left for the trees."

"Moss."

"Sphagnum moss. It's floating on water. But it's so thick a moose can walk on it."

"Well, would you ever."

"Would I ever what?"

The boy's brows were slightly wrinkled, a look of concentrated concern tightening his mouth. It was becoming more and more plausible that he might be an alien after all. Ben checked a smile and attempted an expression of respect.

"I'm sorry. It's a manner of speaking. I've never stopped to think what it means. It's what you say when you hear about something very unusual. Like 'Can you believe that?'"

"It's true."

"Oh, I believe you. I do believe you."

Simon had made a mental notebook from his readings. Heraclitus said that an open-eyed smile was like opening a door and inviting people in. He opened his eyes wide and smiled. "What's in your truck?"

"Mussels. Prince Edward Island mussels on their way to Boston."

"My grandmother lives in Boston. Would you like a hardboiled egg?"

"A hard-boiled egg."

"I boiled them last night."

Simon studied his pack. The man had repeated the word *moss*. Now it was *hard-boiled egg*. Roger did that sometimes. It was a way of gaining time, his father had explained. If you didn't know what to say, you repeated what the other person had said. That was when he had learned the word *hiatus*. When a conversation paused, that was a hiatus.

"They're very good," Simon said. "We have Dominiques." He looked at the ground, waiting to hear the man speak.

"Well, why not? What better way to start the day than with a freshly boiled egg?"

Simon held it out. His hand was small; the egg filled the better part of it. Ben accepted it, admired it, nodding for no reason he could put a name to, then very gently cracked it on his belt buckle. He peeled it.

"Dominiques. Don't believe I've ever seen one. French, are they?"

"No. They are American."

"Rhode Island Reds is what we had."

"They are very nice too. But not as highly-developed."

"Highly-developed."

A third time, Simon noted. This would take some getting used to. Maybe he should try it. But not now, not yet. There were more important things. "Dominique hens are very maternal. More than most fowl. They make good friends. You can tell stuff to them and they stand right there, listening. Most hens just get on with things. And the roosters are very protective. They kill intruders. Like snakes. I've seen one with a garter snake in his mouth. He banged it against a cinder block."

Ben nodded encouragement as the boy spoke. It was fascinating to watch him. He showed no sign of surprise or concern at Ben's presence. Almost as if he were used to meeting people here. He met Ben's eyes only briefly, almost fleetingly, directing his gaze first to one side and then the other, as if to other listeners. Ben took a bite of the egg. He closed his eyes. "Mmmmmmmmmmmm, good," he said, smiling. Now their eyes locked.

"I forgot the salt."

"Not a problem. You gonna have one?"

"Later."

Ben finished the egg and licked the tips of his fingers. "Well, that hit the spot." He looked back at the bog. The landscape glowed in starlight. "Camp out last night did you?" he asked, pointing to Simon's pack.

"No. I walked out this morning."

"It's worth the trip, isn't it?" Ben said, looking back at Curtis Bog. "I lived back up the road when I was your age. About fifty miles back. Never knew about Curtis Bog back then. So what's your name?"

"Simon."

"Mine's Ben." He held out his hand.

"Pleased to meet you, Ben," Simon said, hesitating for a second, then taking Ben's hand and pumping it up and down three times. "Short for Benjamin, right?"

"You got it. Benjamin Pyle. That's Pyle with a Y." Ben winked. Simon winked back and then looked up for assurance that he had winked well. *Boys don't wink*, Ben thought. Had he ever seen a boy wink? Not that he could remember. It was a sort of signature. *Interesting.*

"So what's your last name, Simon?"

"Seeker."

"Seeker?"

Simon nodded.

"Simon Seeker! Now that's a name out of an adventure story. Are you an adventurer, Simon?"

"I'd like to be."

"So I say to you, ask, and it will be given to you; seek, and you will find; knock, and it will be opened to you."

"Is that from the Bible?" Simon asked.

"Right."

"You know it pretty well."

"It wasn't my choice."

"What do you mean?"

Ben laughed. "That's a long story, Simon. And not one that you'd enjoy hearing." A faint line of red was beginning to etch the horizon. He looked at his watch. Ten past five. "Well, Simon Seeker, I've got a load of mussels to deliver. Much as I have enjoyed our conversation, I need to get back on the road."

"What about your story?"

"Come again?"

Come again? This was going to be more difficult than he had imagined. Ben used words in ways all his own. The best thing was just to move on, to pretend that he hadn't heard.

"You said it was a long story. I like to hear stories." People love to tell their stories, his father had explained. If you want people to like you, be a listener. When you listen, you become a part of their story. "You could tell it to me on the way to Boston."

"On the way to Boston."

"That's where I'm going. I'm going to stay with my grandmother."

"Wait a minute. You're telling me that your parents sent you out to the highway to hitch a ride to Boston?"

"My father did. He had to go away. It was very sudden."

"And your mother?"

"I don't have a mother. I mean one who lives here. She lives in Paris. She's a singer."

"Paris, France?"

"I think so. Is there another one?"

"Well there's a Paris in Maine. Northwest of Portland. But I don't think they have any night clubs. How old are you, Simon?"

"Almost thirteen. But I'm very resourceful. I can look out for myself."

"Is your grandmother expecting you?"

Ben was a very nice person. Much better than he had dared to hope for. It felt wrong to tell him fibs. He crossed his fingers and continued. "Yes." He uncrossed his fingers. "It's OK, Ben. Someone will come along. You don't have to give me a ride." He picked up his pack and turned toward the highway.

"Hold on there."

Simon stopped without turning. He knew he couldn't speak right then. He had been so sure of himself. But this was not the world in his books. This is why his father had wanted him to go to that school. *Small steps*, he had said. *One at a time.* But he hadn't listened. He wanted the whole world at once. Simon poked at a stone with his toe, moved it into line with three others.

Ben looked out at the bog, brightening now in the first glow of morning. What was that saying? Be careful what you wish for; you just may get it. *You wanted an alien? No, get serious.* Leaving him here to be picked up by some pervert was not a choice he could make. A smile caught him by surprise. He stroked his beard. It wasn't really so complicated. The kid needed a ride to his grandmother's house.

Chapter 4

Simon
and Ben

Ben put his boot on the throttle and the truck climbed back onto the tarmac. Simon closed his eyes and saw again the bright explosion of flame as the roof had lifted from the farmhouse. The truck accelerated, moving seamlessly from one speed to the next. Simon counted. Two, three, four. A deer emerged from the side of the road, turned, transfixed for a moment by the truck's headlights. Then it turned and darted back into the dark forest. Five, six, seven. Simon watched the road.

"A penny for your thoughts," Ben said. When was the last time he had used that expression? It was his mother's.

"Only a penny?"

"Sorry. It's another one of my parents' expressions. Just wondering what you're thinking about."

"Oh. I was just thinking about Bucephalus."

"Who's that?"

"One of our two Belgians."

"Horses."

"Yes. I told him that there would be someone there to look after him and Empress."

"Do you talk to him a lot?"

"Pretty much. He's my best friend."

"It's hard to say goodbye to a best friend. How did he take it?"

"I told him I'd be back. I think he understood."

"Are you a horse whisperer?" Ben asked, turning his head. He was smiling.

"What's that?"

"A person who can communicate with horses."

"A horse whisperer," Simon repeated, trying out the technique. "Maybe. A little bit. Are you a horse whisperer, Ben?"

"I'm afraid not. I have a hard enough time with people."

"You talked with me."

"Well, sure."

"I'm a person."

"You are quite a remarkable person, Simon."

"Why?"

Ben thought for a moment and smiled. "Well how many people offer you a hard-boiled egg at 4:30 in the morning?"

"Would you like another one?"

"Not right now, Simon. In about an hour we're gonna have some breakfast. Let's save the eggs for later."

"Ben."

"Simon."

"Are you going to tell me your story?"

"My story?"

"The long one."

"Where to begin?"

"Well, you could start with why you are a truck driver. And why you know things from the Bible. Then you might think of other things."

"Why I'm driving this truck? I ask myself that same question sometimes. I guess it's because one day about twenty years ago a fellow I knew got laid up with a bum knee and had this load of mussels that he needed to get to Boston."

"And you drove the truck."

"I did. I'd been working with a construction company, hauling equipment from one place to another. I could handle a semi."

"What's a semi?"

"You're riding in one. Well, not really. It's behind us. A semi-trailer."

"Why is it called a semi?"

"Why is it called a semi? Well I'll be...darned. I don't have the foggiest idea. Sure, it's a trailer. But why a semi-trailer? What would a non semi-trailer look like? Good question. Good question, Simon. Have to look into that."

"How long have you been a truck driver?"

"Twenty-three years? No, more like twenty-five or twenty-six. Anyway..." Ben heard the sound of his own voice over that of the engine, heard his words, his story. The cab was a place where he never spoke, except maybe to swear at another driver. It was a thing you had to be careful about. A habit you could get into. Now and then he sang along with the station he was tuned to, or the CD in the player, if he was in the right mood. But not talking. That would have been too weird. And yet now. Stuff he hadn't thought about for years; attic stuff, cobwebbed in the dark. He forced a laugh to clear his head.

"I never lived on a farm but there was a time when I was about your age when my dad decided to fill up the old henhouse out back with some chickens and ducks and two geese. Mr. and Mrs. Gladstone, I named them. They'd follow me around. Them and the ducks. Single file. Mr. Gladstone in the lead, squawking his head off. Then I'd pick peas from the garden and sit on the lawn shelling them. Mr. and Mrs. Gladstone would try to get the peas out of my hand before I could get them into the bucket. They were something else. I felt like the Pied Piper. Of course there was goose shit everywhere. Loose as a goose, they say." For a second he was there again: a woman's voice singing "Barbry Allen," the sound of plates being stacked, of water running in the sink.

"Geese are good talkers," Simon said.

"That's the truth," Ben agreed. "I can see Mr. Gladstone, head up, yammering the whole time. The ducks quieter, sort of mumbling to one another. Even the roosters fell into line. No cock-a-doodle-doos when Mr. Gladstone was in charge. And the hens. Gossiping like a bunch of old ladies."

"Did you talk to Mr. Gladstone?"

"Oh, you bet. I'd honk back at him and he'd wag his head like…what? Like he understood me. Like he was telling me to get on with the shelling and stop gabbing." Ben glanced over at Simon who was looking straight ahead at the empty road. The boy was thinking. He was, for the moment, someplace else. Ben waited. The sun was up now, behind them, lifting the darkness from the forest, the black from the highway. *How could a father send his kid out to hitch a ride?* There had to be more to the story. Later. Simon, Simon Seeker. He could see Rosie shaking her head. *Whatever possessed you?* she'd be saying. No, she wouldn't. She'd never know. Simon would be with his grandmother and the subject would never come up. Over and out.

"Ben?"

"Yes, Simon."

"What was it like for you when you were a kid?"

"It was OK until my parents died."

"When was that?"

"When I was ten."

"I'm very sorry, Ben."

"It was an automobile accident."

Simon waited. He wasn't good at waiting. His father had told him that. He'd ask a question and before his father could answer, he'd be asking another one, or just chattering. *Whenever you're ready*, his father would say, smiling. He saw the smile right then as if it were on the windshield. He felt his throat tighten. He closed his eyes and breathed in the smells of the truck cab. He couldn't have named them. They were new. Like everything else. At last, Ben spoke.

"That was a long time ago," he said.

"Did they teach you about the Bible?"

"No, that was my foster parents."

Simon knew the word "foster." To nurture, to encourage growth. But didn't all parents do that? "What's a foster parent?" he asked.

"When the state gets hold of an orphan, they put him in a home and pay people to take care of him."

"Were they bad people?"

"Not really. I think they wanted to do the right thing."

Ben spoke in a way that reminded Simon of his father. The words came a little faster, as if they were impatient to be on their way. He smiled and waited a moment, then said, "Oliver Twist went to a workhouse."

"My goodness," Ben said with obvious relief. "Oliver Twist! What a great story."

"He didn't have religion either. They made him learn it."

"They sure did."

"Like your foster parents?"

Ben didn't respond. Simon realized he should have left religion alone, eager as he was to learn more. It wasn't a subject his father liked to discuss. "My father didn't like to talk about religion."

Ben looked over at him with an expression of sudden concern. "Didn't?"

Simon realized his mistake. "Well, I haven't asked him for a long time. I mean he didn't answer back when I was asking him." He smiled. Hoping it had worked.

Ben reached over and patted him on the shoulder. "Well, let me see if I can jump that hurdle." He laughed.

"What hurdle?"

"Oh, it's another silly expression. It means get over an obstacle."

"Like talking about religion," Simon said. "It's OK. You don't have to."

"No, I want to." He cleared his throat and straightened himself a little in his seat. "My foster parents were religious."

"They taught you about the Bible," Simon said in an encouraging voice he had learned from his father but never had much chance to use.

"They did. But I didn't like it." Ben laughed in reassuring way. Simon felt reassured that he was doing OK for his part. "I was full of the devil. And it was their responsibility to get it out of me."

Simon quickly understood why the subject was not one of Ben's favorites. "They hurt you, didn't they, Ben."

"Yes, Simon. They hurt me."

"What did you do?"

"I ran away."

"Did they bring you back?"

"They did, Simon."

"I'm sorry, Ben."

"Thanks, Simon. So what do you believe in?"

"What do I believe in?" Simon thought for a moment, looking out as the road raced by. "Providence," he said.

"Providence," Ben repeated thoughtfully.

"There is a special providence in the fall of a sparrow."

"The fall of a sparrow," Ben repeated slowly. "Is that from the Bible?"

"No, it's from a play that my dad and I read together. It's true. Everything happens for a reason. We can't see far enough ahead or around us to know what that reason is, but it's there."

"Like our meeting at the bog?"

"Yes."

"Providence in the fall of a sparrow. I like it. So your Dad believed that things happen for a reason. Is that right?"

"Yes. But we never know the reason. All we know is that when a sparrow dies, it doesn't disappear. It becomes compost. Then it becomes dust. Then stardust."

Simon turned and looked out his side window. Neither said anything for a minute and then Ben said, "Stardust."

"Stardust and compost. There's a song about that, you know."

"Can you sing it?"

"You want me to?"

"Sure."

"I'm not a very good singer."

"Go ahead."

"OK." Simon recited:

If I should die before I wake, all my bone and sinew take.

Put me in the compost pile to decompose me for a while.

Worms, water, sun will have their way, returning me to common clay.

All that I am will feed the trees, and little fishes in the seas.

When radishes and corn you munch, you may be having me for lunch."

Ben laughed. It was a big laugh. Simon smiled.

"Have you ever heard of the dung beetle?" Simon asked.

"Wait. Save the dung beetle for a minute. I get the compost part. Tell me more about stardust."

"We are made of stardust, Ben. Everything on earth is made of stardust. Sometimes it's called interstellar dust. It came from a supernova billions of years ago. It's what Curtis Bog and this road and the truck and everything you can see is made of. It just cycles and recycles and cycles again."

Ben smiled at the sudden gift of memory. "Matter can be neither created nor destroyed," he said.

"You got it, Ben." Simon let out a big yawn. It caught him by surprise.

"I don't suppose you got much shut-eye last night," Ben said, looking over at him.

"No, I didn't," Simon said. "I'm a little tired."

"You can take a nap if you want to. It's still a ways to Bangor. We'll stop there for breakfast. You'll find some pillows behind that panel," he said, indicating the area between them. Simon opened the panel. There was a whole bed. "Wow!"

"Very nice on a long trip."

"Do you sleep back here sometimes?"

"Haven't for two or three years. You can if you want to."

Simon produced two pillows in blue pillowcases. He tested them. "These are really soft. He put them against his door and re-buckled his seatbelt. "No, I'd rather be up here with you."

Ben nodded, turned and smiled. There weren't words. He put a Willie Nelson CD into the player. Willie sang "Come Back to Boston."

Ben Pyle held no sentimental views concerning childhood. His own had taught him self-containment and wariness. He took his jacket that lay in the seat between them and covered the unlikely boy. He thought of the starlit glow of the tiny tamaracks at Curtis Bog and of the lights there.

Chapter 5

Simon
and Ben

Simon opened his eyes. There were trucks everywhere. Some were being refueled, others idled in their parking places, apparently unoccupied. It was a small diagonal city, fuming and rumbling in the morning sun. A police cruiser glided quietly past and parked. Two troopers got out, laughing, and walked toward a large building.

"How about a little breakfast?" Ben smiled and undid his seatbelt.

"Where are we?"

"Hauler's Truck Stop, the biggest breakfast north of Boston. Hungry?"

Simon didn't answer. He looked out at the large lot filled with cars and trucks.

"We can freshen up. Take a shower." Ben reached back for Simon's pack and handed it to him. Then he reached for the door handle, swung it open, and stepped down to the blacktop. Simon clutched his pack and stared at the field of semitrailers.

Ben opened the passenger side door. "I can smell the bacon frying," he said. "Whaddya say?"

Simon didn't turn. A truck belched exhaust and rolled slowly from its parking space. Finally, he spoke. "Maybe I'll stay here if it's all right, Ben. I could watch the truck. And I have some food in my pack."

"Simon?" Ben stood there, waiting. Simon turned.

"It's all right, Simon. I'm not going to drive off without you. We're going to Boston. You, me, and the mussels." He held out his hands.

Simon was impressed. He wondered how many of his other thoughts Ben had read. Simon undid his seatbelt and turned, and Ben lifted him down from the cab. They crossed the lot to the restaurant.

His familiarity with restaurants was only a little bit greater than his knowledge of trucking and truckers. On their quarterly provisioning expeditions, he and his father always went to a fast food take-out window. Sometimes Simon said that he had to use the bathroom so that he could go inside and see the families around the tables.

LD Hauler's Truck Stop was another world altogether. They walked to a counter. Ben gave the woman some money and she gave him towels. They walked down a corridor with doors on both sides. Ben opened one with the number twelve on it. "This is yours," he said. "There's a sink and shower over there. You got a toothbrush?"

Simon nodded.

"I'll be right next door." He pointed. Number 14, it said. Simon looked for number thirteen. There wasn't any. "Just knock when you're done."

Simon stepped into the small room and closed the door. There was a full-length mirror, a bench, a sink and counter and a small glass room. *That would be the shower.* He took off his clothes. The firefighters would still be at the farm. *Don't think of the farm. Think of the adventure.* He stepped into the shower and closed the door behind him. The stainless steel appliance facing him was unfamiliar. There was only one handle. After some experimentation and several quick retreats, he mastered the control and the hot water cascaded over his head and down his body. There was a small bar of soap neatly wrapped. He opened it, careful to save the wrapper. He had forgotten to bring soap. He tilted his head and closed his eyes.

Simon had known at once that Ben would be his friend. For one thing he had a goatee like his father—whiskers above his lip and on his chin. Neater than his father's, carefully cut instead of wandering down to his shirt. And his belly. Like his father's too, but even bigger, hiding his belt. He had felt Ben's hands under his arms as he lifted him down from the cab of the truck. The strong arms, the smiling face. It wasn't just a reminder of his father's holding. It was something new. A new friend. He was in a new place, the agent sent ashore from the submarine. He was doing OK. Asking Ben to tell his story was good. It made him feel good. It was important to make people feel good. Then they could feel good about you too. Another piece of his father's advice. There were lots of them. He had written them down in his head.

He turned off the water, got out of the shower, and dried himself. Then he reached into his pack, removing his toothbrush, toothpaste, and comb. There was a wallet at the bottom. It had $500 in it. *Just in case*, his father had said with a number four smile. Simon had made a study of his father's smiles. Smile number one was the loving smile that said Simon was everything he should be. Smile number two was the teacher's smile, confident that Simon would know a fact or have an informed opinion about something. How was a star cluster different from a constellation? What is a kettle hole?

Smile number three was the questioning one, for times when Simon did or said something unexpected and his father was caught off guard. Smile four was the mischievous smile, the just-in-case smile. Just in case one or the other wasn't shooting entirely straight. When what was spoken could have been taken more than one way. The $500 was just in case he didn't do as he had been instructed. In case he didn't call Roger after the fire. In case he set out on his own. He looked up at the ceiling. "Thanks," he said. And then in a louder voice, "Thanks, Dad." Silence.

He removed a twenty from the wallet. He would pay for Ben's breakfast. That would show that he was grateful. As he removed the bill he noticed a paper folded beneath the bills. He removed and unfolded it.

My beloved Simon,

I have but a few weeks, maybe days, left to be with you. I know that we will use that time well and perhaps we will feel that we have said to one another all that needs to be said. Or that can be said. I imagine that there are things you would like to say but have spared me the hearing of. It was selfish of me to burden you with this tediously drawn out expiration, and yet you never complained. You never gave a sign that it was too much for you. That was a gift greater than any I have ever received. Well, not any. You were the greatest gift.

You know I was a writer before I was a father. The books weren't really very good. You haven't missed out on much. Roger will tell you about them. Most of the people I have loved were those I invented. And then you came along and put them all in the shadows.

And I put you in the shadows. In my selfish misanthropy I hid you from the world. Like Rumpelstiltskin. I hope as you make your way among strangers that you will forgive me for time lost and think of these years as useful.

You are everything I had hoped you might be, Simon. More than I had the vision to imagine. I wanted to shape your mind, to armor you against the world beyond our valley. I was to be the teacher; you were to be the prodigy. I hadn't counted on having you as my teacher, my best teacher. I hadn't counted on being loved.

I worried that our project was unfinished, that you would walk into the world unprepared, but as you have cared for me, as we have talked, I realized that my fears were mistaken. I had not finished, I reasoned; therefore, you were not finished. But listening to you these last months, seeing you cope with more than anyone should have to bear, I am confident you are ready for the world beyond these pastures. You will make your way wisely. You will love and be loved. You will amaze more than you are amazed.

With all the love I have ever had,
Dad

You can cry later, he told himself. "Yes, later," he said aloud. *When you are alone*. "Yes, when I am alone." He folded the letter carefully and restored it to the place where his father had hidden it. *When? Weeks ago? Days ago?* Secretly, at night while he had slept? His father always knew what he was thinking, what he wanted. And here was proof.

He looked in the mirror, half expecting to see his father behind him, as he had stood every morning on his way down to make breakfast, at Simon's door. His father was an early riser. So was Simon most days. But some days, hearing his father approach, he would pretend to be asleep. He knew his father knew he wasn't really asleep. And he knew that his father knew that he knew this. It was an unspoken secret. It was comforting.

He dressed and re-filled his pack.

On the other side of the wall Ben stood, drying himself, looking at his reflection. He saw a man in his fifties with just the right amount of beard. No white showing yet. Coal black. Eyebrows to match. Fierce if he didn't trim them. If Rosie didn't trim them. Trim his fierceness. Not in everyday things, but in things that got him going. When he was loud. When he felt precariously sure-footed in unfamiliar territory. When he heard his voice come to a hard stop and there was silence. When people no longer met his eye but looked to the arrangement of their silverware.

He slipped a new blade into his razor and clipped it shut. There weren't many things as satisfactory as a new blade in your razor. Then he ran the tap until the water was hot and softened his shaving brush. He soaped it, lifted his head and lathered his neck. A beard needed sharp edges. This far and no farther. There was a wild hair on the bridge of his nose. He sheared it off with the razor.

He thought about the boy, recalling something Rosie had said once. It had caught him off guard. The way she put the words together. Familiar words in an unfamiliar way. She liked to do that. They had been arguing about some little thing. *What are you trying to say?* he had asked. *What are you trying to hear?* she had replied. He had waved the remark away, plowed on with his argument. But that night lying beside her, his mind too full for sleep, he had thought of Curtis Bog. Private crazy thoughts he could never have spoken, not even to Rosie. What *was* he trying to hear? *Tell me your story*, Simon had said. And he had heard himself telling his story. Was that part of what he had been trying to hear?

Cleaning his razor, he returned it to his toilet kit. His routine was to make his deliveries and then drive back to Rosie's in Revere. He'd have a cup of coffee, chew the fat with the girls, and work on his accounts, Rosie looking over his shoulder, making suggestions, correcting his mistakes, massaging his neck. Driving tightened him up. Rosie knew how to loosen. And listen. It was her profession. He smiled at the face in the mirror. Not bad. Not a movie star but solid, real, reliable. *Reliable! Right. With an illegal minor strapped into the passenger seat.*

He took out his deodorant stick. Unscented. He had never been into scents. Scents were for women. "Nostalgia." That was Rosie's favorite. He kept her supplied. He'd never known anyone who smelled like Rosie. *Not smelled. You couldn't say "smelled" about a woman. So what was the word?* He couldn't find one.

Ben put on his shirt: L.L. Bean, red and green checked, a present from Rosie, and buttoned it up. Then his jeans, slipping the suspenders over his shoulders. *Goddamned paunch.* The truck driver's friend.

"Shit!" he said, remembering what he had said to Maryanne at the cash register when he got the towels. *Cute kid*, she had said, like he was into cute kids or something. *My nephew*, he had replied, without giving it a thought. It had just come out. But then he'd gone on. His sister and her husband up in Washington County were going on a cruise along the coast of Norway. He'd offered to drive the boy to Boston to stay with his brother-in-law's sister. *Where had it all come from?*

All that stuff packed in little boxes at the back of his mind, tumbling out. He put on his coat and opened the door into the hall.

Chapter 6

Tom

Mary Potter's office was just down from Code Enforcement in the town office building, a small room divided by a counter, behind which Mary sat at her desk surrounded by a dusty disorder of documents. *Job security*, Tom's father had called it, with a chuckle one night at dinner. *If Mary were to disappear tomorrow, the town would be in chaos. She doesn't keep the records; she is the records*. Mary knew not only the town's business but also that of its citizens. She had mastered the conversational caesura. Sentence followed upon sentence, one snippet of local news tagged the next. A needed document made its way to the counter slowly, very slowly, and once there remained beneath Mary's hand until she had fished and finished.

She looked up from her desk as Tom approached the counter. "Morning," she said.

"Morning," he replied.

"Be with you in a minute."

"No hurry." She closed a ledger, carried it over to the archive closet, stuck it back in its nook and crossed to the counter.

Yes, she had heard about the fire. No, she had never met Larin Seeker, but she had opinions about people who lived that way and had known of several others who came to no good. "Taxes are paid from a trust in New York City," she said, "with the same short letter attached each year." She disappeared into another closet and returned with a file folder. Tom described in detail the extent of the fire, his conversation with Ellie Dawson and that, for the time being, he'd be looking after things at Spruce Valley Farm. Mary opened the folder and handed him a letter.

The stationery bore the name of a law firm: Featherstone, Parks, and Carrington, P.C.

The salutation was standard:

> To Whom It May Concern:
>
> Please be advised that we are the legal representatives of Mr. Larin Seeker who resides at Spruce Valley Farm in Washington County, Maine and that it is his wish that all correspondence concerning that property and his residency there be directed to this office.
>
> Yours sincerely,
> Roger Plummer

Tom took out his pad and wrote down Plummer's telephone number. In all likelihood, no one had called him yet about the fire.

He handed the letter back to Mary. "Thanks. I'll let you know if I learn anything." Mary nodded noncommittally and returned the letter to the file.

Once outside, Tom took out his cell phone and dialed the New York number. The woman who answered said that Mr. Plummer wasn't available but that she would be happy to give him a message.

"I'm calling concerning Larin Seeker, one of his clients." He paused, hoping for some sign of increased interest.

"Seeker?" she asked.

"Larin Seeker, the owner of Spruce Valley Farm in Washington County, Maine."

"Oh, yes. Of course."

"There's been a fire and Mr. Seeker is presumed dead. The fire warden asked me if I would look after the animals and I am doing that. I thought Mr. Plummer would want to know."

"I will give him that message, Mr…?"

"Tom Bewick." He gave her his cell phone number. "Do you have any idea when you'll be able to get this message to Mr. Plummer?"

"He's in conference. I'll give it to him as soon as he's finished." The line went dead. 'In conference' could mean anything. Mr. Plummer might be three feet away leafing through his mail. In movies, secretaries never gave anything away. Well, he wouldn't give much away either.

The phone rang before Tom could clip it back on his belt.

"Hello?"

"Mr…Bewick?"

"Yes."

"This is Roger Plummer."

"Good morning, Mr. Plummer."

"Good morning. I am very sorry to hear the news of Mr. Seeker's death. You say there was a fire?"

"Yes, sir. Spruce Valley Farm burned to the ground last night. I went out with the fire warden. They were able to save the outbuildings, but there's nothing left of the house."

"And it is presumed that Mr. Seeker was inside?"

"Well, his Land Rover was there and there was no sign of him. He could have walked away but it doesn't seem likely. I'm sorry."

"Yes, so am I. It is a great loss."

"We don't know what to do about the animals, Mr. Plummer. You know he had quite a few. I took care of them this morning and I'll put them in tonight, but I don't want to be there if I shouldn't and that's why I was calling."

"That was very thoughtful of you, Mr…"

"Bewick. Tom Bewick."

"Yes, of course. We would be very grateful if you would continue to do that until we make other arrangements, Mr. Bewick. You will be compensated. You say the house was totally destroyed?"

"Totally."

"I see." There was a pause. More coming. "You know, there is something else you could do for us..."

"Sure."

"You might just have a look around."

"Sure, Mr. Plummer. What should I look for?" As soon as he heard himself say, 'sure' he knew he had the right voice. It could almost have been 'Gee!' Naïve, wide-eyed, a boy from Downeast talking to a lawyer from the big city.

"Oh, personal papers that he might have stored outside the house. You might check the barn. It's unlikely, but I'd be grateful if you'd have a look. We'll get someone up there as quickly as we can, Mr. Bewick. We are grateful for your help."

"I'm glad to offer it, sir. Sir?"

"Yes, Tom?"

It had worked. Already he was Tom. "There's a motorhome on the side of the driveway. Doesn't look like it's been lived in for a while. Would it be OK if I stayed there while I'm looking after things?"

"Absolutely. By all means. I don't think anyone's stayed there for a long time. Mr. Seeker bought it when he moved out to Spruce Valley Farm. It took a month or so to get the house up to snuff. Yes, by all means. Make yourself at home."

"Oh and one other thing, sir."

"Yes, Tom."

"There were two pair of boots in the barn."

"Yes?"

"Well, if Mr. Seeker lived alone..."

"Yes. Well, maybe there are some things we don't know about Mr. Seeker, Tom. He was a very unusual man."

"Well, we were just wondering," Tom said. *Your turn, Mr. Plummer.*

"You said 'we,' Tom."

Strike. Keep tension on the line. "Ellen Dawson, the fire warden." It was playing out like *Northern Exposure*. Too good to be true that Ellen was a girl.

"Not the police."

"There aren't any police around. Not yet anyway. I guess they'll probably come though, won't they? What should I tell them?"

"Perhaps you should give them my number."

"OK, sir. Sir?"

"Yes, Tom?"

"What's going to happen to the place?"

"There is a will, Tom. It will have to be probated of course. That's why we will be so grateful for your help."

He felt impatience at the other end of the line. Maybe he had pushed a little too hard.

"What is it you do, Tom? You work with the fire warden?"

"Not really, sir. I'm in school. I just sort of help out."

"Well, Tom, you help out at Spruce Valley Farm, and we'll be very grateful. You have my number."

"Yes, sir."

"Stay in touch. If you find anything, give me a call."

There was no point in an appreciative, respectful, youthful closing. The line was dead. Strange bird. All business. Secretaries everywhere, passing him things even while he was on the phone. Type A but cool. Very professional. Didn't want people messing around with the farmer's stuff. Wanted to be sure the place was gone over before the law got there. That's what lawyers did. Protect people's interests, their privacy. Even dead people.

It couldn't have gone better. Caretaker of the farm and getting paid. Wasn't that called moonlighting? Or double-dipping? Or something. Getting paid twice for doing the same job. And if the story was really big? *Slow down. One thing at a time.*

The State Police would be coming to look things over. Cause of fire, possibilities of arson or some other crime. *What to do then about the boots and the saddles?* He needed to keep that to himself, for now, and hope whoever showed up wouldn't look that closely. News of another missing person would break his story prematurely. It was his ace in the hole with New York, too. Plummer would be working up something to explain it all: the knowing wink, the elbow lightly in the ribs. Larin Seeker liked his women.

As he drove back up the road to Spruce Valley it struck Tom just how idyllic the setting was. The valley with its stream running down from the mountain, the fields green from spring rains, the old trees.

The house was on its way to cooling. Here and there a little steam or smoke, but no longer redolent of that peculiarly sour smell. He walked to the barn to gather his things.

Chapter

Roger

Roger Plummer, a partner in the firm Featherstone, Parks, and Carrington was highly regarded as an experienced litigator of consummate skill. Centered upon his desk, before his chair, a dark blue blotter framed in brown Florentine leather. A tear darkened the blotter. Then another. He removed his glasses and wiped the rivulets from his cheeks.

Placing the receiver heavily onto its cradle he folded his hands. The blood vessels stood out under a fine fabric of wrinkles. He made fists and they disappeared.

He and Reese Larkin had been friends for over fifty years, first as roommates at Wind Lake School, then at Exeter, then once again at Princeton. Then they had gone their own ways, Roger on to law school and Reese writing the first of the Sam Scamper books that would, in a very few years, give him international fame as a writer of books for children. When, years later, he decided to become a hermit and move to the now vacant family farm, he'd called Roger to help him set things up and to be available if he needed anything. That led to a new relationship, he now the caretaker, attendant, administrator. And then there was Simon.

The name Larin Seeker was an anagram, a sign that his friend had not entirely lost his sense of humor when the crisis had hit and he left the world to become a recluse.

Roger had expected a call, but not this one. Not a fire. It made no sense. That a house standing for over a century and a half should suddenly erupt into flame could not be simple coincidence, not with Reese involved. There was some mischief in it. *What? A funeral pyre? Plausibly. But what then of Simon? Certainly not his pyre too, like some Hindu widow.*

Reese's cancer had been diagnosed in November. He had declined treatment. Roger had urged him to enter a care facility or at least provide a nurse to relieve Simon of unseemly burdens. But, no, Reese had dismissed the suggestion. Simon was capable of seeing him on his way and they needed the time alone to get things in order. The boy concurred, soberly. Too soberly for his twelve years. Roger had continued his monthly visits, the last, three weeks earlier. Reese had been surprisingly conversational— an energy at odds with his frailty. Simon, always the precocious farmer and reluctant housekeeper, now seemed to have both tasks well in hand, preparing dinner Saturday night and a breakfast of pancakes and bacon the next morning.

Roger would make the arrangements for Simon's enrollment at Wind Lake School. That Simon should walk the same halls, perhaps even sleep in the same room where he and Reese had come together gave him mixed feelings. Now Simon would usurp their history as well.

When Roger had arrived at Wind Lake School at age nine, Reese was two years older, the brightest boy in his class. Of the eighty boys and girls enrolled, many were wealthy strays whose parents were otherwise engaged: in revolutions, some addiction or other, the secret service, or observing gorillas in the wild.

Roger had been desperately homesick, an easy mark for the older boys. Reese had stepped in, taken him under his wing. They had walked in the woods, sat afternoons in one of the many tree houses built over the past fifty years of the school's history by boys making homes. It was a kind of restitution, Reese playing the parent he had never had.

Reese had never stopped caring for the lost child within him. The first Sam Scamper book had been picked up by Pollywog Press when Reese was only twenty-three. Ten more followed and then Mr. Bumpus and the Lassiter twins. His invented children had made him a fortune, translated as they were into ten languages, selling in the millions.

Did the young man—*what was his name?* He looked at the yellow pad in front of him. *Tom. Tom Bewick*—say it was at night? He should have asked. Both bedrooms on the second floor. The fire would have started below. He pressed the button on the intercom. "Beverly, would you please book me a flight to Bangor tomorrow morning? The 7:30 one. And check my appointments. Thanks."

Roger had never been able to decide whether Simon was a beautiful monster or an angel. Or both. Asymmetrical—an adult brain in a child's body. A mind filled with ideas too heavy for his small limbs, too broad for his short and sheltered life. His edges rough, needing the abrasion of age-mates. But his only friends were the society of the soil. Ants. Beetles. Worms. And of the barnyard. Chickens, sheep, goats, cows and horses, his closest friend a Belgian horse named Bucephalus. Reese had encouraged his precocity with a library of books on botany and entomology. Ants and beetles were his primary interest. His library included several books by eminences at Harvard. He loved to lecture. It was a thing Roger couldn't get his head around. Well, not entirely. Of course Reese encouraged him, applauded his outpourings of insect and animal lore.

It was a sort of Frankenstein experiment. Reese's disregard of convention, his iconoclasm, had deprived the boy of pattern. His habits appeared, as best Roger had been able to infer them, without root. He was a story without a central conceit. *What could the puppet possibly do without his puppeteer?*

He walked over to the window and forced himself to look down the twenty stories to the street below without stepping back. It was not easy; something he did when an unpleasant or difficult task lay ahead. He felt diminished in Reese's death, as if a part of his own history had been erased or could no longer be validated by a reliable witness. It wasn't only sadness; it was disorientation that he felt. He looked down again and then looked away.

There was nothing scheduled for the afternoon. He'd go back to the apartment. He needed quiet. He dropped the file folder into his briefcase, put his cell phone into its small leather case and took his coat from the rack by the door. Beverly, his secretary was hanging up her phone. "You are on the 7:30 flight and I've arranged for a limo at the regular time. Is there anything you want me to do?"

"Not that I can think of. I'll call you from the airport. There's nothing on for tomorrow is there?"

"No, you're clear until you see the Emersons on Friday."

"Give them a call. Make an excuse. Family emergency. You're better at that than I am. I'll call you from the farm as soon as I get there." He walked to the elevator. It was a descent he had made hundreds of times, but this time was different. This time, the doors would open onto an emptier world.

Chapter 8

Simon
and Ben

Lester Thomas was just coming out of another cubicle when Ben emerged. Lester carried airplane engine parts from Quebec to New Haven. Their routes converged in Bangor, sometimes within minutes of one another and often they ate breakfast together. Lester knew all about Rosie's Counseling Center and had even stopped there once. It was acquaintance without consequence—the kind Ben liked best.

"You have breakfast yet?" Lester asked.

"No," Ben said, "I've got my nephew with me. He's been in the shower long enough to get poached."

"How old is he?"

"Almost thirteen," Ben replied.

"Thirteen is when they start worrying about being clean," Lester said. "I got three kids—all boys—all river rats until they got hair on their balls and then the hot water heater couldn't keep up with them. Pimple treatments, shampoos and cologne. Place smelled like a French whore house."

"My nephew hasn't quite got there yet. He's just a little squirt and I don't think he would have taken a shower if I hadn't made it a very strong suggestion. He's not very good with strangers. Maybe not breakfast today."

"No problem. I saw Dominguez' truck in the lot. I'll give him a hard time. He's getting hitched."

"Dominguez? You're kidding me."

"I swear to God. He's a reformed man."

"Right."

Just then Simon emerged from his compartment. Ben introduced him to Lester and then quickly ushered him out to the front of the building. "Let's put our stuff in the truck," he said.

"Aren't we going to have breakfast?" Simon asked, a little crestfallen.

"Sure," Ben said. "I just have to explain something to you before people start asking questions." They left the restaurant and headed back to the truck. "I'm afraid I told a little fib," Ben began. "I've told a couple people that you are my nephew, so I didn't want you to be surprised when somebody brought it up. The thing is, kids your age aren't supposed to be hitchhiking, and there are a couple state troopers in the restaurant."

"Is it because they might be runaways?"

"Right. They'd want to check with your folks, find out just what's going on."

"OK, Ben. Thanks."

"Don't mention it."

"Why not? I mean if you've already told people…"

"Come again?"

"Why can't I mention it if you've already told people?"

Ben laughed. "It's an expression. It doesn't mean you shouldn't mention it. It means…" He narrowed his eyes and studied the boy. "You're kidding me, right?"

Simon shook his head.

"It's an expression: 'don't mention it.' It means 'Hey, that's OK,' 'glad to be helpful.' You don't have to thank me. You say 'thanks.' I say 'don't mention it, my pleasure.'"

"Oh. OK. I'll remember that."

They walked back to the restaurant. Simon studied the room and turned to Ben. "Can we sit by the window?" he asked.

"I don't see why not." Ben led the way to a small table near the door and they sat down. Ben picked up his napkin and put it in his lap. Simon did the same and waited. Ben opened the menu that sat on his plate. Simon opened his. "So, what would you like?"

Simon shook his head. "There are so many things here," he said." I don't even know what some of them are."

"Well, I can vouch for the blueberry pancakes," Ben said. "And the bacon is usually nice and crispy."

"What are you going to have?"

"I'm going to have the finnan haddie, but I wouldn't recommend it for you if you haven't had it before. It's a little bit unusual."

"What is it?"

"Smoked fish and hardboiled eggs in a sauce. They put it on toast."

Simon made a face. Ben laughed. "Yes, you're right. Too complicated. You can have something simpler."

"I think I'll have the blueberry pancakes."

"Good decision." Ben caught the attention of a woman serving the table next to them. She nodded, went to the coffee machine, picked up a carafe and a pitcher of orange juice and came to their table.

"So who is your handsome young friend?" she asked, filling Ben's coffee cup. Her nametag said 'Margie.'

"I'm his nephew," Simon said.

"Would you like some orange juice, honey?"

"Do you have mint tea?"

"Mint tea?"

Simon looked at Ben.

"Simon's into natural foods."

"I'm not sure we have any," Margie said with an apologetic smile. "Do you have a second choice?"

"I'll just have water."

Margie put the order pad back in the pocket of her apron and walked to the back of the room.

"Don't people drink mint tea?"

"Sure they do. Lots of people like it. But it's not big with truck drivers."

"Do you ever drink it?"

"I'm afraid I'm pretty stuck on coffee. Keeps me going on a long drive."

"My father liked coffee. I used to make it for him. I tried it once."

"And?"

"I didn't like it."

"It's an acquired taste."

"Ben?"

"Simon?"

"I wish you really were my uncle."

Ben put a teaspoon of sugar into his coffee. He stirred it. For a second he was standing at the side of the road looking for a light in Curtis Bog. *Crazy stuff.* He looked up and smiled. "It's very nice of you to say that, Simon."

"It's true."

"I believe you. Do you have any uncles?"

"No."

"Well then, I won't be stepping on anyone's toes if I agree to play the part."

Simon made a face. "That's another expression, right?"

Ben laughed. "Right."

Simon nodded. "Did you have any uncles, Ben?"

"No, Simon, I didn't. Or aunts. Most of the other kids in the children's home had relatives, but I didn't."

"Not even grandparents?"

"Not even grandparents."

"So you didn't have anyone at all?"

"My parents left everyone behind when they came to this country." Ben arranged his silverware. Simon waited. Then Ben looked up with a new face. His eyes moved right and then left and there was mischief in his smile. "I made up a brother once. Five years older than me. I told the other kids that he was on a secret mission and had to stay out of sight, but that if I needed him all I had to do was signal at night with my flashlight. If anything bad happened to me, like getting bullied, all I had to do was get out my flashlight."

"What's 'getting bullied'?"

"It's when other kids make fun of you, push you around."

"Did you get bullied?"

"No. Not much. I was big for my age. There was one kid though. Rodney. My Lord, I haven't thought about this for years."

"Did he bully you?"

"Not me so much as he did Jack. Jack was my best friend. Rodney teased him big time. And then one day he was gone."

"Your friend?"

"No, Rodney. Just vanished. Everybody was talking about it, trying to learn what happened." Ben laughed. "I told them it was my brother. I said I had signaled him with my flashlight."

"Did they believe you?"

"You bet. I was a pretty convincing liar back then."

"Did you ever talk with your brother?"

"Like I said, he was made up. I know that sounds crazy, but it's true."

"It's not crazy. I had a friend nobody else could see once."

"You did?"

"His name was Alex."

"And he was made up?"

"No, he was real. He said my name once in a grocery store."

Margie arrived with their breakfasts: three blueberry pancakes with bacon for Simon and Ben's finnan haddie. "Enjoy your breakfasts," she said. "Bob's checking the back pantry for mint tea."

Simon poured syrup on his pancakes. Ben cut into his finnan haddie. Simon took a bite.

"How did he know your name?" Ben asked.

"We were in a big grocery store. We smiled at one another and then he heard my father call me. When my father was paying for the groceries, his mother was behind us. She called him. He was getting something. I think it was candy. When they left, he turned and said, 'See you, Simon.'"

"And?"

"He showed up at the farm one night and he slept in my baleout, and we got to be friends. Not really showed up. Just in my head."

"Right. So what is a bailout?"

"That's what my father called it. It was a place I made out of hay bales in the loft of the barn."

"A fort."

"A place I could go and be alone when I wanted to."

"When you wanted to bail out."

"Yes."

"But now you weren't alone because Alex was there."

"Only if I wanted him to be."

"That's the kind of friend to have."

"I'd like to have some real friends."

"How about a little more coffee, Ben?" Margie stood there, her carafe poised above his cup.

"Sure. Thanks, Margie."

She put the coffee carafe back on the tray and picked up a steaming cup, holding it before Simon. "And guess what Bob discovered in the pantry?" she asked.

"Mint tea?"

"Be careful, it's pretty hot." She put the cup before Simon and smiled. "Can I get you anything else?"

"I think we're set, Margie," Ben said with a smile. "thanks for the tea."

"My pleasure."

Simon couldn't remember a time without mint tea. There was a mint bed on the south side of the house. It was one of the first things to come up in the spring and one of the last to go in the fall. He would cut a handful of leaves, wash them under the tap and put them in the white teapot. Then boil the kettle. When he was little he liked it sweet. Very sweet. Lots of honey. Always there was the aroma. It was magical, calming, a fragrance around which the day gathered, a quiet time. He and his father at first not talking and then telling what was in their hearts. Mint tea wasn't for ideas or argument. It was for quiet and comfort.

Simon leaned over the steaming cup, knowing even as he did what was going to happen. The fragrance filled his head and he felt a tear slide down his cheek. It dropped into his tea with a thunderous splash.

Ben put down his spoon. "Simon?"

Simon picked up his napkin and held it over his face. There was no holding them back. He tried to take a breath and choked.

Ben started to reach over and stopped. It was new territory, the space between them. Like Curtis Bog, daring him to enter.

"What is it Simon?"

"My father."

"Something you didn't tell me?"

Simon nodded.

"What is it?"

"He died. There was a fire."

"Oh, Simon."

The tears had been waiting impatiently since he read his father's letter. He shouldn't have ordered the tea.

Margie arrived with the coffee pot again. She looked inquiringly at Ben, for now Simon was weeping very softly. "Maybe you could put those under the warmer for a few minutes, Margie," Ben said. "I think Simon and I need to get a little air."

"Sure thing," she said.

A moment later, she was back with a box of Kleenex. She put it on the table next to Simon's still untouched mint tea.

Together, Ben and Simon walked out to the fence that bordered the parking lot and watched the traffic on Route 95.

Chapter 9

Tom

The Washington County Star was a weekly newspaper and Tom's deadline was two days away; it would be best to get his thoughts down while they were fresh. He could revise later on. Save the big news. Make a careful plan. For now, just the recluse, the fire, the animals, and…? He walked into the barn and looked again at the small boots. He inspected the workroom again. Nothing he hadn't noticed on his earlier inspection.

He looked up at the loft, its bales silent as sunlight. More hay than you would expect at this time of year. The image came back to him as sharply as its pain. Their barn. He'd been twelve. Jesse, his younger brother, eight. It was spring, the loft nearly emptied of winter feed. Together they had built a fort from the remaining bales. It was an awkward creation within which they occasionally passed a rainy afternoon. It was Tom's responsibility to look after Jesse, autistic, unpredictable, and uncivilized.

Their parents had no idea of the loneliness, the price Tom paid for this caretaking. His friends at school never came to his house, nor was he invited to theirs. Jesse was too strange. He made them uncomfortable.

He wet his pants. He screamed for no reason. He spoke a language of his own. Tom's parents told him he was fortunate to be needed, to learn the importance of caring for others.

Returning one day from school he saw an ambulance in the driveway and knew at once its purpose.

No one blamed Tom, but then no one had ever seen the fort, noticed its precarious design; no one but Tom had imagined that such a thing might happen. Not death. Not smothering, just fright, a few scratches, a scare if someone were impulsive, if someone screamed and flailed his arms, kicked and climbed recklessly within the small, precarious structure. It would serve that person right if a bale should fall, knock him down, frighten him. It would teach him a lesson. That was all Tom had wanted. Not this.

The memory rarely came back to him now, except in dreams. He would awaken, breathless, as if his chest were filled with impenetrable darkness. Untangling himself from the snare of his bedding, he would go to the window and stand, breathing in the night's forgiving calm. And here it was again. Right in front of him. Not a precarious pile but a careful and sturdy construction, something only a boy could have built, only a boy could have wanted to build. He put the memory away, but not entirely. The coincidence was too remarkable, too perfect. Tom was not superstitious. And yet…

He crawled up the ladder. The bales were stacked about six feet high. He walked around behind them and, much to his surprise, came upon a kind of hideaway, with a lamp, a desk and a bookcase made from grey weathered boards. There was also a small mattress. Hung on the wall were deer antlers, artist fungi, and drawings of insects. On the table were boxes with bits of stone and polished glass, jars containing insects. There were also some scrapbooks. He opened one. Dried flowers, leaves, all labeled.

Tom took one of the books from the bookcase. *The Philosophy of Heraclitus*. He opened it. "History is a child building a sand-castle by the sea," he read. "And that child is the whole majesty of man's power in the world." He flipped a few pages. "Time is a game played beautifully by children."

Tom took out several others. *Kidnapped, The Jungle Book, Robinson Crusoe, Dr. Doolittle,* and three books by a man named Edward Wilson. One was titled "Anthill" and another "The Biophilia Hypothesis." And there were other books on insects, several of them.

A small wooden chest contained drawing materials: a set of watercolors with brushes, several charcoal pencils, a nice set of pastel crayons. Leaning against that box were pads of drawing paper. He leafed through them. A man figured in several of them: bearded, a slightly hooked nose, receding hairline, well-defined cheekbones, his age indeterminate. Not particularly old, as best he could tell from the boy's rendering. Most of the drawings were in black and white, impressive in their fine detail but baffling as to their subject matter. More hieroglyphic than pictorial, more abstract than representative. He flipped through them and stopped at what appeared to be the bark of a tree. Yes, definitely. But irregular, and in a way that suggested movement, a tumbling down. *But of what?* He looked at another. A rock, but with a consternation of symmetrical figures. They were familiar. He turned it over. *Of course.* Lichen. It was half-covered in lichen. So carefully drawn. How could a child have the patience—to say nothing of the skill—for such a delicate rendering? Tom held it at arm's length. A face looked back at him, a smiling face.

It wasn't a woman at all. No dark lady. A boy. *Not an ordinary boy.* The pieces didn't fit together. The size of the boots, for example, set against the size of the library. A boy's fort with Huckleberry Finn alongside Emerson and Plutarch. Small for his age? Jesse, too, had been smaller than most 8-year-olds. *No, don't go there.* This boy and Jesse had nothing in common except the loft of a barn and some bales of hay. And…he felt a shudder… the fire. Tom had felt nothing for Reese Larkin except the shiver along the spine that you feel when someone dies in a fire. But now the boy was in the picture. So much of him: his hide-away, his habits of care, his love of nature, animals, even a blanket and pillow. Looking around him, he felt more an intruder than an investigative journalist.

Tom climbed down from the loft and walked outside. So much was familiar. Too much. As if some mischievous puppeteer stood above him. Reporting surrendered its intellectual space to invasive recollection.

He turned. To the south of the smoking ruin of the house was a large garden, maybe an acre in size, which had been planted in expectation of some other future. He saw himself, age nine or ten, following with a basket of seed potatoes, dropping them into the holes his father dug, pushing the dirt back with his black rubber boots. The hard labor of planting and cultivating, the marvel of a brown acre coming to green life, its progeny protected from the freeze of winter in the cold cellar. In August they'd dig the root vegetables and store them—the carrots in sand, the turnips in wax, the potatoes in burlap sacks. But not at once. They had to cool first, out on the barn floor, or they'd rot.

Mr. Seeker's cold cellar would still have had enough in it to get him and the boy through the spring. Now roasted to black ash. He walked the circumference of the still-smoldering ruin. A root cellar required an outside entrance. Typically, two lift-up doors and a concrete stairwell. He found none. The great granite blocks linked without interruption the entire circumference of the farmhouse. So where then?

The barn? Unlikely. But that word was less and less useful. Tom walked to the back of the building. The land fell off to the east of the driveway such that the entrance was almost ten feet higher than the back of the structure. No surprise. Just right for dairy cows, the stanchions below, the stalls, pens, and equipment storage above. More immediately to the point, the area beyond the stanchions would be underground. He went to his truck, took the flashlight from the glove compartment and walked back. Sure enough, there were eight stanchions. Not a big herd. Enough milk for a small neighborhood. Or a large family.

Beyond the stanchions a desk, a chair. A pile of farmer's almanacs. He checked the dates. Ancient. 60s and 70s. There was a corkboard over the desk. Milking records had been tacked up. The latest 1984. *So Mr. Seeker hadn't been into dairy farming.* To the left of the corkboard, a door. He opened it and turned on his flashlight.

Last year's had been a good harvest. There were still three sacks of potatoes, a few sprouts beginning to make their way through the burlap. Root barrels were one-third filled with sand. There was a shelf of canned maple syrup as well. Dusty. *Apparently not from this spring's sugaring.* Well, at least he needn't be hungry while he did his caretaking for Mr. Plummer. Tom pulled a carrot and wiped it off on his sock. Not exactly crisp, but delicious. It took him back. His father kept meticulous records. Numbers of carrots, rutabagas, parsnips, sacks of potatoes. *Don't go there.*

A second desk. *Strange.* Piled with empty crates. He shined his light underneath. Burlap sacks, a pile of them. He stood up, started away, then stopped. Something wasn't right. He knelt and reached under the desk. *That was it: the shape.* You pile up feed sacks and you get a hollow in the middle. The thickness is in the sewn sides. But these were high in the middle. He pulled one away, then another and another. *Yes!* A trunk. A small trunk. He pulled it out.

This was the kind of thing that Plummer probably had in mind. The old man's stash of valuables or porn.

It wasn't locked. He lifted the top. Books, folders of newspaper clippings and correspondence. No hoard of Spanish doubloons; no porn, at least not so far. Tom took out one of the books and smiled. *Sam Scamper in the Palace at Knossos*, by Reese Larkin. He had read it as a child. He had read all the Sam Scamper books. And here they were. *Hannibal and the Alps, Stanley and the Nile*, stories of Vikings, Romans, Spanish explorers and the pyramids. Tom had never read better history. Sam Scamper was a very brave 12-year-old, hooked on adventure but with chronic homesickness, reminding young readers that there's no place like home. Not in high school. Not in college. The television series had been spectacular.

Reese Larkin had also created another memorable character who'd been a part of Tom's childhood: Mr. Bumpus who, to his wife's despair, could never finish building their house and rarely finished a project. Predictably, Mr. Bumpus would want to do something entirely impractical and it would make Canasta, the cat, climb a tree; Luther, the basset hound, crawl under the house; and Mrs. Bumpus throw up her hands in despair. The Lassiter twins figured prominently as did other of the rural neighborhood kids. Mr. Bumpus was the wizard of Monkey Run Road. Tom lifted one of the books from the trunk. It was one he hadn't read. It must have been the last of them. *Mr. Bumpus Builds A Telescope.*

The Lassiter twins. Two of his best friends back then, when the real ones declined to come home with him. Tom had read some of the stories to Jesse before he learned to read on his own. Later they had read together, on the back lawn or in the loft. How he had longed for a twin, someone to share his burden, someone who would understand. They could have taken turns looking after Jesse. The Lassiter twins! *What were their names? Ali! That was it. The girl was named Ali, short for Alexandra. And the boy? Sam. No, that was Sam Scamper.* He picked up one of the books and opened it, skimming the pages. *Silas! Cy! Something like that.* Then there it was. *Simon! Simon Lassiter.* Tom smiled.

He removed the remaining books from the trunk. There were a number of manila folders. He took one out and opened it. Faded newspaper clippings. Hard enough to read in normal light, hopeless with a flashlight. He climbed the stairs to the main floor of the barn, walked out into the daylight and sat on a hay bale. The first article was from *The London Times.*

"Children around the world know the name Reese Larkin, creator of the adventuresome Sam Scamper and the lovably impractical Mr. Bumpus. Patrick Jacobsen has called Sam Scamper "the most iconic American adolescent since Huck Finn, a pickpocket of pretenses and breaker of hearts." Larkin has received both the Newbury Award and the Young Reader's Choice Award.

The stories, which *The New York Times* described as among the best neighborhood adventures ever written, are set in upstate New York on a road called Monkey Run and feature the eponymous Mr. Bumpus, his cat, a dog, and a raccoon named the Lone Ranger. Bumpus works in a toy factory, an occupation that both colors and reveals his love of children. He is the neighborhood's Merlin: wizard, inventor, and spinner of yarns.

But Bumpus is an irreverent wizard and this, it appears, has gotten him and Larkin in hot water. Rock Crosby, director of the Christian League for Decency, interviewed by the *New York Herald*, cites an episode in which Bumpus argues that if cleanliness is nearest to godliness then he'd just as soon have neither:

"But cats clean themselves all the time," Simon said, holding out the can to receive the fat night crawler Alexandra had produced.

"But who'd ever trust a cat. Or for that matter, a preacher!" Mr. Bumpus responded."

And in another of the stories: "Only very clean people who take dressing up seriously create wars."

In the late eighties, the expression "Bumpusite" gained some popularity. Asked if he wasn't worried about the effects of Mr. Bumpus's pedagogy, Larkin replied that he had no such illusions of grandeur. Last week in a press conference, Crosby called upon Christians across the country to 'Bump Mr. Bumpus', holding up a bumper sticker with just those words. He urged that churches petition their local libraries to remove the Bumpus books from their shelves and demand that school boards ban their use in elementary schools."

Yes, it came back to him now. It was his birthday and he didn't get the next Mr. Bumpus book. It hadn't been published, his mother explained. His schoolmates had similar disappointments as the year moved on. So that was it. Mr. Bumpus was ousted. Tom read on.

Crosby's remarks were apparently in reaction to the newest Mr. Bumpus book, in which he and the neighborhood children build a telescope. The Lassiter twins, who figure prominently in all the Bumpus books, ask as they look through the telescope one night where heaven is. Mr. Bumpus responds with a surprisingly didactic discourse on black holes, stars, and other celestial phenomena—a mixture of Greek mythology and modern physics. It is as enchanting as anything he has written, but clearly not to the liking of Mr. Crosby who described it as "pagan, verging on the satanic."

Pierce Fenwick, reviewer for *The New York Times*, interviewed on CNN, said, "The books remain an important part of our culture, a door opened for children which fanatics may try to close but which they will never lock." When asked if the *Times* would be following the case with the same determination as the *Herald*, Fenwick smiled and observed that the *Times* rarely brought to any story the same quality of passion as the *Herald*, being, as it was, a paper that tried to get the facts straight as well as the columns.

So far, neither Larkin nor his publishers, Pollywog Press, have responded to requests for comment, although one source suggests that Larkin's lawyers are filing libel charges against some of the more strident anti-Bumpus groups."

So that was it. And his parents never told him. Neither did his teacher. And his friends? Some of them must have known. They had to; it was in the papers. Well, in London anyway. It made no sense. And it was so wrong. He laid the article beside him and looked at the devastation. And now this. Sure, it was a story, but not one he wanted to write.

Chapter 10

Simon and Ben

The trucks rolled by. Ben's fraternity of long-distance porters, tattooed, carapaced in steel: modern knights on horsepower. He glanced at Simon, his small fingers entwined in the chain link fence, staring ahead. The tears had stopped. Simon leaned his head against the wire netting.

Not being in control of his actions wasn't new to Simon, but it was rare. The world at Spruce Valley was much more predictable than this one. The weather could surprise, but most everything else played out in a familiar pattern. *Where from here?* He felt a numbness in his fingers and relaxed his grip on the netting, then took a deep breath and turned.

"I'm sorry, Ben."

"Of course you are, Simon. No boy should ever have to go through what you've just experienced. And to lose your home and your only family."

"No, I didn't mean about that. I mean about lying to you, and being a crybaby. I think I'm OK now."

"You have nothing to apologize for, Simon. What you've been through? My God! Standing there at the bog as if nothing had happened. Offering me a hard-boiled egg! Listening to me blather on about my life in the truck when you had lost everything. Well, nearly everything. You have your grandparents."

"Sort of…"

"Sort of?"

"I know their names and I know they live in Boston, but I've never seen them. They didn't like my mother having me."

"And she's in Paris, right?"

"She's a singer. She and my father made a deal."

"What kind of deal?

"Me." Simon laughed.

"You."

"My Dad got me and my mother got a lot of money to go to Paris."

"Your Dad got the best part of the deal," Ben said with a generous smile.

"Thanks."

"And your grandparents disapproved of this deal?"

"Yes. But they could still like me. It wasn't my fault that my mother did what she did."

"I'm sure they will be very happy to meet their grandson—a very special grandson. Did your father ever meet them?"

"No."

"So I guess we don't have much to go on. That's OK. We'll stop at Rosie's place on our way into the city and ask for her help. She's good at these sorts of things."

"Who is Rosie?"

"My girlfriend."

"I've only read about women."

Ben laughed. "I think you've got the right idea."

"What?"

"Keeping them in books. You let women out of books and they're nothing but trouble. Except for Rosie. Let's go back and finish our breakfasts and then we'll head for Boston."

"Thanks Ben. You're great."

"I don't know about that, but I'm lucky, that's for sure."

Margie got their plates from under the warmer, brought a fresh cup of coffee for Ben and another mug of mint tea. Simon closed his eyes and took a sip. Then he cut a piece of pancake and put it into his mouth. It was sweet.

"Good?" Ben asked, addressing his finnan haddie.

Simon nodded. He poked at his pancakes and looked up. "They're a little mushy," he said.

"We can order some fresh ones."

"They're OK," Simon said. "How's your fish?"

"It's good. You want to try some?"

"OK."

"Here; give me your fork." Ben scooped a dollop of the creamed fish onto the fork and handed it back to Simon.

"It's good," he said. He picked up a piece of bacon and put it on Ben's plate. Ben ate it.

"Crispy," he said. "You going to finish your pancakes, Simon?"

"No."

"I'll ask Margie for the check, then."

Simon reached into his pocket and found the twenty. He handed it to Ben. "What's that for?" Ben asked.

"For breakfast," Simon said.

"You can pay next time," Ben said. "This is my treat."

"Thanks, Ben."

Ben waved and got Margie's attention. She brought the check. Ben took out his wallet and gave her a twenty. She made change, put it on the table, and turned to Simon. "You OK, honey?"

"I'm fine. Just not very hungry. The tea was very nice, though. Thanks."

"Well, you take care of yourself." She turned and walked to the next table. Ben pushed back his chair.

"You all set?" he asked, turning, seeing the boy's remarkable eyes. *Why remarkable? No, just unfamiliar. Trusting. That was it.* He felt a sense of old loss made new, wanting words. One day they would make themselves known, acknowledge him. That had been his thought yet again as he stood there at the bog. He would see it in their eyes. Then he too would understand: who he was, what he was meant to do. Like now.

Chapter 11

Simon & Ben

Rosie would know what to do. Dealing with people in distress was what she was best at. Ben knew that first hand. So did most of the girls. Rosie was a caretaker. A practical caretaker, but a caretaker nonetheless. He looked over at the boy, asleep again. No wonder, after all he'd been through. He slowed and made the turn onto Route 1.

Simon woke up and stretched. He looked out the window. "Are we almost there?"

"Very close. Did you have a nice nap?"

"I dreamed about Bucephalus. He was running alongside the truck. I hope he's all right."

"Horses are pretty resourceful," Ben said. "I'm sure he'll miss you but I don't think you have to worry." Ben slowed the truck and turned into a parking lot. "We'll leave the truck here," he said, shutting down the engine.

He pulled the seat forward and removed a suitcase from the sleeping cab, then Simon's pack, which he handed to him.

"Are we going to walk?" Simon asked.

"We'll hail a cab," Ben said. He walked around to Simon's side and helped him down, then they walked to the roadside. Simon wasn't sure what was going to happen next. He had never heard the word 'cab' or seen it in a book. Ben held up a hand. A yellow car with writing on it pulled over to the curb and Ben opened the back door. "Climb in," he said. Simon moved to the far side of the seat and studied the interior. It was probably a taxi, he thought, though he had never seen one. *A taxi-cab!* "76 Spruce Street," Ben said. The driver nodded and the car moved out into traffic. He turned off the wide road and started up the hill past a clutter of metal-roofed warehouses, auto repair shops, a number of three-story tenements, a couple small grocery stores, a funeral home, and a meeting hall for the Sons of Portugal.

Yes, Rosie would know what to do. She would unravel the snarl of thoughts at which Ben had been picking for the last five hours. He had told Simon that Rosie's Counseling Center was a place where people went when they were lonely and wanted company. There were counselors there, he had explained, who listened to your problems and helped you feel better. Rosie was the head counselor.

Rosie's place of business had at one time been a merchant's home—the house on the hill, enjoying from its widow's walk a prospect of the sea and of neat, more modest dwellings below. What was now a parking area had once been lawn. A tangle of vines and weeds competed for possession of long-neglected gardens. The building sat back from the street behind a pair of ancient hickories, a verdant shawl thrown about an aging frame, its exterior an intaglio of cracked and curling paint, its large porches long abandoned to the vagaries of New England winters, its chimneys leaning precariously, their backs to the north wind. Rosie's Counseling Center was as timeworn and timeless as the rites and rituals practiced within its walls.

The cab pulled up to the sidewalk. "This is it," Ben said, opening his door and stepping out.

Simon followed. The house was unlike anything he had ever seen, not only bigger but with more complicated parts, like some of the haunted places in his books. "Is this Rosie's?" he asked in a small voice.

"Yup."

"It's big."

"It was a real fancy place once upon a time. A sea captain built it over a hundred years ago. It came down to Rosie through an uncle."

"And now it's a...what did you say?"

"Counseling center."

"What's that?"

"Where people come to solve their problems."

"What kind of problems?"

"Oh, all kinds."

Ben looked up at the many second floor windows, all attractively curtained, inviting. What could he say that would make any sense to a boy who'd never had anyone to talk to—other than his father and a nut-case truck driver who didn't know any better than to take him to a whorehouse? *God!* He turned around. The cab was already on its way. He looked up as if for help. But from whom?

"Should I knock?"

He turned back. Simon was already at the door. Ben took a breath and put together a smile. It worked. Simon smiled back. "Is the door locked?" Ben asked. Simon tried the knob. The door opened. "Just walk right in."

They found Rosie in the kitchen.

The women of Simon's acquaintance lived quietly between the covers of books in a two-dimensional world. Rosie was abundantly three-dimensional. She welcomed Ben with an affection Simon had read about but had never actually seen.

"Well," she said, taking his measure. "What have we here?"

Simon had never thought of himself as a "what" before. "I'm Simon," he said. "Simon Seeker." He held out his hand.

"Simon Seeker," she repeated, taking it in her own. Her hand was large, soft, and fragrant. Not at all like Ben's. She wore four rings. Her nails were painted a soft pink.

She held out her other hand and he knew to offer his own. She examined them as if there was something to be read there. Then she turned them over. "These are working hands," she said, touching the calluses on his fingertips. The whole experience was new to him. It wasn't that she was big; no bigger than many women he had seen on his and his father's occasional provisioning trips. It was the way she took up space. It was a different kind of size.

"How is it that you and Mr. Pyle came to be acquainted?"

"Simon was hitch-hiking," Ben said. "Four o'clock in the morning on Route 9. He and his father live on a farm up in Washington County. He's come to Boston to stay with his grandparents." He looked at Simon. His expression said, *Let's keep it simple. Both of us.*

Simon looked at his hands. He wasn't sure what to do with them. He put them in his pockets. "I take care of the animals," he said.

"And who is taking care of them now?" she asked.

Simon looked at Ben. He was surprised to find his friend's eyes waiting for him. "They're being looked after," Ben said. Rosie looked at Ben and nodded.

So many things not being said, Simon thought. *Or being said without words.* He knew about that. He and his father were like that. A glance would often do. You could say, "Not now...later" with a glance. That's what Ben was saying now. All of this, starting with Ben, then at breakfast and now here with Rosie, was all new and he was doing pretty well. He hadn't really thought about it. Now, a little to his surprise, he did. He wasn't scared. That was good. Ben liked him so he must have done things pretty well. He was doing OK. And he liked it. He looked at Rosie. She looked back and smiled. Then she walked to the stove and turned a flame on under the kettle.

"Have a seat," Ben said, pulling out a chair for himself and indicating another.

Rosie measured instant coffee into the two mugs and paused. "I don't suppose you're a coffee drinker?"

"I'm fine," Simon said.

"There's some juice in the refrigerator," she offered.

"No thanks." He watched as they lifted their cups. Yes, things were going better than he had expected when he was watching his father's soul go up among the flames. His father was watching. Simon looked up and smiled.

Chapter 12

Tom

The other articles were of the same ilk but of later dates, covering altogether the better part of two years. A quick perusal revealed that Pollywog Press had been acquired by a larger publishing house more focused on books with a message, especially picture books for the very young. Larkin had been dropped. Reports on litigation became shorter and finally disappeared. The last article in the pile was from *The Boston Globe* dated 1985. It was from page two and titled "Where is Reese Larkin?" Apparently the writer had been trying to contact the author for an interview and had come to a number of dead ends.

He got up and walked back down to the former milking room. Once dairy cows, and now? A place where Sam Scamper and the Lassiter twins were put to rest in an old trunk, buried. It was hard to get your mind around. Things like this didn't happen. You go to write about a fire and unearth a treasure. He reached back into the trunk.

There were several more folders. Tom took one out and opened it. Carbon copies of letters. When was the last time he'd seen a carbon copy of anything? They went out with typewriters. Ancient.

He leafed through the frail pages. All to Mr. Plummer. Mostly dealing with investments, contributions, maintenance needs, supplies of all sorts. He continued looking through them until he came upon one of a very different character. "It's a boy…" stood out in the second line. He put the other letters back into the folder and pulled up a hay bale.

Dear Roger,

I am back from Boston. It's a boy. 6 pounds, 6 ounces. Alexandra will breastfeed him for the next six months. As I may have told you, my own mother was unable to breastfeed me for some reason; I was on a bottle from the start. Never did understand what that was all about, but I'm sure it had to do with my own failure to create a family. Anyway that's neither here nor there. Alexandra will bring Simon up in May. Sorry, don't think I told you. His name is Simon. More about that later. Sorry to be going in circles. It is hard for me to grasp that this is really happening.

I have been reading about babies. It will be a very different experience, a challenging one. I'm used to children who can be quieted with the closing of a notebook, modified, even discarded if I get them wrong. Simon will ask more of me than anyone ever has and I am ready to meet that challenge. If I had any doubt about that, it vanished as I read through the books you were so kind to send. Sleepless nights, colic, nursing from a bottle, diapers. It makes the enterprise of farming look simple. Most daunting will be learning my role: when to intrude upon his chosen way. What will it be like to hear the cry of a child at night?

When Alexandra brings him up to the farm she'll stay for a couple weeks as we move him to the bottle. I'll do more and more of the feeding as the days pass so that the transition is not so hard for Simon.

I could go on. And on. I have never been more ready and less prepared. I long to hold him in my arms, to see in his eyes the curiosity that will shape him and the trust that it will be my life's work never to betray. It will be a challenge, given the sequestered life he will lead. I will keep him safe, respond to his needs, give him words, the companionship of animals, the fruits of this earth. And I will listen. That will be the most important thing.

Simon will learn from nature, from the society of ants and frogs, the fecundity of gardens, the tempers of the weather, and the moods of livestock. He will be nature's child, and mine.

Best to send the paperwork for Alexandra's letter of credit by courier.

Fondly,
Reese

So, it was a boy. He would be twelve. Twelve! Tom closed his eyes. *Bales in a loft. No, don't go there!* Impossible. But here he was. And where was Simon?

Chapter 13

Simon and Jenna

A woman came into the kitchen wearing only what Simon assumed must be her underwear. It was much more interesting than his own. She had slippers on her feet. Soft, quiet cozy ones. She moved without a sound. Going to the cabinet over the sink, she removed a box of tea bags. She touched the kettle, made a little noise, and licked her finger. Her toenails were painted. They had decorations. Like little paintings he had seen in an art book. He was reminded again of how strange his life had been. No women. Well, in stores when they shopped. But not right up close like Rosie had been a few minutes before. And this woman was as good as or better than any described to him in books. She had reddish hair, sort of like her toenails. Her face was quiet and thoughtful. She looked at him with surprise and then over at Rosie.

"This is Simon," Rosie said. "Ben is giving him a ride to his grandparents' house. This is Jenna," she continued, looking at Simon with a funny smile. "She's one of the counselors. Ben and I will leave you for a bit and catch up on some business. You OK with that, Simon?"

"Sure."

"We'll be back pretty soon." She and Ben stood up, Ben gave a small wave and a large smile and they left through another door at the back of the kitchen.

Jenna brought her hot mug over to the table and set it down. She didn't put out her hand the way Rosie had. Simon wasn't sure what to say. He looked at the steam rising from her mug. "So, are you and Ben related?" she asked.

"No. We met at the bog."

"A bog."

"Near where I live. Curtis Bog. I was by the road looking for a ride. My father had to go away and I needed a ride to Boston to stay with my grandmother. I don't know where she lives. Ben is going to find out."

"Aren't you a little young for hitch-hiking?"

"I'm almost twelve. In June."

"Hey, I'm a June baby, too! What day?"

"The 23rd."

"Cancer. I'm a Gemini. June 17th."

"Cancer?"

"You're actually on the Gemini/Cancer cusp."

Simon looked down and closed his eyes. He saw a boy with a fishing rod sitting at one tip of a quarter-moon. The cusp of the moon. It was a small black and white picture in his father's room. *How could she have known? Did she know about the cancer too?* He looked up. Jenna was smiling.

"We are magical individuals," Jenna said and laughed.

"We are?"

"June 17th to June 23rd is called the cusp of magic."

"What does it have to do with the moon?"

"The moon?"

"That's where cusps are. The tips of a moon before it gets full."

"Really." It was half-statement, half-question.

"Really."

"Well the cusps I'm talking about are..." she paused, "where things sort of come together. Where one thing ends and another begins. Hmmm. Like where one month ends and another begins. No, that's not right. There are six days, seventeen to twenty-three. You know, I've never really thought about this."

"But our birthdays are on the same cusp."

"Right."

"And we're both magic."

Jenna smiled and reached across the table. She opened her hands. Simon looked at them and then up at Jenna. Her face wasn't magic. *Or was it?* He didn't need words. He put his hands in hers. She closed hers softly around his and he felt something he couldn't have given words to.

"Is that mint tea?" he asked.

"Yes. Can you smell it?"

"I love mint tea."

"Really? Well, let's make you a cup." She went back to the stove, dropped a teabag into a big blue mug and added the hot water. As she set it on the table she sat, moving her chair in closer.

"I've never thought of Ben as someone who'd stop at a bog, to say nothing of picking up a hitch-hiker. He's sort of a loner."

"I think he wanted someone to talk to."

"What did he talk about?"

"Mr. Gladstone."

"Who's that?"

"A goose! When he was little. And ducks and chickens."

In the truck with Ben, Simon had been able to keep the face and the words apart, by looking out at the road. Now, sitting across from Jenna, they were together. On a cusp. It wasn't that Simon had no experience of women. They appeared in most of his books, though often in the background. None of his philosophers were women, for example. And it was boys and men who went on quests, had adventures and discovered things, Alice being an exception. And Wendy. But Wendy would never have gone to Neverland if Peter hadn't taught her to fly. Most of the women he could remember from his books got in the way, like Aunt Polly, or worried. The helpful ones were either fairies or elves.

"Tell me about your grandmother," Jenna suggested.

"She lives around here some place."

"But you don't have her address."

"We've never met. She was mad at my mother for having me."

"Really? That's very sad."

"Really. My mother made a deal with my father. He got me and she got money to go to Paris and become a famous singer."

"My goodness."

"Olivia Hardin is her name. I've never seen her. This will be the first time." He felt something on his arm and lifted it off the table. The something was an ant. It passed his elbow and started down toward his wrist. "Did you know that ants make up over thirty percent of the biomass in a rain forest?" he asked. He turned his arm so that Jenna could see the ant.

"Rosie needs to get an exterminator," Jenna said. "You can't leave anything out in the kitchen. And they bite."

"Not unless you're near their colony. If they think their queen is in danger, they'll bite. But usually they're just exploring for food." Simon stood up and walked toward the door.

"Where are you going?"

"I'm putting the ant outside."

"Why not just kill it?"

"It's not right to kill creatures that don't hurt you, especially when they do important work."

"You're a Buddhist," she said, nodding.

"I don't think so. It's just that ants have a right to live too."

"How come you know all this stuff? Like...what did you call it? Bio-something?"

"Biomass."

"Right. What's biomass?"

"Well, it's everything that's living: insects, plants, people, animals. Everything that is born and dies."

"And ants are over thirty percent?"

"In the rain forest they are. Where we are now, maybe ten percent. If you added in all the other insects and bacteria, it would be a lot more. And you know what the amazing thing is?"

"What?"

"Even though they're almost invisible unless you really go looking for them, they're the ones that make life go on. They're the real farmers. It's what you *can't* see that makes everything you *can* see. The ants build whole cities in a compost heap."

"How did you learn all that?"

"I have books and I live on a farm. We have lots of compost."

"What else do you have there?"

"Earthworms, nematodes, red worms, and potworms. You have to have a microscope to see a nematode. A rotting apple can contain 90,000 of them!"

"You're kidding. 90,000 in a little apple?"

Simon nodded with wide and welcoming eyes. He hadn't had anyone to talk with about compost for a long time. A very long time. Forever. "And springtails. They're my favorite. They don't fly, they jump. They've got a spring under their bellies." He demonstrated with his hands. "They eat everything, even the poop of other insects."

"Oh dear."

"It's OK. They clean themselves after each meal."

"That's remarkable!"

"People aren't the only ones who wash up after breakfast."

"What did you call them?"

"Springtails."

"You are pretty remarkable."

"Thanks. You're one of the counselors?"

Jenna took a deep breath and then a slow swallow of tea.

"Ben said that people came here for counseling. I'm not sure what that is. Is it like telling someone your story?"

"Yes." Jenna smiled. "That's very good. Tell me yours."

"I don't have one yet."

"Everyone has a story. You could tell me where you live and what you like to do. You could tell me about your family."

"I live on a farm in a place called Spruce Valley. It's about a mile from Curtis Bog. My dad and I live there by ourselves, just us and the animals."

"Really!"

Simon couldn't help smiling. Talking with new people was much more fun than he had imagined. With his father, it was a little like a book you had read many times. You almost always knew what was coming next. He thought about Ben, saw the profile of his face as he drove, felt the sound of their conversation. It had been easy to learn, easy to know where you were going. Sitting here it was different. Not confusing, not scary, not at all unpleasant. It was full of surprises, like her toenails.

"You know, I think your mother missed out on something that most women would give anything for."

"Having a son?"

"Not just any son." She smiled.

Simon returned it and then continued. "It's all right. Not all mothers want to raise their offspring. Have you ever known any goats?"

"Goats? Have I ever known any goats?"

"Right."

"No. Should I have?"

"You can learn a lot from animals."

"I'm sure. Tell me what I could learn from goats."

"Well our nanny once had a kid. That's what you call a baby goat." Jenna nodded. "Just one, which is unusual. Usually, there are two. Sometimes as many as four. But she had only one and she wouldn't feed it."

"Why not?"

"She didn't want to be a mother. Sometimes that happens. It didn't mean that she was bad. It's like sometimes fathers don't stay around. Dad told me that there were lots of children in the world without fathers. They just walk away and no one pays any attention. But if a mother does, then people think she's bad. But she's not any worse than the father. It's just that she didn't want to do all the stuff that mothers have to do."

"Like the goat."

"Just like the goat."

"So what happened to the kid?"

"I nursed him with a bottle. It was a billy." He looked at Jenna. There was something in her face that had not been there earlier. And then it was gone. "Do you have any children?" he asked.

"Once," she said. "A long time ago. I was very young. So tell me, Simon, how do you feel about that?"

"About what?"

"Wouldn't you like to have your mother come back and take care of you?"

"That wasn't part of the deal she made with my father."

Jenna's focus was on some distant place. Simon wondered if she was seeing herself as a little girl. He saw himself in Jenna's eyes and liked being there.

"I see you've made another friend," Ben said as he and Rosie came back into the kitchen.

"We both have birthdays in June," Simon said. "Jenna's is on the 17th and mine is on the 23rd."

"What a small world," Ben said, with a hint of wonder and a broad smile. Jenna looked at Ben with an expression he couldn't read. He smiled and put his hand on Simon's shoulder. "Six days apart. And you are going to turn twelve. And Jenna? Let's see…"

"Let's not," Jenna said, standing up and walking to the sink.

"Ben's going to deliver his mussels, Simon," Rosie said. "You and Jenna and I can start tracking down your grandparents in the phone book. What do you think of that?"

Simon looked at Jenna. She smiled and nodded.

"OK," he said with a confusion of feelings. *Did he want to see his grandparents? Not really. They couldn't be better than Ben and Jenna.* Things were happening so fast. He looked up at Ben whose hand was still on his shoulder.

"I'll be back in a couple hours," Ben said. "We'll take it one step at a time. You'll be here tonight. Jenna's going to set up a room for you. If Rosie locates your grandparents you and I will drive over tomorrow. OK?"

"I guess so."

Ben was surprised at how well he could read Simon after so little time together. "I'm going to be here for you, Simon," he said. "With or without your grandparents. Our meeting at Curtis Bog was no accident."

Simon stood and put his arms around Ben, and was rewarded with a good hug. Then he took a breath and turned to the others. "Curtis Bog is where we met. It's where Ben stops to see the sunrise."

Ben turned and cleared his throat. "It's a nice place to take a stretch. Very unusual landscape. The kind of place that teases the imagination." He paused, smiled and looked down at Simon. "OK?"

"OK."

Ben walked to the door, opened it and turned. "Good luck!"

Simon stared at the door for a few moments longer. *Good luck. What would that be? Finding his grandparents? Having Ben drive him there and leave him with strangers? No.* He closed his eyes and took a breath.

Simon, Rosie, and Jenna

There were four Hardins in the phone book. Rosie called them all as Simon and Jenna watched and listened. No one had a daughter named Alexandra. No one had lost track of a grandson. Then Rosie and Jenna discussed other research strategies. There apparently weren't many. After agreeing on placing an announcement in the classified section of *The Boston Globe*, their conversation stopped, somewhat abruptly. Each of them smiled.

It wasn't an entirely new experience for Simon. There were times when his father and Roger had done this. Stop strangely in the middle of a discussion, punctuate the silence with a quiet cough and when Simon looked up, smile. *Some things are better left unsaid*, his father later offered as explanation. *What kind of things?* Simon had asked. What had his father replied? He couldn't remember.

"Well," Rosie said, standing up. "What do you say to a little refreshment?"

Simon looked to Jenna, then to Rosie. "I'm OK," he said.

"I've never seen a boy turn down a nice cold root beer," Rosie said.

Simon had the root beer. Jenna and Rosie had the other kind. Simon thought about Ben, wondering when he would be back, sorry that he had not gone along for the deliveries.

"Jenna, why don't you take Simon up to the guest room and make up a bed for him? As I understand it," she said, turning to Simon, "you were up before dawn this morning. You must be tired. You go up with Jenna and get some shut-eye."

That was it. It hadn't taken long to read Rosie. *Stop. Go. Wait. Move. Now. Later.* It was her voice. Words came to a stop and that was that.

Jenna led him to a room above the kitchen. It was small with a window out onto the parking lot. Under it, a small bed. Most of the space was filled with clothing on racks, hats and shoes on shelves, belts, a pocket-watch, and something made of feathers hanging from a pegboard. Simon took it down, ran his hand along the soft surface and looked at Jenna.

"It's called a boa," she said as she wrapped it around Simon's neck. Simon looked for a mirror. Jenna read him and opened the door to a tall, free-standing closet. Inside the door was the mirror. He looked critically at his reflection and then at Jenna. "It's so soft," he said, holding it against his cheek. Then he surveyed the room more intentionally.

"What's it for?" he asked.

"Sometimes clients like to act out their problems or have the counselors dress up like people in their lives," she explained, opening a trunk.

"What kind of problems?"

"Oh, problems at the office, or with their parents, or friends. Just about anything you can imagine." Jenna took out two bed sheets and handed them to him.

"What do you dress up as?"

She handed him a pillow, took out a comforter, and closed the trunk. "I hardly ever dress up. But one of my clients likes to wear military stuff, like he's an officer."

"Does he give you orders?"

"We're not supposed to talk about our clients, sweetie. Sorry. Let's make up this bed. Not very big is it? Here, give me one of those sheets."

He handed her the sheet and together they made the bed.

Jenna explained that she had a couple errands to run before she went to work and that Simon should make himself at home. "You can go down to the kitchen if you want another root beer. There are Cokes, too. And ginger ale. And of course milk. But don't come out front or go outside. OK?"

"Sure."

"Right." She looked around the room as if to be sure that there was nothing out of place, then turned, smiled, and opened her arms. Simon walked over and she gave him a hug.

"Thanks, Jenna. You are a very nice person."

"Oh, sweetie," she said, almost looking sad. Then she turned and left.

Simon knelt on the bed and looked out the window. A car drove in. A man got out and walked around to the front of the house. The parking area wasn't paved. It was dirt, packed down.

He could see behind the parking area what might be an apple or a crabapple tree. He thought of the vegetable gardens at the farm, the peas ripening, all the things he had planted, just as he and his father had every other year as if nothing were going to change. That's what wishful thinking was. He lay on top of the covers. *Make yourself at home,* Jenna had said. *Make yourself useful,* his father had advised. Ben was useful because he could drive a truck and move food from one place to another. Jenna was useful because she helped people feel better. She was very good at that. And Rosie? It was her home. She made herself at home. And Jenna did. And now he was invited to. But it wasn't his home. His home was black ashes. *No. Not that.* Make yourself at home. Make yourself a home. Make yourself. That's what you did. At the end of every day you were different. You had more cells in your body, more memories in your mind, and more things you knew how to do. That's what it was all about.

Making yourself.

It was only early afternoon. Lying down didn't feel like the right thing to do. But this was a different place with different people and different ways of doing things. And he *was* tired. So why not? Going to bed meant putting things in their place, things left over from the day. And thinking about the day ahead. *No, not the day ahead. The afternoon ahead.* The evening ahead with Ben back. At night when he went to bed, he focused on one thing that he would do. It would often be something he had meant to do and forgotten—maybe a place he had passed while riding Bucephalus, disturbed since the last time he had been there, suggesting the presence of new wildlife. Very often it was a task that he had put off in the gardens or the barn. Over the past weeks he had thought about his father, noting the changes as his illness weakened, diminished him. He had thought about the coming of the end and of what lay ahead.

His mind played with that idea, of things lying ahead as if waiting their turn, as if they were trees beside a road waiting to be passed by. But that wasn't the way things were. Nothing lay ahead waiting for him. He had no road. The expression had no meaning, or rather it had too many meanings. Too many possibilities.

The pillow beneath his head was soft and fragrant. The room was more filled with fragrances than any place he had ever been. Rosie had said that they would put "a personal" in *The Globe*. He wasn't sure what that meant and he hadn't asked. He imagined a great sphere in which a very wise person sat. People would come and ask questions the way they had long ago of the Oracle at Delphi. Finding his grandmother was what his father would have called wishful thinking. Another complicated expression. What was the opposite of wishful thinking? He couldn't say.

Make yourself at home, Jenna had said. How do you make yourself at home? Where would he make himself at home? How would he make himself? The pillow was soft. And fragrant. And Jenna was fragrant. He yawned. He listened. A car door closed. Someone laughed. Then it was quiet.

Chapter 15

Simon and The Counselors

Rosie was the first to wake, as always. She dressed quietly so as not to wake Ben. Children meant trouble. They were unpredictable, unfinished and, in Rosie's business, toxic, not to mention illegal. She opened the door to the costume room a crack. Still asleep.

She went down to the kitchen and started the coffee maker. Simon wasn't the first child to sleep in the costume room. And his mother wasn't the first to walk away from her newborn. Rosie had, over 30 years ago. So had several of her girls, Jenna among them. Rosie did the math. Twelve years ago. *Of course. That's what it was all about. Simon couldn't have found a more eligible stand-in.*

The coffee machine gasped. She poured a cup. Black.

Jenna was the first to arrive. Then Rowena, and one by one, sleepy-eyed, half-dressed, a few more. Earlier than usual. There had been no overnight guests. Word had spread about the boy from Maine who talked about biomass and stardust. Jenna alerted them to the fact that they were counselors and that people came there to get help with their lives.

Simon arrived twenty minutes later and conversation stopped. He was given a place at the table and Philemon, the house cat, climbed into his lap. Rowena said she couldn't remember the last time the cat had been that familiar with a stranger. The others agreed. Jenna spoke of a friend who believed that in an earlier life she had been a cat. Clarissa laughed dismissively and poured a glass of orange juice for Simon. Jenna filled a bowl with cereal from a box of Corn Puffs.

"It's really possible," Simon said, between spoonsful. It was his first experience with brown sweetened cereal. The girls smiled, uncomprehending. "About being a cat in another life," he continued.

Encouraged by Jenna, he went on to speak about compost and stardust. He explained how matter, including souls, is recycled; how the remains of breakfast, placed in a compost heap could, over time, birth something as small as a microbe or as great as a pitch pine. Then he spoke briefly of how everything on earth was once stardust. "You don't see it but you know it is there, because you are there and it is you."

Rosie's smile was different from the others. He couldn't read it. Ben's was another matter. It was a familiar smile. It was his father's smile when Simon got something right. He was careful not to look at Ben for fear of scaring the smile away.

Then Rosie moved the conversation to Simon's search for his grandmother. "Are we writing up a personal ad for *The Globe*?" Jenna asked.

"What kind of globe?" Simon asked.

"*The Boston Globe*," Rowena explained. "It's a newspaper."

"Oh."

"He'd probably have better luck on the internet," Cornelia offered.

"What's the internet?" Simon asked.

"It's a place where people can exchange information." Cornelia explained.

"You've never been on the internet?" Gracie asked with an expression of disbelief.

Simon looked at her, his spoon halfway to his mouth. Faces were a big part of this big world. He was an expert at reading Roger's and his father's faces, but had almost no experience beyond that. Never sitting at breakfast with nine women. Reading faces was something he would have to learn.

"Simon has led a very private and quiet life," Jenna said. "Cyber-society is a place he has yet to visit. Isn't that right, Simon?"

"I guess so." He looked at Gracie. "Sorry."

"So," Rowena said. "Let's put something together for *The Globe*."

Cornelia had been scribbling on a small yellow pad. She passed it to Maggie who read it aloud. "Twelve-year-old boy named Simon Seeker would like to find his grandmother." She looked at Simon. "What's her name?"

"Olivia Hardin."

Maggie continued, "He can be reached at…what number should we use?"

"You can use my private number," Rosie said.

"I think it should be an 'I' kind of thing," Cornelia said.

"What's an 'I' kind of thing?" Jenna asked.

"I know what she means," Rowena said. "Like he's the one talking. Like, 'I am an twelve-year-old boy who lives…where?"

"Washington County," Simon said.

"…who lives in Washington County, Maine. I have come to Boston hoping to find my grandmother, Olivia Hardin. If you know her, please pass this number along."

Jenna looked at Simon. He was refilling his cereal bowl.

Rosie had been scribbling on the notepad by the telephone. She tore the sheet off and handed it to Jenna who read it over and then aloud. "Simon Seeker of Washington County, Maine, aged twelve, born—insert birth date—son of Alexandra Hardin, is looking for his grandmother, Olivia Hardin." The girls nodded and went back to their breakfasts, and the topic of conversation changed to some of the people who came in for counseling, and which of the girls was best suited to do the best job in each case. Simon noticed that the girls were saying more than they were literally saying. Again, it wasn't an entirely new experience. He'd had to interpret his father sometimes, and Roger quite a lot. In fact, he had become quite skillful with Roger, who often spoke in code. He had tried it himself but wasn't very good at it. It was hard to find things that you wanted to say without really saying them.

"What's an internet?" he asked Jenna during a pause.

It was apparently the right question. They all joined in again, talking one-on-top-of-the-other about a machine called a computer, a place called cyberspace and about how you used one to 'google' the other. It was the first time he felt he had, in fact, walked into another world. He could summon up neither images nor actions to illustrate what they were saying. After a minute or two Rosie turned to Jenna.

"Why don't you take Simon up to my office and show him?" she asked. "Let him explore this brave new world. Would you like to do that, Simon?"

"Sure."

"You don't have anything else on do you, Jenna?"

"I've got a couple errands but there's no hurry. I'll get Simon started."

"Good." Rosie stood up and started to clear the table. Simon finished the last bite of his cereal and picked up his glass of juice. "You can take that with you," Rosie said.

Rosie's office was just down the hall from the costume room, but it was entirely different. Not in size or shape. In fact, it was just like the room he had been given. But where his room was filled with colors, its edges blunted with soft fabrics, Rosie's room was sharp and colorless. There was a filing cabinet, a table that served as a desk, and three chairs, one with wheels, partly tucked under the desk. No curtain softened the window or carpet padded the floor. Centermost was a screen. In front of it a keyBoard. Next to the keyboard was a small foam pad with a little grey plastic thing on it.

"Bring one of those chairs over here next to me," she said, laying her purse on the table and pulling out the desk chair.

"I'll bet you're a very fast learner," she said, flicking a switch. The screen winked and then smiled. It was the smile of a chimpanzee hanging with one arm from a branch. It looked very real. Simon reached and touched its nose.

"It's a screen saver," Jenna said. She put her hand on the small grey plastic thing and the chimp disappeared. "This is called the mouse. See that little arrow? Watch. When I move the mouse, the arrow moves. That's how you make the screen work for you. You try it." She removed her hand and Simon put his hand carefully on the mouse. Jenna covered it with her own and moved the arrow up to a colorful symbol under which it said 'GOOGLE.'

"You can tell it to look something up. Anything you want to know about. Anything at all."

"Bucephalus," he said.

"What's that?"

"A horse. My horse. At the farm."

"OK. Type the name. Here, use the keyboard." He typed in 'Bucephalus.' "Now click the mouse," Jenna said.

"How do you do that?"

She moved his finger to the side of the mouse and pressed it. *Click*. The screen changed. "WIKIPEDIA, the free Encyclopedia," it read, and next to that, "Bucephalus."

"Why are some of the words blue?" he asked.

"Click on one," she said.

He clicked on the name 'Alexander' and read aloud: "When Alexander was ten years old, a trader from Thessaly brought Philip a horse, which he offered to sell for thirteen talents. The horse refused to be mounted and Philip ordered it away. Alexander, however, detecting the horse's fear of its own shadow, asked to tame the horse, which he eventually managed. Plutarch stated that Philip, overjoyed at this display of courage and ambition, kissed his son tearfully, declaring: "My boy, you must find a kingdom big enough for your ambitions.""

"Ten years old," Jenna said. "How old were you when you tamed your Bucephalus?"

"He was already tame. I mean he wasn't wild. He didn't rear up on his back legs the way horses do in pictures. He wasn't very interested in me. I was five and he pretty much ignored me. But I really wanted him as a friend and so I gave him treats and talked to him a lot."

"And?"

"We became friends. Real friends. We could almost read one another's minds. Not words, I don't mean. I can't really say. Something else."

"Something Alexander would understand. Right?"

"I guess so."

"You have a lot in common."

"I'm not out to conquer the world."

"You've already conquered a small corner of it." Jenna put her hand on his shoulder. "Tell you what. I've got some errands I have to run. You all right here for a while?" She got up and took a step towards the door.

"I guess so."

"You guess so?"

"I mean, sure, I'm fine."

"You're sure?"

He turned and smiled. That always worked with his father. "I'm fine, Jenna. Really."

The door closed and he was alone. He looked at the rest of the screen. There were a lot of blue words. In fact, everything he could imagine anyone wanting to know about Alexander and Bucephalus was in blue. He travelled through ancient Greece, visiting with many of the characters he had learned about in books. Not only people, but the places in which they lived. Had his father known about Wikipedia? He must have.

So why did he keep it a secret? *Dumb question.*

Simon looked at all the blue words at the left of the screen. He clicked on 'About Wikipedia.' "Please help improve this article by adding citations to reliable sources. Unsourced material will be challenged and removed," he read. Even more amazing. An encyclopedia that you could change.

He went back to the place where he had typed in 'Bucephalus' and typed 'ants.' "Ants have colonized almost every landmass on earth," he read. *All except Antarctica*, he thought. That was the kind of thing you remembered because of the words. Ant-arctic? Every fourth word was in blue, leading someplace else. He wandered for some time and then sat back. No names. Not even Professor Wilson. So who then? It said unsourced material might be challenged. But no source was given. And it was wrong. About Antarctica. He clicked on edit.

Chapter

16

Roger and Tom

It was early afternoon. Tom was sweeping the barn floor when the car appeared, stopped, and sat for a moment in the settling dust. It was a Ford Mustang. A man got out, possibly in his sixties, graying at the temples. Tall, high forehead, hatless, expensive designer casuals, designer nose. He stood looking at the ruin of the house, then turned and approached the barn.

"Tom Bewick?"

"Yes, sir."

"Roger Plummer. We spoke on the phone."

"Mr. Plummer! I didn't expect you so soon."

"Yes," Plummer said. "Well."

"Pleased to meet you, sir." They shook hands and Roger turned to once again address the devastation.

"It's certainly a total loss, isn't it?"

"They say it burned like tinder. By the time the forest service got here there wasn't much left." Tom was still holding his push broom. He looked for a place to put it.

"Don't let me interrupt you," Roger said. "I'll just have a walk around. Stretch my legs."

"I was just cleaning up in the barn."

"You go right ahead."

Roger walked over to a rectangle of charred wood and poked at it with a loafer. It rolled over softly in the ash. He took out his handkerchief and wiped his shoe. His imagination hadn't prepared him. *This finale! And Simon. Where the hell was Simon?*

When he turned back, the young man was still at work. Attractive. Nice voice. Poised, but a little nervous. Shrewd. Roger had picked that up at once in their telephone conversation. Wanting to know about Simon. He had decided on the drive up not to say more than necessary. It would be Mr. Seeker, Larin Seeker, at least until he was sure of his ground. The longer he could keep Reese's death from the media, the better. He walked the perimeter of the ruin and returned to where Tom stood waiting.

"I haven't said how grateful I am that you were willing to take care of things here, Tom."

"I'm glad to, sir."

"So the Belgians weren't too intimidating for you?"

"No, I grew up on a farm."

"You said you were in school."

"Yes, I'm a senior at Orono."

"University of Maine."

"Yes, sir."

"Rudy Vallee."

"Who's that?"

"'Lift a stein to dear old Maine.' You've never heard of Rudy Vallee? Not surprising. He was even before my time. 1920s. The Elvis Presley of his day. He went to your school."

"I guess I'd better brush up on my local history."

"I wouldn't bother. I'm sure there are more distinguished graduates. What are you studying, Tom?"

"Journalism. Actually that's why I came out here. I have an internship at *The Washington County Star*."

"I don't know it."

"A weekly. Local news."

"You were covering the fire."

"Yes sir."

"I see." When the young man had called, he had placed him in that tedious category of Yankees with whom he had dealt on Reese's behalf over the years—people whose conversation was a clipped monotony of complaints about the weather, the government, and the price of fuel oil, with an ear cocked for the slightest hint of gossip.

Roger looked around at the remaining buildings, his eyes resting on the chicken coop. The door was open and the birds clawed the shredded brown earth for grubs.

Roger had been in charge of the hen house at Wind Lake School his last year. Chickens were the only animals for which he had developed any affection. He turned to face Tom. "Do you know what those exotic fowl are called?" he asked.

"No sir," Tom said.

"They are called Dominiques. They're true colonialists, Tom. Came over with the first settlers from England. They were an all-purpose bird. Big brown eggs and very meaty. Even the feathers were valued. Mattress stuffing. Mr. Seeker had a book on them."

"I've seen it," Tom said.

Roger looked at him and wrinkled his brows. Then he looked at the smoking ruins of the house.

"In the barn," Tom said. "There's a kind of fort up in the hayloft. Made of hay bales."

"Ah, yes." Roger paused, pursed his lips. "Yes of course. I'm sorry that I haven't been more straightforward with you, Tom. It's all been so sudden and Mr. Seeker was a complicated man. He had a son. Simon. Just coming up on his thirteenth birthday."

"I thought it must be a boy's place," Tom said.

"Mr. Seeker called it Simon's baleout."

"Bailout?"

"Mr. Seeker was fond of puns. Outrageous, actually. Real groaners. It was Simon's retreat." Roger paused, took a pipe from his pocket. "Do you mind?"

"No, sir. My dad smokes a pipe. Now and then a cigar if someone gives him one."

"It's very much frowned upon nowadays," Roger said, taking a leather pouch from his jacket pocket.

"Really, sir. It's fine."

Roger packed his pipe and lit it. He needed the time and the ritual. He didn't inhale, never had. The taste was comforting. He asked Tom how he liked the University of Maine.

"It's OK." He thought, reconsidered. "No, that's not fair. It's very good. I just wanted a break, time in the real world. I'll go back and finish up next fall. It'll be good to be back just like it's been good to be away." He laughed. "Sorry."

"Variety is the spice of life," Roger said. He pursed his lips. "I've no idea who wrote that. Hmm."

"You got me," Tom said. "I'm not a literature buff. I can do some Shakespeare from high school, but that's about it."

"But you are a writer; I mean you write for the local paper. Did I get that right?"

"Right. *The Washington County Star*." Tom turned towards the charred remains of the farmhouse. "The fire," he said. "Do you think...?"

"I don't know what to think. Both bedrooms were on the second floor. Usually Simon slept in his loft but these last months he has been looking after his father."

Tom turned with a puzzled expression.

"Oh, sorry. Larin had cancer. He decided against treatment. Came back here to spend his last months."

Tom turned with open mouth and no words.

"Yes, I know. Hard to imagine how he could ask that of Simon. But he did. And Simon seemed to cope. I came up every other week. Larin was pretty normal until about a month ago."

"And then?"

"Bedridden. I begged him to let me hire a nurse. For Simon's sake if not his."

"And?"

"Simon said he didn't need a nurse. "I'm fine, he said. Can you imagine that? Twelve years old, talking like he's the daddy and Larin is the kid."

"My God! That's...."

"There isn't a word to describe it. Not in my vocabulary anyway." Roger kicked at a burnt timber that crumbled into small pieces.

Tom looked at the blackened ruins and felt a shiver. "And then the fire."

"Right."

"So where is Simon?"

Roger spoke in a quieter voice as if to himself. "I have to believe he got out." He thought for a moment, then continued with an attempt at self-assurance. "He could have jumped from his window if he couldn't use the staircase. Second floor, but not all that high really."

"Would he have run away?"

"He must have."

"Maybe he got lost in the woods."

Roger took a breath, looked around, then another.

Tom thought it best to change the subject. "You asked me to have a look around."

"What? Oh… right…did you find anything?"

"Yes."

"Oh?"

"A trunk with some file folders, some kids' books, and a couple newspaper articles. In the lower level of the barn."

"Ah, yes. I apologize a second time for these omissions. It's been my job to protect Mr. Seeker and his son from exposure to the wider world for quite some time now; the habit is a difficult one to break."

"Hey, it's all happened so fast. No problem. But you did invite me to have a look around."

"And I'm so glad you did. I would never have found them. I always thought of the office as a repository for ancestral leavings. I'd like to have a look."

Tom led Roger down to the office behind the milking area and opened the trunk. Roger pulled up a milking stool and looked at a surprising orderly arrangement of books, newspapers, and file folders. He lifted out several of the Sam Scamper books, holding them as if they might break. Tom watched, sensing that perhaps his visitor wanted to be alone. "I've got more work to do in the barn. Can I get you anything?"

"Thank you, Tom. I'm fine. I'll sit here for a bit and sort through things."

It was an hour later when Roger came back up to the driveway.

He found Tom cleaning out one of the stalls. He watched for a few moments before speaking. Tom was clearly familiar with the work at hand. He had hung the stall mats on the divide wall and cleaned the straw of turds which lay in a tin pail. Now he was filling the water trough. Roger cleared his throat and Tom turned.

"Did you find everything?"

"Yes. Thank you so much. I'm sure that I can count on you to keep things in the trunk a little longer. There are matters of the estate that are a little tricky, especially with Simon potentially out of the picture."

Tom inspected the water trough for a moment as he waited for the specter of Simon's potential fate to fade. "I figured out the anagram," he said.

"Ah, yes. Reese the writer couldn't resist that mischief, chancy as it was. Larin Seeker, Reese Larkin."

Tom put away his broom. They walked outside the barn to where he had put a couple of hay bales and sat down.

"Did Simon ever read any of his father's books?" Tom asked.

"Reese didn't want Simon Seeker's life complicated by his namesake," Roger responded, finding a comfortable position on the somewhat prickly bale. "Understandably. And Reese was done with his made-up companions, now that he had a real one."

"I read that article from *The London Times*," Tom said with some caution.

"Yes, it's all there. The Christian Right bumped Bumpus when he started talking cosmology...that was Reese all over. He threw out those celestial ideas on a take-it-or-leave-it basis. It wasn't heavy-handed. But it was just that kind of mischievous detachment that infuriated the Christian Right. They can't stand ambiguity. He could have handled the financial reverses. I'm not sure how much was in the clippings you read. His publisher dropped the Bumpus books."

"The Lassiter twins were a big piece of my childhood," Tom said, thoughtfully.

"Yours and hundreds of others."

"Thousands, I'd bet. So Mr. Larkin—excuse me; Mr. Seeker—moved out here to get away from it all. Do I have that right?"

"You do."

"I was re-reading a couple of the Bumpus books last night," Tom said. "It took me back. The Lassiter twins were my pals when I was nine or ten. They were so believable. They said things that I might have said." Tom chuckled. "More often, things that I would like to have been quick enough to say. They were so real."

"Reese loved children, Tom. More than anyone I have ever known. A child's trust was sacred. As small a thing as sarcasm would get him going. He wasn't as fond of adults. 'Great oafs from little acorns grow,' he used to say."

"Should we file a missing persons report on Simon?" Tom asked.

"Not yet. Let's give him a day or two. He might very well be out at one of his bases, pulling himself together. It's hard to imagine Simon in shock, but I can imagine him out there somewhere with his friends, watching us."

"Friends?"

"Animals, birds, ants. They were all his companions. His only ones." Roger stretched and turned, with a swift smile. "He would have turned to them for comforting." Roger paused, considering. "No. That is unfair. I'm sorry, Tom. He is a puzzling child. He could quote philosophy to you but knew nothing about how the world worked. He was good at chess but had never kicked a soccer ball. Husbandry, horticulture, and Heraclitus. Did you ever read *The Once and Future King*, Tom?"

"Merlin and Arthur. It was one of my favorite stories."

"Understand Merlin and you'll understand Reese." Roger picked up a stick and cleaned out his pipe, turning the ashes over with his fingers to be sure there were no live ones.

"There were books on ants up in the loft," Tom said.

"Oh, yes. Wilson. One of Simon's heroes. I think he read everything of Wilson's, and any number of other naturalists. Thoreau, of course." Roger banged his pipe against the heel of his shoe and put it into his pocket. "The house is a total loss. If Simon is out there, he must be in a state of shock. Everything gone. His father, his home…"

"But not his place in the loft."

"Right." Roger laughed quietly. "Makes you wonder." He looked at the ruins and shook his head. "Ridiculous."

"What's that?"

"Nothing. Crazy thought."

"Can you tell me?"

"You promise not to put it in your column?" Roger asked with a grin.

"Of course. I'm not going to put anything in that you don't approve."

"I know. Just kidding. Simon's baleout. A place of his own. Just in case? Planning for the future? Crazy. I knew Reese as well as anyone in his life, but I never knew what might come next."

They walked over to the remains of the farmhouse. There was nothing now but a square foundation within which the grey ash rested, almost seductive in its softness. Here but not here. Hidden but in plain sight. It was one of the many things the critics had commended Reese for. Helping children understand that life was complex. Never one thing or the other. Not absolutely. Opposites depended on one another. One possibility might go into hiding for the sake of the momentary clarity that comforted young readers. But it never went entirely into hiding. Time would do its mischief, have its laugh.

Tom tossed a stone that disappeared soundlessly.

"They don't make foundations like that anymore," Tom said, clearing the ashes away from one of the granite blocks that stood naked and speckled in the sunlight. "When did you say the first Larkin arrived here?"

"Around 1735. Josiah Larkin. Not unlike Reese in some ways, if the record is correct. A loner. Imagine back in 1735 how primitive this part of the state was. Didn't cost King George much. Like giving away a crater on the moon today." Roger got down carefully on one knee and examined the granite. "It wasn't until quite a few years later that the house got built.

I imagine it took a pretty good road and a pair of hefty Belgians to haul those granite blocks."

"It's quite a story, Mr. Plummer. How much of it can I use?"

"I keep forgetting that you are a journalist. I should be much more close-mouthed." He stood up and dusted off his knees. "Let's start modestly."

"That's fine with me, sir."

"You can certainly write about the fire, and the loss of the house. How the animals were let out by the fire-fighters. When does your paper come out?"

"Wednesdays."

"That gives us almost two weeks until the second installment. The more we can slow things down the better. Once word gets out about Reese there'll be a stampede. Reporters, TV crews. My God, the press will have an orgy. Let's take time to catch our breaths, Tom. And if Simon is hiding out there, we need to give him some time to come to terms with the situation."

He stood up and turned to the barn, then scanned the rest of the buildings, finally looking once more at the ruins. He took in a deep breath and stood there for a moment. Tom watched with sympathy, glad to be there, glad to be needed. Roger turned. "There is one more thing I'd like you to undertake if you feel comfortable with it. It's no small task. I must restore the farmhouse. It's in Reese's will. I had never really given much thought to that request until these last few days. Whether or not Simon turns up, the house is part of the Larkin trust, part of the Larkin history. And of course it's the only home Simon has ever known. Do you know of anyone in the area who might take on such a restoration?"

"Yes, I think I do. Bob Thibodeau has a construction company. He's done some work for my father. And he's active in the Maine Historical Society. Big on restoration."

"Excellent. Talk with him and give me a call, please."

"By the way, Bob is the pilot for the forest service. He's the one who saved the barn and the outbuildings."

"What could be better? He already has an investment in the place. Knowing that you are here looking after things gives me peace of mind where I never expected it. I have something for you." Roger turned and walked to his car. Tom followed. Opening the passenger door, Roger removed a box from the seat. He turned and handed it to Tom. "This is a satellite phone. My secretary says it will work anywhere in the world. She put my number into the memory and your number into mine." He took another phone from his pocket and held it up. "Call me any time. If I don't hear from you by tomorrow morning, I'll give you a call. If you need anything, let me know." He took out his wallet, removed five one hundred dollar bills and handed them to Tom. "This will help you get provisioned."

"Wow. That's a lot of provision."

"You may be here for a time. I hope you will be." He held out his hand. Tom took it. Roger covered their clasped hands with his other hand. *Was that too much?* He hoped not. "I can't tell you how fortunate I feel Tom, that you should have been the one to show up. If Simon is out there someplace, watching us, he will be very fortunate indeed to have you as a friend."

"Sure thing, Mr. Plummer. Is there anything else you would like me to do?"

Roger smiled and put his hand on Tom's shoulder. "First off, let's leave Mr.Plummer in his office. Please call me Roger."

Chapter 17

Simon

Sunday morning Simon was first up. He studied the kitchen, carefully opening drawers and cupboards, observing the contents of the refrigerator and then examining the coffee machine. Ben, like Simon's father, was a coffee lover. One of his tasks during the last months had been to brew his father's coffee. His father would taste it carefully and then smile. *Parfait*, he would say. *Absolument!* What would Ben say? Or Rosie? Or Jenna? It was something he could do.

The settings were straight-forward, the water tank where it should be and a filter holder that swung out. He took a filter off the pile in the cupboard just above and inserted it. Then he looked for the grinder. No grinder. His father would have had a fit. *What? Canned coffee? Tired-out, flavored-out ground coffee.* He opened the bag of ground coffee and filled the filter. Then he filled the tank and clicked the switch. He watched. It gurgled. He smiled at the familiar sound. It was a new world but not an entirely different one.

The room where he had slept had nothing familiar about it. All those strange clothes, smells he had never encountered, the softness he had felt lying on the bed. From the moment he had climbed up next to Ben and looked out at the highway, everything had been new. His father had told him he must walk slowly into the world. Wind Lake School would be a good first step. Things would be familiar: sights and sounds, routines, the cooking smells, the animals. He could take small steps and feel secure, like first learning to walk. He couldn't have explained to his father that he wanted to take bigger steps and more quickly. He had waited so long. If he must lose all that was familiar, all that he had known, he did not want to be reminded of it.

He walked to the back door and out onto the porch. It needed paint. The railings were flaked and peeling. Behind the parking area was a field of weeds from which a red-flowered tree broke free into the brightening sky. He knew it. It was a crabapple.

He walked down the steps and across the parking lot. The tree was surrounded by a thicket of wild raspberries. Very carefully he pushed them aside. About two feet in front of the crabapple, completely hidden by the raspberries, a rose bush, a very healthy climber, had used the crabapple as a trellis. Hundreds of buds speckled the vines as they reached sunward. In another month they would flower. The "natural reciprocity" appealed to Simon; it was a phrase he had come across in one of his books. Like egrets and cattle, or mistletoe in a tree. He looked more closely at the exploring tendrils of the rose bush, hugging the crabapple's branches. Hugging, not choking, the way bittersweet vine would. But what was the crabapple getting out of the deal? Companionship. Nature was full of surprise friendships. Things that made you know you weren't alone. The farm had been filled with friendships. Sometimes they needed help. That was what people were for.

And now this new world. Not only a reaching rose bush; open arms. Smiles. A hand on your head. A kiss good night. He had been given so much in the last two days. Ben, Jenna, even Rosie. *But what had he done? Where was the natural reciprocity?* A pot of coffee. It was a start.

Once someone had tended this garden, planted the rose bush. Someone with tools. A shovel, rake, and spade. A wheelbarrow or a cart. He scanned the yard, then the back of the house. Nothing. *Wait; under the stairs.* A trellis. He walked back and parted the morning glories. Yes. A door. Carefully he raised the vines. It had a rusty knob. He turned it and pushed. There was a quiet rain of dust and rust and a rise of disturbed air. Simon breathed respectfully. He was an intruder.

He stepped over the rotting threshold and onto a dirt floor. The only light came from the open door, enough to see that every distance a spider might have traversed was woven with elegant and dusty cobwebs. In one corner he found a wheelbarrow and in it the tools of a gardener, left as if for a next day that had never come. He tried to imagine the gardener, old and hunched, wheeling the barrow under the stairs one last time. That thought led to others, unwanted. On a counter was a stack of gardening magazines. He opened one. The date was 1968.

Pushing the wheelbarrow and its contents out into the sunny morning he crossed the parking area to the raspberry patch. It was familiar. You couldn't change too many things at the same time or you'd get lost in your head. That's what his father had said when he was talking about that school. The important things would be familiar. The company of animals, the gardens... things that he knew about. Things where he could show people he knew his way around. But people ran away from schools in his books. They didn't want people telling them how to use their time. They didn't want to be surrounded by copies of themselves. They wanted to meet real people, make their way, make up their own minds.

This was right. A garden just waiting for him. He took out the sickle and swiped at the tall grass. Then the goldenrod. He piled the cuttings to one side and took the spading fork from the wheelbarrow. It wasn't easy. The soil wasn't used to the seasonal attentions of a gardener. He had to jump on the fork to sink it. Getting the first several clods broken away took all his strength; but as he moved along and began to cut smaller wedges the routine became more manageable. And satisfying. Spaded earth held the promise of new life. Life that he could create and that others would admire.

He had no idea how long he had been working when he heard Rosie's voice. "I don't think anyone has turned this weed bed for 50 years," she said. Simon looked up. In one hand Rosie held a cup of the coffee he had brewed. In the other a cigarette. She took a puff and exhaled.

"I'm making a garden," he said.

"What kind of garden do you have in mind?"

"Well, it could be a vegetable garden. It's near the kitchen so you could come out and get things for dinner."

"And just what kind of things should we grow?"

"Whatever you like. Beans, peas, squash. Oh, and watermelon. You can watch it get bigger and bigger."

"Well, that would be very nice. Where on earth did you find that decrepit wheelbarrow?"

"Under the porch. Didn't you know it was there?"

"I've never been much of a gardener. I guess I didn't notice it."

"So what do you think?"

"About what?"

"About having a garden.

"Who's going to take care of it?"

Simon turned away and looked at the crabapple tree. It was just a common crabapple until the rose had made a home there. "Ben did gardening when he was a boy."

Rosie laughed quietly, as if it was unintended. She took a puff on her cigarette, dropped it to the ground and stepped on it. "The paper should be here." She turned and walked back to the outside stairs.

Chapter 18

Tom

On Sunday Tom had called Ron Thibodeau and described the project. Ron was not a man given to public enthusiasms, but Tom detected a slight change of conversational tempo as he responded to the builder's questions. As it turned out, the Brothers Thibodeau were between projects. They would come out on Monday.

They arrived just after eight as he was collecting eggs in the chicken coop. He had brewed some coffee and the three of them walked over to the foundation that had survived the conflagration without alteration. Not surprising given the monumental sizes of the granite blocks which, like those in the pyramids, inspired speculation on their transit and assembly.

"Big horses," Ronnie said. "And a sledge."

"Very big horses," brother Bob said. Several of the blocks were eight feet in length and three feet thick.

"We've never built a house on a rock foundation before," Ron said. "Poured concrete was a great invention, allowing you to set your bolts for the frame," he explained. "Not many people in this part of the country go in for restoration," he said. "They're glad to modernize. How faithful to the original design do we have be? I'm not sure there's anybody around who still does lathe and plaster work." Tom had to say that he didn't know. It wasn't a detail that he and Roger had yet discussed. He promised to do that by tomorrow.

"We should have a close look at the barn," Ron said. "They would have used the same basic techniques. We can get an idea of timber sizes. It's all mortise and tenon, of course. We've done plenty of that. I hope they don't expect us to hew the logs by hand. I'm not sure you could find a working adz anymore in any case. Maybe at Charlie's. I know he still stocks the old river runner gear. Mostly for tourists. You know, pikes and the like. I did pick up a draw plane there once."

"It's lucky we have the barn at all," Tom said. "I still can't figure out how the out- buildings survived. It's a miracle."

"Partly miracle and partly good fire-fighting," Bob said, grinning. "If I'd got here ten minutes later it would have been a different story. That's for sure."

"So what'd you do, drop your chemical on the outbuildings instead of the house?"

"Most of it. There was no saving the house. First load I dumped on the barn and the shed. I dropped three loads before the pumper got here. By the way, thanks for the nice piece in *The Bangor Daily News* this morning. The forest service can use all the kudos it can get. The state budget's coming up for review next month."

"I'll make a note of that. I might not have another shot at *The Bangor Daily News* right away. Maybe as things unfold. Anyway I'll make a point of it in *The Star* this Wednesday. I meant to mention that you had let the animals out in case the fire spread. I'll put that in."

"I didn't let the animals out. They were wandering around when I arrived. Horses were pretty spooked by the chopper."

"Ellie said you probably let them out."

"The animals weren't let out at night," Ronnie said. "Ellie should have figured that out."

"Why?" Tom asked.

"Well, for one thing, the chickens. You don't move a roosting chicken. Not unless you want to get pretty scratched up. And you certainly don't move thirty of them. The chickens were out, right Bob?"

"Why would someone shut them out?" Tom asked.

"Maybe to clean the hen house," Bob said. "And then forgot that they had left the door closed."

"What about the goats and the horses?"

"Same person forgot to put them in. Maybe the old man got sick, couldn't go out, knocked over a lamp. Bang. There's your fire." Ronnie was so pleased with his theory that he wrapped it up in some advice. "What I always say is, look for the simplest answer. Don't go off half-cocked with complicated theories when common sense will do the trick." So saying, he turned to inspect the barn. "Here you got the same arrangement as the house," he said. "Sills on the granite foundation." Bob joined him and they walked behind the building for a closer inspection.

Tom was left with his thoughts from a childhood spent as a farm boy. There had been times when chores had been forgotten in some small crisis, a door left open, lights left on, water running.

Still, this was more complicated. These animals had been out before the sun went down. They were let out before the fire had started. He took out the cell phone Roger had given him and googled Maine Forest Service. It rang four times before the message. "You've reached the office of Elias Compton, Game Warden. I am out on the road right now, but I check my messages regularly and if you leave one, I will get back to you shortly." Tom waited for the beep. "Elias. It's Tom Bewick. Ellen must have told you that I'm looking after things out here at Spruce Valley Farm. Look, I need your help on something. It's a little bit unusual, but does anybody use dogs anymore for tracking people? My cell phone number is 365-6677. It might be important, Elias. Give me a call as soon as you can. Thanks."

Tom closed his phone and clipped it to his belt. Empress whinnied and cantered over to where he stood. She nuzzled his shoulder. "You think so too, huh, girl? Well, we'll see. We'll see."

Chapter 19

Simon and Jenna

Simon awoke on Wednesday morning with a word in his mind. It was comforting. It took him back to the farm and his baleout. When he slept there among his many books, he felt their companionship. Their breadth of settings and circumstance somewhat quieted his need for adventure. Their authors spoke as if to him alone. New words opened new thoughts and helped to order what was random. Often when he awoke, a word would be waiting for him, offering to accompany and perhaps even order his thoughts of the day past.

Today it was the word "routine," one that he heard many times without giving it a thought. His father used it. Roger used it. And he used it. But without reflection. Hearing Jenna, Rosie, and Ben use it was different. It served to make order of so much that was new, confusing, and sometimes frightening.

He had never spent time with so many people so different from one another, and yet, through their common routine, alike. The girls, for example. Breakfast time was spent sharing the evening before, with familiar friends, mostly approved and rarely quoted. Then there was breakfast itself, each eating as she chose but with the same habits of table and sink.

Routine, he realized, was a way of relaxing. It was the quiet stride of Bucephalus or the soundless work of ants.

He had continued to make coffee, an old routine that made the unfamiliar comfortable, habitable. And thanks from the girls, from Rosie, from Jenna gave him a sense of being useful. They shared a routine. There would be others, especially with Jenna. And Ben. And there was Ben's routine: up to Prince Edward Island on a Thursday, back on a Friday. Some day he would go along. Not now. Not yet. Someday.

When the coffee was on its way to brewing, he went back out to his gardening plot and continued to turn and pound the soil. He had made good progress in the past three days. Better even than he had hoped. It was going on nine o'clock and his mind went to the cereal cupboard. His father was not enthusiastic about cold crunchy things in a bowl, but he had provided three kinds of cereals that Simon might choose from. They were OK. But nothing compared to the colorful fragrance of Rosie's cereal cabinet. He thought about it now, seeing how many boxes he could name. Each name gave a nudge to his appetite, and finally he put down the spade and made his way back to the house.

"Good morning Johnny Appleseed," Jenna called from the porch.

"Good morning, Jenna," he replied, making his way up the steps. "I have a pair of those," he said, pointing to the binoculars around Jenna's neck. "Well, I did have a pair."

"We can share these. I'm taking you out to breakfast at Marcellino's, after our bird walk."

"Bird walk? Oh, that's what the binoculars are for."

"Right. You ready to go?"

"I guess so. I mean, sure. Does Marcellino's have cereal?"

Jenna laughed. "I don't think so. Do you need to go inside first?"

"No. I peed behind the tree; I'm OK."

Jenna laughed again, put her hands on his shoulders, and kissed the top of his head.

Simon quizzed her with a few birdsongs as they walked and was pleased that he did them well enough for her to name the singers. Her favorite was the cardinal. His was the catbird, plainest of all the local population but the only real composer, he explained. The other birds had maybe two or three songs at most. Most had only one.

The catbird never sang the same song twice. Well, maybe. That would be something interesting to research on Wikipedia. When they got back.

Jenna pointed out a number of birds, most of which he knew; but this was Jenna's walk, and he didn't want to show off. He asked how long she had done bird walks. Jenna told him about her father, who had died in a war but had once worked for the Parks Service and taught her about birds. She handed him the binoculars and they watched a mourning dove that was all alone. They waited for him to show them his nest, but he didn't, so they walked on.

A gray squirrel ran across the road in front of them and Simon pointed to it. "Do you know about grey squirrels?" he asked.

"I know they like sunflower seeds and that you have to have a baffle on your bird-feeder pole."

Simon laughed, "Baffling squirrels. That's good. It's not easy. Squirrels are really, really smart. They have lots of tricks to fool people and they can almost fly. A grey squirrel can jump ten times the length of his body. And he can turn his ankles 180 degrees. And they're really good farmers. When they gather nuts and things—mostly acorns where we live—they check them over to see if they're sprouting. If they are, they throw them out, because they'll go bad. But that's not the most amazing thing."

"What is the most amazing thing?"

"They know if you're watching them. They've got wrap-around eyes. If they think someone's watching—or maybe another squirrel is—they'll only pretend to bury the acorn. Actually, they keep it in their mouth. But they go through the whole routine. They dig the hole, poke their noses in and fill it up. But there's nothing there."

"You've checked."

"Lots of times."

"Birds, horses, squirrels. Tell me about your other friends at the farm."

"There are a lot." *Friends,* Simon thought. *Yes, they were his friends. His only friends. What was it Ben had called him? A horse-whisperer.* So he wasn't the only one. There wouldn't be a name for it if there weren't people who earned the name. *Were there also bumblebee, dragonfly, and cricket whisperers?* Ants were different. Ants and honey bees. With their signals, their language, their loyalty to royalty. That's what his father had called it. His father was much better with words. But never a horse-whisperer.

"Well?"

"I'm thinking. There are lots. OK. Chipmunks."

"Cute little guys, but they can be a real…" Jenna seemed to reconsider her words. "Tell me what you know about chipmunks."

"Well, one way they're different from squirrels is that they don't eat the seeds that they find. They fill their cheeks and take them back to their homes. They have a special place where they put them away for the winter."

"Underground?"

"Yes. They have several rooms. One for storage and others for living and sleeping. I'd sit outside with some sunflower seeds in my hand and they'd crawl up my leg, check me out, and then pack away the seeds. I can get a red squirrel to eat out of my hand but it takes a lot of sitting still."

They turned a corner onto a street with more traffic. Jenna reached out and took Simon's hand. The light changed and they crossed. "This is all new to you, isn't it, sweetie? Crowds, traffic, crosswalks."

Simon nodded.

"You are straight out of a book."

"Which one?"

"One that hasn't been written yet. Here we are." They stopped in front of a storefront with the name MARCELLINO'S in dancing black script over the door. He followed Jenna inside. It was nothing like Hauler's, Simon thought. Tiny by comparison. And quieter. The people were different as well. More women. Mostly women. Happy women, talking and laughing quietly, in twos or threes. Jenna walked to a table by the window and took off the binoculars. She put them on the table as if to mark it theirs. Then she walked up to the counter.

"What will it be?" the man asked. Simon smiled to himself. His mind ran back to his first moments in Ben's truck. "Buckle up," Ben had said. Not a new language, but a new way of using it. And that was only the beginning. Phrases he had to decipher like code without letting on that he didn't understand. *What will it be? What will I be?* Choices.

Jenna picked up a couple menus from the counter and handed him one. "OK, what would you like for breakfast?"

He looked it over and the name 'finnan haddie' came to mind. It wasn't on the menu. Not here. He closed his eyes and saw Ben across from him at the table at Hauler's.

"How about some scrambled eggs and bacon?" Jenna said.

It was a much shorter menu than the one at Hauler's, but not all that different. "I'll have the pancakes," he said.

"Anything with them?" the man asked.

"Just maple syrup."

"OK," he said. "And you, Jenna?"

"I'm good with the biscotti," she said. She handed him a twenty-dollar bill. He rang up sixteen seventy-five and gave her the change.

They walked back to the table and sat down. Jenna offered Simon a bite of her biscotti.

"Good?"

"Very good. Biscotti?"

"Right."

"From biscuit?"

Jenna took a bite and rolled her eyes. "They're Italian. Italian was Latin once. So was English. They are probably distant cousins."

"Much better than a biscuit."

"Depends on the biscuit. Rosie makes really good ones with cheese."

"Cheddar cheese?"

"Asiago. Oh my goodness."

"What?"

"Asiago cheese is Italian."

"First cousins," Simon said. "Roger always brought a box of croissants when he came to visit. Sometimes they had things in them. Like cream cheese or nuts. The nut ones were the best."

"Who's Roger?"

"He's a lawyer in New York City. And he was my dad's best friend."

"Ben told me about your father. I'm so sorry."

"So am I."

Jenna reached across the table and put her hand on Simon's "Would you like to tell me about him? I know that might be hard."

Simon looked quickly at Jenna and then away.

"You can tell me about him later. I'm not going anywhere. We'll have lots more time."

"It's OK. I can talk about him. I was just remembering a time when he and Roger were having a fight. Well, not a fight. Just yelling at one another. Roger called him a hermit."

"A hermit?"

"He called himself that but he didn't like it when Roger did. When my dad got grouchy he'd say that he was a hermit crab. "What's it like to be holed up with a hermit crab?" he'd say."

"What was it like?"

"He was almost never grouchy, unless we had to go out shopping and he had to be around other people. Mostly Roger arranged for things to be brought. And money stuff."

"So Roger sort of looked after your dad?"

"Sort of. He's my guardian. I was supposed to call him when Dad died."

"But you didn't?"

"No."

"Have you told Ben about Roger?"

"No."

"Does Roger know about the fire and your father?"

"I think so. I saw the helicopter from the Forest Service before I walked to the road. They'd probably call up Roger to tell him about the fire."

"Oh, Simon. This isn't good. He might think you died in the fire."

"That would be OK."

"Simon!"

"He never liked me very much. I'd just be a problem for him. He wasn't like my father. I don't know how they got to be friends. Anyway, if I called him, he'd send someone after me and then I couldn't be with you."

"You need to tell Ben. And Rosie."

"Why?"

"Well, she's the boss. You can't have secrets from her or you're out on the street. No, I don't really mean that, so don't repeat that. What I mean is it's best to be up front with her."

"Up front?"

"Honest."

"They'll make me call Roger."

"You have to do that, Simon. I'm sorry that makes you unhappy, but there are things called legalities. Ben and Rosie could get in trouble."

"Not if they don't know. You wouldn't know if I hadn't told you. Please, Jenna. I know I have to let Roger know I'm alive some time. But I don't want to go to that school."

"What school?"

"The one he and my dad went to. It's up in the mountains, away from everything. I've been away from everything my whole life. I want to be here. With you and Ben…and Rosie…and the others. I want to be in the real world. I've been waiting my whole life."

"Don't you think you should do what your father planned for you?"

"My father knew what I was going to do."

"What are you saying? He made all of these arrangements. He appointed Roger as your guardian."

"He wrote me a letter and hid it in my backpack. When we get back to Rosie's I'll show it to you." The man arrived with his pancakes and syrup, setting the plate before him.

"Sure you don't want to share these?" he asked Jenna.

"Thanks, but no thanks. I've got to watch my figure."

"Your figure?"

"I don't want to put on weight."

"Oh." Simon swallowed his first bite and smiled. "You would still be beautiful," he said.

113

Chapter 20

Tom and Roger

Bumpus Twin Frees Animals, Flees Fire
Special to *The Boston Globe*
Thomas Bewick

Simon Larkin is alive. So say authorities in Baxter, Maine, where the boy was thought to have died ten days ago in the fire that destroyed the family home. Simon, the son of Reese Larkin, creator of the Sam Scamper and Mr. Bumpus stories, is now believed to have fled the farm at the time of the fire and made his way to State Highway 9, several miles to the south of the property.

The discovery was made when an earlier report concerning the farm's livestock was found to be erroneous. Fire Warden Ellen Dawson reports that when she arrived at the fire site the livestock had all been released from the buildings. Contacted by phone, Ronnie Thibodeau, the fire service helicopter pilot, tells us that when he landed after dousing the fire he found that the animals had already been let out of their pens. With this information we report that the boy, Simon, aged 12, is in all likelihood still alive. Why the boy fled the scene is still a matter of speculation, but Karen Pollard of Maine Youth Services, told this reporter that the boy was probably in shock and fearful that he himself might be consumed as the blaze spread. "It is not impossible," she said, "given the magnitude of the boy's loss, that he could be suffering from temporary amnesia."

Using the boy's jacket, which was found in the barn, the police employed tracking dogs in an attempt to locate him. William Casey, who headed the search on behalf of the Maine State Police, said that though the fire occurred six days ago, the dogs were able to pick up the boy's scent and follow it to Route 9, where presumably he hitched a ride. Anyone with information on Simon Larkin's whereabouts is urged to contact the Maine State Police in Bangor at 207-973-3700 or 1-800-432-7381.

Roger Plummer, attorney for Larkin and executor of his estate, said that this is very good news indeed. He described the boy as extremely resourceful for his age and well able to take care of himself. Plummer also announced a $25,000 reward for information bringing about the child's return.

Putting down the paper, Roger called Tom. It was nine o'clock. Tom answered after only three rings. "Hey Roger. Have you seen my story?"

"Yes and it's excellent. Any calls yet from the State Police?"

"No, but it's still early."

"Well, we can hope. How are things at the farm?"

"Everything here is moving along pretty well. Ron and Bob are leveling the old foundation. Not leveling, I don't mean. You know, straightening it out. The lumber has arrived. Beautiful stuff. Big beams. Like the barn."

"You're not getting cabin fever?"

"Knowing Simon is alive makes the place less haunted. I really want to meet him. I'm going through his books. It's an amazing collection. Every adventure story I've ever heard about. Stevenson, London, Dumas, and of course Twain. He must have been a pretty precocious reader. And not just adventures! Lots of books on nature. I skimmed a few by a guy named

Wilson. On ants. One of them was about his childhood in the South. Not a lot different from Simon's in some ways."

"Simon read everything he could find on ants. Wilson was his hero."

"And drawings. Lots of them. Not so much of ants as of trees and plants and decaying stuff. That really caught my eye. Oh, and stars. The kid really knew his astronomy."

"Reese bought him a very fine telescope."

"I don't think it was up in his loft."

"No. You walk down by the pond and you'll find a small shed. The telescope's in there. On rollers."

"I'll check it out. By the way, speaking of telescopes, would it be OK if I got Direct TV to install a satellite receiver? Not so much for entertainment. I just want to stay up on the news."

"No problem. So great to have you there, Tom. If you need anything else don't hesitate to ask."

"Thanks, Roger."

Tom put the phone on the table, sat back in his chair and closed his eyes. There was much more to all of this than a press release. The story into which he had found his way was one in which he might have been a part. Not as a reporter, but as a character. Jesse had left without any possibility of returning. None at all. Of course not. He was dead. Gone from the world. But never from Tom's mind, and now he had come out once again to watch and wait. Would Tom do it right this time? Would he be there?

Tom shook himself and stood up, turning to the motionless morning, listening to the sounds of chickens clucking, flapping their wings, warbling discoveries to their companions. One of the books up in Simon's loft had been about chickens and the sounds they made. Simon had written his own notes in the margins and marked many of the sounds, presumably the ones he had himself heard. One of them was short and low-pitched, meaning, "Stay close." Another was a vibrating sound that said, "Danger is near. Stay put." And there was a hiss that said, "Stay away. These are my eggs, not yours."

Simon. Simon Seeker. Simon listener and learner. And now Simon lost. But not as Jesse had been lost, to the real world. And Tom was the one who had discovered that, who had shared it with the world so that Simon might be found, brought back.

To what? The ruins of the only home he had known. To all that he had shared with his father: the trails they had ridden, the animals they had raised, the gardens they had planted and harvested. To sad memories.

But it didn't have to be like that. *No, it wouldn't be like that.* He would make sure it wasn't. He would be here as much as Simon needed him. It couldn't have been an accident. No, he was being given another chance.

Tom walked outside and headed for the pond and the shed that Roger had described. Looking at the landscape as he walked he could imagine Simon on one of his explorations. His books on ants and animals were both a product of and an inspiration for those wanderings, uncoverings, and studies. He couldn't have had a better place for all of that, at least not in any landscape Tom had ever seen or imagined.

He got to the shed, opened the door and there it was. Mounted on a tripod, the telescope stood at his chest, about right for an twelve-year-old boy. It wasn't a toy; no, it was very impressive. The tripod was wooden with extendable legs. On its top a black mount with adjustments. The telescope itself was white with black fasteners. He started to take it outside and stopped. *No point. Not in the middle of the day. Later maybe.*

Tom stepped out of the shed, closed the door securely and walked to the pond's edge. How many times had he stood at the edge of the pond up by Baker's place trying to catch frogs? With Jesse. It was one of the few places Jesse would go with him, mainly because there wouldn't be anyone else there. And because he liked to fish. Never with much luck. He was impatient, jerking the line too quickly. He'd land a carp now and then but that was it.

Did Simon like to fish? Probably. Not so that he could eat them but so he could study them. *No, come to think of it, there hadn't been a book on fish up in the loft.* Well, not one that he had found. *There had to be.* He'd have to look again.

Tom started back to the barn with a different sense of things, a set of feelings that had been arranging themselves over the past days as he explored, read, listened to Roger tell of Simon and his father, and as he'd spent time with his own thoughts of the past and what the future might hold. Now those thoughts and imaginings had found a new home, and that home was filled with new hopes.

Chapter 21

Simon and Jenna

The movie was in downtown Boston, and they'd gone down into a cellar to take a subway train. It wasn't very clean but it was interesting. From a distance, he heard the painful squeal of steel on steel as the train rounded a curve, a momentary quiet, a rush of air and a flashing presence cushioned on a bed of blue sparks. Impossibly, it stopped, twenty doors slid, like one, open. Like a reversible falls, people flowed out and then in. At this concatenation he froze, mouth agape. Had Jenna not led him by the hand he would still have been staring as the doors slid shut and the train disappeared into the darkness.

He sat very close to her, his heart racing. *It would be like this*, he realized. He remembered his father's description of cities: "Too many people in too many machines, going too many places too fast and for no very good reason."

He was squeezing Jenna's hand. "It's a short trip," she said, squeezing back.

She was right. Too short to have gotten them anyplace, and yet when they walked back up to the sidewalk it was another world. Rosie's neighborhood was nothing compared to Brookline Avenue. Walking with Jenna to the theater, he became mechanical. His feet operated on their own. His eyes could never have done the job of choosing direction. Jenna had her arm around him now as they walked the crowded street. Simon had never seen so many people hurrying in so many directions.

Destination had been a simple matter at home, a friendly and familiar path where everything was known, expected and reassuring. Novelty and surprise were rare but welcome, contained as they were in the larger quiet.

The brightly lit marquee of the theater announced, as Jenna had that morning, that the name of the movie was *AI*. Simon asked what that meant and she said "artificial intelligence." *And what is that?* he had asked. *Robots*, she had said. *Things that aren't really human.* He thought of Pinocchio and the Scarecrow.

Jenna bought tickets at a window and a bucket of popcorn and they entered the theater. It wasn't very full and they took seats about halfway back. There was a giant white screen on which someone was projecting announcements about things to buy, places to visit, and reminders to turn off cell phones. Then the lights went down, people stopped talking and the screen exploded. It was as if someone had harnessed the energy of a thunderstorm and the spectacle of an aurora. The sudden vastness and discontinuity of the images and the penetrating barrage of sound were beyond anything Simon had anticipated. He sat rigid and white-knuckled as the previews cascaded over him, image upon image: cars flying through the air, buildings imploding, and bald men in leather making love to empty-eyed women. When the feature began, things slowed: names came and went on the screen. Writers, actors, special effects, crew members, a director. Simon was able to collect himself, close his mouth, moisten his lips, and relax his grasp on the arm rests.

Jenna reached over and held his hand. "Do you want to leave?" she whispered. He shook his head, not daring to speak. Leaving was out of the question. He was in the presence of greatness. He squeezed Jenna's hand to say that he was all right. The story began. Now the images stayed longer in front of him and, for the time being, he did not feel the sound in his legs. A man told about making a robot boy, but when the boy appeared, Simon knew that he wasn't a robot at all. The mother didn't know that, however. She left him and went away, just as Simon's mother had done. He hadn't thought about his mother for a long time. She had left, too. Not because he was a robot but because she had made a deal with his father. He had never really thought much about her with his father there, but now his father was gone.

Leaving the theater two and a half hours later, they stopped at a Burger King. Jenna ordered two Whoppers, fries, and chocolate milk shakes. His Whopper sat on the tray in front of him, untouched.

"It made you sad, didn't it?" Jenna asked.

Simon nodded. "I never really thought my mother did anything wrong. She gave my father what he wanted and he gave her what she wanted. I never really missed her. My dad was all I needed. But now he's gone."

"I'm sorry. It may take a while but you'll find her. Or she'll find you. When your grandparents find your personal in *The Globe*, they'll know where she is."

"If they find it. If I have any grandparents."

Simon looked past Jenna at a family having their dinner, a boy and girl both under ten, a mother and father who looked to Simon like the mother and father in the movie. The little girl said something that made them all laugh. The mother kissed her. They seemed very happy together.

"You going to eat your Whopper?" Jenna asked.

Simon looked at the cheeseburger and at Jenna. "I miss my father," he said.

"Oh, sweetie," she said. She got up and moved across to sit beside him. She put her arm around him and cradled his head against her breast. "You know what the two best things in the world are?" she said. He shook his head.

"Laughing and crying. Only human beings can do it. Everything can have sex but only human beings can laugh and cry. A guy told me that once and I think it's true."

121

The family at the other table had finished. The boy gathered their trays and dumped them into the trash containers. The little girl took her mother's hand, they turned and left.

Simon didn't know why he was crying but he wasn't sorry for it. He liked the warmth of Jenna and felt sheltered enough to ignore the world around them for the few minutes it took for the storm to pass. Then whatever thoughts he might have framed about his mother were elbowed out of his mind by the realization that dogs do cry, or at least whimper, and that loons laugh, in a way. He said so.

"Maybe it's the tears," Jenna said. "I don't think animals have tears."

"That's probably it," Simon said. He liked the idea and didn't want to examine it more closely.

Jenna wrapped the burger in a few napkins and put it in her purse. Simon took another sip of his shake and they left.

The kitchen at Rosie's place had acquired an audience, all of them facing the door as if waiting for a screen to light or a curtain to rise.

"Hello?" Simon said slowly as he and Jenna walked in.

"What's all this?" Jenna asked, hands on hips.

"Your grandmother called." Ben said.

"My grandmother?"

"Your grandmother."

"I really do have a grandmother?" Simon asked, looking at him with surprise.

"You really do!"

"Wow."

"She wants you to call her," Rosie said, standing up. "Here's her number." She handed him a sticky note. He looked at it, then at Jenna, his eyebrows bunched together slightly. "I've never done this before."

"Well, of course. You never knew you had a grandmother."

"No, I mean... I've never..."

"Used a telephone!" Jenna finished the sentence, walked over and gave him a hug. "We'll do it together. OK?"

"OK."

The phone rang six times. Simon was about to hang up with a mixture of relief and disappointment when there was a voice at the other end.

"Grandma?" Simon asked. "This is Simon. Hello? Are you still there? Yes, it's really me. Is it really you?"

There was a long pause. "I'm in Boston with friends of mine. They thought I should call you." Another pause.

"Where is your father?"

"He died of cancer."

"Oh, I'm so sorry."

"So am I." "Where are you? Who is looking after you?"

"My friend, Ben. I'm here at Rosie's Counseling Place. She's a friend of his." Simon listened, nodded and turned to Ben. "She wants to know if somebody can bring me to see her."

Jenna held out her hand. "Here, give me the phone." Simon handed it to her. "And some paper and a pen." Simon went to the counter and opened a drawer he had put in order on that first day to be helpful. Seeing it, he felt a little odd, almost dizzy, and held onto the counter for a moment. So much had happened in so short a time. He took out a pen, closed the drawer, and picked up the shopping list pad from beside the refrigerator. He handed them to Jenna.

"I'm ready," she said. Bent over the kitchen counter, she listened and wrote. Simon looked over her shoulder. "Right… Yes, I know the area. Claremont… right… third left… grey Cape Cod. Got it. When would be a good time for me to bring Simon out? OK… I see… No problem. We'll see you then." She hung up the phone.

"When are we going?" Simon asked.

"She wants us to come over on Saturday when her husband will be out at his men's club."

"She doesn't want him to be there?"

"I think she wants you to herself."

"You'll be there?" It was as much a plea as a question.

"Grandmother or not, I'm not going to leave you with anyone I haven't checked out."

"Good."

Chapter 22

Simon and Bill Miller

Simon lay awake. So much was happening. So much was new. The world was new; he was new. He lay in bed among a sad clutter of memories. Of his father reading to him every night before he went to sleep, sitting in a chair at the side of his bed. They weren't fairy tales and they didn't always have a happy ending. Sometimes he carried the unhappiness, the unfinished-ness, into his sleep. *Dreams were the architects of invention,* his father had said, *and through their richness, the framers of intelligence.* New words, new places, new ideas weren't always the best things for sleep. But they were pretty good for dreams.

One night it was Phaedrus: the story of the soul's journey through the heavens in a winged chariot, its brief acquaintance with perfection before taking up residence in a human being. Simon had wanted to know how a soul could live without a body and where they were stored among the stars.

His father had asked him if he had ever read the words, "ashes to ashes." Dust to dust, he'd responded. He had read it in Huck Finn. His father asked him what he thought it meant. It was like compost, he'd said. Plants die and become food so that other plants can be born.

At the farm, the seasons, the weather, the predictable needs of the animals, had given everything a place, a time, and an order. Discovery was quiet. The world was quiet. The outdoors was a place where you were a part of things. And a place filled with things to discover. He thought of lying outside, high up on the hillside watching the northern lights, hearing the sounds of night creatures. A raccoon, a fox, always a few bats, and occasionally the louder footfalls of a moose.

The past days had been of a different order. He looked out the window next to his bed. The parking area was quiet, the night moonless. He walked down the stairs and listened. No sound from the kitchen. He opened the door and quickly walked to the back porch, down the steps and across to the tall grass. Finding a soft place, he lay down.

Because of the moonless night the sky was bright with constellations. Not as bright as at the farm where there was almost no artificial lighting, but bright enough so that he could see his guardian, Orion. He lay there for a long time, the movie running through his head. He saw the boy sitting in the seat of his little airplane as it filled with water, in the flooded city, waiting for the blue fairy to turn him into a real boy. A real boy. Then it came back to him. They had been to the hospital in Bangor, Simon, his father, and Roger.

His father had decided not to do the treatments that the doctor had recommended. *Without them he might have as much as a year,* the doctor had said. *Or less.* Sitting in the back seat, Simon had felt the tension in their silence. They spoke of the weather, predictions of a severe winter. It was September. He and his father had been harvesting, carrying carrots, turnips, and potatoes to the cold cellar beneath the barn. His father had pain, but not enough to stop him or even slow him down. Lying there now beneath the comfort of the night sky, it all came back to him. They'd had a late dinner and he had gone to bed. Roger and his father had stayed up talking and drinking. He had awoken some time later to the sound of an argument. He walked to the door, opening it a crack.

"It's outrageous," Roger was saying. "He's a child. You are asking too much. This is not a fairy tale!" In a slower, quieter voice Roger said, "You are dying, Reese. Your Pinocchio cannot bear you from the belly of the whale." *Why couldn't he say my name?* "You will need a nurse," Roger said.

Roger didn't know about dying. He hadn't helped animals through injury and illness. He hadn't buried a best friend as Simon had buried Barker. He didn't know as much about death as Simon did. *Yes, he would do what had to be done.* He, Simon Seeker. Not "The Boy," not Pinocchio.

And he had. And he was real now in the real world. Jenna thought so. Ben thought so.

He heard a door close, then conversation. A match flared, burned, and went out. A car started, backed up, its lights sweeping the lot, and drove away. Then quiet and darkness.

What is it? his father would ask, when Simon stopped to listen as they walked in the woods. Sometimes a sound, a twig broken, a ruffle of feathers; but more often a sense of presence. Then his father would hear it too: the sound of a deer retreating into the woods or a sudden partridge breaking its cover. But Simon always knew first. As he knew now that a man, a large man, was approaching. He was just a few feet away. There was the sound of a zipper. Simon stood up.

"Oh my God!" the man said. "Where'd you come from?"

It was amusing, the look on the man's face. He had been about to pee. Now he zipped up his pants. He was not at all frightening.

"I'm not really here," Simon said, feeling a percolation of mischief. He pointed to the sky.

The man looked up, then back at Simon. "You're a space alien?"

It was an invitation Simon couldn't resist. "I am a stranger in a strange land," Simon intoned.

The man took a step back. "Fuck," he said, "and I'm the Gnome King." Then he turned aside. "Sorry," he said. "Got to take a piss."

Once finished, he zipped up and turned back. Simon had thought of making a quick getaway, but he was having a kind of fun he had now and then with his father when he was in a silly mood.

"You are a kid, right? You're not just small," the man asked.

"I am Simon Seeker," he said.

"Simon Seeker."

The man was doing what Ben had done. Repeat things. Rosie and Jenna didn't do it. It was a man thing.

"Yes," he said.

"That's really your name."

"Yes."

"And what are you seeking at Rosie's, Simon Seeker?"

"Ben brought me here."

"Ben."

"Ben Pyle."

"Ah, Rosie's friend."

"He's my friend too."

"So what are you doing lying in the grass?"

"Watching the stars." Simon looked up and pointed. "That's Ursa Major. Also called the Big Dipper."

The man looked up. "Oh yeah. How long has it been since I've looked at the stars? They are beautiful, aren't they?"

"It's where we come from," Simon said.

"Is that right?" The man studied him; his eyes said he was available and interested. Simon was learning about people. Slowly. His father would have been proud of him. You had to read the other person, know what he was prepared to hear, say it in a way that he would be comfortable with. It had gone well with Ben. But this man was not Ben. He needed to look into the man's eyes, watch the way he moved, study his face.

The man glanced over his shoulder and made a movement with his head toward the picnic table. "You got a few minutes?" he asked. Simon nodded. The man walked to the picnic table and he followed.

"I like your shirt," Simon said.

"Are you a Red Sox fan?"

"It's our favorite team."

"You and who else? Your father?"

"And Ben. He's going to take me to a game."

"Your first?'

"Yes."

"Well, I'm sure you'll have a great time. Tell me more about the stars."

"Did you ever look at the Milky Way?"

"Lots of times when I was your age. Not so much nowadays. I should. It's so beautiful."

"It's where everything comes from. All the planets. Everything started there. From dust." He stood and pointed as he spoke. "The picnic table, the driveway, the house, everything you see. And us." He sat down and smiled a new smile. It felt right for the occasion. His companion seemed surprised at it. He'd have to practice with a mirror.

"Where did you learn all that?"

"I have lots of books."

"On stardust."

"And other things. I have four books on ants."

"Tell me about ants."

"What do you want to know?"

"Well, let's see. OK; how many are there?"

"About a million billion. They weigh four times as much as birds, amphibians, reptiles, and mammals combined."

"Really?"

"Really."

"Tell me about stardust."

"A plant dies. You pull it up and put it in the compost pile. Then you put other things on top. As the pile grows it gets hotter and hotter. It doesn't explode, but sometimes it starts a fire, which is why you should *never* put compost in a building." He was all but scolding his listener.

"My father did that," the man said. "Outside, not in a building. In a year or two it turned back into dirt. Really good dirt for making a garden. My mother was a serious gardener."

"Humus."

"Humus? Right, humus. Good soil. Humus."

"And human." Simon smiled.

"Humus and human. Right. And humble. How about humiliate?" The man laughed.

"What's funny?" Simon asked.

"Nothing. Sorry. Go on."

"The words all mean "low down." Like the soil. Underneath, where seeds come to life. And where lots of creatures live, like tiny little farmers."

"Making new life."

"All from stardust."

They both looked up at the bright night sky, and for a while neither spoke. Then the man said, "So how did you learn all of this?"

"At my home in Maine."

"Where in Maine?"

"Washington County."

"Washington County. That's really up country. I went fishing there once, a long time ago." The man looked carefully at Simon and smiled. "I don't think I've ever met a boy who's developed his own theories on ecology. And that's really your name? Simon Seeker?"

"That's me," Simon said and held out his hand.

"Sorry," the man said, extending his own. "Bill Miller."

"Pleased to meet you, sir," Simon said, giving three firm shakes.

The man smiled as Simon knew he would. He'd have to ask Jenna about shaking hands.

"That's a real name," Simon said.

"Real?"

"Miller. It's medieval. Your ancestor was a miller. That's where names come from, what people did. Like Carter or Smith or Mason."

"And Seeker?"

"I don't think so, but maybe." It was a new thought. Surprising that it should be, but it was. Simon smiled.

"Well, I'm not a miller. And my friend Terry Smith has never seen a horse's hoof, but you…. Tell you what. I'm going to give you my card."

He stood up and reached into his back pocket, removing a very fat black wallet. Simon wondered what it must be like to sit on something like that all day.

"I'd like to hear more about stardust. Stardust and compost. And maybe about ants as well. And I think some other people might be interested also." He slipped a card from his wallet and handed it to Simon. Simon read it. *The Bill Miller Show*, it said in bold across the top. Then underneath: *Tomorrow's Talk Today.*

Simon read it aloud and looked up at Bill Miller. "What does that mean? How can you have tomorrow today?"

"You can't. Well, not really. It's an expression. You know about expressions, right?

"Like, 'the early bird gets the worm.'"

"Exactly. Perfect example."

Simon studied the card again. "So what about tomorrow's talk today?"

"It means listening to people who have an eye on the future, who have a pretty good notion of what lies ahead." He put his hand on Simon's shoulder. "Like you, my young friend. From compost to stardust. I think my audience would love to hear you talk about stardust. What do you think?"

Simon wasn't sure what to think. Bill Miller wasn't like anyone he had ever known. Not that there were all that many. But his way of talking, the way he moved words around, his smile. They were all new. He took a breath. "I'm not sure what an audience is."

Bill Miller laughed, "Well, right now I'm your audience."

"Oh."

Bill Miller took a breath, studied Simon's face and continued more carefully. "I'm sorry. I have a program on television Saturday afternoons. I interview interesting people. Do you know about interviews?"

"No."

"Well, it's when someone is asked questions before an audience. You do know what an audience is." He looked at Simon more quietly, taking a short breath.

"Like people watching a movie."

"Right." He continued slowly, watching the boy's face with a new curiosity. "So I sit on a stage with my guest and ask him to tell the audience about his favorite subject. Something he knows more about than the audience. Or something he has new ideas about that the audience would like to hear."

"Like stardust?"

"Yes. Like stardust. And compost. What do you think? Would you like to do that?"

"I think so. I'll ask Ben."

"You do that." He reached out his hand again.

Simon took it with a grateful feeling in his body. He held it and looked up. "Thanks."

Chapter 23

Simon and Ben

When they entered the stadium, Simon had reached out for Ben's hand. The crowd at the movie theater was nothing compared to this multitude. Every kind of person he might imagine was there. Every age, every size, every color. And the sounds! More voices than the forest held. Too much to take in.

And yet, when they were in their seats, all those differences merged into one voice, a familiar one. The one he and his father had heard on the radio. The voice of baseball fans becoming one. He had compared it at the time to a chorus of singers on one of his father's CDs.

There was no announcer. He was somewhere, watching the game just as he and Ben were. He felt the energy of the people around him. It was catching. Little by little he added his own energy and voice, checking Ben's expression for encouragement. Louder and louder, standing, waving his arms. It was all new. He was a part of something much greater than his mind could take hold of. His energies were something other, outside of himself.

After the first three innings, Ben got Cokes and hot dogs. They were a perfect fit, the bun filled with cheering colors and loud tastes. A boy about his age sat next to them with a pair of binoculars. He must have seen Simon looking at him. He cheered a two-bagger by Pedro Martinez and Simon cheered in synchrony. The boy looked at him and gave a thumbs up. Simon returned it. What the boy did, Simon did. He was a good teacher. He even handed the glasses to Simon, and Simon was able to see up close the faces that went with the names he knew so well.

On the way back to the Counseling Center in Rosie's car, he took out the card that Bill Miller had given him the night before. "What does 'tomorrow's talk today' mean, Ben?"

"What?" Ben glanced over at Simon quizzically. "Whatcha got there?"

"A card a man gave me the other night."

"What man was that?"

"Bill Miller."

"Well, I'll be. How did you meet Bill?"

"I was lying in the weeds watching the stars."

"Bill Miller. My goodness. And he gave you his card."

"After we had a conversation. We sat at the picnic table."

"Let me guess: you told him about compost and stardust."

"Well, he asked me." Simon shrugged a shoulder.

"Hey, I'm not criticizing you. People love to hear you talk about the things you've learned from the land. So what did he say?"

"He said there were people who would be interested in hearing about… the stuff I talked about. Then he gave me the card and said I should call him."

"He wants you on his show," Ben nodded as he spoke. "'Tomorrow's Talk Today.' And you are tomorrow. I swear, Simon, anybody comes near you walks away in a different place."

"What does that mean?"

"It means you get people thinking about things they've never thought about before. Like me. Telling you things about growing up that I've never told anyone, not even Rosie. Don't get me wrong; I'm not sorry. Nobody is sorry for meeting Simon Seeker. No, kiddo, you are a very special person."

Ben's words took Simon by surprise. He didn't know whether to be pleased or not, whether Ben was saying something nice about him or that he was some kind of dark wizard. His father had said to let people tell their stories. And he had told his. He was just like other people. Or was he? He thought about the robot boy in the movie and his throat tightened. He said nothing.

Ben looked over at him. "What's wrong?" Simon shook his head. "Did I say something to upset you?" Simon shook his head again. Ben considered his words carefully. "Simon, what I was trying to say is that you bring out the best in people. You are a very special boy. Did you think I was saying something else?"

"I just want to be a real person like you and Jenna and everyone else."

"You *are* real. That's why people like you. That's why Bill wants you on his show."

"What's a show?"

"On television. Saturday afternoons. He sits on a stage with his guests and they talk about themselves. People my age or older, mostly. Now and then a pop star or an athlete."

"What's a pop star?"

"A singer. Someone who creates popular music and goes on television now and then."

"Like the Beatles?"

"How do you know about the Beatles?" Ben was truly surprised.

"My dad loved them. He had CDs."

"So you *did* have some electronics!"

"Electronics?"

"A CD player."

"Yes. And we had a radio. My dad and I listened to baseball games."

"Of course."

"Did Bill have the Beatles on his program?"

Ben laughed. "Only Ed Sullivan was lucky enough to get the Beatles."

"Ed Sullivan?"

"Way before your time. He had guests perform on stage before a big audience, on television."

"Am I going to be famous like the Beatles?"

"Do you want to be?"

"I don't know. I don't think so. It's scary to think about." Simon paused in thought, and decided, "No, I don't. No. I just want to be with you and Jenna."

"Are you saying you wouldn't want to be on the Bill Miller Show?"

"No, I'm not saying that. I don't know. But I like these new things. The game was great. Really great." Simon beamed at Ben.

"Well, let's take one step at a time. No need to rush. I'll call Bill and see what he has in mind."

"Does he get counseling at Rosie's too?"

Ben coughed. "Uh…right…yeah. Yes. He's got a very busy life. Very busy. He needs to relax now and then."

"Rosie's is a good place to relax. I love Rosie's. If I don't go to my grandmother's, do you think I could stay there? I could do the gardening."

"And I'm sure Rosie would love that. Nobody's going to put you out on the street; you can be very sure of that. You are a gift, Simon. We will be there for you as long as you want us."

"Well that's easy. Forever."

Chapter 24

Simon and Jenna

Olivia Hardin's home was suburban textbook: a two-story cape, shaped cedars to screen the foundation, fronted by a mixture of salvia and dusty miller, the lawn neatly edged and chemically perfect.

"You ready?" Jenna said.

"I guess so."

They got out of the car and walked up the front steps. Jenna rang the bell. It played a short scherzo. "Some day when I have a house of my own," Jenna said, "I want a doorbell like that." Simon smiled. He hoped the friendly bell was a good omen.

The woman who opened the door was older than Jenna had expected. And there was a problem. Her lipstick wasn't on straight. Jenna's heart sank. Simon saw something as well: a too-careful smile that didn't quite fit the features of her face. But also hopefulness, something he had begun to recognize in a mirror.

"I'm Simon," he said.

Olivia reached out and touched his cheek with the back of her hand, gently as if she might be brushing away a tear. "I never believed…," she began. "I never hoped to believe…" She withdrew her hand and covered her mouth, apparently with no idea what to do next.

"I'm Jenna," Jenna said, holding out her hand. The familiarity of the gesture was enough to automate a response. Olivia took it, smiled, shook herself free of amazement and escorted them into the living room.

It was, in a word, colorful. The sofa and chairs brightly upholstered in designs vaguely tropical, the wall-to-wall carpeting rose or perhaps salmon. Several paintings decorated the living room walls, none with a subject that might have been given a name. Textures, strokes, daubs— nothing geometric or vaguely representational. Fascinating nonetheless. Simon walked up to one and studied it.

"Your mother did those," Olivia said. "Art was her favorite subject. Well, after music. Olivia studied him as he stood there and glanced at Jenna with a quick wipe at her eyes, "I made a pitcher of lemonade and some chocolate chip cookies." She indicated a glass coffee table by the sofa. "Please help yourselves."

They sat, Jenna and Olivia on the sofa, Simon across from them. Offering the lemonade, Olivia remarked that she had already helped herself. She held up a glass with what looked like ice-water. She urged Simon to try the cookies. He did. He pronounced them very good.

"I'm not a very good cook, really," Olivia said. "Grandmothers are supposed to be, I know. But I never really got the hang of it. Paul and I usually go out to dinner." She poured a glass of lemonade for Simon.

Jenna recited the ritual of arrival. "Your directions were very good, Mrs. Hardin," she said. "We made only one mistake."

"*You* made only one mistake," Simon said teasingly. "I told you it was the second street after the stop light."

"I didn't think the first one was really a street. It looked more like an alley," Jenna explained. This was familiar territory for Olivia and she joined in. There was traffic to discuss, the behavior of cab drivers in

Boston, the recalcitrance of the town in the matter of repairing frost heaves, and the legendary corruption of government when it came to highway construction. There was no originality in the conversation for anyone except for Simon, for whom such discourse in this new world was novel and instructive. He looked around at the room and back to his grandmother and asked, "Did my mother live here?"

"Yes. Your grandfather bought this house. It was the first real house that either of us had ever had. We both grew up in triple-deckers in Worcester. Thomas worked hard to get this house."

"That was my grandfather's name?"

"Yes. Thomas Hardin. He had a drug store. He built it up from nothing." She spoke with regard and a suggestion of something lost. "When the chains started coming along, he had to work twice as hard to keep up. You see, they sold everything at a lower price to drive out the competition. His customers were loyal, of course, after all those years, but then they started to drift away. The harder he worked the worse things got."

"What happened?"

"He had a heart attack." Olivia reached unsuccessfully into her pocket, apparently for a handkerchief. Simon had noticed a box of Kleenex on the table below the pictures. He got up and brought it to her. "Thank you, dear." She took one, wiped quickly at her eyes and continued. "The doctor told him he had to stop working."

"Did he stop?"

"Thomas Hardin stop working? No, dear. Your grandfather wouldn't have known how to stop working. Three months later he had another heart attack and it killed him."

Olivia got up and walked to a secretary that nested under the stairs. She opened the drawer and took out a photograph. "He was a handsome man," she said. "And a good provider and a good father." She handed the picture to Simon. "You look like him," she said. "Your mother took after me."

It was difficult for Simon, whose sense of his own appearance was pretty vague, to see anything familiar in the face before him. "He looks very serious," Simon said, handing the picture to Jenna.

"Yes," Olivia said somewhat wearily, "he was. But he could have a laugh when the time was right for it."

"What is my mother like?"

"You have her eyes. And her hair. What is she like? Full of life. Full of plans for the future. She always wanted to be a star. Even when she was a little girl. When she was your age, she was in a school play and one of the parents asked us if we'd let her do a screen test for advertising. You know, like children who do cereal ads."

Simon looked at Jenna with puzzlement. His grandmother was naming things he'd never heard of. Jenna smiled and held her hands up gently. Be patient, they said. His grandmother was continuing. "We said sure, and she did and then nothing happened. She was very disappointed. The painting happened in high school. Her teacher had studied with Josef Albers. Can I pour you some more lemonade, dear?"

"Yes, please," Simon said, holding out his glass. She filled it and then offered some to Jenna, who declined.

"Now where was I?"

"Josef Albers," Jenna said.

"Ah, yes, well it never happened. She didn't get to do advertising. I hadn't realized how much it meant to her. And of course there was Paul." She played with the ring on her slightly skeletal hand. It was loose. Simon wondered why it didn't fall off. After a moment she looked up and smiled. "And what do you do, my dear?" she asked, turning to Jenna.

"She's a counselor," Simon responded quickly.

"Are you with Social Services?" Olivia asked.

"In a manner of speaking," Jenna answered carefully. "I'm with a private organization."

"It isn't Catholic Charities is it?"

"No. It's a very small organization."

"I see." Olivia smiled at Simon and said quietly, "I haven't seen your mother for a long time. To think what she has missed."

Simon told the story he had told Jenna about the nanny goat who didn't nurse her baby. "Not all mothers want to be mothers," he said.

"Oh, you dear child," Olivia said, again putting her hand to her mouth.

"But now I have a grandmother," Simon said.

Open your arms, Jenna thought. *Accept him. He's your fucking grandson.* But Olivia just looked at him. "Yes," she finally said. "And I have grandson."

Jenna wanted to scream at her. It was all so familiar and painful. She looked at Simon who appeared unfazed. Olivia stood up. "There's something I want to give you," she said, walking to the secretary and returning with a small box. "These are all I have, dear," she said, handing the box to Simon. "We weren't much of a picture-taking family, I'm afraid."

Simon held the box for a moment, then stood up and crossed to the sofa, sitting beside Jenna. He took out the first photograph and examined it. His mother might have been in her late teens.

"She's very pretty," Jenna said. "Look. Her hair is the same color as yours." Simon said nothing. He put the photo on the table and took out a second. Glanced at it briefly. He looked up. "Can I see my mother's room?" he asked.

It was clearly not the question Olivia had expected and she hesitated. "Why, dear, she hasn't lived here for fourteen years. There's nothing of hers there now. It's a guest room."

"Can I see it?" he persisted.

"Why, of course you can." She led them up the stairs to a comfortable room at the back of the house. It had a view over the back lawn where a rusted swing set gave sole testimony that there once had been a child in the house. Simon said nothing. He opened the box of pictures again and took one out.

"I'd love to see the rest of the house," Jenna said, "if you don't mind giving a little tour."

"Not at all," Olivia said. "Would you like to stay here for a few minutes, dear?" she asked, but Simon was lost in his thoughts and didn't respond. "Fine. We'll just take a little walk around. You make yourself at home."

Jenna was glad for the opportunity for some time alone with Olivia. It was a small house and after a short tour they returned to the living room.

"He is so like his mother," Olivia said. "Not his looks. I'm not sure how to say it. The way he asks a question, does things the way he wants to. I don't mean willful. He knows his mind just the way she did. She broke my heart."

Jenna was afraid that Olivia might become maudlin. She had learned from her own parents that alcohol could have that effect. She was trying hard to like Olivia and to feel some sympathy for her, but there was too much familiar in all of this.

"You say she didn't get along with her stepfather."

"Oh, my dear, it is so complicated. So very complicated." There was no pretense now. "Paul abused Alexandra. I only learned about that a year after she left home. She came by one day to collect her things. She had been living at a friend's house. A member of the band that she joined. I asked her why she never told me, and she said I wouldn't have believed her. She didn't like Paul. She probably thought I would have dismissed the charge, that I would have sided with him. And maybe I would have. It was very bad of me."

"And that's when she left?"

"Yes. This is not a good home, my dear. It never has been. I was not a good mother. Paul wouldn't make a good grandfather. It's complicated. There's a good deal I haven't told you. No, this is not a place for a child. To see him breaks my heart." Olivia shook her head and turned to look at the staircase. They listened. There was no sign of Simon. "What will become of him?"

"He'll be fine, Mrs. Hardin. Maybe he can't live here, but you can be in his life. I'm sure he will want that. He was so excited when we told him you had called."

"He's very fortunate to have a friend like you. And a counselor, no less."

Jenna hesitated. She was again tempted. Secrets bear the weight of other secrets. They could have talked about how mothers don't always do the right thing and how daughters find themselves in places they shouldn't be. "Yes," was all she said.

"She's the best counselor in the world," Simon said, crossing the room.

"You've been eavesdropping," Jenna said.

"I just heard you say you were a counselor," Simon answered in his straightforward way. He put the box on the coffee table.

"You can take those with you if you'd like to," Olivia offered.

"I'd like to take one of them," Simon said. He opened the box. He had put the picture on top. It had been taken when his mother was about the same age as he. She stood between her parents in a pretty white dress. He showed it to Olivia.

"Your mother's confirmation," she said. "Does she look the way you imagined her?'

Simon hesitated, lost for a moment in his thoughts. "I tried to think of what she would have had in her room and where she would have had her bed and I thought about her sitting there and looking out the window."

"She had her bed just under the window."

"So that she could feel the fresh air?"

"That's what she said."

Simon looked at Jenna. The look said *I'm ready to go now*; it was unmistakable. Not impatient or insisting. Perhaps a little wistful. Something had happened. Simon would tell her about it.

Jenna looked at her watch and said that she had a client at four o'clock. They stood up and Olivia accompanied them to the door. Simon turned. "Thank you, grandmother, for the lemonade and the cookies. And the picture."

Olivia opened her arms and Simon closed the physical distance between them. Other distance would take more time. She held him for a few moments, kissed the top of his head and he stepped back. There were tears on her face. Simon turned and walked down the steps.

"I'll be in touch," Jenna said, extending her hand.

Olivia took it absently, her eyes on Simon as he walked to the car. "Yes. If only things were different. I…"

"He's only twelve, but I think he does understand. He's quite a remarkable boy. I'm sure he won't want to lose touch with you."

"Yes. Well."

Jenna walked to the car, turning once with a sympathetic smile and a small wave of her hand.

She backed the car out of the driveway and started back toward the highway. Simon was studying the picture of his mother. *What would that feel like?* she wondered. *Seeing your mother's face for the first time at the age of twelve.* Reading people was a part of her profession. Fail and you could get into trouble. But she had no experience with children. Well, very little. Her own long gone, and a good thing too. Still, she searched her memory. It smirked at her. She had been a secretive twelve-year-old—with others, with herself. That part of her wasn't about to yield its secrets now. Simon was different, unguarded. He had no capacity for mistrust, or so it seemed. Alexandra. Alexandra Hardin. If she only knew what she had missed, what she was missing. Jenna looked over at Simon. He smiled and slipped the picture of his mother into his pocket. "So what do you think?" she asked.

"About my grandmother?"

"Uh huh."

"She was tight."

"Lord. I haven't heard that word for a long time. Tight." She laughed.

"It was my dad's word. When he had too much to drink."

"Did he do that very often?"

"No. But when he did he'd get strange and I'd go out to my baleout."

"Your bailout?"

"My place in the barn. In the loft. I built it out of hay bales so I called it a bale-out. I had lots of my stuff there."

"Your private place. Baleout. I love it."

"Do you think she wants me to live with her?"

"Yes, but it can't happen."

"Because I don't want to?"

"That's one reason, but she doesn't know that."

"Why then?"

"After your grandfather passed away, she married another man named Paul. He's a little complicated." She paused.

"What does that mean?"

"He wouldn't be a good person for you to live with. He drinks a little too much and loses his temper."

"When did she tell you all that?"

"On the phone and while you were upstairs."

"What else?"

"That he's not very good with kids."

"I wouldn't want to live there even if he liked kids."

"Well, you won't have to."

"Thanks. Where are we going now?"

"Well, we could go back to Rosie's and make some lemonade."

"I'd rather have another biscotti."

"You've got it!" Jenna sat back and pressed the accelerator.

"Jenna?"

"Yes, sweetie?"

"I wish you were my mother."

"Oh, Simon," she said, slowing the car and moving to the curb. She put it in park, unbuckled her seat belt and reached over. Simon unbuckled his as well and moved over into her arms. Neither said anything for a couple minutes, then Jenna said, "I can't think of anything in the world that would make me happier."

Simon moved back so he could see Jenna's face. "Well?"

"We'll have to work on that."

Chapter 25

Simon
Seeker
Larkin

It was Simon's first lobster, Bill's treat at The Chart House. He wasn't exactly the man Simon had remembered from their first conversation. This time more a talker than a listener. Not loud, but energetic in a way that made Simon a little nervous. And the way he watched Simon was puzzling as well. As if he were sizing him up. Ben and Simon sat opposite him in the booth. Simon glanced at Ben from time to time and what he read in his smile was, "You're doing fine."

Bill seemed particularly interested in the subject of recycling and the environment. Simon recalled his father talking about how our buried yesterdays threaten to haunt our tomorrows and repeated the phrase, knowing that his father would be glad and wouldn't mind not being given credit. He shaped with his hands as well as his words the vastness of space and the invisibilities of life as it renews beneath the soil. He told of the dung beetle and the industry of ants, of how nothing is ever lost, but reborn as something new.

"Tell me again about stardust," Bill urged, breaking off a very small piece of his roll and waving it as if to scoop up Simon's thoughts. Simon smiled. Bill looked for the butter, found it, put a large piece on his tiny bit of roll and held it, waiting.

Simon repeated what he had said that first night about how life was born of stardust, how every element except helium had to have come from an exploding star because they were older than our sun. He spoke of how things rise and fall. Not in the way of empires or famous people, but like a tree starting from a tiny seed gets nourished and rises; if it's a sequoia, to over 350 feet.

"And then?"

"Someday it falls," Simon said. "Termites, ants, beetles of all kinds, grubs, small animals, thousands of bacteria move in and live there. The tree is like a giant feast, for years and years. And when it falls, it lets in sunlight so other plants can grow. Up and down, up and down. Nothing is wasted."

"What if there's a forest fire and the tree goes up in flames instead of falling to the ground?" Bill asked.

Simon glanced quickly at Ben and continued, "It becomes trapped in clouds, traveling to another continent and falling with the rain."

Bill put his piece of roll back on his plate very carefully, watched it for a moment and looked up. As he was as about to speak, the lobsters arrived. Simon glanced at Ben whose eyes were rolled practically up under his eyelids. "Well, at last," Bill said, clearing the place in front of him for the platter. "What do you think of that, Simon?"

The waitress had to move Simon's bread plate, and re-set his silver to make room for the platter. Then she handed Bill a bib which he tied around his neck. Simon laughed. Ben smiled at Simon as he tied his own bib. Then came Simon's lobster and after the lobster, his bib. He couldn't tie things behind his head so he put the straps over his shoulders and leaned back.

"OK," Ben said, "start with one of the claws." He twisted one free and held it up. "They're already cracked. But these are hard shell." He took the claw and broke it using both hands. Simon tried to do the same but without success. "There's a nutcracker by your plate," Ben said, holding up his own. Simon applied it and the claw came apart. "Take that little fork," Ben instructed, holding up his own. "OK, now take the meat out and dip it in the butter." He demonstrated. "Deee…licious!" he said.

Simon tasted his and smiled. It was delicious. He was eating a giant beetle and it was delicious.

Bill, released from the spell that had momentarily frozen his limbs, looked at his lobster and then at Simon. "Stardust," he repeated. "The tree becomes stardust? Have you ever seen a forest fire?"

"Not a forest fire," Simon said. He looked at Ben who tightened his face a little and did a quick twist of his neck that said, *No*. Then he looked at Bill. There was something he couldn't have explained to Ben, or even himself; a sudden need to say aloud what sat in his heart, to free it as the burst roof had freed his father's soul to live on in the night sky, in the rain that fell to make new life. What would be the point in saying any of the things Bill wanted him to say if he couldn't say the most important thing?

"Not a forest fire," Bill guessed.

Simon shook his head. "My father died last week," he said, very quietly, "I saw his soul go up among the stars. It was like sparks only they didn't go out. They just went up and up and up."

No one said anything. Ben's eyes were closed. Finally, Bill spoke. "Holy shit!" he said.

Ben and Simon looked at one another. Simon hadn't really had time to imagine what Bill's reaction might be. Sympathy probably. Maybe after that, explaining why they couldn't do the show. But this was something else.

Bill turned to Ben. "You haven't seen *The Globe*? No, of course not. You just got back here."

"The boy," Ben said. It sounded scolding.

"Sorry," Bill said. "I'm sorry, Simon. I mean I'm really sorry. Oh my God! Simon Larkin! They thought you were dead. At first. After the fire. I don't believe this."

"Who is Simon Larkin?" Ben asked.

"He doesn't exist," Simon said. "It was my father's name before he changed it to Seeker. Same letters put in a different way."

Bill took a pen from his pocket and a napkin from the dispenser. He wrote "Reese Larkin." Then circling the letters one at a time, he wrote "Larin Seeker."

"Well I'll be!" Ben said. "Reese Larkin. Simon Larkin."

"Simon Seeker," Simon corrected. "And Larin Seeker. Larkin went in the wastebasket when I was born. Reese Larkin made up boys. Larin Seeker *made* a boy. Me."

Ben sat for a moment with his mouth open, as if searching for words.

"I should have told you, I guess. I'm sorry, Ben. I didn't think it mattered."

"No. You were right. It doesn't matter. No. Really. It doesn't."

"My goodness!" Bill said. "What you have been through! You are a remarkable young man. Truly remarkable."

"Why did they think I was dead?"

"Well, you weren't there after the fire. They thought you might be in the woods, safe from the fire, but when you didn't show up the next few days they didn't know what to think."

"Except that I had burned up."

Bill opened his mouth but without sound.

"But I didn't! How did they figure out I was alive?"

"You had let the animals out."

"In case the fire spread."

"They only just figured that out. They thought that the helicopter pilot had done that. They thought you were probably in the house when it burned. Then they found out that the animals were already out when the chopper landed. They got some tracking dogs." He paused. "You OK with this, Simon?"

Simon nodded.

"They got a coat of yours. You know about dogs and scents and tracking, right?"

"Barker could find me anywhere."

"Barker?"

"My dog. He got caught in a poacher's trap and died."

"Sorry about that. Oh dear."

"It was a long time ago. So what about the dogs they got?"

"They followed your trail out to Route 9."

"Where Ben picked me up."

"Right." Now there was something new in Bill's face, something he was sorting out. This time he was doing it without fiddling. No roll, no napkin scribbling, just with his head slightly back, working on it.

"Do you still want me on your show?" Simon asked carefully.

Bill wrinkled his bushy eyebrows and smiled. Simon could feel Ben relax. "You are a celebrity, Simon. Any talk show host in the country… heck, any TV host of anything at all would give his eye teeth to have you on his show. You're the mystery boy, the son of one of the country's most beloved authors. No one knew you existed. Then everyone thought you…," he paused, "…thought you were stardust. And now here you are. The Stardust Kid. Simon Seeker, Simon Larkin Seeker! Come fresh into the world with things to say. Things that people will want to hear. What's the saying? A child will show them the way?"

"The wolf will live with the lamb," Ben recited, "the leopard will lie down with the goat, the calf and the lion and the yearling together; and a little child will lead them. Isaiah 11:6."

Bill's eyebrows did their caterpillar thing again. "Ben knows the whole Bible," Simon said.

"Not all of it," Ben said, off-handedly, awkwardly. Simon could tell that he had said the wrong thing. He had embarrassed Ben.

Bill was still someplace else. Then, with a serious smile, he was back.

"There's something we have to talk about." He reached across the table and covered Simon's right hand with his own. It was their first contact. Simon welcomed it. "Are you OK?" he asked.

Simon nodded.

"OK. Here's the thing…"

Simon smiled. It was a funny thing to say, "Here's the thing." He had never heard anyone say that before. He looked at Ben. Ben was looking at Bill.

"There's a lawyer," he began. "He's quoted in *The Globe*. He was your father's lawyer."

"Roger," Simon said.

"You know him," Bill said.

"He's my guardian. I'm sorry, Ben. I knew I should have told you but I didn't want to. There's this school that he and my dad went to. I didn't want to go there. I didn't want to be looked after. I didn't want people telling me what to do. And Roger doesn't really like me anyway. I wanted to find some people of my own." He looked at Ben. "Like you and Jenna and Rosie."

"I think you need to call him," Bill said. "He's very worried about you. Will you do that?"

Simon nodded.

"OK. We'll call him together. Then I'll talk to him about the show. He'll have to sign off on it. He'll have to give his permission. You with me?"

Simon looked from one to the other. "Yes, I'm with you, and Ben and Jenna…and Rosie. You are my new friends. Ben is my uncle." Bill looked surprised. He sat back in his chair the way his father had when Simon surprised him. Simon smiled. "My pretend uncle."

"Oh. Right. Well…" Bill took a ball point pen out of his pocket and started making marks on a napkin. Not words. Not pictures either, really. Simon squinted his eyes. Designs, whirls, and three-dimensional boxes and stars. He drew a circle around a box and looked up. "Background. We need to work on background. The whole world knows that Simon left the farm the morning of…what was it?"

"May tenth," Ben said.

"Four a.m.," Simon added. "That's when Ben and I met. At Curtis Bog."

"And you rode with him to Boston."

"After we had breakfast at Hauler's."

Bill looked up. "Hauler's?"

"It's a truck stop," Ben said.

"Right. Then to Boston."

"To Rosie's," Simon added.

"No, definitely not Rosie's." Bill stopped, looked at Ben, then at Simon. "Rosie doesn't like to be in the limelight."

"Limelight?"

"Limelight. In the news. It's an expression from the movies." He paused, looked at Ben. "The movies? No. Older than that. Vaudeville? Anyway. She doesn't want people knocking on her door asking about the Stardust Kid."

"Because of the counseling," Simon said.

"Right. It's a private thing, the counseling. Her clients talk about their private lives. They say things they wouldn't say to most of their friends. Newspaper reporters would be a problem. So, not Rosie's. You and Jenna are going to have your own place. An apartment. Not too far away from Rosie's but far enough to be separate."

"What about Ben?" Simon asked.

"Ben can be there with you, too. You and he and Jenna can do things together."

"Ben took me to a Red Sox game and Jenna took me to a movie. And shopping," Simon offered.

"Perfect. You with me on this, Ben?"

"Sounds good to me."

"Are you OK with all of this, Simon?"

"Sure." He looked at Ben.

"I'll be there on and off. We'll do stuff together. What do you say to another Red Sox game?"

"Yes!"

Bill drew a square on his napkin. Simon watched, keeping his curiosity quiet. Inside the square he drew a circle. Then pointing at Ben and Simon with his pen he continued. "OK, let's take a minute to sketch out a schedule. It would be great to settle you in at the apartment for a couple weeks. That will give you and Jenna a little more time together before the show. But the first thing we need to do is call your guardian. Ben and I can't pretend not to have read the piece in *The Globe*. We've got to be up front about this. You with me, Simon? Is that OK with you?"

"I guess so."

"He won't be at his office 'til Monday. We'll call him then. OK, Simon?"

"OK."

He turned to Ben. "Can you and Simon come by some time after nine?"

"We'll be there."

Bill picked up a lobster claw. "Great. Shall we finish our lunch?"

Chapter 26

Simon and Bill

Simon listened as Bill and Roger talked. His father had a word for the way Bill was speaking. *Deferential! That was it.* His father had used it in a story he told Simon at bedtime. It was about an owl and a large grey squirrel. The squirrel was cornered and didn't want to be the owl's dinner. He tried to make the owl feel very important. He was being deferential. *I can be very useful to you*, the squirrel was saying.

The story came back to him now as he sat next to Ben watching Bill listen, close his eyes, nod his head, and smile. "Yes, he's here with me now," Bill told Roger. "Yes… yes…yes." Bill drew on his desk pad. He wasn't someone who could just sit there and listen. Simon could almost hear Roger's voice. Not the words, just the going on and on about something. Then Bill told of Ben picking him up at the bog and their driving to Boston to find his grandmother. Roger said something then, and Bill said things like, "Right. I see. Of course." He tried to imagine what the words were in response to. Nothing bad, it seemed. Bill was being friendly. And nodding. Roger talked for a while and Bill listened and once he rolled his eyes. In an easy voice he said, "Yes, but…yes, I understand, but…" Then in a firm voice, a no-messing-around voice, he said, "Well, the article came out on Saturday." Then there was a pause. Simon could see Roger checking the buttons on his cuffs, brushing off his knees. "No, no, no need to apologize," Bill said. "You must be at your wit's end. So good that your young man got the tracking dog. Yes, yes. I'm sure he is. Right. Right."

Then the conversation and Bill seemed to relax. He leaned back in his chair. Simon wondered if he would light a cigarette the way his father did. He didn't. Once, Bill laughed. Then he told Roger about Ben introducing them and some very serious things about Simon's philosophy of nature. It was strange to hear a person talking about you. His father had done that now and then with Roger, but not often. Probably only when Simon was there with him.

It was obvious that Roger didn't know anything about The Bill Miller Show and from the way Bill scribbled to fill in and darken the designs he had made on the pad on his desk, Simon guessed that he wasn't very pleased about that. Then Bill was boasting. Well, it sounded a little like boasting. Talking about how many viewers the show had. Something about ratings, whatever they might be. And then a lot of "nos" and some laughter without his face changing. "Yes," he said, "the show can be seen anywhere. It's on cable." That seemed to make a difference. Bill looked at Simon and smiled. "Right. Right. Good. He's right here. I'll put him on." And then he handed the phone to Simon.

Simon looked at Ben for reassurance. His friend nodded with a smile. Simon took the phone.

"Hello?" Simon said. "Yes, it's me."

Roger said how worried they had been, he and a guy named Tom. It was Tom, he said, who had gotten the tracking dogs that had followed his scent to the highway the week after the fire. Simon explained that he didn't want to go to Wind Lake School, he didn't want to be cooped up again. He said he hadn't told anyone about having a guardian and so it wasn't Ben's or Jenna's or even Bill's fault that he hadn't called.

"I'm very disappointed to think that you didn't trust me," Roger said. Then quiet. Simon couldn't find a response. It was true. "You know, I wouldn't just pack you up and ship you off." No, he didn't know that because it wasn't true. "You might at least have called on the phone I gave you. Just to let us know that you were all right. You still could have walked out to the road and hitched a ride, if that was your plan."

"I forgot about the phone," Simon lied, his fingers crossed. "Everything happened so fast. I left everything behind. The fire was chasing me. I'm sorry. I just wanted to be away." Simon was good at crying when things didn't go his way. Not often, but when it seemed the best thing. Like when his father sold livestock or evicted spiders—especially when they were surrounded by newly hatched babies. It would probably work now, but that wasn't the way he wanted to have his relationship with Roger. Not as 'the boy,' not as Pinocchio. Not even as a philosopher. Just person to person. *Talk slowly, quietly, as if you are ashamed of yourself.* "I know. I shouldn't have left you worrying. I'm sorry."

"I can understand, Simon. I don't mean to be critical. It's remarkable that you had the strength to do anything, watching what you had to watch. It's just that we were worried."

We were worried. He hadn't quite picked up on that the first time. A new place to go.

Tom. The person who got the dogs. "Who is Tom?" he asked.

Roger's tone changed. It was as if he had set down a heavy bundle and taken a deep breath. He spoke then at some length about Tom: how he had hired builders to reconstruct the farm house. How he had discovered the baleout, read his books, admired his drawings. How he looked forward to meeting Simon.

Then he asked about the broadcast. Did Simon really want to be seen on stage by millions of people? "Bill says I can make a difference in the way people feel about nature. He says I have a responsibility to share my ideas…. Yes…yes. It's because of Ben. He's one of the best people I ever met. He's like my dad. He cares about me. He wants to help me."

"Are you excited about going on television?"

"I'm a little scared. No, I'm a lot scared. But I'm a lot excited too. We're going to practice. Just Bill and me. It'll be OK. Bill is a really nice man and he thinks I have some good ideas."

There was more conversation about the days past, and how he felt about being on Bill's show. Simon was careful, as he had been instructed, not to talk about Rosie and the counseling center. Just about Ben and Jenna, about the baseball game and the movie and Bill. Then Roger asked him to give the phone to Bill.

Bill listened, nodded, smiled and then said, "Great. OK. Absolutely. We'll save a front row seat for you. I look forward to meeting you. Have your secretary call so we can arrange to have you met at the airport. And don't worry about a hotel. We'll take care of that. Right. Thanks." He put down the receiver. "Well, that couldn't have gone much better. What do you think, Simon?"

"It was OK. Roger was pretty nice."

"Who's Tom?" Ben asked.

"The guy who's looking after the farm. He's read my books and seen my drawings."

"And he's the one who hired the search dogs, right?"

"Right."

"I'll bet he's looking forward to meeting you."

"Roger says he is."

"Good."

Chapter 27

Tom and Roger

Tom was up in Simon's loft. He had been looking through one of the books by Edward Wilson. A number of them had page corners turned down and pencil lines next to paragraphs Simon had wanted to come back to. One began, "I redoubled my efforts and began to discover unusual and interesting species. One day I found a marching column of army ants in my backyard—not the famous voracious hordes of the South American rain forest, but miniature army ants of the genus Neivamyrmex, whose colonies of 10,000 to 100,000 workers search for prey through grass clumps around human habitation and across the carpeted forests…"

His phone rang. He set the book aside and took the phone from his pocket. "Hello?"

"They've found him." It was Roger. Tom caught his breath. For a moment he couldn't speak. He looked around the loft and took a breath. Then another. "Are you still there?"

"Sorry, Roger. Is he OK?"

"He's fine and in good hands. He's had an adventure and a half and that's only the beginning."

"Thank God! Have you talked with him?"

"I have."

"Is he coming home?"

"Not quite yet. It's complicated. Where to start?"

"Where is he?"

"Oh, sorry. He's in Boston. With the fellow who picked him up. He walked out to the highway before the firefighters got there. I don't have the details. Simon persuaded the guy to give him a ride. I haven't talked with the guy yet. Simon is great at making up stories. I'm sure it was a good one. Anyway, he ended up in Boston with this guy and his girlfriend, and one night he met Bill Miller."

"*The* Bill Miller?"

"You've seen the show?"

"Yeah. It's good. He gets really interesting people. Once he had a guy who had discovered a shipwreck while he was scuba diving."

"Aren't shipwrecks usually deeper than that?"

"Right. And, not many people scuba dive in the Arctic. So what about Bill?"

"He wants Simon on his show!" Silence at the other end of the line. "Tom?"

"He wants Simon Larkin on stage before a million viewers?"

"Is the show that popular?"

"It gets clipped on YouTube and a hundred other places. It's big."

"Well yes. He does. And he's not Simon Larkin or Simon Seeker. He's the Stardust Kid. It's all about ecology, saving the planet, the sacredness of life and its continuity. Simon has been remarkably fortunate. I don't mean the show, or not *only* the show. But he sounded very secure and happy in his new life with his new friends. I had a hard time finding words."

"That's all great, that he's safe and happy, but isn't putting him on stage a little over the top? Do you think he can really handle it?"

"He's never had an audience. A real audience. Anything is possible. We've got nothing to lose. By the way, Miller asked if I could send some of Simon's drawings down. I was telling him what a precocious artist Simon was and he said he'd like to project some of Simon's work on a screen during the interview."

"I'll get them out tomorrow. You want me to send them to you or Miller?"

"Send them to Miller. I could take them, but he will want some time to look them over."

"Excuse me, but I think I'm missing something…"

"Oh. Sorry, I haven't told you. I haven't really told myself. I'm going to Boston for the show. Miller is putting me up at his club."

"That's great. Wow. Simon will love that."

"What makes you think so? I had a sense during our conversation that he was quite happy to have me at a distance from his new life. Perhaps that's over-stating, but you know what I mean. Our conversation wasn't bad. In fact, it was quite good. Generous? Maybe. He has others in his life now. So anyway, yes, send the drawings."

"To Bill Miller?"

"Right. I'll send you the address."

"Simon really wants to do this."

"Right."

"By the way, where he's staying?"

"He's staying with the truck driver's lady friend. In south Boston. I didn't inquire further. Miller is at some risk in all this. I'm sure he isn't taking any chances."

"When's the show?"

"Saturday the eighth. You want to come down? I'm sure Miller would be glad to have you there."

"Thanks but I have too much to do here. And Simon will have a pretty full plate. I'll watch it here. Will he come back here after it's over?"

"If he isn't swept off to Hollywood."

"Well, let's hope for the best."

Chapter 28

The Bill Miller Show

"It's the Bill Miller Show, Tomorrow's Talk Today. And here he is, Boston's favorite listener, Bill Miller!"

Simon stood at the side of the stage out of sight as Bill Miller walked through a lighted doorway, his arms spread in greeting as the audience cheered. The lights on the stage were brighter than any he had ever seen. There was a glass of water by the chair he would be sitting in. That was good, for suddenly his throat felt very dry.

"Ladies and gentlemen. Friends. We have with us today a very special guest, a boy with a remarkable story and an even more remarkable gift for telling it. Many of you will have read or heard in the news over the past few days that one of America's—indeed one of the world's—most beloved writers of children's stories, Reese Larkin, a man lost to the world for the past thirteen years, died a recluse at his home in Washington County, Maine last week. That farm was about as far from civilization as a person can get and still be in these United States. You will also have heard that he had a son who escaped the conflagration, made his way to Route 9 and hitched a ride with a truck driver delivering a load of mussels from Prince Edward Island. Ben Pyle, will you please stand so that our studio audience can thank you for bringing this wonderful young man into our world?"

Ben stood, turned to the rest of the audience, nodded briefly, and resumed his seat. "Ben is an old friend of mine, though we have seen little of one another these last few years. He is a very loyal listener to the show. Right Ben?" Ben gave a thumbs up. "One day he called me up and said, 'There's someone you have to meet. His name is Simon Seeker, he's twelve years old, he's read books I've never even heard of, knows more about the woods than a forest ranger, and talks to animals.' So I dropped by and Simon and I sat out on a moonless night watching the stars. He told me about watching his father's soul ascend among the flames to become stardust, how the soul of a plant or a person creates new life, how compost and stardust remake the world. Ladies and gentlemen, please welcome Simon Seeker Larkin!"

It was his cue. That's what they called instructions on television: cues. Simon took a deep breath and stepped out onto the lighted stage. Bill stood there smiling. What he remembered as a quiet and empty space was ablaze with lights and sound—the sound of applause. He stepped out, stopped halfway to center stage and looked out into the packed hall as people rose from their seats. They clapped their hands and cheered. Bill had told him this might happen. The thing to do was to smile at them and then join Bill at center stage.

Ben, Jenna, and Roger waved from the front row. He waved back. Then he turned. Bill held out his hand. Simon took it. He was much better at shaking hands now. Bill indicated the chair beside him and Simon sat. The applause quieted; its energy remained. He turned to Bill, glad for the simplicity of a single smile.

"So, Simon, you're the youngest person ever to have sat in that chair."

Simon smiled, looked at the chair, sat up straight as if trying to more adequately fill the space. The audience was with him at once. There was approving laughter.

"And yet," Bill continued, "I can say without exaggerating that you are one of the most well-read and thoughtful guests I have ever had." He turned to the audience. "Those of you who are regular viewers—and I do thank you for being there—realize that most everyone who has shared a part of this hour with me is pretty well-known. A personality, if you will. Someone in the spotlight, whose message or achievement is out there in public view. What I am trying to say is that there is always a starting point, a set of givens, a history. As it is with this young man. You are twelve, right Simon?"

"I'm almost thirteen."

"And you have lived your whole life on a farm deep in the heart of Washington County, Maine, with your father, pretty much in isolation."

"Yes."

"No traveling?"

"Only a little. Sometimes we went shopping, but most of the time my father's friend, Roger, brought what we needed."

"Only a little, you say. How much was only a little?"

"Maybe once a month."

"How did you feel about that? About not getting out more?"

"I didn't think about it a lot. I don't know. I liked being at the farm. It was quiet. The city was noisy."

"I'd better explain to our audience, just in case they haven't got the whole story, why your father liked a quieter world...unless you would like to do that..."

"You do it."

"OK. As many of you in our audience know, when Simon's father decided to leave the world for a quieter place he changed his name. Take the letters of Reese Larkin, rearrange them, and you get Larin Seeker. Having already created some of the best fictional children of our time, he decided to have a real one. He worked that out with a woman he knew. She wanted to be a singer and he wanted to be a father. She delivered Simon and he set her up with a career. How'd I do?"

"Great."

"It's true, isn't it, Simon, that you knew your father had been a writer, but you hadn't read his books?"

"Yes. He told me stories and I told him stories. It was one of the things we did together. But not Sam Scamper or Mr. Bumpus. He was a really good storyteller."

"And he was a really good father."

Simon paused, looked up at Bill with some surprise. It had been agreed in their earlier talk that Bill wouldn't say things like that—things that might make Simon sad. Bill caught his expression.

"Sorry," he said quietly. Then to the audience: "Simon and his father used to go for long rides through the forests and meadows that made up their farm. By the way—and again I'm probably repeating something you have read or heard in the news—Spruce Valley Farm isn't just a farm as you and I ordinarily think of farms. It is an entire township that came into the Larkin family in the 18th century, a land grant from King George." He turned to Simon. "You tell me when I don't get things right, Simon."

"You're doing fine."

Laughter from the audience again.

"As you have probably already concluded, ladies and gentlemen, Simon's want of society hasn't left him socially or conversationally handicapped."

More laughter.

"On the contrary, he has developed communication skills beyond anything most of us can boast of. Simon is a serious rider. He and his horse, Bucephalus, are explorers of the northern wilderness." He turned to Simon and smiled. "Tell us about Bucephalus."

"It was the name of Alexander's horse," he began.

"Alexander the Great," Bill elaborated for his audience.

"He named him that because his head was so big. As broad as a bull's. That's what it means in Greek: Ox-Head."

"And you named your horse after Alexander's."

"Yes. He's a Belgian. The biggest horse there is. And smart. You can explain things to him and he'll understand. Not the words. Well, some words, but mostly he reads your face." He paused, smiled, and added, "And your mind." There was a small approving laugh from the audience and he continued. "Philonicus brought Bucephalus to Alexander. He was wild and Alexander's father, Philip, King of Macedonia, was angry at him because Alexander was only twelve years old. But he saw things that a lot of people didn't. He noticed things about animals that most people wouldn't have."

"Like what?"

"Well, he noticed that Bucephalus was afraid of his own shadow. When he led him into the sun, he quieted down. There were lots of people watching. Then Alexander stroked Bucephalus' head and spoke to him."

"The way you speak to your own Bucephalus?"

"Well, no one knows what he actually said, but Bucephalus became very gentle and Alexander climbed up on his back. Maybe Philonicus helped him. The story doesn't say. But anyway, there he was and everybody was quiet. Then King Philip said something very important."

"And what was that?"

"'He told him to look for a kingdom that would be his own. And he did. He conquered all of the known world."

"How is it that you learned all this ancient history?"

"My father bought me lots of books. They're up in my baleout."

"And what is that?"

"It's in the barn. Up in the hayloft. It's my private place."

There was laughter from the audience. Bill joined them. "What a perfect name. Bale-out. I love it. So, tell us about your books."

"Mostly they're about insects and animals. I love ants. I learned about them from a man who studied them when he was about the same age as me."

"And that man is?"

"Edward Wilson."

There were murmurs of approval from the audience. Bill continued. "And who else?"

"Lots of people. I can't remember all their names. My father found them. And Roger. Roger found a lot of them."

Bill smiled at him and turned again to the audience. "That's Roger Plummer, Simon's guardian and a great friend of his father's. He's here with us today. Would you stand up please, Roger?"

Roger stood to approving nods from the audience. He sat and Bill continued.

"So, Simon. One of the questions I'm sure many of our viewers, as well as many in our audience, have is: what's it like to be all by yourself for your whole life? Was it hard not to have friends?"

"I had lots of friends. Not people friends. My Dad helped me build a sort of tree house in the woods. Not really a house, just a ladder and a little floor."

"What did you do there?"

"I'd wait for a bird or a raccoon or a fox. One of my raccoons was named Specks. I'd bring a piece of bread or something and he'd climb up and sit there eating it and I'd talk to him and he'd look at me. I don't think he knew the words. I mean I *know* he didn't know the words, but there aren't only words."

"Not only words?"

"Well, animals and birds and even ants can communicate. Not with people, I don't mean. Not usually with people. Now and then with people."

"Go on."

"Do you know about Epimetheus?"

"Do you mean Prometheus?"

"No, Prometheus's brother."

"Oh, of course, *that* Epimetheus." Miller looked at the audience. Simon couldn't see his face. The audience laughed. "Remind me about him."

"Well, he and Prometheus had the job of giving creatures their special qualities. Like good eyes and fast legs and wings and all the things that are important for getting along."

"I didn't know that. And I'll bet not many people in our audience did either." He looked at his audience again. There was a chorus of agreement. "So what about man? Humans."

"Well there wasn't much left. He gave them fire."

"And that's it?"

"Well, they learned a lot of other things from animals and birds and fish and insects and all the rest of nature."

"So what should we learn from this?"

"That they belong here as much as we do. We need to make sure they're safe and have homes and food and places of their own."

The audience broke into another round of applause. After a few seconds Miller held up a hand and they quieted. Anyone could tell there was a new and as-yet-unnamed energy in the room.

Miller looked out over the audience at the light booth. "Can we get some of those projections on the screen?" He turned and looked up at the projection screen. On it appeared a drawing of a raccoon. The audience spoke delight in unlettered sounds whose meaning was unmistakable. Simon looked at Bill and smiled.

Simon continued. "That's Specks. He couldn't talk but I knew what he was telling me. He liked to ride on my shoulder. He'd show me things in the forest."

"How did he do that?"

"By chattering and wiggling his tail against my head."

"What kinds of things?"

"Where other animals lived. But mostly birds. He liked birds. There was a white dove. He would walk up and eat out of my hand, even if Specks was on my shoulder."

"Specks looks pretty small for a raccoon. Didn't he have a mother?"

"I think something must have happened to her. Probably a hunter's trap. That's what happened to Barker."

"Your dog."

"Yes. He got caught in one and died. I made a grave for him so that he could still be a part of things."

"Ah, yes. Tell our audience about that, Simon. Tell them about continuing to be a part of things. Tell us about compost and stardust."

Simon had worked on this part of the show for several days, trying to get things in the right order. Should he begin with stardust or compost? He wanted people to be able to see things in their minds.

"Well," he began, "there's this insect called a dung beetle..."

Chapter 29

Return to Spruce Valley

Roger had called to let Tom know that Simon would be arriving at the farm on Thursday. The truck driver would drop him off on his way to pick up his load of mussels. It was a little after 11am. He sat at his computer in what had been one of the barn's storage rooms, now converted to a work room. Simon Seeker, the Stardust Kid, was in the headlines and on the internet around the globe.

A video made by a member of the audience during the broadcast had made its way to YouTube and had over a million views in the first forty-eight hours. Simon had the world's environmentalists at his feet.

The Times and *The Globe* were after Tom for updates. Soon he would be in a position to offer them. After a little research, he had also discovered an organization that would act as an intermediary with papers around the world. The International Consortium of Investigative Journalists would work as his agent. He would be paid, but he was surprised at how little that mattered. He didn't negotiate. He didn't set a price. His goal was to keep Simon and his concerns for the natural world before the public.

And then he heard the engine and walked out of the barn. There it was, a very large semi-trailer crawling up the dirt driveway, fresh PEI Mussels appetizingly emblazoned on its side. It came to a stop a hundred yards from the barn. A red-haired woman stepped down from the passenger's side, a boy behind her. She took his hand and they walked toward the construction site. A burly man with a trimmed beard got down from the driver's seat and stood watching them. *That would be Ben*, Tom thought. He looked like an OK guy. Not the way he remembered the truck-drivers in his father's work, pushy, loud, making space for themselves as they talked. Ben seemed very comfortable. He waved. Tom waved back.

Simon and the redhead walked to within fifty feet of the presumed restoration and stopped. The woman put her arm around Simon. She leaned over and spoke. He shook his head. She pulled him closer. Then Ronnie walked to the newly framed entrance and took off his hat. "Want to see your new house?" Ronnie asked. If Simon answered it was in a small voice Tom couldn't hear. "We only just arrived," Jenna said. "Simon wants to show us around. Maybe a little later."

"We'll be here. Whatever works for you. Just give a yell. It can get pretty noisy over here."

"Thanks," Jenna said. Then she spoke quietly to Simon who nodded and leaned into her. They stood there. Tom watched and waited. He felt an outsider. They had arrived as three. They were Simon's friends. *No, they were his family.* And now? He turned back as Jenna and Simon walked towards him.

"You must be Tom," Jenna said, holding out her hand. He took it. "I'm Jenna, Ben is over there by the truck, and this young man is…"

"Simon Seeker," Simon said, holding out his hand. Tom took it. Simon had learned over the past weeks that you could learn a lot from hand-shaking. With a woman it was almost always gentle. Sometimes a woman would look at your hand, turn it over, touch it with her other hand. They were learning about you. If she held it for a while it meant she didn't want you to go away. If it was quick, it was because you were just another kid and she had plenty already. If it was a man, you paid attention to the pressure and the up-and-down. Women hardly ever did the up-and-down, at least the ones he had met at Rosie's. He'd learned to let the other person decide how it would be. Tom took his hand, held it gently and then covered it with his other.

Simon looked up. This was new.

"It's great to have you here, Simon. I've really been looking forward to meeting you." He paused. They looked at one another. Simon smiled.

Ben had been walking towards them. He held out his hand. "Very glad to meet you, Tom. Simon is lucky to have such a competent guy looking after his place, aren't you Simon?"

"Did you send my pictures to Bill Miller?"

"I did. And very nice pictures they were!"

"Thanks a lot. So you've seen my baleout."

"I have."

"You are the first person ever. Not even my father saw it. It's my secret place."

"I was very careful not to disturb anything. I'm sorry."

"It's OK. I'm glad you went there. You hired the dogs too, right?"

"Right." Tom wondered where this was going. Simon smiled. His tone was approving. Not so complicated. He was giving Tom a place in the story, a place at the farm.

"Can we be friends?"

"There's nothing I would like better!" Tom smiled broadly, somewhat relieved, more than a little grateful. Opening his arms, kneeling, came without thought. Simon looked quickly at Jenna. She smiled and nodded. He walked into Tom's arms. A quiet few seconds passed.

"You've come back to the right place, boy," Ben offered.

There was a call from the corral. Simon turned. "Bucephalus!"

"I told him you were coming. He's really missed you. He's been pretty restless."

Simon ran towards the corral. His friends followed him and watched as he greeted his life-long friend. He stood outside the enclosure; Bucephalus whinnied happily. Simon stepped up on the bottom log and leaned in. Bucephalus nuzzled his face, then his neck, stepped back, whinnied, nodded a few times and put his head on Simon's shoulder. Simon embraced it as best he could. They were still for a moment and then Simon climbed up to the top log, sat there and they talked.

Jenna looked lovingly at the reunion and then turned. "He's been looking forward to meeting you," she said. "You've done good, Tom. Really good."

"Having Simon back here makes it all worthwhile."

"Are you going to stay around?"

"I hired Ronnie and his crew. Roger will probably want me to stick around until the house is finished. And help Simon with the livestock. I go back to Orono for my final year in September."

"Orono?"

"University of Maine. I have one more year."

"Who will look after Simon?" Ben asked.

"He'll be going to the school that his father and Roger went to. It's a sort of farm school with livestock and gardens. Lots of nature. It should work pretty well for Simon."

"Oh dear," Jenna said, with a worried glance toward the corral.

"What's wrong?"

"He doesn't want to go there. It's the reason he left. Well, one of the reasons." She turned and looked again at the frame of the new farmhouse. "But I guess there's no real alternative. His house won't be finished and even if it were there's no one to look after him."

"Well, we've got a couple months before school starts. I'll see what I can do to help him with that move."

Jenna looked back at the corral. Simon was inside now with his t-shirt in hand, cleaning Bucephalus' ears. The stallion had spread his front legs and lowered his head for the remembered care. "And Ben and I aren't going to disappear. Not a chance of that. Simon has a place in both of our lives. When he goes off to school we'll stay in touch. I'll visit him there."

"It would be great if you could stay on for a while here. Help him make the transition. But that's probably impossible with your work." Tom turned to Ben. "But you're going to stop in aren't you, Ben?"

"Oh, for sure. And maybe Jenna will be able to get away as well. What do you think, Jenna?"

"Sure. But things are a little bit up in the air right now for me. I'll come up and spend time with the two of you if that's all right."

Tom looked at her more closely and with delight. In just these few moments he had been surprised by a hope that there could be more.

"That would be terrific."

"Great," Jenna said, smiling.

Simon led Bucephalus over to where they stood. He studied the new arrivals with a lift of his head and a few hoof scrapes.

"That's one very happy horse," Ben said. "He sure is glad to have you back home again."

"Tom has taken good care of him," Simon said, smiling at his new friend. "He's taken good care of everything here."

"He sure has," Jenna said. "And now he gets his reward."

"Reward?" Simon looked at Jenna, then Tom, then Ben.

"Am I right, Tom?"

"You sure are."

Jenna reached up and held Simon's hand. "You, sweetie. He did it all for you."

"Oh."

"We can leave without any worries. You and Tom are going to be great friends."

"Leave? What do you mean?"

"Just for a while. Ben's got his delivery."

"You aren't going too are you?"

"There are things I need to take care of. I'll be back. After you get settled in."

Simon grabbed the rail of the corral fence, and Ben reached over and lifted him out to where they stood. He looked at Jenna with confusion. She pulled him close and he started to cry. "You think either of us could just walk away from our boy, Simon?" Ben said, putting his hand on Simon's back. "I'll be up every week and Jenna will come with me when she can."

"You promise?" Simon said with a hard look at each of them.

"I promise. Cross my heart," Jenna responded. "I love you so very much and I couldn't bear not to see you for more than a short time."

"OK. I believe you. You wouldn't say it if you didn't mean it. Right?"

"Right."

"OK."

"So, walk with us to the truck," Ben said.

He walked between them holding each of their hands. Tom walked along beside them. After final hugs the two of them climbed into the cab. Simon stepped back as Ben started the engine. The truck moved slowly down the driveway.

Chapter 30

Simon and Tom

Simon guessed that it was about six o'clock. He got up, dressed climbed down from his bailout and walked out into a bright morning. As he approached the trailer he smelled bacon frying and realized that he was hungry. Tom turned and smiled as he entered.

"Hey, Simon."

"Hey, Tom," Simon mimicked.

"You have a good sleep up in your aerie?"

"Yes. You can come up there with me some night if you want to."

"I'd like to do that."

Simon looked at the bacon and then checked out the table and opened the refrigerator. "Want me to collect some eggs?"

"Absolutely."

The familiar complaints of the chickens made him smile. He had come back to them. It was all right. It was going to be all right.

"Fried or scrambled?" Tom asked when Simon returned with four warm eggs.

"Fried please. Sunny-side up." He smiled. "It's funny, isn't it, about things like that?"

"Like what?"

"Sunny-side up. The way words make something good or bad. I mean you'd never say "sunny-side down." Over lightly, you could say. I don't know. It just seems funny the way words can make something sound like you'd like to have it or not like to have it."

"Once I wanted to be a writer," Tom said.

"I thought you were a writer."

"I mean a real writer, like your father. Probably not children's stories. You have to have a special gift to create a Sam Scamper."

"What kind of stories?"

"Once I tried to write a detective story."

"Like Sherlock Holmes?"

"Not like Sherlock Holmes," Tom said, laughing. "That was the problem. I didn't know the first thing about how to do it. What about you?"

"Maybe a naturalist."

"You mean like Professor Wilson?"

"Yeah."

Tom took a plate from the table and carefully laid two of the eggs on it. "Help yourself to the bacon. I didn't make any toast."

"I'll make it." It was a new pop-up toaster pretty much like the one at Rosie's. As he stood over the fragrance he closed his eyes and was back among the girls, the bubbling coffee pot, the breakfast conversation, the shuffling of chairs. There was a soft click and the toast rose. He took it to the table, sat down, and looked at Tom's smile. It felt good.

Then he looked out the window as Ron and his crew drove in. It was hard to think about the house coming back without his father. Ron had been very nice, asking his advice on where to put a wall or how high to make a ceiling. He had drawings from some history place but they didn't tell him everything he needed to know. *Would the house be easier to have if it was different?* He couldn't decide.

He buttered the toast, put a piece on Tom's plate and one on his own. Then he took a couple pieces of bacon from the plate and took a bite. Crispy. Tasty. *This would be a good time to ask about Jenna*, he decided. Ben and Jenna were back in the city. Jenna had called and given him her number. When he asked about returning she had asked him to be patient. She had some things to finish up, she said. But she would come. He hadn't felt that earlier; not so clearly. Hearing her say it a second time cleared his mind for other things.

He tipped one of the fried eggs onto his toast and took a bite. "When do you think Jenna will come up?" he mumbled between bites. He watched the expression on his friend's face. Reading faces was yet another skill to be mastered in his newly populated world. Ben had been a good person to start with. He was what he seemed. Rosie was much more of a challenge. Tom he was still learning. He watched as Tom arranged his toast carefully and then centered his eggs perfectly in the middle. Hearing of Jenna's promise Tom's brows had done a quick wrinkle, then a thoughtful purse of the lips, a nod and a smile. Simon tried to guess at the series of thoughts beneath his features, but he was quickly relieved of concern.

"We'll need to get to work on converting the milking shed," Tom said, taking a bite of bacon. "Ron went through it with me a few days ago. The parts that made up the office are already in pretty good shape. Taking out the stalls, putting in a floor will take a while."

"Is that where Jenna will live?"

"Not yet. Not until we get it finished. She'll get the trailer. I can sleep in the milking shed and you've got your baleout."

"I'd rather sleep with you. I can bring my mattress down."

"Great. There's plenty of space, even with the construction."

Simon nodded and finished off the last strip of his bacon. It was crispier than his father's. It was good. Really good.

Chapter 31

Tom and Simon

After cleaning up the breakfast dishes, Tom and Simon set about the morning chores. Simon looked after the sheep while Tom saw to the pigs. Then the chickens. Simon filled the feeders and Tom checked the nests for eggs. There were only nine hens but their offerings were bountiful. Ron and the guys had been well supplied and there were a good many hard-boiled eggs in the refrigerator. As he collected, Tom was reminded of Ben's story about Simon's offering on their first meeting.

Finally, the horses, the high point of morning chores. Once the feed and water containers had been freshened Simon had a conversation with Bucephalus. Tom retrieved the grooming tools from the closet and began to groom Empress. Simon was a serious groomer. There were two curry combs, one plastic and one metal, a dandy brush, two body brushes (one for the body and one for the head), a grooming rag, a pulling comb, and an assortment of hoof picks. Tom had not been religious about grooming, a fact that gave him pause as he watched Simon and Bucephalus in intimate and affectionate conversation. But to his surprise, when Simon came over and joined him it wasn't to pick up a brush or a pick but to mention an even more essential equine need. Exercise.

Tom gladly concurred and together they set about saddling Empress and Bucephalus. It would be their first ride together. Simon had ridden Bucephalus around the farm a couple of times, never, at Tom's request, getting out of sight. Now they would explore Simon's wilderness.

Simon and Bucephalus led. Tom and Empress followed as they crossed the lawn and headed toward the pond. Soon they reached an outlet stream with a small but steady current. Simon dismounted and knelt beside it. Tom followed, standing beside him. Simon paddled in the water with his hand, disturbing the bottom so that it clouded the shallows. The cloud moved slowly away with the current and out through the outlet of piled stones, like something disturbed from its darkness, then disappeared in the commotion of water below.

"There are turtles here," Simon said. "I've seen them. A razorback, too. A great big one."

"What's a razorback?"

"A snapper, but his back looks like a roof."

"Oh."

"Not an ordinary roof. Like the one over our picnic table. They're called shakes."

"Oh. Cedar shakes. I know what you mean. So that's like the back of a razorback?"

"Not really, but sort of." Simon walked down the stream and then waded into the middle where he appeared to be searching for something. Tom looked around, never having seen a ravine before except in movies. It was different from the world above, but not merely in its daylight darkness, or from the cool air which gathered in its hollow. It was the way in which it gathered and concentrated other things: fragrances, compressions of rotting leaves, tight mounds of mosses, rocks which in their wetness were also denser and more secret. In the same way it concentrated Tom's thoughts and gathered together feelings which had rarely visited his mind. An expectation, an immanence, formless but filled with longing.

But it was Simon who was most in his mind at that moment as he stared at the tangle of vines above their heads and watched him foraging in the creek.

"Have you ever seen one of these?" Simon asked, a tiny chrysalis in his hand.

"What is it?" Tom asked.

"I don't know," Simon said. "Something makes it and then ties it down on the bottom of the stream. Maybe it's a small amphibian. A baby one. Then it comes out and this is all that's left. Tom held out his hand and Simon tipped the tiny jewel into his palm.

Tom touched it carefully. It was a perfectly shaped tube, an aggregate of grains no larger than the head of a pin and altogether about the size of a dime.

"Amazing. It looks like a piece of jewelry."

"I'm going to give it to Jenna."

"She'll love it."

"How did you ever find anything this tiny?"

"I have a pair of goggles. They're great for exploring under water."

"What else have you found?"

"Some stoneflies and roundworms. That's about all."

They got back into their saddles and rode deeper into the forest. Tom urged Empress up alongside Bucephalus and they rode quietly for several minutes.

Stopping, Simon pointed up at a small platform in the triangular crook of an oak tree. "That's one of my forts," he said.

"Wow. Pretty impressive. Did you build that by yourself?"

"My dad helped me. We made the platform back at the farm and brought it out on the cart. With ropes and pulleys, it wasn't so hard. He had to do the heavy lifting."

"A good place to watch what's going on without being in the way. Right?"

"Right." As they rode on, Simon pointed out places colonized by ants and bees, trees that were home to porcupines and several rabbit burrows.

Then he stopped. "I need to check something," he said, dismounting and walking a short distance through the brush. Tom dismounted and joined him. "There was a family of foxes here in the spring," Simon said. "If I walked over and sat on that dead tree…" he pointed to a fallen birch, "… one of the cubs would come over. Not to be petted. Just to watch me. One day I came out with a book and read for a while. He curled up near me. Foxes are nocturnal. It was pretty unusual."

"For most of us. But not the Stardust Kid."

Simon reached into the opening. "They're gone now. Like the beavers." Simon stood up and looked at Tom. Gone. Gone.

"You aren't going any place, are you Tom?" he asked.

"What do you mean?"

"I mean you're going to be around here for a while, right?"

"As long as you and Roger want me."

"We make a good team, you and me."

"You think so?"

"Sure. I want you to stay. Really. A lot. And Roger wants you. He hired you. The farm wouldn't still be a farm if you hadn't been here to take care of it. Did you know Roger before?"

"No. I came out to cover the fire for *The Star*."

"A star?"

"It's a local newspaper. Small-time. Anyway, I was here for the Fire Warden, and after I found Roger he asked me if I'd look after things for a few days and I said sure. One thing led to another and here we are."

"I like that."

"What?"

"One thing led to another."

"You've never heard anyone say that before?"

"No. There are lots of things Ben and Jenna say that I've never heard before. Some of them are pretty funny."

"Like what?"

"'You don't miss a trick,' Ben said. It means that I pay close attention to what people are saying."

"That's right on the money," Tom said with a grin.

"Huh?"

184

"You're hitting the nail on the head."

"Oh. I know that one. Roger uses it. It means you're right. You've got it right. Right on the money! Right?"

"You've got it."

"Roger used another one when we talked on the telephone. He asked how I felt about being in the limelight."

"How did you feel?"

"It was OK. Jenna and Ben were there. And Roger. And Bill made it easy. He asked me easy questions."

"You were great and the audience loved you."

"Thanks."

"There's quite a lot going back and forth about The Stardust Kid. I've come across a few conversations where people are talking about coming to Spruce Valley to be in the presence of the boy wonder."

"I'm no wonder. I'm just me."

"So, how do you feel about it? Visitors, I mean."

"It would be OK, I guess. Did you talk to Roger about it?"

"No."

"He let me be on the Bill Miller Show. I didn't think he would."

"Why is that?"

"Roger wanted me to go to the school that he and my father went to. They call it a farm school. Jenna says he is my guardian and he's in charge of me until I get older. I'm supposed to do what he tells me to do."

"And that's why you hooked up with Ben. Right?"

"Right. I didn't want Roger to be my boss. But I couldn't be on Bill's show unless Roger gave permission."

"Were you afraid that he wouldn't?"

"Sure, but I had a plan. If he said no I would disappear again before he could take me away."

"I'm sure glad that didn't happen."

"So am I. Bill is good at getting people to go along with him."

"Like you."

"Right."

Chapter 32

Tom and Simon

Tom hadn't expected to be returned to his own fairly recent childhood, but he wasn't displeased. Looking after Simon was, in many ways, a redemptive experience. During those first days when there was a likelihood that Simon had not survived the fire, he could think of little else. Too parallel for coincidence. The barn, the loft, the bales of hay, not to mention the ages of the two boys. Discovering that Simon had walked out to the road changed everything.

They had spent little time apart over the past two weeks. The vegetable gardens had doubled in size and promised a fine harvest. The Thibodeau brothers were major beneficiaries. Baskets of tomatoes and a number of other fruiting vegetables had gone home with them.

The Bill Miller Show had gone viral. YouTube and social media had anointed the Stardust Kid "Nature's Guardian." It helped that he had entered the world from a land far away in the Maine woods. He was a child of nature and spoke on its behalf. By the second week of July, forty-four visitors had pitched tents at Spruce Valley Farm to hear Simon reveal the secrets of soil, the workings of worms, the romances of dragonflies, and the industry of ants.

With Simon's approval, Tom directed the visitors to the meadow that led down to the pond. There they set up tents and arrangements for cooking. Many of them were activists in the environmental movement, well-practiced in the arts of simple living.

Some drove small campers that they parked along the road.

At first they ate independent of one another, but as the days passed and acquaintance grew, the tasks of cooking and cleaning up were passed around and dinners were shared.

The visitors were a mixture of ages and experiences as well as education. What they had in common was a serious concern for the environment. A number were educators, writers, and activists. And there were the pilgrims, seeking a better land and leader. A man named Professor Jack Benson from London had written widely on bird populations. Another named Milton Schneider was widely regarded as a leading authority on endangered sea creatures.

Simon welcomed them with a grateful and open heart, not effusive but appreciative. They soon began to share meals and walks as well as afternoon gatherings and evenings around a campfire. Tom took pains to make conversations casual and simple. This was not the Bill Miller Show. Simon should not be asked to perform as the Stardust Kid. This was an opportunity for him to learn as well as teach.

One of them was different from anyone Simon had ever seen or heard. He was black and he spoke with a different sound. His name was Afua. He was from Africa, studying now at Harvard. He described the loss of his home and his loved ones in the desertification of Ghana. He spoke of his friend and benefactor, who arranged for his study in the United States. And much to Simon's delight, spoke of his hero, Edward Wilson.

Simon's knowledge of the insect world was mostly first hand. With Afua's help they put together a number of demonstrations. Within the first few weeks they had discovered several colonies which they shared with the visitors. Lawn ants and Cornfield ants were easily found. The winter wood pile offered a large community of Carpenter ants. Yellow ants were harder to find, but after some careful searching among the barn's foundation stones, they too were a presence and the subject of an afternoon talk.

One afternoon, Simon had taken a group of visitors into the forest to observe various insects. With Simon it was a hands-on affair. The ants crawled up his arms. He held beetles in his hands.

"Don't they bite?" one visitor asked.

"Not very often," Simon replied.

"Have you ever read any Charles Darwin?" one of the young men asked.

"Sure," Simon replied. "He loved insects. Once he put a beetle in his mouth."

"What happened?"

"It burnt his tongue." There was laughter and a little mimicry.

"But really," Simon continued, "ants and worms and other insects make it possible for there to be trees and everything else that grows. Ants especially collect and store large amounts of nutrient-rich prey. After they eat it their waste fertilizes the soil and the soil makes things grow. And of course the trees feed the ants. They are partners."

"So where do earthworms fit in?" one woman asked.

"They are very important but they couldn't do it alone," Afua said. "Ants create soil up to ten times faster than earthworms, excavating as much as thirty thousand pounds of soil per acre every year, creating about four inches of new soil per millennium in the process."

"And they do it all alone north of here," another visitor said.

"They have to," Simon agreed. "Earthworms would freeze."

"In forests near the Brazilian Amazon, ants and termites together make up more than one quarter of the biomass," Afua said. "Ants alone weigh four times as much as the birds, amphibians, reptiles, and mammals combined."

Evenings around the fire people sang and played harmonicas, guitars, and a few other exotic and portable instruments. Visitors were rarely disappointed in having made the journey to meet the Stardust kid.

Simon and Tom both shared in the collective dinners, providing fresh vegetables from the gardens and some eggs from the hen house. Simon also contributed a variety of mushrooms from his walks in the woods. There was predictably a good deal of skepticism when he presented his first cutting of boletes. Few of the visitors had seen them before. Simon sliced them and instructed the cook how to fry them up. Then he ate a forkful with the rolling eyes of a French gourmet chef and others followed suit. In the days following boletes begat Chanterelles and Puffballs. One of the guests filmed Simon as he presented an elegant array of Chanterelles. It appeared the next day on YouTube under the title "Stardust Mycology."

Everybody sang. He joined in eagerly and learned songs quickly, singing them to himself as he lay in bed awaiting sleep.

Chapter 33

Simon and Jenna

Being in someone else's mind was what Simon had missed the most after his father's death. That had begun to change with Ben and Jenna. Being in their minds he found new places in his own. Working alongside Tom, he was reminded of doing chores with his father, times when the task set the pace and thoughts waited 'til later. When the work was completed, there was a quick review to be sure that you hadn't forgotten anything. Then there was looking away, in a different direction, at a new scene.

Not having Jenna by his side had been hard. Or Ben. He knew that because he had woken up several times in the night and cried. Into his pillow, so as not to upset Tom.

With help from two of the visitors, he and Tom had converted the once milking shed into an apartment. The cow stalls were gone, the walls refinished, and there was a carpet on the cement floor. The office had been made into a bathroom. There was no need for a kitchen given the one that Tom had converted from a couple of stalls. Tom spent a lot of time with his own thoughts. Simon watched him, trying to read from his actions his state of mind.

It was the opposite of his experience with books. There, you would have to make a picture of a character while the author told you all of his thoughts. With Tom it was the reverse.

Now and then, Tom would look for a bench or a bale and sit down with his thoughts. "Reflective" was a word that came to mind. It was a word his authors liked to use. When the characters in books became reflective they would fiddle with something, pick at a tooth, examine an irregular fingernail, arrange things on a table, trace a surface with a finger. Tom didn't do any of those things. He wiped immediate purpose from his hands and sat. He might look at the floor for a moment, but never for very long.

Prologue actions were another thing Simon was noticing. Pauses, facial changes, breaks in the rhythm of an activity or a conversation. The characters in the stories he read were often complex and original. Following a line of thought, predicting a behavior, even imagining stature and movement were things he could do turning the pages of a book. Faces were another matter. He studied them now with great interest, his father's face being his template. And Roger's. Roger's wasn't very complicated. What he said was often at odds with his expression.

Jenna's was comforting. Looking into her eyes he felt the same embrace he had felt with his father. He challenged his father, explored limits, watched for new signals, but never with anything like fear of losing his love. With Jenna that was different. It was partly a matter of time. Because they shared no past, he feared for the future.

Tom was different from all of them. For one thing, he was only a few years older. And he was a farm boy. The two of them could do a whole morning's worth of chores without a need to explain anything. He could imagine, and did often, that when he grew up he would be just like Tom. But there was something he hadn't been able to name.

Partly it felt like protection, of the kind he had known with his father. With Tom, he felt safe remembrance.

It was almost one o'clock. Ben and Jenna were late. A stretch of roadside just past the trailer was marked off for Ben's truck. RESERVED, the sign said. Ben had been able to stop off to catch up and have lunch with Tom and Simon for the two past weeks. He had taken a walk around the farm on his last visit and met some of the visitors.

Simon heard the truck before he saw it. The sound clicked switches in his brain the way a hamburger on a grill got his mouth watering. The sense of leaving one world for another in a machine that moved with slow but powerful purpose, indifferent to the presence of one so small as he, who couldn't even see out its window.

Ben stopped. Simon ran over and jumped up onto the running board holding onto the mirror. "Hold on," Ben said reaching a hand to muss his hair, then back to the steering wheel, turning the large circle of the driveway, heading back toward the road and pulling over to his parking space. The engine sighed and quieted. Simon jumped back to the ground and around to the other side as Jenna opened her door. He stood there. He felt water in his eyes. He blinked and wiped with his sleeve. Then Jenna was there, holding him close.

Tom had heard the truck and was walking towards them, a big smile on his face. Simon looked to see if Ben and Jenna were answering with their own. Jenna was. Ben didn't do that kind of thing. Not at first. He was careful to size things up, make sure all the pieces were in place, just as he had been the first day by Curtis Bog. Simon smiled quietly and counted. One, two, three, four.

"How great to see you," Tom said, walking up and extending his hand to Ben.

Five, six, seven. Ben took it firmly. Eight, nine ten. "Good to be back, Tom. I see you're looking after the young man. Hope he isn't giving you any trouble." That was it. First one cheek rose, then the lips tightened and the other cheek rose and then the laugh. It was a great laugh. Not one of those throw-away things that people did when they really weren't interested.

One of the things that fascinated Simon as he met more and more people was the different ways they used words. His father's way was clean and uncomplicated. His face changed in simple ways that suggested surprise, happiness, puzzlement, annoyance—simple every-day things.

Roger, though often louder and sometimes corrective, wasn't very hard to read. Ben, Rosie, the girls, even Jenna were straight-talkers. Tom was different, harder to be sure about. His face might say one thing and his words another. Or his posture. He might speak as if certain, his face or his posture suggesting something else. It wasn't upsetting. It was a new thing he was learning, to his advantage. He looked up at Tom.

"He's a real handful," Tom said, shaking his head slightly.

Jenna and Ben laughed. "He isn't letting all this hero-worship go to his head is he?" Ben asked.

"Not all of it," Tom replied. They laughed again. It was at times like this that Simon didn't wish he was older.

The days passed under a blessing of good weather. It was the end of Jenna's second week at the farm. She had made friends quickly and was with Simon for most of the day, listening to the visitors discuss the problems the planet faced. The topic was new to Simon as well, or had been before the pilgrims arrived. The visitors, in gatherings throughout the day or around a campfire at night told of worldwide threats to animals, birds, sea creatures, and soil dwellers that disturbed him greatly. Afua had quickly become a close friend. When he spoke of the devastations in his homeland resulting from overcutting and the measures that were being taken to restore the forests, Simon lay awake wishing he could join the hundreds of children in Ghana who were planting trees, trying to restore homes for the thousands of creatures made homeless.

He spoke to Jenna of all that he was learning and how that knowledge was changing him. One thing that his father had taught him was that things don't happen accidentally. *No out-of-the-blues*, was his expression. *Don't feed the chickens and they won't lay eggs. Don't feed Bucephalus and he'll stop talking to you.* Sure, there were forces in nature that could cause bad things to happen: a big storm, an early frost, a takeover by bad bugs or a tearless sky. But he did his part to get things right by being a responsible farmer. He could make things happen, make things appear, turn a brown bed into a vegetable garden.

It was on a Sunday afternoon when many of the visitors napped or read and the meadow was quiet that he told Jenna what he had decided.

"I'm not going to that school," he said.

"What is it called?"

"Wind Lake."

"Oh yes. I think you said it was in New Hampshire, right?"

"Right. I don't know maps very well but it's somewhere in New Hampshire."

"But you don't want to go there."

"No."

"Why not? It sounds like a really nice place. Your father must have really loved it there if he based the farm on it. Do you think you could at least give it a chance?

Simon remained silent.

"Anyway there's time to think about it. You've got the whole summer ahead. We'll talk more about it. One day at a time. OK?"

"OK."

Chapter 34

Roger and Tom

Roger had driven Route 9 from Bangor to the farm countless times, but never with quite this sense of anticipation. There were some decisions he would need Tom to help him enforce. First off, the visitors, as Tom called them, would sail back to their own lands. Nothing personal, but common sense, legal sense, required that the farm and Simon not be liable to suits of misfortune. Someone drowning in the pond, falling from a tree, eating a poisonous mushroom. And Simon. Just a boy needing what a child needs: the security and care of professional people. Educators, house parents, psychologists. A return to the way of life he had known. The farm. Then gradually, year by year, out into the world.

And that truck driver and his mistress. She was there. Living there. Acting as Simon's caretaker. *No thank you.* This was a harder issue to think about. *Where was Tom in all of it? Tom, who had been a gift from the sky, who had performed miracles to get the farm put back together and discovered Simon's trail out to the road. What was going on?* But that he had allowed that woman to move in, even temporarily, was not right. Simon needed Tom. He needed his horse and his animals. Simplicity. Life as he had known it. Life as the farm knew it, as Reese had known it.

He had meant to ask Tom about the university's vacation schedule. If it matched that of Wind Lake, that would solve the problem. If not...well, something could be arranged. Maybe Simon could go back to Orono with Tom. Something.

As he approached the lane leading to the farm his mind tossed up a memory of his own last year at Wind Lake. It was a tradition that the eighth graders put on a play the week of graduation. Reese had written it. It was about getting lost in a deep wood and encountering strange creatures. He had been one of the creatures. He smiled as he recalled the ending. The lost boy was rescued by his fellow students and the play ended with their leaving the woods singing that old song about a hole in the bottom of the sea. With some new verses. He tried to remember them as he turned and drove into the driveway of Spruce Valley Farm. He couldn't.

Tom had brewed a pot of coffee for the building crew and was about to take it over when the car drove in, predictably a Chevy from Avis. *What would Roger make of all this?* It was hard to imagine him in conversation around a fire, joining in the story-telling, the singing. The car sat for a couple minutes adjacent to the space where Roger usually parked. That space now hosted a Volkswagen bus, something of a relic, but still on its feet. He tried to get into Roger's head. Not all of the visitors were automotive archivists, but the vehicles decorating the farm's entrance did have something in common.

Roger drove past the parked vehicles and right up to the front of the barn, turned off the engine and got out. He looked out over the meadow where most of the visitors had set up their tents and then at the construction. Tom walked over and joined him.

"I can't believe what your builders have accomplished, Tom! I know I haven't been here for over a month, but my goodness. The house is actually taking shape."

"Ron says he's aiming for Easter."

"That's great. I never would have guessed things would move along so swiftly." Roger turned toward the barn. Tom had erected a simple gazebo with a table and chairs and a grill. "Very nice," Roger said. "Are you still cooking in the barn?"

"Not very much. Jenna has been doing most of the cooking in the Trailer. Simon and I have moved to the bottom of the barn. It's coming along pretty well. The stalls are out and there are a couple beds. I rented a composting toilet just outside. It's not the Hilton but it meets our needs. By the way, Simon will be moving in with Jenna so that you can have the other bed."

"Oh. Jenna. I had forgotten," Roger lied. "So she's moved in, has she?"

"It's been really great for Simon. They spend a lot of time together. He's taught her to ride."

"Really." Roger turned and looked at the trailer, then at the visitors wandering the meadow. The tone of Roger's response put Tom's unrealistic hopes back in the drawer.

Jenna had described their meeting in Boston at the time of the broadcast. Roger had said little when the broadcast ended and the audience made their way to the doors. Simon had jumped off the stage and run up to her. She had given him a big hug, Ben a smaller but equally affectionate one. Then he had turned to Roger, awaiting his response. He had held out his hands, palms up, and Simon had matched them palms down, what appeared to be a ritual greeting. And that was that. Roger had looked first at Ben, then Jenna, nodding to each with a careful smile, excusing himself from further conversation with the apologetic urgency of an emergency room physician.

Jenna had watched for Simon's reactions, prepared to lessen his disappointment with remarks on how busy lawyers were and how good it had been of Roger to make room in his day for a trip to Boston. But none of that was necessary. Simon seemed unsurprised at the abruptness of his guardian's departure. Clearly it was consistent with their long relationship, but nonetheless hard to grasp. Simon had had two people in his life. How had he ever learned the open and trusting affection that he had offered her?

"So what's the plan?" Roger said, turning back. "As I explained, the office is a madhouse and I will have to leave the day after tomorrow."

"Well, Jenna's cooking dinner for us tonight, just the four of us, and I think Simon will want to show you around."

"Show me around? Oh, you mean the gypsies. Right. Well, that should be interesting."

Tom couldn't completely suppress a smile. *Gypsies, of course. Rootless nomads without a key or a mailbox. Nobodies, traveling from one amusement to another, ungrounded, looking for the next free meal.* "I think you'll be surprised," he said.

"Oh?"

"Seriously. They aren't all wanderers or worshippers or transients. There are some major movers and shakers in the crowd."

"Movers and shakers of what?"

"You know: environmentalism, protecting wildlife, saving the planet. The stuff that got Simon on TV. The stuff he talked about with Bill Miller."

"Right. Right. I just can't get my head around it. Any of it. Most especially Simon. How in God's name did a kid who has no social experience, no social skills, no practice in real conversation, suddenly end up as the Stardust Kid?"

"I can't explain it. It's just that Simon is so…what's the word? Available. Friendly. Sociable. I keep looking for strangeness. Like he's from another world or something. I don't know. I just know that he's one fantastic kid." Tom waited for a response. There was none, just another glance at the meadow, then down at his shoes. "He certainly is lucky to have you in his life, Roger," Tom continued respectfully, hopefully. "Someone who's been there all those years to help him tie up the past with the present." When Roger once again said nothing, a disappointed Tom laughed as best he could. "And someone whose head isn't up in the clouds like the rest of us."

"So when are we going to see the boy wonder?"

"He and Bucephalus are out on one of his trails. Simon likes to have his time alone."

"Good. I was afraid he might be heading for Hollywood."

"He's glad to be back here on the farm. He and Bucephalus have been catching up on things."

"So very glad to hear that. I didn't know what to suspect with all the publicity. I don't do that thing on the computer that everyone's talking about."

"You mean YouTube?"

"I guess that's what it's called. The office staff can't get enough of it. They keep me up to date. I gather he's the center of attention for the... visitors."

"He certainly is that. I guess you've heard about the ants and the mushrooms. Yesterday it was seeds. He apparently had collected them at the end of last summer."

"What kind of seeds?"

"Vegetables. The garden has been well taken care of by the visitors. Under Simon's supervision. The harvest is modest, however, so they're turning over new ground and Simon is planting the seeds."

"What on earth for?" The question was sharper than Roger had intended.

Tom picked up on that without surprise. *Gypsies were one thing, settlers were another.* "I'm pretty sure it was Simon's idea. He's great at coming up with ideas for projects. Things that he and the visitors can do together."

Roger turned and studied the arrangement of tents between the barn and the pond. Then the seven small pop-up campers along the driveway. There were even a couple motorhomes.

Tom could sense his disapproval. Not surprising, but nonetheless disappointing. "Simon is totally into his relationship with the visitors," he continued. "Not just because they love him. They do love him. We all do. He's a gift. Like, none of this goes to his head. He doesn't get puffed up the way a teen idol or an actor might. And one of the really great things is that he hasn't given up who he was in order to join the crowd. I've watched him with Bucephalus, or just sitting by the pond, or gardening. He's his own person more than most grown-ups are." He cleared his throat and brought up a smile. "Sorry, I didn't mean to make a speech."

Roger was quiet for a moment, nodding, as if thinking the thing through. Then he looked up. "Simon is a very lucky boy. Coming back to a place that was empty of everything and almost every one he knew, and finding you here. We might never have seen Simon again if it weren't for you."

"And Bob. If he hadn't told me that his brother hadn't let the animals out, I wouldn't have known that Simon was alive. By the way, Simon and the Thibodeaus are getting along pretty well now."

"Good. It's not hard to understand his reluctance earlier on. Rebuilding the place where his father had died. Very tough. But that's changed?"

"It has. Having Jenna here has made lots of things easier for him. It's almost like he's found a new parent."

"Really. And she's been able to take time off? That's not an easy thing to do when you are a counselor. Do I have that right?"

"Yes. I think she's been cutting back on her clients since Simon came into the picture. She was spending a lot of time with him in Boston."

"And she can afford to do that."

The conversation was making its way into Roger's office, Tom thought. *Cross examination. Was Jenna guilty? Professionally irresponsible?* "I don't know, Roger. All I know is that she loves Simon and he loves to have her around."

"I'm sure she is a fine lady," Roger said. "A very caring lady. I look forward to getting to know her better."

"And she you. She's been looking forward to having more time with you. I gather you didn't have much time for conversation after the show."

"Right. Damned divorce cases."

"Divorce? You've never spoken of divorce cases. I thought you were doing wills and stuff like that."

"I am. This is temporary, and very annoying. Covering for a colleague."

"How long will you have to deal with that?"

"God knows. Anyway, getting back to Simon. You say he's getting along well with the visitors."

"I'd love for you to see Simon at one of the campfires."

"What are those?'

"Sorry! I guess I haven't done much to bring you up to date."

"Well, Tom, I've only been here for about ten minutes. I think you've done brilliantly. What do you say we retire to the new guest quarters? I'm eager to see what you've done. I must say this farm hasn't seen such creativity and care-taking in a very long time. You are a great gift, not only to Simon, but to the estate itself."

"Thanks Roger. You are very generous. I see all of this as a gift to me. One of the best, maybe *the* best, I have ever received."

Chapter 35

Simon and Roger

Simon chose a shorter route home. Instead of coming out at the end of the meadow by the pond, he took a trail directly to the field below the house, a short way from the barn. It wasn't that he didn't enjoy the shouts and cheers, the walk-along-sides, the invitations to stop and chat; it was Roger's arrival. He had never been particularly eager to see Roger in the past three or four years when, despite being older, Roger still treated him as a little boy. Tom had explained what a guardian does. Makes sure you are looked after, makes decisions about where you go and what you do. Makes sure you are safe. But Simon had his own plans and his father had approved of that.

He rode out of the forest to the meadow, below the house rising from ashes. For the first few weeks it had been a reminder of things lost. But then, seeing the changes Ronnie and his crew were making, he saw it filled, like spring, with promise. New growth from old roots. The past was down below among the ancient megaliths, the future in fresh smells of fragrant wood taking on new shapes.

He rode to the gate, got down, opened it and led Bucephalus in. He removed the saddle and put it in the box that his father had made for it, so that he wouldn't have to carry it into the barn. It was heavy. *Maybe next year.* He was much stronger than he had been then. And not just with saddles. He talked with Bucephalus for a few minutes, explaining about Roger being back and sharing a few other thoughts.

He walked down to the old milking shed and stopped. Roger and Tom were inside. He walked to the window and peered in. Tom was showing Roger the changes they had made. Roger nodded with approval, looking closely where Tom pointed, asking a question, getting an answer, approving with a pat on Tom's back. Roger had been different when they talked on the phone before the Bill Miller Show. It wasn't a difference Simon could have named. *Had Roger ever been in the room before?* Why would he have? He had never had any interest in the barn or the animals. At least none that Simon had observed. Roger was a house guy, a kitchen table guy and sometimes a front porch guy when he and his father had drinks before dinner. This was a new Roger. Especially his energy. It had to be Tom. Roger liked being with Tom. *How could anyone not like Tom?* Simon opened the door.

"Well, here he is, the twelve-year-old celebrity," Roger said, turning, with a friendly smile.

He held out his hands. Simon walked up and matched them. Roger looked at them, let go, and put his hands on Simon's shoulders. "So you and Tom have become partners in carpentry. Very nice work. Your father would be proud of you."

"It's mostly Tom. I just hand him things and move things around."

"That's only part of it," Tom said. "Simon has a very good eye for design. I was going to put the beds against the back wall. It was Simon's idea to put them where they are now. Much more convenient and leaving lots more room for other things."

Simon took a quick step back in time. Two people in the same room as he, one praising him the other looking at him with an expression his father never got to see. He couldn't have given it a name but it said something like, *You and I know better, don't we?*

"And Simon has been a big help to the Thibodeaus as well. Tell Roger about the kitchen."

"They had it turned around."

Roger wrinkled his eyes. "Turned around?"

"They had the stove where the windows were supposed to be."

"How did that happen?"

"They have old drawings from before the new kitchen was made."

"Well, well. It's a good thing you were back to get things straightened out. There will probably be a lot more things you can help them out with."

"I guess so."

Tom suddenly felt an impatience, for no reason he could find. Without examining it further, he took charge. "How about the two of you take a walk around the farm? Simon can show you what's new and introduce you to some of our guests. Would you like to do that, Simon?"

"I guess so."

"Bring Roger up to date on everything. I've got to take a quick run into town to do some shopping for dinner tonight. Is that good with you, Roger?"

"Um…yes…sure. I need to catch up on things. It's been a while."

They left the milking room and headed back up to the barn. Tom gave Simon a pat on the back and turned to Roger. "It's great to have you back, Roger. Simon has been counting the days. Right, Simon?"

It was an expression he hadn't heard before. He looked at Tom with some confusion. Tom winked at him. *It was OK; they were on the same side.*

"Right." Just then there was a call from the edge of the meadow and a man of color approached.

"This is my friend, Afua," Simon said, grateful for his friend's welcome appearance. "He's a friend of Professor Wilson."

"Professor Wilson? Oh, of course, your ant man." He said it dismissively.

Afua looked puzzled. "I can't claim to be a friend, but I've taken his course." He extended his hand. Roger took it with a smile that took Simon back. It was the smile he used when Simon interrupted a conversation between Roger and his father to show them something he had found.

"Look at that!" his father would say with a big smile. *Very nice, very nice,* Roger would say with impatience, wanting to get back to whatever they were talking about before he'd showed up.

"Are they waiting for me?" Simon asked with suggestively bright eyes. Afua read them accurately.

"Yes. The meeting's about to start." He turned to Roger. "You are welcome to join us, sir…"

"Roger Plummer. I am Simon's guardian."

"Very glad to meet you, Mr. Plummer. We have a get-together every afternoon to share ideas. Simon has a lot to teach us."

"And you teach me too." Simon offered.

"Are you going to be here for a while, sir?" Afua asked.

"I'm afraid not. Much as I would like to. Too many cases waiting for me back in New York."

"Oh, you're a lawyer."

"Yes. Now if you'll excuse us. There are some things Simon and I need to discuss."

"Sorry to interrupt. I'll catch you later, Simon." He started to turn. Simon grabbed his hand.

"Wait." He turned to Roger. "We can talk later. This is a really good time for you to meet some of my friends. Especially Jed. He went to a school like yours and Dad's. You'd like to meet him. He really loved it."

"What school was that?"

"I don't remember. I know that it was in the mountains and that they rode horses a lot and grew things."

Roger said nothing for a moment. He looked at Afua.

"They'd sure like to meet you, Mr. Plummer. Hard to imagine anyone more important to all of this than Simon's guardian."

Roger couldn't help a smile. *Simon's new friends and worshippers. Even one who might speak well of farm schools. Give a little, take a little more.* He smiled. "Sure, I'd be glad to meet Simon's new friends."

"Great! Let's go." Simon ran toward the meadow and turned. Afua and Roger followed, in conversation.

"We have a get-together every afternoon. It's a chance for Simon to tell us about life here at the farm and for Simon to learn some things he might not have read about. Our leader is Jack Benson, from London. He's major in the environmental movement there. I think you'll find him pretty interesting."

"I'm sure I will."

Simon led them to a gazebo not unlike the one Tom had erected by the barn. Bigger, and brown instead of blue. There was a folding table at the front.

Simon walked up and was greeted with a friendly nod by a man of about seventy, Roger guessed, white-bearded, bespectacled, erect. Benson raised his hand and the crowd of eighteen or twenty men and women took their seats. "Well, my friends…" he began.

Afua stood up and waved. "Yes, Afua. I see you have a new guest with you."

"I would like to introduce Mr. Roger Plummer, Simon's guardian. He's here for a couple days to see Simon and meet his friends." He held out his arm. Roger stood. The group applauded. Three of those nearest reached out to shake his hand.

"Would you like to say a few words to Simon's tribe of uninvited guests, Roger?" Benson asked.

"Thank you, but I'm afraid I'd be a poor second to the boy wonder. No, you carry on." There was an awkwardness in his tone, and a feeling that the group was waiting for him to continue. "Please." He held up his hands briefly and sat.

Jack Benson re-started the discussion. "Today we're going to talk about noise pollution. Not something we have to worry about here in your quiet valley, but something that is getting a lot of attention from congested areas or communities near factories, airports, and highways."

"I heard it in Boston when I was there," Simon said. "Lots of noises. More than I had ever heard. Well, not ever. My Dad and I went shopping a couple of times a year. Into noisy places."

"And I'll bet you didn't hear many song birds."

"No. I saw some but they weren't singing."

"That's a problem. They sing in order to find mates and build nests together." Benson said.

"Oh they still sing," a woman said. "At least some of them. The problem is that the friends they'd like to make can't understand a note that they're saying." Several in the group commented on this to their neighbors. There was small laughter.

"It isn't just birds," Simon said, standing up. The group quieted. "It's frogs and bats and lots of other animals."

"Frogs?" a heavy-set fellow asked. "I hadn't read that."

"It's true," Simon responded. "Frogs are supposed to talk way... .d.o.w.n...here," he said, trying for a voice that was still some years off. His friends warmed at his attempt and smiled. "There's one in Australia called the Pobblebonk. It could send its croak a long ways. But it's disappearing because of all the noise."

Roger closed his eyes as he had at The Bill Miller Show. The boy he saw then, and again now before an audience, was as unlike the boy he had watched over the past twelve years as anything he could imagine. He spoke and people listened with approving nods, smiles, and quick words of agreement.

Another member of the group of participants, wearing a t-shirt that said Earth Day Every Day, raised his hand. "Yes, Simon, and it's not only a matter of volume with birds or toads. It's frequency," he said. "When they raise their voices," he turned to a woman beside him, "just like Maggie, it goes up an octave or three."

A few examples were offered, then laughter, then Jack raised his hand and they quieted. He looked affectionately at Simon and smiled. "The population of house sparrows in my country has declined by two thirds over the past two decades. It all has to do with their songs of courtship. They have had to raise their voices to compete with the volume of Great Britain's industry and commerce. Those they would mate with have a limited range of hearing, too low for their high-pitched attempts to woo."

He had everyone's attention as he reached out and put his hands gently on Simon's shoulders. "The world depends more and more every year on assurances that those who speak of our planet's needs are heard. All of us here devote a significant amount of our time to be sure that we are heard. Never before have we had a voice like that of Simon Seeker. Nor are we likely to in the future, at least not in the futures we share. Being here with

Simon is a gift without measure. Thank you, Roger, for allowing our visits." He turned Simon to face him. "Thank you, Simon, for your gift to us and the planet upon which we are still able to live."

Simon had experienced lots of commendation, appreciation, and affection over the past months but this was different. Roger was listening.

Chapter 36

Roger and Jenna

Roger was talking with the Thibodeau brothers as they finished up for the day. It was one place he could collect his thoughts. Not only collect but focus them, grasp the present in the context of the past. The arrangement of rooms was as it had once been. He could sit in what had been the living room where, during the last year, after Reese's diagnosis, they had talked into the night. Reminiscences, resolutions, regrets, a reconstruction of the years that had brought them to this moment. Then Simon would arrive with updates on his afternoon wanderings with Bucephalus. Roger tried to work up a believable curiosity about the various insect migrations and vegetative transformations, but Simon rarely responded with more than a few words.

He had spoken with Mark Williams, the head of Wind Lake School several times over the past months. Williams had called when he'd read of

Reese's death in the local paper. Roger had assured him that Simon would be there in September. In a more recent conversation he had apologized for the confusion the Stardust Kid might bring to the quiet world of Wind Lake. Mark dismissed his concern, reminding him that Wind Lake had a tradition of protecting the children of celebrities from the outside world.

There had always been children of movie stars, writers, politicians, even of royalty. That was one of the school's major attractions. It was a quiet place where children could take their time, find themselves. *But what about celebrity children?* he wondered. Mark was right, of course. It would be as good as he could find. And it wasn't as if he was asking Simon to abandon his commitment to nature. The students lived off the land at Wind Lake. They took care of the gardens, the creatures who howled at night, whinnied in the stables, nested safely under eaves or swam in the lake.

Sitting there now as the house regained lost dimensions, he listened to the saws, sanders, and hammers that were so much more promising than the sounds of guitars and fiddles that arose from the fireside gathering in the meadow. He walked over to the house and up to Ron who was marking out the kitchen pantry. He complimented him once again, said how very fortunate Simon was to have the two of them rebuilding his home. He played for and received some agreement from Ron about the gypsies. It was only four o'clock.

As he approached Tom's improvised outdoor dining room, he saw Jenna walking up with a box of groceries.

"Well now, isn't that a luscious looking thing," Roger said as she brought a blueberry cheesecake to the table and set it down.

"I'm afraid I can't take any credit for it," she said with a friendly smile. "It's a Hannaford's creation."

"Ah, yes, Hannaford's. I haven't been there for quite a while. I used to stop on my way up to see Reese and do his shopping. I'm surprised he never put it on his list. But then, he wasn't much into desserts, or sweets of any kind for that matter."

"What about Simon?"

"Candy. Simon loves chocolate. I was always a little surprised, given its side effects."

"Side effects?"

"You know. Caffeine. High energy. As if Simon didn't have enough as it was. And acne, but that would have come later. Yes, Simon is a devoted chocolatier."

"I know."

"Ah yes. Of course you would. Looking after Simon as you have. That was very good of you. And Ben. He was very fortunate to have found the two of you. When I think of what might have happened, him standing out on the road that way. And that you should be a professional counselor. Very fortunate indeed." Roger smiled. "Please. Sit down. Tom and Simon are off discussing the perils of the planet."

Jenna looked up toward the pasture, considering. *Roger had certainly been pleasant these last few minutes.* It wasn't what she had expected. *What had she expected?* To be ignored, distanced from Simon. Someone who had no place on this stage, no lines to speak, who should go back to her own troupe of players. She turned. "You are very kind."

Roger indicated the bench with his hand. She sat. "So what do you think of this turnout of gypsies?" he asked.

"Gypsies? I hadn't thought of them as gypsies. On the road, sure, but several of them are pretty important people in the environmental movement. Like Mr. Benson." She turned for a moment to where the caravans and travel trailers were parked. "But you're right; I guess a few of them just travel from one place to another. Tom says it was YouTube that brought a lot of them here."

"I had a chance to meet your Mr. Benson. Jack, I should say. Conversation here is on a first name basis it seems. Yes, indeed. He is a serious environmentalist. He was talking about birds and how they are affected by noise pollution. They have to change their tunes because of urban development. Something along that line. Must be hard for Simon to get his head around all this, never having heard much more than a tractor engine."

"He heard plenty of noise in Boston."

"Oh, of course. Your apartment. Where was it again?"

"South Boston. Not so much industrial as crowded. Lots of traffic. Simon would sit at the window and watch when people went to work in the morning. For a while with the window open. Then he'd close it. It's hard to imagine what it must have been like for him, moving into another world. I took him to a movie once. He cried."

"Scary movie?"

"*AI.* Artificial Intelligence. Spielberg. It's about a robot boy. I didn't understand at the time what it was that got to him. Sure, it was the first movie he had ever seen and it was about a boy his age. I should have thought it through more carefully. Just the fact that he had never been in a movie theater. I tried to be more careful after that."

"A robot boy."

"It was nominated for two academy awards."

"But tell me more about the robot boy."

"The woman's son dies and she adopts a robot. Then the son gets better and she dumps the robot in the woods. I've been more careful about stories since then." She smiled. "I'm reading "The Adventures of King Arthur" to him now. Before he goes to bed. I thought it might help him feel better about leaving the farm. Oh, by the way, did he tell you that we visited with his grandmother?"

"Tom did. I gather it didn't go very well."

"She's re-married to a guy who wants nothing to do with children. That was part of it."

"And the other part?"

Jenna laughed, with some relief. The conversation was easier than she had anticipated. "Simon said she was tight," she said, still laughing. "It's a term I hadn't heard in a very long time. It was his father's, he said."

"Right," Roger said. "It's pretty dated. I believe Reese got it from his parents. So there was no suggestion of their taking Simon in, I gather. Tom hasn't really filled me in on what Simon told him."

"Well it's not just the drinking. Her husband, the new one. Well, not new but not the father of Simon's mother. It just wouldn't be a good or safe environment for a child, especially not one as open and vulnerable as Simon. The grandmother herself said as much to me when we left there. Have you tried to reach Alexandra?"

"No. We've heard nothing from her since she left. Reese helped her get established. Quite handsomely. And she has stayed out of the picture as it was agreed she would. I really don't know what came of her ambitions."

"To be an opera singer? That's what Simon said."

"Right. Interesting. I haven't thought about Alexandra for years. I never did meet her, but then, why would I have? Simon was conceived in Boston. I never even knew about it until he was born. But it's interesting that you should bring this up. Alexandra has no legal rights to her son. She signed those away. But she is his mother. Hmmm. What do you think?"

"About contacting her?"

"Yes. With grandmother in the picture I suppose it's possible she might learn about your visit to the house."

"I don't think so. They are pretty well estranged as I understood it."

"What about Simon? Did he ask about her?"

"Yes. Olivia gave him a box of photographs. He went up to her room for about a half an hour while Olivia and I talked. When he came down she said he could keep them. He chose one and left the rest."

"Only one?"

"Yes. I think Olivia wants to love him, but she's afraid it would be like it was with Alexandra all over again. All this must have been hard for her."

"Not being able to keep Simon?"

"Yes, and memories. Her second husband, to whom she's still married, abused Alexandra. Sexually. She left home quite young."

"One sad tale upon another."

"When we were back on the road I asked Simon whether he would like to see his mother."

"And?"

"He said he wouldn't. She had given him away without ever coming back. She didn't want him; he didn't want her. "But that was your father's decision," I said. "It was part of the arrangement." He still said no." She took a handkerchief out of her purse and wiped her eyes.

Roger watched. She put it on the table and covered it with both hands. "Sorry. I was back there with Simon for a moment. Something he said."

"Tell me."

"It's not important."

"Let me decide. You were quite moved in remembering."

"Well, all right. Simon said he wanted a mother who wanted him. Like me. Who didn't go away." Once again she put the handkerchief to her eyes.

"Just like that little robot boy I guess. Simon and I had become very close in those two weeks. We talked a lot, we went places, we laughed. I'm telling you more than you want to hear."

"On the contrary. I am very interested; please go on."

"Well. I'm here. Don't misunderstand me. I know I have no right in Simon's life. But I couldn't just walk away. As his mother did. Very different circumstances, of course. I don't mean to make too much of this. We could stay friends, be pen pals. I could visit now and then." She stopped, took a breath, and smiled. "Simon's world is here with Tom and Bucephalus. And for a while I guess, the visitors. Tom tells me there are plans for Simon to go to the same boarding school you and his father attended. That's wonderful, though I'm not sure Simon agrees yet." She put the handkerchief back in her bag and smiled. "I have talked too much. Sorry." She stood up. "Well, I guess I'd better get a start on dinner."

"Thank you for sharing. And thank you for being there when Simon needed you." He couldn't have said more. Not just then. Things were more complicated than he had anticipated. It had been his intention to send her back to Boston, break the ties that complicated Simon's life. But now it seemed one of those ties might help him achieve his goal. Reese's goal. With Jenna making the case to Simon things would go more smoothly. He must keep an open mind.

It had been a long day or so it seemed, out of regular routine, over-spiced with unwelcome flavors. He watched as Jenna unpacked the rest of the groceries, stood and looked back up at the meadow. The gypsies were singing. *Unreal. Woodstock. How many years ago had it been?* He walked down to the milking shed, sat on the bed, took off his shoes and lay back on the pillow. It was soft, very soft. Almost fragrant. Of course it was new. The beds, the bedding, the carpet still rolled against the wall, the dresser, the table. Even the room was new. A new place, a new chapter. He closed his eyes.

Chapter 37

Simon, Jenna, & Roger

The afternoon sing-along over, Simon ran back to the barn where Jenna was setting up the grill.

"Can I invite one more person to dinner?" he asked.

"Who's that?"

"Afua," he replied. "He and Roger are friends now, so it won't be a problem."

"Already? Roger just got here."

"Afua brought him to a meeting this afternoon."

"Oh. Well maybe we should ask Roger. The dinner is really for him. I mean for him and you. And Tom. Your family."

"Roger's not my family; he's my guardian."

"Well, he's known you your whole life and he was your father's best friend. They went to the same school, right?"

"Right."

Jenna asked, "Have you thought any more about Wind Lake?"

"I don't need to think about it. I don't want to go. I need to do what Jack says we all need to do. He says I can make a difference. It's not something I can do locked up in a school."

"From what I've heard, it sounds to me like Wind Lake might be the perfect place to start."

"I don't know. I guess so. But if it is then it doesn't need me."

"But maybe you need it."

Simon checked the un-shucked corn in a basket by the table. He reached into the basket with a practiced hand for an ear. He shucked it, carefully removing the silk and making a small pile. Jenna unwrapped the steaks and trimmed them, adding some seasonings and then re-wrapping them.

Simon looked up and saw Roger walking towards them. "Here comes Roger. You won't tell him what I said, right?"

"I won't. But we need to talk more."

"We will. Lots more. So what about Afua?"

"Let's ask Roger."

Simon walked over to join Roger. Jenna watched as they came together. Roger smiled and put a hand on Simon's shoulder. Simon asked his question and Roger looked back up the meadow for a moment, then back at Simon. He nodded, said a few words, and Simon ran off and out of sight.

Jenna walked to the grill and spread the charcoal, sprayed it and lit a match. Roger walked down to the gazebo and took a seat at the table. "I gather we're going to be five for dinner," he said.

Jenna closed the top of the grill and walked over to join him. "Simon says you've met Afua."

"Yes, he walked me up to the lecture on birds earlier. He's at Harvard, from somewhere in Africa."

"Ghana. He's into ants. He and Simon have run some field trips for the visitors. They've become buddies."

"He seems like a nice enough guy. Not quite so energized as a lot of this crowd." Roger looked at his watch. "Five o'clock. That's when Tom and I usually start the cocktail hour." Afua and Simon waved as they approached from the meadow. No sooner had they walked up than Tom joined them from out of the barn carrying an ice chest.

He made Roger's gin and tonic and poured a glass of the white wine that Jenna had bought on their shopping trip. It wasn't cold. He added an ice cube. Then a light gin and tonic for himself. Roger had introduced him to cocktail hour. His parents didn't drink and at the university it was beer, rarely scheduled but always available.

Tom handed Jenna her wine, Roger his gin and tonic, and walked back for his own glass. He took a healthy swallow. He did not look forward to dinner. The script which he had pretty well mastered with Roger was inadequate for the scenes that lay ahead. The pilgrims were the least of his concern. The summer was coming to an end and they would soon be packing up for other explorations. If Roger wanted them out tomorrow that would be another matter. But that was unlikely. His major concern was getting Simon off to school. Kicking his friends out the door would make that even harder. Let them stay for a couple more weeks and maybe even enlist a few of them to talk with Simon about the importance of school. Tom walked over to the table, holding up his glass. "Here's to new acquaintance and friendship," he said.

"I'll drink to that," Roger said. "Jenna and I had a very nice conversation." He smiled at her and held out his glass. She raised her own. They drank.

"Jenna's not your only new acquaintance, I gather," Tom said.

"No, she isn't. I was invited to join one of the afternoon lectures. That fellow from Britain. What's his name?"

"Benson. Jack Benson."

"Right. I gather from Afua that he's a scholar of repute."

"Oh, you met Afua?"

"Yes. Simon introduced us. He introduced me to the group. By the way, I believe he's joining us for dinner." He looked at Jenna.

"Yes. It was nice of you to go along with Simon's request."

"It seemed like a good idea. Studies with that fellow Simon admires. The expert on ants. I mean it could be valuable to have him tell Simon how important school is." Roger looked up toward the meadow and then at Tom. "They'll be joining us in a few minutes. There are a couple things I'd like your help with when they arrive. It's about Simon going off to Wind Lake in a few weeks. They start the second week in September."

Chapter 38

Family Dinner

There was a shout from the meadow. They turned to watch Simon and Afua quickstep through the grass in their direction, hand in hand. The scene took Roger back to the many times Simon interrupted a conversation with Reese, took his father's hand and led him to the site of some new discovery: a first-ripening vegetable in the garden, newly hatched chicks, or a small visitor from the wild.

"Very nice to have you join us, Afua," Jenna said, making room for him at the table. "What can I get you to drink?"

"Water will be fine," he said. "Unless you've got some iced tea."

"I'll get it," Simon said, walking to the counter. He put ice cubes in two glasses, filled each with his mint tea and brought them to the table. He sat across from Afua. "Afua led the exploration this afternoon," he announced. "You all should have been there. It was really good."

"Exploration?" Roger asked.

Afua smiled and put his hand on Simon's. "It's Jack Benson's expression. When we first arrived here he introduced the idea of afternoon gatherings. 'We've come to explore your world,' he said to Simon. The term stuck. It's a good one. Simon has been our guide."

"So has Afua," Simon said, smiling at his friend. "And Jack Benson and lots of others. We are learning from one another."

"Well, of course you are," Roger said with a generous nod and a smile which Simon didn't return. "Learning is what it's all about. Simon knows this place like the palm of his hand. You and your friends have been fortunate to meet such a young man."

"By the way, thanks for coming to the talk," Afua said.

"My pleasure," Roger said. "Watching Simon with all you folks has been very reassuring." He turned to Simon once again with a smile, this time edged with appeal. "Living mostly alone for twelve years isn't an easy thing. It's remarkable how well Simon has adapted. And not just adapted, inspired others. I'm not surprised that you and the others have come to meet him first hand."

Jenna stood up. "I think the grill is ready for the steaks. You carry on. Simon and I will get dinner ready." She looked at Simon, who smiled at a welcome reprieve from Roger's charm. He followed her to the grill.

The conversation at the table turned to Afua's cutting a path for himself to Harvard. Roger listened with nods of approval and words of encouragement. Tom watched with a mixture of surprise and mistrust. *Roger, the lawyer*, he thought. *This must be what it's like in a courtroom. Yes, court. Court the audience, the judges. Confuse the suspect. The gypsies had become pilgrims. And Afua! A black African pilgrim.* He wondered if he should redirect conversation.

Simon approached the table with one steaming plate in each hand. "These are the rarest ones. The others will be more well-done. Who wants rare?"

Afua held up his hand and Simon put a plate in front of him. Then he looked at Roger. "You always liked rare."

"And I still do. I was just waiting to see if anyone else does. I know you don't. How about you Tom?"

"I'm easy. Give the plate to Roger, Simon. After all, he is the guest of honor."

Simon put the plate before Roger and stepped back. Then he hurried back to the grill, took two more plates from Jenna and returned, putting one at Tom's place and the other at his own. Jenna joined them, setting down her own plate. "Well, to reunion and new acquaintance," Roger said lifting his glass. The others lifted theirs and drank. Simon watched and picked up his ear of corn. He took a bite, then another, and quickly nibbled his way down the ear. He held it up and looked across at Afua.

Afua laughed. "Simon holds the record for corncob racing."

"You beat me once," Simon responded, pointing his cob at Afua."

"Once. Only once."

Roger put his own ear back on the plate and cleared his throat. "So, Afua, you're still at Harvard, yes?"

"I've got another couple of years to my degree in environmental science. I'm taking it slow, mixing things in, traveling a little."

"Sounds like a very good approach," Roger offered. "They're both important, and one supports the other. Look at Tom. Back to school in a few weeks after taking care of the farm. With Simon's help. And hosting our dinner tonight with help from our cook."

"University of Maine, right?" Afua asked.

"Right. Actually, I took this year off to do some hands-on stuff. I'm aiming for a career in journalism."

"You've certainly made an impressive start."

"Thanks, Afua. I can't take much credit though. I'd still be writing about the debate over new parklands if it weren't for the Stardust Kid."

"And I would be counting ants in New Jersey," Afua added. "The Stardust Kid has changed all our lives for the better. Here's to Simon," he said, lifting his empty glass. The others joined him with equally empty glasses.

Jenna laughed and reached for the jug of iced tea. She filled her glass and reached out to the others, adding a little to each of their glasses. "Let's try that again," she said. "To Simon."

"To Simon," they said in chorus.

"And to his entry into the world we have all known and loved." Roger said, lifting his glass one more time.

"The world we have known and loved," Simon repeated. "Right. And that may not be there for much longer."

"Oh, I think it will be for a little while longer," said Roger with a dismissive smile.

"Not if we keep destroying the places where creatures live."

"But that's been going on for millennia hasn't it? I read somewhere about what our race did in Australia. Totally transformed the place."

"Right." Afua responded, putting down his silverware. "This isn't a new thing. Homo sapiens drove to extinction about half of the planet's big beasts long before they invented the wheel, writing, or iron tools."

"So this is a part of natural history," Roger offered.

Afua nodded and pushed his chair back. "That's true. But it has sped up. And there are things we can do about it. Things we *have* to do about it."

"It's killing off animals," Simon said. "It's destroying their homes."

"Ah, yes," Roger said, nodding. "Animals. Of course."

"Roger thinks I'm an animal lover."

"That's not a criticism," Roger offered with a reach of his hand. Simon stiffened. "They have been your only companions for most of your life. It's time to broaden your acquaintance."

"Right. Locked away in a school."

Jenna interrupted. "We're getting off the subject. So, Afua, just what is happening to animal populations?"

"Well, what Simon says is true. Eighty percent of Earth's land animals live in forests and many cannot survive the deforestation that destroys their homes. And it's not just animals. Without the protection of forests, soils dry out and become barren deserts. Half of all the forests in Ghana have been burned for grazing and farming. And there is comparable devastation in Togo and Nigeria. It's a very serious issue." Afua paused, and Tom watched him attempt to discern whether Roger was hearing him or just being polite. He continued, "In moderation, deforestation is not a problem. But it can have a negative impact on the environment. The most dramatic impact is a loss of habitat for millions of species."

Tom felt a need to join the conversation while things were still under control.

Jenna had redirected things a moment ago. She shouldn't have to play that role alone. Roger's willingness to include Afua in the gathering was not offhand. He was to serve a purpose. "I think we're all on board when it comes to global warming. Wouldn't you agree, Roger?"

"Most certainly. I didn't mean to suggest otherwise. I share that concern with all the good people gathered here. And with Simon. Your concerns, Afua, have brought you to this country to study at one of our foremost universities. That you have taken time to come up here on your vacation is much to your credit." He turned to Simon. "You are fortunate to have a friend like Afua who has devoted himself to learning." He turned back to Afua. "So tell me: is it graduate work you have undertaken at Harvard?"

"Yes."

"Excellent!" Roger said, relieved at the possibility of an ally in his quest to convince Simon that he should go to school. "I believe Mr. Benson has an advanced degree as well."

Afua smiled. "Several, actually."

"Well, the more the better. People listen to serious scholars."

Jenna stood up. "So what do you say to a little dessert?"

"Wonderful," Roger said. "Can we help you clear?"

"Just pass me the plates and keep your silverware." They passed their plates to Jenna who handed half of them to Simon and then walked with him back to the grill.

"Thank you for joining us, Afua," Roger said. "Simon is very fortunate that you have taken him under your wing. Anything you can do to encourage him with regard to schooling would be much appreciated."

Afua nodded. "What was it he said? Locked away in a school?"

"Right."

"It's a boarding school, right?"

"The same school his father attended. It's where he and I became friends. There couldn't be a more perfect place for the boy, but given his life up to this point, it's hard for him to imagine living with a couple hundred age-mates."

"His father was an author, right?"

"A very fine one, yes. He tangled with the Christian Right. The hero in a number of his books was an eccentric fellow who downplayed religion. The churches went after him. It's a long story, but in a word he became a hermit. Got ahold of this place, partnered with a gal in Boston to bring Simon into the world and raised him here on these eleven hundred acres. They went into town three or four times a year. That was it."

Afua nodded thoughtfully. "I read about that in the paper. What a story."

Roger glanced to where Simon watched as Jenna sliced the cheesecake. "As you may have gathered, Simon is not keen on going to boarding school. It was his father's wish and it's my responsibility to make sure it happens. Becoming a celebrity and enjoying the worship of these followers—sorry, no criticism intended—well, it complicates things."

Afua nodded. "Yes, I can see how it might. I will do what I can to help, but..."

"Yes?"

Afua looked at Tom. Tom looked down at the table. "Well, it's just that Simon isn't your typical prep school boy. Nothing in his life, as I understand it, has been typical, conventional, or ordinary. How to say it?"

Tom smiled. "You're doing fine."

Roger looked at Tom with a slight frown of disapproval. Afua continued. "Well, it's just that he really could make a difference. He has already invigorated the environmental movement."

"He's a boy, Afua. He's not even n his teens. Well, almost. Anyway, he needs the companionship of peers, not worshipers. And, more to the point, it is our—or at least my—responsibility to do what his father intended should be done."

Tom cleared his throat as if to make a rough passage smoother. "I guess Simon hasn't told you about the letter then."

"Letter? What letter?"

"I'm sorry, Roger, I should have told you about it. There's so much going on. I have trouble keeping track."

"A letter from whom? One of his worshipers?"

"From his father."

"From his father?"

"It was in his pack. He found it on his way down to Boston with Ben. He says his father gave him permission to do as he wished. That he would understand if Simon wanted to have an adventure. Those were Simon's words. I haven't seen the letter. I should have told you. I'm sorry."

"This is much more complicated than I thought. Reese trusts me to send him to Wind Lake and then tells him he should run away. Crazy. Totally crazy!" He studied the table top as if it might offer an explanation. Then he looked at Tom but without speaking, as if waiting for something like a retraction.

"I'm sorry I brought it up."

"Tom! For Christ's sake. You should have told me this weeks ago."

"I know, I know. It's all so complicated."

"What's complicated about it? I'm Simon's guardian, appointed by his father, trying to do what I was asked to do. I hired you to help me, and…"

Afua looked over at the grill where Jenna and Simon were putting the slices of blueberry cheesecake on plates. "Excuse me, but Simon's going to be here in a second. Should we take a breath and save this for later?"

Roger looked over his shoulder, turned back, and put his head in his hands.

Tom and Afua exchanged glances that spoke of their need for a plan and a means to act upon it. Simon wasn't the boy Roger had once known, if indeed he ever had been. The path ahead for him might not be one anyone had ever walked, certainly not one that led indoors or to a row of desks.

Chapter 39

Simon and Roger

After finishing their dessert over a conversation about laying hens and blueberries, Jenna collected the plates and carried them to the barn. Afua accompanied her. Tom said that he needed to get the new milking shed quarters ready for its new tenant.

Simon stood up to accompany him.

"You stay here with Roger and get caught up on things." Tom said. "He's come all this way to see you and the two of you haven't had any time together since he arrived."

Simon looked at him with a mixture of appeal and annoyance, then took a breath and turned to Roger with a half-decent smile. "OK. You want to take a walk, Roger?"

"Sure. I'd like that. After a deliciously full meal. What do you say we head over to the pond?"

"Great."

Roger stood and pushed his chair under the table, feeling suddenly much older.

They walked up toward the meadow where the visitors waved from their dinner groups. Simon waved back and carefully matched Roger's slower stride.

"You certainly have a great many admirers, Simon. I'm very happy for you. Going out into the big world for the first time, all on your own, and winning so many hearts."

"They're really nice people. And they all get along with one another."

"It certainly seems that way."

When they arrived at the pond's edge, Simon picked up a stone and tossed it near the shore. A fish swam out, a very tiny fish wearing a red hat. Roger chuckled.

"It's a koi," Simon said. "One of the guests brought it. They are illegal in Maine but I guess it will be all right since it's alone."

"It certainly is interesting. Very colorful. Very nice."

They stood quietly for a moment and then Roger continued. "You have had some remarkable adventures, young man. Your father would be very impressed. Doing that show with Bill Miller! Very impressive. Very very impressive."

"I'm very lucky."

"Yes, you are. But there's more to it than simply luck. You made an amazing leap from a world of two to a world of millions. Your father would be proud. Not amazed, because I'm sure he knew of your potential, but proud. Quite proud."

Simon tossed another stone further out. The pond was quiet. Perfect rings appeared, following one another back to the calm and reflective surface. "I don't want to go to that school."

"It's not up to me, Simon. And until you are of age, it's not up to you either. Your father wanted the best for you. He wanted you to be in a safe and caring place where you can grow up to become the best you can be. Your running away after the fire was understandable. Watching the house you had grown up in go up in flames with your father inside was more than any boy should ever have to have lived through. I can understand you wanting to get away from it."

Simon was silent throughout Roger's monologue. None of it surprised him, except perhaps the suggestion of regard or affection. Only a suggestion. He knew Roger too well to argue or agree. He just listened, watching a parade of ants carrying crumbs to their nest. He had thought for a moment he would tell Roger about the letter in his pack and the money. But no, that was just between him and his father.

"Do you understand what I'm saying, Simon?"

"Yes."

"Do you have any concerns?"

"No." Simon had to look away. Roger was good at reading people's faces.

Chapter 40

September

The meadow was a map of the summer past—geometrically browned where the tents had been, webbed with paths of trodden grass, black where fires had burned. The last of the visitors had left the day before, cleaning up as carefully as those before them. It had rained the last few days and the field grass was making a last grasp at color as fall arrived. Simon walked the empty paths collecting memories and trying to picture the days ahead. He would try the school. Afua and Jack had both encouraged him to give it a try. There would be lots of people his age whom he could get on board the movement. It's what Tom and Jenna both asked him to do, at least until one of them could be at the farm with him. Only a year, then Tom would have finished school. He wouldn't want to be there without Tom. And Jenna. *Would Jenna come?* Maybe if he did as she said, she would do as he hoped she would. Until they could be back at the farm together, the Thibodeau brothers had agreed to look after things. They'd be there to work on the house and said they'd be happy to feed the animals as well. In return, Simon assured them, they could have all the eggs.

Roger had talked more about the school before driving back to New York. He talked about the staff. They were there because they wanted to be with young people. They would watch closely to be sure things were going well for him. Like the visitors who had come to Spruce Valley. And there was horseback riding. It was very big. All the kids rode. Simon could teach them a lot. And not just horses. Animals were fed every morning before students had breakfast. Eggs were gathered and brought to the kitchen, if not for that very morning, then for the next day. Milking the cows came later, just before lunch. And the goats, but not every day, only when the head of farming made an announcement at breakfast. Simon had tried to picture it as he listened, but he couldn't.

It had been arranged with Mark Williams, the Head of Wind Lake, that both Bucephalus and Empress should accompany Simon down to the school. Roger had rented a large pickup truck, and Bob Thibodeau had found a horse trailer at a farm near Marshfield.

The next day Simon and Tom drove to Marshfield to pick it up. It looked much too small for both Bucephalus and Empress. *Horses like to be close together when they're on the road*, the owner explained. *Having the side close gave them a sense of security.* The man spoke to him as if he were a child. Simon listened with a serious face, nodding. And he thanked him, extending his hand. The man looked surprised, but he took it and Simon did his best to get a good grip.

The things were pretty well closed up, but he and Jenna finished tidying and enjoyed some time alone. The four days were filled with promises, affection, and assurances. Yes, Jenna would be there for Thanksgiving. She couldn't come for the feast because, as Roger had explained, it was an all-school celebration. All school and only school. They sat side by side at the picnic table finishing their cheeseburgers and fresh corn. He asked her if she would be going back to Rosie's to do counseling, and she said that she probably wouldn't. She would go back to the place where they had spent those last days in South Boston.

"But what about all the people you take care of?"

"They've been doing pretty well without me these past weeks," she said with a smile. Then more seriously, "You've met Rosie's other counselors. They can take over my clients. They're glad to have more work."

"But what will you do for work?"

"I'm not sure. There are lots of opportunities out there. Something that will give me time off to be with you." She reached and put her arm around him. He slid close and leaned his head against her shoulder.

"Why can't I go to school in Boston and live with you?"

"The schools in Boston are nothing like Wind Lake. You'd hate them. Seriously. Wind Lake is the right first step for you. Please believe me. Roger isn't being mean-spirited. He's doing what your father knew would be best for you. And the more I've heard, the more I am on board too. And so is Tom. We are all going to be with you, sweetie. You will be in our hearts and thoughts."

"And you will be in mine."

Chapter 41

Wind Lake School

Simon and Tom arrived at Wind Lake School on the 14th of September. A little girl named Charlene, whose parents worked at the school, was at the stable visiting with a young colt. She helped them move the horses into their stalls and showed Simon where everything was. He noticed that Empress took to her at once and was glad that she had shown up to welcome them. She was a couple years younger than he, but very sharp about horses. It was a nice start. More than he had expected. She asked if she could ride Empress tomorrow. Simon said sure. They could ride together. If Bucephalus would go along with that. He said it loud enough to be sure Bucephalus heard. If he did, he didn't let on.

After seeing to the horses, they went to the cafeteria and had left-overs from the staff lunch: some chicken soup, home-made bread, and a salad.

The salad greens were from the farm, the cook explained. And the chicken. Simon held up one of the rolls, questioning.

She smiled. "Not yet. Not grinding our own flour. Maybe someday."

As they finished, a man walked into the dining room and up to their table. Tom started to stand but the man waved him back into his seat. "No need to stand, my friend." He held out his hand. "Mark Williams. Hope you had an easy trip down from the north woods. May I join you?"

"We'd be honored," Tom said with a nod. "I'm Tom Bewick and I guess you know who my companion is."

"The Stardust Kid! Simon Seeker! Or is it Simon Larkin now? Never mind. You can be anyone you want to be. I am so very happy to have you here with us."

"I'm just Simon," Simon said, putting down his fork and sitting up straight. "Thank you for letting me come, Mr. Williams."

"By the way, you can call me Mark. We all go by first names here. I hope you will find this a friendly place, Simon. Roger has explained what a very big change it will be for you to be surrounded by so many people your own age. But from what I have heard…" He smiled broadly. "… and seen rebroadcast to millions of kids and grownups around the world, you will quickly find a place for yourself and make a good many friends." He turned to Tom. "And you're invited to stay for a few days as well."

Tom smiled, turning to look at Simon and then back at Mr. Williams.

"That's very kind of you, Mark, but I've got to get on the road after breakfast. I'm already two weeks late for classes at my own school." He laughed. "Not exactly the right example to set for my friend here."

"He went up and registered a couple days ago," Simon said, as if to make sure Mark wouldn't really think Tom was a bad influence.

"Well, I'm sure your professors appreciate and respect your time with this young man. I assume they have followed Simon's adventures in your column."

Tom smiled and looked at Simon. "This guy has launched my career in journalism. Way above anything the folks up at Orono could have done. I'll spend the night if you can put me up, but I'll need to head back first thing in the morning."

"No problem. There are plenty of beds here. In fact you can stay with Simon in Lance Cottage. That's where he will be living." Mark addressed Simon. "It's where your father lived when he was at Wind Lake," he said with a glance that invited approval. Simon said nothing. "Is that OK? I mean, I don't want you to be sad. I thought it might give you a sense of connection. What do you think?"

"It's fine." Simon said, "Is it the same room?"

"That I can't tell you," Mark replied. "Way before my time."

"Does everyone here live in a cottage?" Simon asked.

"Wouldn't that be wonderful!" Mark said with a small laugh. "No, there's only one cottage. The other students live in houses up the hill behind us. They all have house parents just as you will. But there are three or four times as many rooms as Lance Cottage has. I think you'll like it. Only four bedrooms. Four girls on the first floor. Rodney and Stefan across from you on the second floor. And of course, The Fentons, your house-parents."

"What floor are they on?" Simon asked.

"They are on the first floor. By the way, would you like a roommate?"

Simon looked at Tom for help. They had talked about this on the drive down. "I think Simon might like to take things slowly," Tom offered. "He's been a loner for a long time. A very long time. Maybe as he gets used to things."

"No problem. I understand entirely. One step at a time." He looked at Simon with affection. "There's a very nice room on the second floor with a nice view of the mountain and a bathroom a few steps away. Would you like to see it?"

"Sure."

"OK." He got up. Tom and Simon pushed back their chairs and stood, waiting for him to lead. "Let's get your things out of the truck and we'll walk over to Lance. By the way, how did your horses handle the ride down? Bucephalus? Do I have that right?"

"And Empress," Simon said with something close to comfort. "They didn't like it very much. Especially Bucephalus. They've never been away from the farm before. They didn't want to leave."

Mark glanced at Tom who was quick to make use of the moment. "But Simon promised them that they would love Wind Lake. Right, Simon?"

It took Simon a moment to realize what he must say. He had learned over the past weeks to think twice. "Right," he said, smiling at Tom.

Lance Cottage was something of a surprise to Simon. In many ways it reminded him of the house he had lost. It was old. The woodwork was scratchy, the floors worn and there was a creak in some of the steps as they walked up to his room. Unlike his old house, the walls were newly painted and the curtains looked fresh and colorful.

There was art on the walls. Not like his father's collection. Not old things done with oils, but drawings of all sorts. Not all that great. Probably done by students, but not all that bad either. Some almost as good as his own, and like his own, of animals and fields and barns.

He carried his suitcase and backpack; Tom and Mark carried his trunk.

They set it down at the foot of his bed. He sat and gave the bed a bounce. *Not bad.*

"Well," Mark said, "I'll let the two of you get settled in. The room across the hall is yours Tom. I think you'll find everything you need there."

Simon walked over to the dresser and pulled out a drawer. Mark asked Tom to tell him a little bit about Orono. A cousin of his had gone there a number of years back. As they talked about University life and their pasts, Simon opened his trunk and started removing the clothes Jenna had bought him and a number of books from his bailout. *You could dress any way you liked at Wind Lake,* Roger had explained. The words had stayed with him. Any way you liked. They relaxed him a little. Just a little.

Chapter 42

Tom and Roger

Tom hadn't told Simon that Roger had asked him to continue on to New York after getting him settled at Wind Lake. He didn't look forward to the visit. He had felt more and more over the past weeks like a middle-man, encouraging Simon's trust in his guardian while hiding his own concerns.

He had a responsibility to Roger; a major one. He wouldn't be here now if it weren't for Roger.

And Roger had been generous. Very generous. Being there for two people at odds with one another was not an entirely new task, but it had been tiring.

Tom arrived at Roger's building just after three and took the elevator up the twenty floors to the offices of Featherstone, Parks, and Carrington. Roger's secretary stood to greet him with something better than a professional smile. She might have been Roger's age, dressed in a grey skirt suit. "He has been so looking forward to your visit," she said. "You have no idea how much your taking care of things at the farm has given him room to relax. He speaks of you with the greatest affection." He thanked her and she led him to the door to Roger's office. She turned and put her hand on his shoulder. "And gratitude! Losing his only life-long friend was a heavy blow. And then having to put up with that boy." She knocked and opened the door. "He's here!" she said with the pride of a provider. Tom thanked her once more and walked in.

Roger got up from his chair and held out his arms. Tom walked up to the desk and reached across to take his hand. Then he turned to see where he might sit. Roger gestured to the leather sofa and they sat, each at one end, diagonally, one arm on the back, the other available for conversation.

"So, Simon has moved to his new world." Roger said. "With the help of his great friend," he smiled broadly and continued, "and the company of his life-long companions. How did that all go? The horses I mean. The trailer worked all right?"

"Oh, fine. No problems. It'll take a while for them to get used to the place, but they'll be fine. Jeez, there must be twenty horses there. I've never seen so many in one place."

Roger stretched his legs out, put his hands behind his head and looked up at the ceiling, "Ah, yes. The soul of the school is in its thoroughbred stock."

"Did you ride?"

"Oh yes. Not very well, but I enjoyed it with Reese riding ahead of me." No one spoke for a few seconds, then Roger sat back up and laughed. "So how did our young fellow do? Is he comfortably moved in? What house have they put him in?"

"Lance Cottage. With Bob and Sara Fenton."

"I don't know the Fenton's. Of course. How could I? But Lance Cottage I know well."

"So how's the boy handling the move?"

Tom had tried to prepare a right answer to this question on his drive down. He didn't want to say anything that Roger wouldn't hear, and yet he felt a need to keep things open so that he would understand if Simon needed his patience or intervention. "As you can imagine it is all very new to him. His relationships with the visitors and his Boston friends and Miller and Afua…"

"And that prostitute."

"Excuse me?"

"Jenna."

"What are you talking about?"

"Rosie's Counseling Center is a whore house."

"Where did you hear that?"

"On the evening news. Some guy's wife apparently followed her husband there and told the police. They raided the place and arrested the counselors. They've been indicted."

"Jenna's a prostitute? That's impossible!"

"Impossible, but true. I'm not really that surprised. She's a pro. She made good conversation. Too good. Too professional. I might as well have been a customer." He laughed. "That's not quite fair. She was an excellent hostess and was good to Simon."

"Good? My God, she's like a mother to him! This is terrible." Tom stood up and walked to the window. He stared into the street. Jenna in jail. And Roger amused, indifferent. *No, not indifferent. Pleased to have her out of the picture. Getting Simon free of yet another gypsy.* And where did he fit in all of that? *Not here. Not now.* He walked to the door and opened it. "I've got to go. Sorry."

He walked out to the elevator. Roger followed quickly, catching up to him as the door opened. Tom stepped in. "Sorry. I have to have time with this. I'll get back to you." The elevator door shut. Roger stood there as it descended. The elevator that took you to emptied places. Or from them. He turned and walked back to the office.

Tom walked across the street to the garage and up to the second level where he had parked. Unlocking the door, he climbed in and rolled down the window. He had no desire to drive, no place to go. *She loved Simon. He was a gift. To both of them, giving them a chance to make right what they had done wrong all those years back, abandoning their own. How could this be true?*

His phone rang. It would be Roger. *Who else was there now? No, don't go there.* He took it out of his pocket and checked the number. Right. "Hello, Roger."

"Sorry, Tom. I shouldn't have spoken so offhandedly about Jenna's arrest. She was very nice to me at the farm. Very nice. I'm a judgmental old fart and there's no way of denying it. I am very sorry to have been so insensitive just now."

Tom let the apology lie, untouched. "So do you know anything about how long she's in for?"

"A year at most. Probably less. Could be as little as six weeks."

"Let me know if you learn more, please. Simon isn't expecting to see Jenna 'til Thanksgiving. That's more than two months from now."

"I really am very sorry to have been so flippant about this, Tom. What do you say we get together for dinner?"

"Thanks, Roger, but I really have to get on the road. I've missed almost two weeks of classes. If you learn anything about Jenna, please let me know. If she doesn't get out by Thanksgiving we've got a problem. Simon is counting on her visit."

"I understand. I'll check with authorities and let you know what I learn." *No, that was too easy. After his thoughtless laughter. What then?* "In fact, I'll drive up to Boston and inquire at the courthouse. I have some acquaintances there."

"Let me know what you learn."

"You can be sure of that. And once again, Tom, I'm very sorry for my thoughtless behavior."

"It's OK, Roger."

"I'll be in touch. Drive safely."

"I will."

Roger put down his phone and closed his eyes. He saw Tom's face as, with intended off-handedness, with a smile and chuckle, he had told of the arrest. He imagined himself in Tom's eyes as he had laughed: a cynical, dismissive observer of people, their misfortunes much more entertaining than the daily drab of their lives. No wonder Reese had kept a kindly distance all those years, caring but careful not to get too close, a friend, a best friend, but no more than that. Reese was a client, a cook, a conversationalist, even still a caretaker. And a man who trusted him, for the most part, to look after things. Even Simon. *Simon. Yes, that was his biggest gift.* Reese's trust that he would do right by Simon. And in a way he had. He couldn't have found a better caretaker than Tom. And he'd done right by Tom also. Meeting his needs at the farm, paying him well, praising his articles in the press. And then this. How could he have been so stupid?

He got up, walked to the bathroom and splashed water on his face, dried it and wondered what Tom saw there. Earlier, before all this. Something he trusted. *No, it wasn't the money. There was much more to it.* Simon, of course, but even before Simon. Could he earn it back?

He'd drive to Boston on Saturday. Get a room at the Marriot just across the street from the courthouse; he had known it well a few years back. And the courthouse. And those who sat its desks. *Yes, it would be worth a try.*

Chapter 43

Simon

The international students had been the first to arrive, two days before the other students. Most of them were returning and went directly to their houses. At Mark's invitation, Simon had joined him in the main building to greet the new ones. Lethabo was from Africa but not the same place as Afua. He was in the seventh grade. Greta was from France. Her father was in the Foreign Service. Her parents moved around a lot. They wanted her to go to school in the United States. She was to live in Lance Cottage on the first floor. Simon walked her and her parents over and introduced them to Bob and Sara. Then he returned in time to greet a new boy named Rainer, from Germany who had come without either parent. A friend of his family had driven him all the way from Washington where he had spent the last month. He was the same age as Simon. Learning that Rainer was new, he began to tell him about the days ahead. He had a room in Durgin House, which was further up the hill from Lance and had many more students. Simon had been there with Laurie, the riding coach. She and her husband were two of the four house-parents. It was not a place he would have wanted to live. Much too big.

Two of the remaining newbies were from Japan, twin brother and sister. Simon was still surprised to see people with such different faces. None of his visitors that past summer had been from that part of the world. There had been some in Bill Miller's audience, but he hadn't seen them up close. It was a lot like meeting Afua, the kind of thing that reminded him of just how far out of the big world he had lived. The last boy to arrive was from Brazil. Roberto was, like the Japanese twins, a year younger than he, close to the man who had come with him, probably his father. Simon decided that if the man *was* his father, the kid was lucky to be coming here. The man was loud, pushy, and in a big hurry. *Maybe he's someone I can help out,* Simon thought. He looked like he might be trying not to cry.

They were sent up to Wentworth house, another of the big houses, but not one he'd been in.

The other students had arrived on the weekend and things had gotten underway quickly. The pace of life was more than he could have imagined after twelve years at the farm. Chores, then breakfast and announcements, then classes, lunch, more classes, recreation, more chores, evening meeting and bed. Morning chores were the best part: chickens, goats, sheep, and of course the horses and their young ones. Mark had been sure to get him assigned to the barn and he looked forward to that part of his day more than any other. The stable-master was named Luke. He had given Bucephalus a stall near the entrance and Empress one further back. The stalls were well kept and the stable was an inviting place.

Potato harvest started the first week in October. It was an enormous undertaking, so much more than the small gardens at Spruce Valley. Rows and rows of potatoes dug up by the farmer and his tractor, lying in the sun, the students picking them up and filling carts.

Living in Lance Cottage was a good thing. It was small and there were only two rooms on each floor. In addition to Greta, on the first floor were Clara, Jean, and Marla. His second floor mates were Rodney and Stefan. They shared a room.

He was getting the hang of things. *What a crazy expression.* Roger used it now and then. And so had Ben. He had overheard him say it to Rosie one morning after he had spaded the garden.

You could ride by yourself or with a friend in the corral, or on one of the several school trails with a group led by a teacher, but you couldn't ride alone. It was for safety reasons, Mark had said. Simon had tried to explain that he wasn't going to get lost, that he had ridden many miles around the farm, that the woods were his home, that he and Bucephalus had to have time together. Mark had smiled at him with his official smile. It was a nice one but it didn't reach out to him the way Tom's or Jenna's or even Roger's did. It was his school smile. He had seen it at mealtimes and with other kids. He had also seen his angry expression when a kid did something wrong. Mark didn't get angry very often. Once when Jud had tried to carry his lunch on his head and it crashed all over the dining room floor. Another time when Fred climbed up on the roof to get a Frisbee.

Riding the trails he kept pretty much to himself as the others talked or sang. Juliet, who ran the science program, liked to name things: trees, plants, outcroppings of rock and an occasional peak in the distance. The peaks often had stories attached and some of them were interesting, one in particular about a group of students who had climbed it once in the winter and couldn't get down. They had to be rescued by a helicopter.

Simon knew he was different. He had expected to be. The teachers were nice people and reminded him of Dr. Schneider and Jack Benson. They weren't the problem; it was the kids. Not all of them. Some were what he had hoped for, remembering the stories he had read. There was a boy actually named Sam who had come from New York City to live here near the mountain. And there were the kids from other countries who must have felt even farther away from home than he did. But all of them were from a world he had never known, filled, like Boston, with hundreds of other kids. Their language was something he had to learn as well as their way of relating to one another and the many interests they shared. Oh, he had read some of the same books, but never seen a television set except in a store window when they shopped. And of course there was baseball, where he held his own and could keep up with any of them.

There were a few toughs who pushed other kids around, but no Draco Malfoy. Oliver Twist would have been very happy here. They were never alone. Always three or four or six or seven, all tied together by the way they walked or ran or shouted. He caught himself and smiled. Not all that different sometimes from the visitors at the farm. Singing at the campfires, agreeing in a buzz of sound at things he said or they said. All together. Yes, he had been in a crowd before this. *So why was it so strange?* Because they were all pretty much his age? *No, it was something else.* He'd have to work on it.

The staff explained things to him and tried to help him with being at a desk in a classroom. It was important. He knew that. It was part of being in a school, but the desks, the rows of things, the blackboard, permission-asking and what Miss Leonard called 'classroom decorum' were hard. He had learned to sit at the meetings in the meadow when Jack or another one of the pilgrims talked. But they didn't bounce and yell; they were different from each other. Not all the same age wearing the same clothes wanting to be somewhere else.

It was complicated and often confusing, but nothing he couldn't deal with. Getting in the truck with Ben all those weeks back had been the beginning of his new life, of which meeting Jenna had been the greatest gift. And Tom. Tom and Jenna. He looked at the school calendar on his door. Only six weeks until Thanksgiving.

It was a Wednesday morning. He crossed the hall into the bathroom. It was pretty nice. Small, but everything you needed was there. He peed and brushed his teeth.

Looking in the mirror had always been important. Not just to make sure your teeth were clean but to see yourself as real and not just what you imagined some of the time, especially in dreams. He walked back to his room, changed out of pajamas, opened his door and listened. The others were up now. He could hear doors opening and closing on the first floor. He walked down the stairs.

Bob and Sara were sitting in the common room with their coffee and book bags. Bob taught mathematics. Sara was the school nurse. She looked up and smiled. "Good morning, Simon. Help yourself to the orange juice."

"That's OK. I'll wait 'til breakfast."

"Did you have good sleep?" The question was predictable. There were nights he hadn't, at the beginning, and she had come up and sat with him. They had talked about how much he missed the farm and she had assured him that it was all right to be a little homesick—that it was a part of going away to school. She had listened as he told about the summer past. He was careful not to talk about his father and she was careful not to ask, knowing of his loss.

"I did. Thanks. Good morning, Bob."

Bob looked up from his book. He was not as much there for you as Sara was. As Rodney, who lived with Simon on the second floor, put it, he was a master of formulas rather than feelings. "Good morning, Simon." He folded one of the cover flaps into the place where he had been reading and closed the book. As he did, Greta came out of her room and Stefan and Rodney came down the stairs. "Well," Bob said, standing up and rubbing his hands together as if ready to put them to work, "I guess we should head over to breakfast. Simon and the others followed him out the door and across to the dining hall in the main building.

Tom and Roger

Tom was walking back from breakfast and stopped at the mailboxes. There was a letter, hand-addressed. He recognized the script at once. Looking at it, he recalled a conversation with Roger after he had gathered together Simon's drawings for the Bill Miller Show. They were remarkable in their capture of detail and grasp of proper proportion. He remembered how frustrated he had been even in high school trying to get human limbs the right size on paper. But even more impressive than Simon's drawings were his captions. To Tom it seemed there was no way the small hands of a twelve-year-old—to say nothing of a ten- or nine-year-old—could've shaped such words.

Simon had composed the address on the envelope with the same skill. And patience. That was the reassuring part. Reason to hope that he was equally patient with his new environment. Closing the door, he sat in the recliner his father had brought to Orono that first year. Three years ago. *Was that all?* He unfolded the pages and lay them on his desk.

Dear Tom,.

I hope you get this. I have never written a letter before. I hope it's right. Sara gave me the paper and the envelope. The pen is the one you gave me. I am in my room. It's OK. I have it to myself. Well, you know that. The other students have arrived. About a hundred of them, boys and girls. The oldest ones are thirteen. The youngest ones are 8. I'm in the middle. That's OK. I haven't gotten to know many of them yet. Mostly the ones in Lance Cottage. There are seven of us. Rodney and Stefan have the room across from me. Greta and Clara have one of the rooms on the first floor. Jean and Marie have the other one. Bob and Sara are our house-parents. They're nice. Well, Sara is. Bob doesn't say much. He's fussy about keeping things neat, but that's OK.

The worst things here are the classrooms. Fifteen or sixteen kids. My science class has twenty! It's crazy. Raising hands, yelling out, scribbling, walking back and forth to the blackboard. You never told me about blackboards. I don't like them. It's really different. Mark introduced me one day as the son of Reese Larkin, who wrote the Sam Scamper books. Then he told about my father being a graduate of Wind Lake. A couple of the kids at my table had read the books and said how much they liked them. I couldn't tell them that I had only read two of them. I said I didn't like to talk about them and Terry, one of the kids at my table, explained that my father had died. Then the kids were nice, but I wish Mark had never said what he said.

Oh, Bucephalus and Empress are getting along pretty well. Empress anyway. Bucephalus is being difficult. I got him to go with a kid named Ryan the other day. Ryan is

thirteen and knows horses. I walked with them for part
of the way. It was OK. Greta who lives with me in Lance
House rides Empress. She's pretty good with horses. They
are her favorite thing. OK. I'm going to bed now.

Love,
Simon.

Tom smiled, carefully refolded the letter, put it back into the envelope
and slipped it into the pocket of his shirt. He couldn't have asked for more.
The Consortium of Investigative Journalists had been after him for weeks
now to update Simon's story. He had provided updates during the summer
as Simon worked with the visitors at the farm. A newspaper in Ghana
had done a feature story on the friendship between Afua and Simon. Jack
Benson had done a piece for a British environmental journal and several
of the visitors had done stories for their local papers.

He owed them an update, something that might bring a few of Simon's
followers back to the farm next summer. The letter was a start but he needed
to walk with Simon in his new world. He had spoken to his journalism
professor whose response had been disappointing. And condescending;
or so it felt. Chastising him for his late arrival, trivializing his work of the
last summer. It had caught him totally by surprise. No one in his class had
been published as widely as he. Very few had been published at all. He had
tried to get his mind around it with little success. Professor Meridan was
new to the college. Dr. Coppersmith, who had encouraged Tom to take the
year off, had taken ill. He had mentioned this to Roger, who attributed it
to ownership. *When you replaced a popular person at an institution, or in an office,*
Roger explained, *you had to take charge in several ways, one of which to show your
superiority to the person you succeeded.*

Coppersmith had taken a number of careful hits, one being Tom. That
Tom had arrived two weeks late because of the Stardust Kid just added to
Meridan's case. *No,* he had explained, *forget the boy and get back to work.* Tom
wondered if his new professor had read any of his articles. His reference
during their first meeting had been off-hand at best and when he spoke of
the Stardust Kid it was with a dismissive smile.

Simon had become much more a part of Tom's life than he had ever imagined might happen. Sure, there was Jesse, and what he had said to Roger a couple weeks earlier was true. Truer than he had known until he heard himself speak it. Part of it was Jenna, their shared sense of loss and recovery. That had made his bond with Simon even stronger and had moved it from his own mind into the world outside. He was impatient with university life. A year away had distanced him from the friendships. His classmates had graduated and his acquaintances among the juniors, who were now his peers, were few. The year away had put all of what had been familiar and routine at a distance.

Then his phone rang. He took it out of his pocket and checked the number. Roger. He clicked on the speaker. "Hello, Roger. What's up?"

"Jenna wasn't arrested."

"Oh, that's such a relief! How'd you find out?"

"I went to the courthouse in Boston. It's a long story. Best over a drink or two. Anyway, we don't have to worry about her being there for Thanksgiving. Thank goodness."

"So she wasn't at Rosie's after all."

"No, she never went back. She went directly from the farm to the apartment Bill Miller had gotten her before the show. He rented it for a year. Don't ask me why. Anyway, it's a good thing he did."

"How did you find it?"

"I had the address from when I was in Boston for the show. I got a room at the Marriot and she came up for dinner. We had a very good conversation."

"That's wonderful."

"And mind-changing. I have been wrong about a number of things, Tom. And not just Jenna. It's hard to admit how wrong. Less hard to admit why. Anyway, as I said, that's a conversation for another time. She told me about your plans to visit Simon on Thanksgiving."

"Yes, but actually I might stay on a little while after. I'm being pressed by my news organization. They want a follow-up piece on Simon at school." There was a moment of silence on the line. "I won't write it if you don't want me to, Roger."

"No. No. You write it. Everything you have written has been good. Good writing and good for Simon. No, you go ahead."

"Are you sure?"

"I am sure. I have as much to learn as Simon does, Tom. And thanks to you…and Simon…and Jenna, I am. I count on your patience… and Jenna's." He paused. "And Simon's."

"Thanks Roger. How about coming up to the school on Thanksgiving? Simon would be happy to see you."

"I wouldn't count on that. Not yet. But I am going to work on it."

"Well, if you change your mind let me know."

"I will."

He put the phone back in his pocket and watched his fellow-students as they walked from the dining hall to their dorms or a class. *Their worlds were so much simpler,* he thought. *Listen to the lectures, write papers, pass tests, party, date…* He had been there in full swing. Loving it. A year ago. *Was it only one year he had taken off? One year and a lifetime maybe.*

OK. Get real. Time for French class.

Chapter 45

Roger and Mark

It was the day before Thanksgiving and the traffic had been predictably heavy. The distance between Belleville and Manhattan wasn't that great, but Roger had been driving for over three hours by the time he reached the hotel. It was a familiar sight from many years past. His parents had stayed there when they drove him to and from school. As he parked and retrieved his bag from the back seat he noticed not much appeared to have changed.

Not structurally in any case. The siding was new—a natural wood shingle over what had once been white ribbed siding. A new porch and front entrance, but otherwise just as he remembered it.

He checked to be sure that the three rooms he had reserved were on the same floor, that the small private dining room was theirs for Thanksgiving Eve, and then he walked up one flight to his room. It was small but comfortable, with a tiny kitchen containing a two-burner hotplate, a fridge, and a coffee machine. He walked over to the bed, unpacked his pipe and tobacco, his sleepwear, a change of clothes, and his toilet kit.

Then he turned on the coffee machine, popped in a cartridge of dark blend and waited for the light to flash. There had been no kitchen in his parents' days and the décor had been much homier. Now the drapes were fringed in a light gold braid and the bed cover was fluffy with a simple geometry of gold threads.

He had called Tom the week before to tell him of his plan to join them for the evening before Thanksgiving. He would arrange rooms for them at the Belleville Inn. They would have dinner together and he would leave the next morning before they went to the school. The visit was the result of a call he'd had from Mark. Something the school head wanted to talk with him about. Roger hadn't said more, other than that. *No, Simon was not in trouble. On the contrary*, he had said, leaving it there. He checked his watch. 3:40. Mark had said he would be there by four. The light on the machine flashed and he pressed the button. He carried the cup to the easy chair and sat down.

A week had passed since Roger had spoken with Mark on the phone. He had assumed the call had to do with Simon; a problem of some sort needing his advice. *It did have to do with Simon,* Mark had said, *but it was part of a much bigger picture. It had to do with the school itself.* He had asked Mark to expand on that, but he'd declined. Instead, he'd asked if Roger could extend his Thanksgiving visit by one day so they could get together at his hotel. Mark had been kind enough two weeks earlier to reserve the rooms Roger requested. Roger had agreed.

There was a knock on the door. He got up, opened it, greeted Mark and offered him a cup of coffee, which he accepted, following him to the small press.

"We need one of these at school," Mark said, in a voice that didn't suggest intention. Roger understood. When he had visited several months ago to begin their conversation about Simon he had noticed that the same Hamilton Beach tank that had sat at the staff table all those years ago was still there. The school's embrace of tradition expressed itself often in puzzling ways.

"Tradition, tradition," Roger sang.

"Right. Well, it serves its purpose. Sometimes." Mark lifted his quickly-brewed cup from the machine and tasted it. "Delish!" he said.

"Well, have a seat and tell me how things are going."

"Pretty well. No, very well. Good enrollment, as good a faculty as I've ever worked with. Really good. I haven't had an issue for the first two months. Not that I ever have very many. But the three new staff members are tops. Jeff Barlow has taken over the math department. Pauline Grassley is looking after the fourth-graders and Tom Harkness has taken Bob's place as farm manager. Of course Tom isn't really new."

"When did he graduate? Before my time?"

"And after mine."

"Anyway, things are going well. And Simon is doing fine. He's made friends and he's done his part with daily chores. He's having some problems with his classes, but he'll get those under control."

"What kind of problems?"

"Impatience mostly. Understandable. He's far ahead of his classmates in several areas. Hell, he's far ahead of most kids in the country. His knowledge of natural science is awesome."

"Ants."

"Not just ants. Anything that lives anywhere around here is a friend of his. And literature."

"Reese saw to that. So, is he acting like a know-it-all?"

"Not really. How can I describe it? He looks bored. He fiddles with things. He's not used to sitting in a classroom, or at a desk, for that matter. At least I don't think he is."

"No, he did his stuff up in his loft in the barn. Oh, he had a desk there, but not one someone *told* him to sit at. In fact there weren't many things he was told to do. Reese let him find his own way, being more a listener and provider. Like most parents. You must have other kids who've been home-schooled."

"Sure, but not the way Simon was. At least as far as I know. Anyway, Simon is making his way. One day at a time."

"So, what is it that gives us this gift of time together?" Roger asked. Had he said that right? He smiled to make sure."

"The other part of my job."

"Fund-raising."

"You've got it."

"I was thinking about that on my drive up. You probably know that Reese did quite well for himself. His books sold all over the world. There's almost a million dollars in the trust fund. But it's not something from which I can make withdrawals. It's Simon's money and yes, I'm his guardian, but that doesn't extend to gift-giving. Tuition, sure. Living and travel expenses. But not donations."

"I understand that and it's not what I was going to suggest or ask for. No, it's broader. It's Simon."

"Help me out."

Mark took a breath and let it out. He looked up and smiled. "The Stardust Kid."

"Go on."

"He's an international figure. I have to turn people away. Two weeks ago a guy with a truck and a camera crew. They wanted to film him at work on the farm."

"And?"

"I said no. We can't allow that sort of thing. You know Wind Lake; it's apart from that world. The opposite. Kids don't even watch television except at selected times with selected programs and staff presence. Not much different from your time here, I suspect. Cell phones get turned in at the office and used only there for conversations with parents."

"How about the internet and computers?"

"Again, with faculty supervision." Mark held up his hands. "I know, it sounds crazy and it isn't easy. For the kids or the faculty. But there we are." He laughed and looked up. "Or there we were."

Roger stood up with his empty cup. "Would you like another cup?"

"Sure. Thanks." Mark rubbed his hands together and looked at his palms. They were a farmer's hands, calloused and not great for typing. But he managed. He managed lots of things. Even this.

Roger handed him his cup and sat down. "So where are you now?"

"Underfunded. Under-enrolled. Under pressure."

"From your trustees."

"Yes." He took a sip and continued. "It's not just us. Independent schools around the country are having the same problems. Many of them, anyway. The approach to the enrollment issue has been to recruit from abroad. I visited five countries this summer, mostly Asian. But Germany and Norway as well. We have good alumni representation in several European countries. Japan and China are coming along fast. As is South Korea. You wouldn't believe the influx of Asian students all over the place. I saw a picture of the freshman class at Exeter and lots of the kids were Asian. I know a gal who runs a day school in Kansas City. They have created an offshoot campus in Beijing."

"Offshoot?"

"A school. A day school. For locals."

"Why?"

"Income. To help pay the bills at the Kansas City School." He shook his head and stood up, walking to the picture window that looked out onto the street. "That's the main reason. But there's more to it. As there is for us. International students have always been welcome at Independent schools and not just for the tuition income. The world's a smaller place. Kids need to know who's out there. They need to know people other than their neighborhood kids. That's always been a part of Independent education. Teaching kids about the world through companionship as well as books." He turned back and looked at Roger. "I'm blathering."

"No, you're not. Not at all. I had no idea there were so many students coming from Asia. And a good thing too, in many ways, I gather."

"Oh yes. I'm all for it. But as has always been the case schools compete for these students, and a farm school with barn chores and mountain climbing isn't what most of them are looking for." He sat down and studied his hands again, then looked up at Roger and smiled. "But there's someone who might be able to change that."

Roger looked at him, puzzled, and then it came to him. "Simon?"

"The Stardust Kid. You wouldn't believe how many pictures I saw of him, taken, I'd guess, by your summer visitors at the farm. Sorry. Anyway, he's out there. Everywhere. He's become an icon for 'Save the Planet' movements. Not many people know he's at Wind Lake. We've been careful to protect his privacy."

"But now you think you might want to change that."

"Yes. I think we do."

Chapter 46

Tom, Roger, and Jenna

Tom and Jenna arrived in Belleville shortly after six, and after checking with Roger and then into their rooms, joined him at the bar where he was sipping a martini. Jenna ordered a glass of white wine and Tom a stout beer. "I thought you were a gin and tonic fan," Roger said.

"I'm not really a fan of anything. Depends on the season and the occasion. At school, mostly beer." He took a sip and smiled. "Very nice. So here's to Thanksgiving." They raised their glasses.

"And to Simon," Jenna said.

"Simon," they chorused.

"So have you seen him yet?" Tom asked.

"No. I got here a couple of hours ago," Roger responded, setting his glass carefully on the marble counter-top. Mark Williams wanted to have a meeting."

"He's the head, right?" Jenna asked.

"He is. And a very good one. The school was fortunate to find him."

"So how is Simon doing?" Tom asked.

"Apparently he's doing very well. But that wasn't what Mark wanted to talk about."

He summarized their conversation and Jenna turned to Tom, open-mouthed. They exchanged quick glances of puzzlement and Tom spoke.

"He wants to use Simon to sell the school?"

"Well, I suppose that's one way of looking at it." Roger laughed.

"You said no, right?"

"It's more complicated than that."

Jenna turned and looked at him, waiting for more.

"Wait a minute. I'm confused," Tom said. "I thought that the whole idea of Wind Lake was its isolation. That's why we thought Simon might make a go of it. Am I right?"

"Yes, you are, and I haven't made any commitment. None at all. It's not for me to decide alone."

"You're his guardian," Jenna offered.

"And you are his family. You and Tom. And, as I've said to each of you over the past weeks, I hope to be a part of that family as well. This is not a decision that is mine alone to make. As I said, I have made no commitment to Mark whatsoever. I just listened. So what do you say we go in for dinner and catch our breath?"

Tom and Jenna exchanged glances, looked at their glasses for a second and stood up.

"You can bring those with you if you like," Roger said.

"That's OK," Tom said. "It's not that great."

"Jenna?"

She picked up the half glass of wine that remained and they followed Roger into their private dining room. A young man wearing a much older tweed jacket brought them menus and rubbed his hands together just below his carefully arranged smile. "The specials tonight are country ribs with sweet potato and fresh beans from our gardens, and fresh caught lake trout served with bacon, fingerling potatoes, and a fresh garden salad. Can I get you anything from the bar?"

"I'll have a martini," Roger said, turning to the others.

"I'm good for now," Jenna said.

"I'll have a martini, too," Tom said, smiling at Roger.

"So, where were we?"

"About to put Simon back on stage," Tom said, lifting his glass. "Here's to The Return of The Stardust Kid."

Roger lifted his glass and looked at Jenna. She looked at him and then Tom. "I'm confused," she said.

Roger and Tom exchanged glances and put their glasses down.

"It will be up to Simon," Tom offered. "Right, Roger?"

"Yes, of course. Absolutely."

"Then I'm missing something," Jenna said.

"What?"

"Help me out, Tom. I thought in his letters to you Simon has said he didn't like it when the kids called him Stardust."

"Yes, you're right. But he didn't mind when the visitors to Spruce Valley called him that. At least I never heard him complain about it."

"I'm even more confused."

"Excuse me," Roger said. "It is confusing. To anyone. Even those of us who have known Simon for a long time. I think what Tom is saying is that Simon has never had friends his own age. His father, you and Ben, me, Tom and then the…visitors. And Bill Miller's audience. He's learned adults. He's comfortable with them. He likes their approval." Roger paused and looked at Jenna with some affection. "Yours as much as anyone's. More than anyone's." She opened her mouth to speak, but Roger held up a hand to stay her protest. "No, don't disagree. It's true. You are the person he never had in his life."

Jenna relaxed and resigned herself to the praise. "Thank you."

"It's true. He has said as much to me. When we talked about Wind Lake he asked if you could be there with him. By the way, thank you so very much for agreeing to move up to the farm when the house is finished. Does Simon know that?"

"No. I wanted to tell him tomorrow, in person."

"Have they set a date yet?" Tom asked.

"Mid-March," Roger replied. "They are ahead of schedule. But getting back to this audience issue. I recall your saying something to me, Tom, about his feeling like one of the internationals."

"Yes. In a couple of his letters he said they speak another language. Not just words. He didn't elaborate, but I think I understand. Kids share lots of things in our culture, from toys to television. You don't make it in your school or neighborhood or anywhere else if you aren't cool. It's hard to describe. And really I never thought about it before Simon brought it up. I grew up with neighborhood kids. We played the same games, worshipped the same heroes. You know what I'm saying?"

"Yes, all too well," Jenna responded with a glance up at the ceiling. She paused. She took a deep breath and smiled. "It's one of the reasons that Simon and I became close. How could I have forgotten?"

Roger had been listening with an affectionate, if somewhat condescending, regard for the remarks of his young friends. Now he looked at Jenna with real curiosity. "Go on."

"I never fit in as a child. Or an adolescent, until sex came into the picture. And even then I wasn't very good company. I didn't like the things I was supposed to—the things girls like. Dolls, jewelry, fashion. I never had many friends. A few neighbors and three or four friends at school, but I was never a member of a crowd or even a team. I don't mean to overdramatize, but I was pretty content with my books and pets."

Tom thought of asking what kind of pets but thought better of it. *Just listen.* She was saying things that he never would have imagined hearing. Jenna, who had the social skills of a...*stop. Listen.*

"My older brothers weren't school heroes but they had lots of friends. Friends their age, mostly. Some older. Not many younger. The house was filled with them. I stayed in my room a lot, unless my parents had people over, and they did that quite often. Dad bartended at a hotel and my mom worked at the post office. They had lots of friends." She stopped and took a sip of her wine. "Sorry. I didn't mean to go on like this. It's been so long. And Simon! All this time we've had together and I never put two and two together. You know, when we'd go out for lunch or shopping, he never gave kids his own age a second glance."

"You never told me any of this," Tom said.

"It never occurred to me that it was worth telling until now. I never realized how much Simon and I had in common. Not until we started this conversation."

"'There's a divinity in the lives of men'...." Roger began, then laughed. "And women and twelve-year-old boys. It's just the coincidence of it that, on some plane, isn't a coincidence at all. That you should have met and bonded and understood one-another...it's remarkable. So what do you think we should do?"

The waiter arrived with their drinks and asked if they were ready to order. They looked at their menus. "I'd like the ribs," Tom said. "And a simple salad with a blue cheese dressing."

"And you, madam?"

"I'll have the same with just oil and vinegar."

"I'll have the duck leg," Roger said. "Nice and crispy. And no salad." He looked at Jenna. "How about another glass of wine?"

"Sure. Make it red this time. I'd like a blend. Whatever you have."

"Why don't you bring us a bottle of that blend? You up for that, Tom?"

"Sure."

The waiter took the menus and crossed to the kitchen. Tom watched him go and turned to the others. "I think we should leave it up to Simon. Let him know that whatever he decides we'll be there for him." He looked at Jenna.

"Yes, I agree. I don't think we have any choice. I want to be there for him when he needs me but I don't think I'm someone who should be telling him what to do unless he asks me, and even then..."

"Yes?" Roger asked.

"I'd try to help him think it through. The positives and negatives. I don't know. You're in a different position, Roger. You're his guardian. Whatever you decide, I'll go along with."

"And you, Tom?"

"I'm with Jenna. My guess is that he'll want to. It will mean hanging out with adults again. We all know how much he likes that. And now with the kids there too. That could be really good. But where are you in all this? Like Jenna said, you are his guardian. You have to think of a lot more things than we do. How do you want to deal with it?"

"I'll have to admit that I have some reservations about putting him out there in front of the cameras. It won't be a totally new experience, given Bill Miller and the visitors, and it can be kept within limits. Mark isn't about to do anything that would put Simon at any risk. I think we're pretty much in the same place on this."

Jenna and Tom exchanged affirming glances.

"And if it were possible for either or both of you to be here with him for the event that would be an added incentive and assurance for him"

"I wouldn't miss it for the world," Jenna said with broad smile, glancing at Tom.

"Nor would I," he assured.

"That's great."

"And you?" Tom asked.

"I'll be here. I have to," he assured with a dutiful smile. "After all, I'm his guardian. And if all goes well and he becomes more at home here, we might become friends."

"What do you mean?" Jenna said with an attempt at puzzlement. "You've been friends since he was born."

"Sorry," Roger said. "Of course we have." He took a breath and glanced toward the kitchen, ready for an intermission. "Oh, by the way, I'm going to head back first thing in the morning. I think the whole thing will be easier for Simon if I'm not here. I don't want him to feel under pressure as he makes his decision. Let him know that I will be happy with whatever the three of you decide. Hearing from you that I can be trusted will mean much more than hearing it from me. I'm sure you understand. I still have a ways to go before I've earned Simon's trust. I'm working on that. But, one day at a time. Better not to mention that I was here." He smiled at Jenna and then at Tom with an expression new to both of them. Jenna stood up from her seat, walked over and gave him a kiss on the cheek.

Roger felt surprise, and gratitude. "Thank you. Thank you both for all you have done, given...are. My love of the school is old. My love of Simon is new. The school gave me a new life once. Simon is giving me a new one now."

Chapter 47

Tom, Jenna and Luke

It was Thanksgiving morning, and after having an early breakfast at the hotel, Tom and Jenna drove to the school. They would have the morning with Simon and then head back to Boston before the school gathered for the holiday feast.

They parked in the visitors' lot at the entrance and started down the drive to the school. On their left stood the barn and its various animal enclosures. A large corral stretched out toward a pond, and beyond that a rich woodland that quickly rose up the side of a mountain. To their right, gardens and more gardens already attended by students with gathering baskets.

"My goodness, it's the farm all over again." Jenna said. "So sad that Simon doesn't like it."

"He likes the farm fine. Speaking of which, let's have a look in the stable. Bucephalus and Empress might like to see some familiar faces." They stepped onto the ramp and Tom slid the door open. It was a surprisingly sunny room, much more so than at the farm, and the floors were immaculately clean. They were greeted by a small chorus of sniffs and snorts, and they walked along the stalls until a large familiar muzzle poked out at them. Jenna reached out her hand slowly and stroked Empress on her withers, then gently touched her nose. Empress pressed against it. "I think she knows me," Jenna said with a little laugh.

"Of course she does." He walked past her to the stall where Bucephalus stood watching. Seeing Tom he stood up on his hind legs. "It's OK, boy. Take it easy. I'm so glad to see you." Settling his front hooves carefully, he nodded his head and advanced, practically poking Tom in the nose with his muzzle. They exchanged a few words and sniffs and Bucephalus looked at him as if waiting for more. "How's it going, boy? Is Simon looking after you?" There was a call from behind them.

"Can I help you?"

Tom turned. "Oh, sorry to just walk in like this. We're friends of Simon. Simon Seeker."

"You'd have to be," the man said with a laugh. He was a small man of middle age, with classic overalls bearing a Wind Lake emblem on their bib. "Bucephalus and Empress haven't greeted anyone like that since they moved in. My name's Luke. I run the stable." He held out his hand and Tom took it.

"Good to meet you, Luke. I'm Tom, and this is Jenna." Jenna held out her hand and they shook.

"So, come up to visit the Stardust Kid have you?"

"We have. For the morning. We don't want to interrupt the big event. Just wanted to catch up on things with him."

"I'm sure he'll be real happy to see you."

"How's he doing?" Jenna asked.

"He's doing great. What a rider; makes me feel like an amateur. And horse-whisperer too! My Lord. The two of them go on for half an hour. I've read about stuff like that but never seen it before. I keep out of the way, but I can't help listening."

"Does he do it in front of the other kids?"

"Yeah. Not all of them. I suggested he save it for times when he and Bucephalus were alone." Luke put his thumbs under his overall straps and twisted them. "So, are you related?"

"No, just friends," Tom said. "We help run the farm."

"That must be quite a place."

"Simon tell you about it?"

"You bet. He talks about it all the time." He laughed. "I don't want to hold you up. I'm sure he's dying to see you."

"No, that's OK. We've got time. We've got plenty of time. It would be great—I mean if you have the time—to hear a little more about how Simon's doing."

"Heck, I've got all the time in the world. Can I brew you a cup of coffee? Jenna and Tom exchanged glances. "Sure," Tom responded.

They walked to the back of the stable and up a flight of stairs to Luke's apartment. They entered the kitchen, a small room with a window's view of the corral. Off to one side a small living room with a fireplace. An open door suggested a bedroom. Luke invited them to take seats at the kitchen table, strewn with crossword-puzzles. Luke cleared them with a chuckle.

"You are a serious puzzle maven," Jenna said.

"They keep me company," he replied, walking to the counter. He took three coffee mugs from the cupboard and placed them on the table. Then he removed a nearly full coffee carafe from its machine and filled their cups. "My wife works in the kitchen," he said, sitting down. "Not breakfast, but from ten 'till seven she's straight out. I stop by for lunch and an afternoon cup of tea, but I'm pretty much tied up here with chores and riding lessons and trail work."

"How long have you been here?"

"I grew up here. Then off to college and a stint in the Navy, and then back here. So you said you help run Simon's farm?"

"We look after it together, with a lot of help from some others as well. I'm a student—a senior thank goodness—at UMaine and Jenna is a professional counselor. Roger Plummer, Simon's guardian, hired us."

After the introductions, they covered the parts of Simon's story that Luke didn't already know. There weren't many. He'd read the newspaper stories. Everyone on the staff had. After all, Simon was Reese Larkin's kid. It was obvious Simon had trusted Luke as a friend, and as they talked Tom and Jenna could understand why. It wasn't only his affection, it was the measure of his sensibility. Clearly, working for what must have been a good thirty years and being himself a product of the school's culture, he knew how to deal with its students.

"So, from your perspective, how's Simon doing?" Jenna asked.

"All things considered, pretty well."

"What things?"

"Mainly routines. Wind Lake is different in lots of ways, as you know, sitting here in the stable. Any kid new to the school has to take it one step at a time. And for Simon the steps have been a little harder. He's not used to other kids. Or schools of any kind. Or routines that don't have to do with a farm. Classrooms, blackboards, announcements, games. You name it. Practically anything that most of the kids have grown up with."

"I know," Tom said, "he's told me about a lot of that in his letters. And the problem of being Sam Scamper."

"Mark never should have mentioned it. I don't know what he was thinking. Anyway…"

"Is he making progress in dealing with it?"

"A little. It's complicated. He'd be having a hard time fitting in even without that. And there's the rule about riding."

It was Jenna this time. "Wait, I thought that was the best part of the place for Simon."

"Oh, it is. But there are rules that he's not used to and struggles to understand."

"About riding alone?"

"Yes. He's told me about the rides he and Bucephalus took up on the farm. Miles and miles through the forests. Is that right?"

"It is. Spruce Valley Farm is part of a land grant that goes back a few hundred years. It's practically the size of a county. All undeveloped."

"Except for Simon," Jenna added, smiling at Tom.

"Right. You wouldn't believe the trails he's cut. With his father's help."

"Well," Luke continued. "He can't do that here. It's against school rules. As you can understand. We can't have kids wandering off."

"So when *can* Simon ride?"

"With others. Trail-riding. I supervise a lot of it. Once or twice a week."

"That's not much."

"Not for Simon. I let him spend a lot of time here, riding around the corral. Now and then he and I take a ride up one of the trails."

"Does he like riding with the other kids?" Jenna asked.

"I think it's probably the best part of his day. Most of the kids—the girls especially—like his guided tours."

"You mean he picks the trails?

"No, they're as old as the school. What I mean is that he points out things along the way. You know, birds and places where animals probably live."

"No ant colonies?" Tom asked, immediately regretting the tone of his question.

Luke laughed. "Not yet. I'm glad you brought that up. Reminds me of The Bill Miller Show."

"You saw it?"

"Not live. Later on YouTube. Anyway, Roger told the staff about it and asked us not to bring the subject up unless Simon did. He hasn't, and to everyone's surprise neither have any of the kids."

Luke asked Tom and Jenna to tell him about their roles in Simon's life and they went on, with encouragement, at some length. When they had finished their coffee and invited Luke to tell more of his own story, he smiled and stood up. "That will have to wait till another time. Much as I'm enjoying our conversation, I need to get back to work."

They stood up and walked back to the driveway, now unpopulated by feeders and gatherers. They thanked him with warm hand-shakes. "We'd like to stay in touch if that's OK," Jenna said, looking at Tom.

"You can count on that," Luke assured her. "Enjoy your visit."

Chapter 48

Tom

After showing Tom and Jenna his room, introducing them to the Fentons and giving a quick tour of the classroom building, Simon offered to take them for a short ride on one of the trails. Tom said that that the two of them should have some time together and that he wanted to pay a visit to Mark. Simon smiled without argument and set off with Jenna for the barn.

Mark, was in the dining room, his secretary explained, up to his ears getting ready for the Thanksgiving feast. Tom thanked her and walked back outside. *Up to his ears? Elbows he knew. Ears he didn't.* Anyway, it was just as well. Roger was the one to deal with the Stardust Kid stuff. Better to walk around, get a sense of the place, maybe chat with a couple kids.

He walked out to the gardens. Three kids were pulling up root vegetables. "What are you harvesting?" he asked.

A girl held up a long white root. "Parsnips," she said. "And carrots and some onions. We already did the potatoes."

"Two tons of them," a red-headed boy said. "And we still have some broccoli to bring in."

"That's very impressive," Tom said with a broad smile.

"Are you staying for dinner?" the girl asked.

"No, just stopped by for a quick visit with one of your fellow students. Are you harvesting for the Thanksgiving feast?"

"No, the dinner is already cooked. These are for the root cellar under the barn. Who are you visiting?"

"Simon Seeker. Do you know him?"

"Everyone knows Simon," the girl said with a big smile. Tom studied it, quickly returning his own. It was an approving smile. *Good.* "Are you his brother?" she asked.

"No, just a friend. I look after the farm up in Maine."

"That's where Bucephalus and Empress grew up," the girl said.

"Right. Do you ride Empress?" Tom asked.

"Only in the corral."

"But not on the trails?"

"Not yet. But I will. Simon's helping me make friends with her."

"That's great! Actually Simon's riding right now with my friend, Jenna. By the way, my name's Tom, and you are?"

"Leona," she said, dropping the parsnips into a crate and wiping her hands. She turned to the others. The red-head waved.

"I'm Robbie. Simon and I are in the same grade."

"Jason," the other boy said. "I'm in fifth grade."

"Hi. Good to meet you. So, Robbie, are you and Simon friends?"

"Sort of."

"Good," Tom replied, thinking he should leave that alone.

Robbie continued, "Simon's brilliant. He knows a hundred times more stuff than I do." He laughed. "Or even Kamil knows."

"Kamil?"

"Our teacher. Simon is a genius."

"I don't know about that." Tom said with a chuckle. "But he has read a lot more books on nature than I did at his age."

"It's funny," Robbie said. "Kamil has to be careful. Simon corrected him a couple of times. He made him stay after class. I asked him what Kamil said but he wouldn't tell me. Anyway, Simon doesn't say much now."

"That's too bad. I'll have to talk with him about that. He hasn't had a lot of experience with teachers. Or with other kids. I'm glad he has you as a friend."

"He invited me to come up to his farm in the summer."

"Really? That would be great."

"He invited a bunch of kids in our class. We'd really like to. It would be cool to see where Mr. Bumpus lived."

"You've read his father's books?"

"Not all of them. I liked the Mr. Bumpus ones. Mr. Larkin went to school here and his books that are in the library have places where kids have underlined stuff that sound like he got some ideas here when he was a kid."

"Interesting. I never thought of that but it makes sense. Funny, Simon hasn't mentioned that."

"He hasn't read the books," Jason said, with a dismissive laugh. It was the first suggestion of something less than approval.

Tom smiled, a little tightly. "Well they were written before Simon was born. And his father never showed them to him."

"I think that's good," Robbie said. "That would be hard."

"What's hard about it?" Jason responded. "Scamper and Bumpus and the others are just made up."

"I understand what Robbie's saying," Tom offered. "I think his father wanted him to have his own life and not have to live up to some imaginary ones. Would you want to have to do that?"

"No, I guess not," Jason conceded. "Yeah, you're right."

Tom relaxed. "OK. Well, I'll let you finish your harvesting. Great to chat with you. Hope you have a great Thanksgiving."

He walked past the playing fields where various groups were playing soccer or lacrosse, or playing on a large assembly of wooden bars: climbing, swinging hand-over-hand from bar to bar, or just sitting aloft with their friends or their thoughts. He could see only two staff members, not obviously supervising, casual, chatting with kids.

He continued to the road that led up the hill to the other residences. They were very much in the same style: two- or three-story wooden buildings with large porches and gardens, a few students sitting reading or playing board games. He could picture Simon among this quieter crowd much more easily than among the athletes and gymnasts. He had spoken of playing cribbage and a couple card games with his father.

He checked his watch and headed back to the barn. Simon and Jenna would be there shortly. They'd have the rest of the morning together, Simon showing them around, maybe introducing them to a few friends, but mostly sitting together, getting a better sense of his feelings about the weeks and months ahead. Mark's proposal could wait until he and Jenna had a better sense of where he saw himself here at school and how going back on stage would fit into that.

Simon, Tom and Jenna

After giving them a tour of the campus Simon took them to his favorite spot beside the pond. There was an old wooden bench just back from the shore. He sat in the middle and they sat on either side of him, Jenna putting an arm behind his head. Simon asked about the other farm. *How were the animals? Had they filled the root cellar? How was work on the milking shed coming along? Were any new visitors stopping by?* There weren't, but that question opened the door to the topic they had been rehearsing since their conversation with Roger. Tom began with a broad and encouraging smile.

"Speaking of your visitors, something has come up here at school that might put them back in your life."

"Really? Here at school?"

"Well, not like at the farm. That will have to wait until next summer. But in a different way that you might like."

"OK, how?"

"Remember why your visitors came from all over the place to meet you?"

"The Bill Miller Show. And then they saw me on YouTube."

"Right.

"And your stories in the newspaper."

"Well, yes, they helped."

"Big-time."

Jenna laughed. Then Simon. Then Tom. It was a familiar and much missed sound that made its way across the pond in a comforting way reminiscent of times they'd shared by the pond at Spruce Valley. Jenna took a turn. "Mr. Williams—"

"Everyone calls him Mark," Simon interrupted. "Everyone here is first name."

"Right. Well, Mark has a favor to ask you."

"He's asked me some already," Simon said in a way that couldn't be dismissed.

"Oh?" Now it was Tom, whose expression was a mixture of curiosity and concern. "What kind of favors?

Simon laughed. "Like not correcting my science teacher when she gets something wrong."

Jenna laughed. "What did she get wrong?"

"She told Billy that if he was a strong as an ant he could lift his desk."

"Was she wrong?"

"No."

"So why did you correct her?"

"I didn't really correct her. I just said that he could lift a car if he was that strong. She laughed and said she didn't think so. Then she went back to the blackboard and I said it was true and she told me to be quiet. Anyway, what kind of a favor does Mark want?"

Tom said, "I'll let Jenna explain. She has done a lot of thinking about this. She had a lot of questions for Roger when he told us about it."

"Roger?"

"Oh, sorry," Tom apologized. "This all started in a conversation Mark had with Roger."

"Does Roger want me to do this favor?"

"Only if you want to. Roger wants you to be happy; that's number one. Anything else takes second place."

Simon stood up, walked a couple steps, reached down and picked up a stone and threw it into the pond. "Then why am I here?"

"Because Roger thought it would be the right thing for you," Jenna said standing and walking over to his side. "…a place where you could make friends and learn…and…"

"Do what he and my Dad did."

"Yes, that too. A family tradition."

"Roger isn't my family."

"He cares about you very much. He had no choice, Simon. I'm working. Tom's in school. There's was no one to look after you. Roger has to be sure you are safe and that people are there when you need them. We'll be back with you next summer for sure." She paused and then continued, "We love you Simon. There's no one we love more. That's true. I think you know it's true. Of course you know it's true."

"And Roger's on board for you in a way you haven't gotten to see yet," Tom said.

Simon turned and looked at Tom with some mistrust. "What does that mean?"

"We've had some good talks. He's listened to Jenna and me. Really, he has. Please believe me. I don't lie to you, Simon."

"I know."

"So, can we talk more about the favor?"

"I guess so."

"You're not sure."

"Yes, I'm sure."

"Good. Go on Jenna."

"Well. In a nutshell…"

Simon laughed. They looked at one another and joined him. The laughter was healing.

"The school needs your help."

"They don't want my help."

"Luke told us that you were a great help with the horses."

"That's different."

"How is it different?"

"I don't know. It just is." At the sound of a splash Simon turned to the pond. A widening circle of tiny ripples interrupted the water's stillness.

"What was that?" Jenna asked.

"Probably a frog." He turned back.

"You know why your visitors came to the farm last summer…" Jenna began.

"Yes. What does that have to do with Mark?"

"Mark would like more people in the world to know about the school. He'd like to have more students from other countries."

"There are a lot here now. I know some of them." Simon brightened. "They've got pretty interesting stories. I got to meet some of them before the other students got here."

"Well this is your chance to bring even more here."

"How can I do that?"

"By getting on YouTube again."

"How do I do that?"

"Your turn, Tom."

Tom stood and joined them. "Mark wants to invite TV crews to the school at spring vacation. He wants you to give them a tour, show them around, take them on a trail ride."

"Why me?" He looked at each of them in turn. They smiled expectantly and said nothing. "I'm not The Stardust Kid anymore. I'm just me."

"And that's all you ever have to be for us," Tom assured. "But your visitors, including Afua and Jack Benson and Dr. Schneider, came to meet The Stardust Kid. And they stayed. And they listened to you."

A frog croaked loudly, as if wanting attention. They turned. It took a jump towards them. They watched. It sat back, looked at them and croaked again.

"Is he trying to tell us something?" Jenna asked with a mixture of amusement and relief.

"He's telling us to get out of here," Simon said. "This is his territory."

"So what do you think?" Tom asked.

"About the frog?" Simon asked with a mischievous smile.

"About Mark's request," Tom said, smirking. "It would just be for the second week of vacation. You would have the first with us at the farm. We'll bring you down from the farm and stay around for the shooting."

"Shooting?!"

"Sorry. Making films. It's called a shooting."

"Why?"

"Good question. I never thought about it." Tom looked at Jenna. "Jenna?"

She shook her head. "Neither did I."

"OK, never mind. But there are no guns."

"Right. No guns. Just cameras. By the way, it isn't just the school that would benefit from your showing people around. Sure, they'll get a few more students from abroad, and it will be good for the school to be better known as a place that cares about looking after our planet. But it also gives your friends from the summer and lots of others a chance to catch up on how things are going for you."

"Why would Mark want to do it when no kids are here? I mean, he wants people to see kids from other countries, right?"

"Oh, the press will come after the kids are back. Mark wants the vacation time with you alone to plan. Then the students arrive and get on camera as well. They will love you for it! I promise you."

Simon looked at each of them and turned back to the frog. Like Tom and Jenna, it was waiting for him to speak. There was no sign of life. He looked up into the maple tree by the pond. A grey catbird sat on a branch. No song. *Wrong season. Sugaring season. That would be good. Take them sugaring. And snowy owls. And beavers down by the lake. There would be things to see.*

"Look sweetie, you don't have to do this if you don't want to. It's just an idea Mark had. You don't have to do it."

"Can I have some time to think about it?"

"Certainly," Tom assured. "All the time you need. It's only November. See how things go. Think about what you would show the guys with the cameras. Mark won't bring up the idea even to the staff until he's spoken with you. He doesn't want to put you in a tough place. He wants to do it only if you do."

"But when you think about it, think about more than the school."

"That's easy."

"You know what I mean? Think about all those people out there—not only your summer visitors—who want to hear more from you, who want to do the things that you and Afua and the others care about."

"Does Afua know about this?"

"Nobody knows except the three of us, Roger, and Mark."

"Can I talk about it with Luke?"

"You should ask Mark about that. OK?"

"OK."

"So, let's head back to Lance House. You don't want to miss the Thanksgiving Feast."

They walked back on to the road and then to Lance Cottage. Sara was over at the dining hall helping to set things up for the celebration. Bob sat on the porch playing cribbage with Rodney. The sight reminded Tom of his grandfather's house where a small cribbage table sat sacred by the fireplace. He had never played or had any interest in the game, but for his father it was ritual. Bob walked over to greet them.

"So how's our boy doing here?" Tom asked.

"Very well. Very well indeed," Bob said, smiling at Simon. "He does his chores without complaint, he's a good housemate, and he keeps his room neat." He put an inquiring hand out to Jenna who took it with a smile and said simply, "I'm Jenna. I help out at the farm now and then."

"Well, I'm sure Simon wants to show you around."

Simon opened the door and they followed him up to his room.

"Hey, this is very nice!" Jenna said, checking the bed for softness, the window for its view and the neatness of Simon's desk.

"There are only three of us on the second floor," Simon said. "Stefan and Rodney have the room on the other side. Greta, Clara, Jean, and Marla are downstairs. Greta rides Empress."

"Well that worked out nicely, didn't it?" Jenna said, sitting on the bed. "It's nice to make friends and even nicer when you like the same things."

"She said she's going to get her parents to come up to the farm this summer."

"That's great!"

Tom, who had been looking out the window, turned. "Speaking of the summer, Simon, I don't think we told you. Roger is planning to spend more time up at the farm. He really wants to spend more time with you."

At a skeptical look from Simon, Tom insisted, "Honest. I'm not making this up. He thinks he's missed out on a lot, not being a better friend. And there's something else too." Tom looked at Jenna, excited for her to deliver the news.

"I'm moving out of my place in the south end this March, and I'm going to move up to look after your new house. I'll be your maid!" She laughed.

"Really?!"

"Really! It will be all ready for you when you come back."

"That's great!"

Simon walked to the window. "Nobody's going to the dining hall. There's still lots of time."

"We've got some packing and driving to do," Tom said, his hands on Simon's shoulders. "The traffic will be pretty bad if we don't get an early start. We'll be in touch. Oh, I forgot to mention: If you agree to Mark's plan he'll give you a kind of phone access that most kids here don't have. In case you need to talk with us about things. All you have to do is go to Mark's office and he'll connect you with Jenna or me. I'll be at school and she'll be home, but we'll both have our phones nearby."

They walked together down the stairs and outside to the porch. Greta was standing there waiting for her new best friend.

"It's will be really great if you do this for the school,"

"I guess so," Simon said.

"You guess so?" Jenna questioned with a smile.

Simon laughed. "OK, I know so. And you'll be here, right?"

"We promise," Tom said. "Just as we were with your visitors this summer. Wouldn't miss it for the world."

"You coming?" Greta asked.

"Yes," Simon said, in a voice of assurance…and confidence.

Chapter 50

Simon

Simon awoke from a set of helpful dreams about the weeks that lay ahead. He would tell the visitors how much he needed to take his message beyond the school. Then they would understand that he wasn't leaving because he didn't like Wind Lake, but because he had done his work here and needed to move on.

He brushed his teeth, got dressed and walked down to the first floor. He was, as usual, the first one up, but instead of taking the opportunity to walk in the woods he sat on the porch, waiting for the others. First to arrive was Greta. She sat beside him on the bench and reminded him that it was Tuesday and that meant pancakes for breakfast. That led to a discussion of maple syrup and sap harvest. Greta had been at Wind Lake only one year but had helped to gather the sap buckets that spring. Simon listened with the pleasure of shared experience, though his had been on his own land. It was as if they had been side by side in harvesting. They were joined by Stefan, who liked the pancakes but not as much as the crispy bacon that came with them. Only two slices, which wasn't fair, but Rodney didn't like bacon and so he'd give a piece to Stefan for half of a pancake.

"At least we don't have to slaughter them," Rodney said with a laugh as he joined them. "Unlike the chickens."

"Do we kill the chickens?" Simon asked with lightly contrived horror.

"Chicken Harvest! One of the major fall events," Stefan confirmed. "The eighth graders chop off their heads and gut them. Then the seventh grade plucks and the others cut them up and bag them for the freezer."

"Do we have to talk about this before breakfast?" Greta pleaded.

"Oh, sorry. I forgot. Greta and some of the other girls go to the library during Chicken Harvest."

"I didn't come here to kill things," Greta said with a lift of her head.

It was a lift as well to Simon's spirits, which had brightened during the last few minutes, the topic notwithstanding. His three housemates were friends who could talk like this without discomfort or even disapproval. It was better than he expected. He should have spent more time with them. From now on he would.

Several students ran past Lance House toward the barn. Rodney got up. "Let's go."

"Are you still doing the sheep?" Simon asked.

"Yup."

"And I've still got the hen house," Stefan said with a laugh. It's amazing they don't attack me."

They headed up the drive, Simon and Greta to the stables. Luke greeted them as they entered and told Simon with a familiar smile that Bucephalus had been asking about him. Greta opened their can of rotting banana peels. They each took a couple. Greta walked over to Empress' stall and greeted her with one of the peels. Such gifts had helped to secure their relationship over the past month. She ate it with a grateful nod of her head and waited for the next. That horses loved rotting peels was something Greta had learned from Simon.

Simon spoke softly to Bucephalus, who nuzzled his ear as if to convey his own thoughts. It had been like that for years. He was a great listener. "Guess what?" Simon said. "I had a great time with Greta and Stefan and Rodney. Just the three of us there like we were friends." He took one of the banana peels from his pocket lifted it to Bucephalus' open mouth. "I mean, sure we're friends. We're in the same house but… I don't know. It was different. I think things are going to get better." Bucephalus shook his head. Simon gave him the second peel. "I know you want to be back at the farm and you will be sooner than I thought. I've got a plan."

Greta walked back from Empress' stall. "You ready?"

"I'm ready."

They walked out of the stable and down the road to the dining hall.

After breakfast, Simon went to Mark's office. He was greeted warmly and knew he would see an even bigger smile on the man's face when he gave him the news.

"So, how are things going for you? Getting used to your new life here by the mountain?"

"Pretty good."

"Did you have a nice time with your friends?"

"Yes."

"Jenna and Tom, right?"

"Yes. They told me about your idea."

"I'm glad to hear that. Would you like to sit down?"

"No, that's OK. I've got a class."

"What do you think of it?"

"I'll do it."

Mark's smile gave way to an expression that brought back glad but sad memories for Simon. It was the smile he remembered on his father's face when he surprised him with unexpected agreement.

"That's wonderful! Oh, Simon. This is so generous of you." Mark put his hands on Simon's shoulders. Simon smiled at him. Simon hadn't seen that expression on Mark's face before, a mixture of surprise and delight. It seemed as he blinked that there might be tears coming, but they didn't. "It will mean so much to Wind Lake. Oh my goodness." Mark caught his breath. "You don't mind being the Stardust Kid again?"

"No. It's OK. It will help outside Wind Lake too. I think."

"Oh, absolutely. What you have to say about caring for our environment and all the creatures who live with us is so important. So very, very important. This is wonderful. Do you have any questions or concerns about the project?"

"Not now. Maybe later."

"Well, I'm here any time you want to talk. By the way, Bob and Sara tell me that you and your housemates have become close friends."

"We get along pretty good."

"And your trail-riding companions. And your table-mates. More friends every day. Isn't that true?"

"I guess so."

"It is so. They are getting to know you and discovering what a caring and well-informed boy you are. You have made great progress. And you will make much more. Especially when your friends return and get their own time in front of the cameras. You will be giving them something they never dreamed of having."

Simon was pleased by Mark's reassurance. In any case it would be a fair trade. *But that wasn't something to bring up now. That was for later. Waiting 'til then was important.* Mark couldn't say no. Not after he had done his part.

"We'll have lots of time to plan for this. For now, let's just keep it between ourselves. Is that OK with you?"

"Yes. When will you tell them?"

"As soon as my board approves the idea and the press accepts the invitation."

"What's a board?"

Mark smiled and nodded. "They are my bosses. The people who tell me what I can or can't do as head of the school."

"Is Roger one of them?"

"Wouldn't that be nice! No, he's not. Not yet anyway, but that's a very good suggestion. Thank you."

"You're welcome."

"A school's board is made up mostly of people who attended the school years back and who still want to be involved. They are very good people. Very generous people. We meet every two months and discuss ways to make the school better."

"Like bringing more kids from other countries?"

"Yes. And getting word out to people about the things we think are important. Like caring for our environment. And I can't think of anyone who could get people thinking about that more than the Stardust Kid. Thank you very much for helping out with this, Simon."

"You're welcome."

"So what can I offer in return?"

"Well, maybe I could do a little more exploring. Maybe take some rides by myself to come up with good ideas. Maybe find places to take the visitors. I know that's against the rules but I do my thinking best when it's just us."

"You and Bucephalus?

"Yes."

"Well, I'll tell you what. You wait until I hear back from the board and we have some assurance that the press will come. Then I'll tell the school about the plan and that you have been given a special privilege. That way the students won't think you're breaking the rules. More than that, they'll understand why you've been given this special privilege. Is that OK?"

"Yes. When is the next meeting?"

"In early January. Then I'll see about the press, and if all goes as planned I'll tell the school. I'd guess sometime in early February. How's that?"

"OK."

"Thank you, Simon. This is a very generous gift and I appreciate it."

They walked to the door; Mark opened it. Simon walked into the hall, then out into a sunny and fragrant fall morning.

Chapter 51

Simon and Jenna

When the snow fell, life at school changed. The outdoors became an even more inviting world than he had known at the farm. Flying down a snowy hill on a sled, a board, or skis was much more fun with friends. Rainer, the boy from Germany, was a competitive racer and taught Simon new ways to turn fast and jump high. Only very briefly was he kept in bed with a twisted ankle. Then back out as if it had never happened.

His thoughts of the future gave him a much more comfortable place in the present. It must have shown, for the other students opened doors to amusements he had never known. And not just amusements. They spoke of feelings he had known but could never have shared with his father, fantasies that he thought were his alone. He was no longer different from those around him. They were of his age and knew his thoughts as he was learning to know theirs.

He knew about ants and antlers. They knew a great deal about aunts and uncles, brothers and sisters, and next door neighbors. The expression "next door" was one he had never had reason to use, but now it was very much a part of his life.

He had become a listener as much as a talker, a gatherer of expressions both vocal and facial, of feelings new and surprising. Friendships with those a little younger had given him a chance to offer help; friendships with the older students had taught him to listen and take more careful steps.

There were games that he had to learn and mischiefs that he had to weigh, heroes he had never known and some he could share. It was all much more than he had imagined and much less than he had feared.

It was the night before Christmas vacation. There were small celebrations in all of the houses with treats from the kitchen. At Lance Cottage, his friends told of their plans for the weeks ahead, remembered Christmases past and sang a few songs, led, much to their surprise, by Bob. Then they went to bed. Simon couldn't sleep. So many things contended for his attention. The new house which would be nearly finished, his baleout, memories of his summer friends, the excitement of seeing Jenna and Tom.

Then the morning bell and his friends running down the stairs. He got up and dressed. Then he packed his small bag with enough clothes for the two weeks ahead. He included his school sweatshirt.

Most of the students would leave that morning on chartered buses traveling to Boston and New York, with stops along the way where their parents would be waiting for them. For Greta, Rainer, and a number of others, after the buses it was on to the airports where they would board international flights. And there were others picked up right at school by their parents or friends of the family. It was a very busy morning with more traffic than Simon had seen since leaving Boston months before.

Tom arrived shortly after lunch. Simon was packed and ready to go. The Fentons wished them both a happy holiday and they drove down the school drive and out onto the highway. Simon had been looking forward to the journey home for a long time. Jenna would have arrived the week before, riding north with Ben. Roger would be there as well. Simon was curious in a way that surprised him. If what Tom and Jenna had said to him over the past weeks was really true, Roger might be a different person. He had begun to learn that things like that were possible. Even perhaps for older people.

And the house was ready to be lived in. Well, almost. There was a lot still to do on the outside, Tom had said in one of his letters. But inside had heat and beds and a kitchen that worked, pretty much.

"So Jenna's already moved in?" Simon asked.

Tom nodded as they drove onto the highway. "More or less. Sort of. No one can really move in quite yet. The floors still need to be finished off and some of the woodwork needs painting. But yes, she brought her stuff up and she'll stay there after you and I go back to school, getting the place ready for summer."

"All by herself?"

"The Thibodeaus are still looking after the animals and finishing up work on the house. They'll look after her."

"What about beds and stuff?"

"The house is pretty well stocked with towels, bedding, even soap in the bathroom." He laughed. "I drove over a couple weeks ago to check on things and I was amazed at how much they've done. You won't believe it."

"Yes I will. They're good guys."

Simon turned and looked out the window. Houses with Christmas decorations, telephone poles wrapped with colored lights, a few small snowmen. It reminded him of the farm and of the decorations he and his father put up to welcome Santa. *Santa!* When was the last time he believed in Santa?

"So, how were the last couple of weeks?" Tom asked. "Pretty crazy with vacation around the bend?"

"No, not really. We did a lot of skiing. I'm getting pretty good at it." Simon sat back and told about his new skill and a couple of others, his new friends and the things they did together, his conversations with Luke and Bucephalus, Rodney's teaching him how to play gin rummy and other news of the weeks past. He asked Tom how things were going at his school and listened as his friend told him stories about his college friends and his teachers.

The comforting sounds of quiet highway travel reminded him of his time with Ben, sitting there so comfortably beside him as the highway unrolled beneath them. He hadn't thought about Ben for quite a while. Uncle Ben, who had brought him into this new world. Suddenly he was standing there beside him at the bog, the sun just coming up, the branches reaching toward it. And then his voice. His smile. Standing by the road at Hauler's, telling him of the fire, Ben holding him close. He turned from the window.

"I haven't seen Ben for so long," he said.

"He's going to be with us!" Tom said.

"What?"

"For a couple nights. He'll drive up on his way to the island on Tuesday instead of Thursday."

"That is so great! I haven't seen Ben for a long time. Not since he and Jenna brought me back to the farm. That's one of the best Christmas presents I could ask for." He paused, smiled and continued. "Almost as good as you and Jenna."

"I thought it might be. He's been asking about you. He can't wait to see you."

"What about Roger?" Simon asked in a less energetic voice.

"Like we told you, Roger is looking forward to having more time with you. He's very proud of what you've accomplished at school." Tom turned to read Simon's face, but he was looking out his window. "Really. I'm not just saying that to make things easier. Trust me. OK?"

"I guess so."

"He might be there when we arrive if he got an early start. If not he'll surely be there by dinner time." Tom slowed the car and drove into a gas station. He stopped by the pump and turned off the engine. "I'll fill the tank and make a quick trip to the men's room. You OK?"

"I peed before we left."

"OK, sit tight. I'll be right back." He closed the door and Simon yawned, stretched out in his seat, closed his eyes and thought about the farm. In a few moments he was asleep.

There was much more snow at the farm than there had been at Wind Lake. Ronnie had plowed the driveway and the mounds to the side were even larger than he remembered them. As Tom drove slowly in, the barn emerged to the right, itself deeply decorated in white. Simon leaned ahead and there it was; just as he remembered it from the summer, but now painted a warm and welcoming yellow.

Tom stopped the car. Simon opened his door, jumped out, and ran up to the front door of the house. Opening it, he stopped, an unexpected confusion of feelings catching him by surprise. He took a breath. The front hall was not all that different from the one he had known. About the same shape and size. A closet, a small table, a carpet along its length. He walked slowly into the living room where things were much different, and relaxed. For a moment he had been back there. Just a moment.

He walked on into the kitchen. Jenna stood at the sink. He guessed from the movement of her arms that she was peeling potatoes. Just as his father had. *Enough of that.* "Jenna!"

She turned with a half-peeled potato in one hand and the peeler in the other, tossed them in the sink, and held out her arms. *Yes, this was now.*

"Home for the holidays," Tom said in a quietly celebratory voice.

Simon turned. "And am I ever glad to be here. What can I do to help?"

"Well," Tom said. "I'm sure we can put you to work but first let me show you your new bedroom."

Simon followed him down the hall to a sunny room overlooking the pasture. A twin bed sat against one wall, a dresser across from it and that was it. Simon put his small suitcase on the quilted cover and walked to the window. White as far as he could see. Like the room, waiting for things to come.

"I told Roger that I was going to move the things in your baleout over here and he told me not to."

"He did?"

"Yes, he said that was your private space and no one should mess with it."

"He said that?"

"Yup. So I'm sorry they aren't here in your new digs."

"No, that's OK. They belong over there. I mean that's where they've always lived." He had to look away for a moment to get his thoughts together. Roger had done right. He could have just gone along. But he didn't.

"Oh," Tom continued. "By the way there's something else that you need to see."

"What's that?"

"I want to surprise you. Ready?"

"Sure." They walked out to the kitchen where Jenna was putting the newly peeled potatoes in a plastic bag. "We're heading down to the new construction," Tom said. "Want to join us?"

"Of course," she said with a smile that Simon remembered from back at Rosie's. It was the smile that promised a new discovery. They grabbed their coats from the hall rack and stepped outside. It was colder than Simon had noticed on his way in. He took the gloves out of his pocket. They headed towards the barn and then passed it heading down towards the milking shed.

It looked neater than Simon remembered it. Maybe it was just the snow. Mark opened the door and Simon had to catch his breath. The interior was entirely new. Well almost entirely. What had been a single space was now divided into three separate rooms. The first where the stalls had been, then up the five steps to a landing and off the landing three doors. Tom opened the first into a small bedroom with two comfy cot-like beds and a dresser.

"What's this for?" Simon asked. Then he noticed on the wall a picture of Lance Cottage. "What the heck…"

"Roger knows how much you look forward to having your friends from school here next summer. Greta and…what's the boy's name?"

"There's Rodney and Stefan and Rainer and quite a few others others."

"Well, whoever you choose. There are three rooms, each with a couple beds like these, and that third door is the bathroom. It even has a shower."

"Roger did all of this?"

"He did." Tom started to say more and decided to let the room do the talking. He was right. Simon stood for a moment trying to soak it all in. There were no words that seemed to want speaking. Telling Tom that his baleout was a private place, and now this. And Tom and his new home and Jenna invited to stay there. This wasn't the Roger he had known. Not even that summer at the farm when he had been a little better. This was over the top. Then he remembered what Tom—or was it Jenna?—had said about Roger wanting to be a better friend. There were so many surprises. How had he managed all those years being alone? *No, don't think about that. It's over.* He looked at the cots and imagined Stefan sitting there.

"So what do you think of it?" Jenna asked.

"It's fantastic," Simon said. "And Roger did this. At your suggestion, right?"

"No," they said in chorus.

"It was all his idea," Tom assured.

On their way back Simon said he wanted to have a look at his baleout and walked over to the barn. He climbed the ladder to the loft and around the bales of hay where his many treasures sat, undisturbed. A number of feelings ran through him, which he tried, as had become his habit over the past months, to sort through and weigh. Major among these as he stood there was a sense of distance. Not simply the distance between the farm and Wind Lake, but between this quiet inner space and the world he now lived in and loved in a way he had never known possible.

His immediate thought as he looked over his treasures was that they needed a new home, a place where he could share them with others. And that home had just been built. By Roger. For him and his friends. And all of these old treasures from the past. He smiled at the thought. *The past! Right. Less than a year ago.*

Then a voice caught him by surprise, "Simon? You up there?" It was a very familiar voice, in one sense. In another it was new.

"Hi, Roger. You made it! Good! I'm on my way."

Chapter 52

Mark

It was on Saturday the 24th of February when Mark announced, at breakfast, his plan to welcome the visitors from the press. It was, he explained, a way of letting the world know how much they all cared about making the world a safer place for all living things.

"Most of you don't know this, because your friend Simon is a modest young man, but he appeared last year on a television show talking about his concerns for the environment—concerns that we all share."

Instead of the dismissive mumblings that might have disquieted the room months earlier, there were nods and smiles of approval.

"Simon tells me how much he has learned being among us these past months and how much he appreciates his good fortune of being among such a fine group of friends."

There were now some chuckles and moving of chairs. Mark was known for his approving speeches and often spoke of student achievements. The students heard them with a mixture of gratitude and dismissiveness. They were often a bit over the top. He explained that the plan was to have the visitors the week after spring vacation. A hand went up.

"Yes, Lonnie?"

"Isn't March a bad time to do that? I mean there's still snow."

"That's a very good question, Lonnie, and I'm glad you asked. There are a couple of answers." Several other hands went up. "Yes, Verra?"

"The snow is beautiful and we still ride the trails. And the animals are all here."

Now it wasn't hands, just voices, and Mark let that pass.

"Simon knows where the animals are in the woods. He can show them the owls and turkeys."

"And cottontails."

"And bobcats." There were growls and a few screeches.

"And river otters."

"And the red foxes!"

"And maple-sugaring," a girl yelled, holding up her table's syrup canister.

Mark held up his hand and smiled. "Yes, indeed. That will be a high point. And the foxes and wild turkeys. There was a gobbling sound followed by others.

"There's plenty of life here at Wind Lake year round."

"And lots of vegetables in the cold cellar!" another boy called from the back of the dining room, pumping his arm to mark his role in the harvest.

Mark quieted them again. "I'm sure Simon will be glad to have any suggestions you might make about his showing the visitors around. We originally planned to do it during vacation but Simon has asked us to change that. Simon said he didn't want to do this unless you were all here at school. He wants you to be a part of it. And he's right!"

There was a chorus of cheers and table chatter grew. Mark held up his hand a last time.

"So, we have three weeks until the visitors arrive. I'm sure Simon will be eager to hear your suggestions. Is that right, Simon?"

Simon nodded, looked around and smiled. He hadn't expected any of this.

Tables were cleared and students made their way to their classes with new and outspoken approval of the Stardust Kid. There may have been a few salutes from some of the older kids but nothing that gave support to the concern Simon had carried to breakfast. Mark giving him credit for including the others had a very good impact. Simon respected him for having the idea and appreciated its effect.

As they headed off to classes he was thanked in a chorus of new voices by his fellow students. His summer visitors had shown approval with broad quiet smiles collected around a fire. His schoolmates expressed it with energetic offers of places he should see, things he should say, and offers of accompaniment in his explorations.

The next week was good. Eager to be a part of the big event, several of his schoolmates showed him places he hadn't seen and worked at making them accessible and attractive to the visitors. Four of the older students introduced him to farm animals they had befriended over their years at Wind Lake. One was an elderly ewe with generations of offspring who enjoyed milkweed. Bertha, a seventh-grader, gave Simon a bag of milkweed pods she had gathered in the fall and kept refrigerated for him to use when the cameras arrived, in case her friend the ewe became bashful. Leon, an eighth-grader, cared for the geese and had befriended the leader of the flock who followed him out to the pond during the fall to graze on aquatic plants. He introduced him to Simon with whom he quickly made friends, Simon breaking the pond ice for him to expose the tasty milfoil.

Friendship with Bertha and Leon was just the beginning of what turned out, over the next two weeks, to be a whole new life at Windlake. It had started months before with his house-mates and those he rode trail with, but now there were many others. And it wasn't simply that they hoped to be on camera. It had become much more. Simon had become a listener and a learner. Not only about geese and milkweed pods but about being with age-mates as well as elders. Empathy wasn't new to him, but feeling it for those who had been around no longer than he, was. Oh, his father had allowed him to be a boy, to be silly, even mischievous once in a while. But it was never very rewarding. Not in the way it was now with age-mates. Now it was give and take, laugh and be laughed at, speak and be spoken to in a new, sometimes mischievous and private language. For the first time in his life he wasn't alone in his feelings, frights, and fancies. He would lie awake at night hearing his friends' voices, seeing their faces, thinking of things he might say and do.

He explored with them on foot and on the trails. And he explored alone early in the morning astride Bucephalus. Though, at Mark's invitation they now had more time alone, it was not time that Bucephalus appeared to enjoy as he once had at the farm. His impatience had become a little hard to deal with. He had explained to his friend weeks before his plan to ask Mark tit for tat, this for that, his home for his hosting. But now he had second, third, and even fourth thoughts about that.

Simon no longer felt an outsider. His father, Roger, Ben, Tom and Jenna, were all he had known. They were all he had wanted to know, in the real world. There were his books. Huck and Tom and lots of others. But they were made up by grown-ups. Greta, Rodney, Rainer and the others were real, with feelings and thoughts so amazing like his own.

There was nothing new in Bucephalus' skill at mind-reading. He hadn't said a word about his thoughts of staying here at Wind Lake, but Bucephalus appeared to have read his mind. Having the time alone with him on the trails he hoped might put his friend more at ease.

The trails weren't all that different from those at the farm. They could explore and talk just as they had all those years. *How many years?* He had to count. He had started to ride when he was five. Not in the woods. Just around the farm with his father alongside. Then, when was it? Six? Six or seven he stared to ride alone. Close by. Then farther and farther and farther, always feeling safe because Bucephalus was with him.

Simon had more time with Bucephalus but his companion's energy and sociability diminished as they made their way back to the school after an afternoon's explorations. It was clear Bucephalus wanted to be back at the farm. When they were together at the stable and no one was around he would reassure his friend that they would soon be returning there, that Mark couldn't refuse after he'd done his part. Still, Bucephalus would turn his head and walk away, letting Simon know that he was upset. Simon hoped that in the next few days things would change back to the way they'd been in the old days.

One week remained until the visitors would arrive. On Tuesday, before the others were up, Simon decided to take Bucephalus for a longer ride on a trail they had never ridden. It ran north from the school, first along the highway, gradually disappearing into the deep woods. He saddled his friend and led him out to the sunny and quiet afternoon. Once he was in his place he loosed the reins and they started down the road toward the woods. Simon spoke as he always had and Bucephalus listened. Or so it seemed, for he had a way of responding with a nicker or a neigh occasionally. Not often, but at surprising moments. Mostly he spoke through his movement, quickening, slowing, moving his head, seeing things that Simon hadn't seen, stopping to show him.

Simon hadn't been able to talk to Bucephalus while riding with others. He had kept his thoughts to himself. He owed his good friend something. Back at the farm he had often let Bucephalus do the exploring. He was never disappointed. It was almost as if his friend was interested in showing him new things. So why not now? Bucephalus would stop now and then, looking from side to side in search of something that might interest his rider.

But not today. Bucephalus' attention was directed entirely at the trail ahead. For a while Simon could understand that. Unlike the trails at school, it was cluttered with fallen branches and required careful attention. There had been other explorations back at the farm on abandoned trails, but this time was different. It wasn't just one step at a time. It was a more dedicated commitment indicated by a pulling away of the reins and a nodding of his head, as if he were saying, "Yes, yes, yes. This is the trail we have been looking for."

They rode for a good half hour before Simon decided to explore on foot. He pulled on the reins. Bucephalus slowed, whinnied and moved on. He pulled again, harder this time. Bucephalus whinnied his discontent. Simon pulled harder. Bucephalus stopped. He dismounted and walked to face his friend. "It's OK," he said. "We're just stopping for a bit so I can look around. OK?" Bucephalus didn't respond. Not so much as a nod or a sniff. He looked ahead.

A fox ran by. Then another. The second one stopped, turned and looked at him. He knelt down. The fox took a few steps towards him, then turned and followed his companions. Simon walked on a little further to a trickle of water, apparently from a spring. It ran over some stones and into the ground. He knelt and collected some of the water in his hands and drank it. It could be the purest water he had ever swallowed. New from beneath where he knelt, like a welcome. The thought led to others. Being welcomed. Invited in by others.

He thought of Greta and the boys in the house. The thought of all the friends he had made over the past weeks. Here he was once again in the woods with Bucephalus as he had dreamed he might be on so many nights over those first months. But now it was different. Their exploration hadn't reminded him of times past. It brightened his thoughts of times to come. With his friends. And not just their explorations and showing the visitors around. Well beyond that. Most surprising of all was an out-of-nowhere reluctance to leave for spring vacation. The thought of asking Mark for a payback of departure no longer put him to sleep nights. No, now it was the thought of his friends coming up to the farm in the summer to stay in the milking shed. No, not the milking shed. He had told Roger that he wanted to name it Wind Lake Cottage, and Roger had said he'd make a sign for the entrance. He looked increasingly forward to welcoming spring here at Wind Lake with his friends. Not riding the old trails with only his thoughts, but now with others, listening, learning how to be a part of this much more interesting world.

He walked to where Bucephalus stood and remounted. "OK, boy. A little bit further. We're here today for you." He settled back in the saddle as Bucephalus continued on. The trail became more inviting. Less deadfall. More open spaces. Quiet, except for the familiar sounds of animals and birds.

His tummy mumbled agreement. They would save some breakfast for him. They. The staff. And then he would sit with his friends in class, no longer as Sam Scamper or even The Stardust Kid, but simply as Simon, a classmate, an age-mate, a friend. He smiled, remembering when he and a couple other boys in Mrs. Blummer's class had put a mouse in her desk drawer. She had let out a scream. They had laughed and confessed and been sent to Mark's office. Mischief. He had read about it, but that was all. He smiled at the memory.

He pulled on the reins. "OK, boy, time to head back." Bucephalus pulled back and took a few more steps. He stopped, apparently awaiting approval. Simon dismounted and walked around to face him. "I know," he said. "It's like the old times and we'll do it again. But not now. OK?" Bucephalus responded with another loud whinny and pushed against his hand. Simon stepped aside. Then he understood. His friend had thought they were going home.

He started back down the trail on foot and turned. "Come on, boy. We'll come back."

Bucephalus took a few steps forward and stopped, as if waiting for Simon to follow. He turned his head and whinnied. Then he looked ahead and took a few more steps.

Now Simon spoke more loudly and with a tone unfamiliar to his friend. Well, not entirely unfamiliar. There had been other moments of disagreement over the years. But this time he didn't condescend to reluctant obedience. He started off again, this time at a faster pace. "Come back!" Simon called. "Bucephalus, come back!" Bucephalus continued on. It was a dense forest. Soon he was out of sight. Simon watched with a confusion of disbelief and understanding.

Chapter 53

The Search

Simon had been doing a lot of trail-riding over the past weeks, so no one was surprised not to see him at breakfast. He was an early riser, wanting to be there when his fewer and fewer furry companions came out of their winter quarters to search for breakfast. He was very conscientious about being back for his first class. Mark had explained to him how his special privilege might work against companionship with his classmates if he wasn't sitting with them each day.

When Rhonda, Simon's English teacher, told Mark that Simon had missed class he walked over to Lance cottage to check with Sara. *No, she hadn't seen him that morning. Probably another early trail ride.* They went up to his room to check. Not there.

He walked to the stable to talk with Luke. They agreed that it would be a good idea to check out the trails if he wasn't back in the next hour. He wasn't. Luke found four staff members who didn't have classes and sent them to ride the school's four trails. They returned in less than an hour without having seen him. Now Mark was seriously worried. *Where could he have gone? He had ridden Bucephalus. There had to be a trail. But where?*

Mark arranged for Simon's companions in Lance Cottage to leave class and join him in his office.

"Sorry to take you out of class," he started. "I'm a little concerned about your friend, Simon," he said.

"He wasn't at breakfast," Rodney said.

"He's probably doing a trail ride," Greta said. "He gets up before any of the rest of us."

"He's been taking a lot of rides lately, as you know, to find interesting sites for our visitors next week," Mark said with an appreciative smile. "But he's never taken this long. And I've sent some of the staff out to check our regular trails without success. I've invited you here to ask if Simon has ever spoken to any of you of any off-trail explorations."

"You can't ride without a trail," Greta said.

"I know," Mark acknowledged with a respectful nod. "Not on a horse. That's what's perplexing. He left with Bucephalus before breakfast."

"I'll bet he went north," Stefan said with a smile.

Mark looked at him with encouragement to continue.

"He said Bucephalus likes to go north," Rodney offered. "Like when they're out on a trail and you can go one way or the other. He pulls on the reins toward the north. Like he has a built-in compass."

"Horses do have built-in compasses," Greta assured. "Not the kind you put in your pocket, I don't mean. But inside their heads. Isn't that right, Mark?"

"It is. That's why you can count on your companion to bring you home if you get lost."

"So maybe Bucephalus showed him a trail to the north, up beyond the potato fields," Stefan said.

Mark glanced quickly out the window to the north and then back. "Thank you. We'll check that out. You have been very helpful."

"Is there going to be a search team?" Rodney asked.

"I'm not sure," Mark said, trying to imagine where a northern trail might exist. "Simon is probably on his way back as we talk. I just wanted to be sure we had some plan if he isn't."

"So if there is a search can we be on it?" Rodney asked. "We're his housemates."

"We'll see about that," Mark said. His visitors looked at one another with disappointment.

"No, I take that back. If there is to be a search team I promise that you shall be on it."

"How will we know?" Greta asked.

"I promise. No search team without his family. Now, back to class. I'll be in touch."

"I hope he's all right," Greta said with an appealing look at Mark.

"I'm sure he is. Simon is as comfortable in the woods as any person I have ever known."

Luke arrived just as Simon's housemates were leaving. They exchanged a few words, Luke assuring them that Simon would be fine and that they'd be the first to know if he had fallen or gotten hurt in his explorations. Then he closed the door and put an aerial photo of the area surrounding the school on Mark's desk.

"I called the town office," he said. "There's a trail to the north of the school on what was once the Turner property, now state land. It starts about two miles north of the river. Pretty much overgrown, but probably there's still a path he could have followed."

Mark examined the map and turned to Luke. "We'd better have a look. You think it would be safe for kids?"

"With enough staff, sure. If he left the trail and got lost we'll need some searchers. Just make sure they all have their contact devices."

"How many do you think we will need?" Mark asked as they walked out into the hall.

"Let's start with eight or nine. We can take the wagon out to where the trail starts and walk from there."

"No horses?" Mark asked with some confusion.

"No. Like I said the trail is pretty well overgrown. We don't need another accident. Much better on foot. We need to be sure everyone is well-outfitted. Hiking boots, warm pants and jackets."

They walked out of the building and stopped. "You get Lance House kids out of class and outfitted," Luke instructed. "I'll find Rainer. He and

Simon are pretty close friends. And I'm sure I can find others there who'd like to join us."

"I'm sure Laurie would want to be a part of this if she's free," Mark suggested.

"Right. Good idea. She was at the stable when I left. I'll ask her. Let's meet as soon as everyone's ready, at the stable."

They separated at the bottom of the steps, each to his destination, each with his head in a place it had never been before. No student in either of their memories had ever gone missing from Wind Lake School.

Luke found Rainer and several of his housemates in the library and invited the five of them to join the search. He didn't have to say more than a few sentences and they were on their feet, their books closed, ready to go. He sent them up to their houses to get properly outfitted and walked to the stable where he found Laurie grooming her horse. He explained the plan and she looked at him with deep concern.

"It's OK, Laurie," he reassured her. "We'll find him. He couldn't have gone very far. It's an old trail. Not one for trotting as best I've been able to find out. My guess is that Bucephalus has had an injury and that Simon is hanging in there with him."

"Or the other way around," she said with a break in her voice.

"Either way, we'll find him," Luke assured her. "Are you with us?"

"Of course. I'll start getting the horses ready."

"We'll only need the cart horses. Like I said, the trail isn't horse-friendly." He started out the door and stopped, thought for a moment and turned. "On second thought, maybe you should saddle up Empress. She might see some things that we miss. She's known Bucephalus for quite a while."

"Good idea. See you in a few minutes."

It took a while for the searchers to get themselves properly outfitted but within the next half hour they had all gathered at the stable. They were proud of having been selected, a little bit nervous at the prospect of searching new territory, but ready for new adventure and inspired by the possibility of saving their friend.

Laurie had harnessed the horses to the cart and helped the searchers climb aboard. Luke took the reins with Stefan beside him. Laurie and

Empress led the way through the pasture gate, across the three acres of field to the edge of the Wind Lake Campus. Reaching the end of the school property, they stopped and everyone got down from the wagon and waited for instructions.

Mark took a few steps north through the brush and stopped. "There's no sign of hoof prints that I can see," he said. "Let's spread out and see what we can find." The students and staff made a line and began exploring about ten feet from one another. They walked for several yards without finding any indications of hoof marks in the spring-softened soil, or even tramplings of the still-brown grasses. Then Laurie, who had dismounted and joined them, spoke. "Maybe Empress and I should do a little exploring. What do you think, Mark?"

"Yes, good idea. OK, let's the rest of us go back to the wagon for a bit, until Laurie finds something."

"Maybe they went on the road," Rainer suggested, pointing to the highway, which was about a hundred yards to their left.

"Why would Simon do that?" Greta asked. "He's not a highway kid."

"I dunno. Maybe Bucephalus told him to." There was a comforting chuckle from the others.

"Good thinking, Rainer," Mark said. "That's a possibility."

"I don't think so," Stefan offered. "Bucephalus doesn't even like to walk on the school road. Isn't that right, Luke?"

Luke nodded. "Good observation." He smiled. "Even when we go trail riding he heads to the roadside."

Just then Laurie returned with a pleased look. "We've found their trail. Not sure how they got there but Bucephalus's prints are pretty clear where they crossed a creek not very far in."

"Excellent!" Mark said. "OK everybody, ready to trek?"

There was a chorus of agreement and they followed Laurie single-file through the grass to the edge of the woods.

Once there Mark gathered them together and described the plan. "Now we all know that Simon is more of a woodsman than any of us. He would have had no trouble finding his way along the trail, overgrown as it is." The students underscored his observation, pointing to fallen trees, moving around trying to find a clear view ahead. "My concern is that he may have fallen. You know, even Bucephalus would find this trail pretty difficult. Or perhaps the trail pretty much disappears some distance from here and they got lost in the woods."

"Simon? Get lost? No way," Greta said.

"Well, we have to consider every possibility, don't we?" Mark responded. There was general assent from the students. "So, what we'll do is spread out to both sides of the trail as far as we can, always keeping the person nearest to you in sight. Be careful. We'll go slowly so that no one falls behind. Ready?"

After a chorus of reassurances Mark walked one group to the right of the trail, each within sight of another and Luke spaced the other half of the group to the left.

They walked for some time without any sign of him. Laurie assured them, however, that they were on the right trail, that Bucephalus's hoof prints were still there and that they mustn't give up. After half an hour of tough walking, Mark told them to gather back at the trail and take a break. He had brought some cookies and lemonades from the kitchen and passed them around.

Then Greta and Clara started to sing:

> *Wind Lake, Wind Lake, that's my home*
> *Away from home where I can roam,*
> *Learning lots of whys and hows,*
> *Growing gardens, milking cows.*
> *Learning new tricks and feeding the chicks,*
> *We learn all day and harvest the hay,*
> *Take our courses and feed the horses,*
> *We weed and we sow.*
>
> *And grow and grow.*
> *Cleaning the stables*
> *And setting the tables*
> *Wind Lake, Wind Lake, that's my home*
> *Away from home where I can roam.*

The other kids and Laurie joined in for a second round and then, with an energy that surprised them, Mark and Luke as well.

It wasn't the official school song. It had been written a couple years before by one of the students who played the piano.

After finishing his lemonade, Rodney started them on another favorite school song.

> There's a hole in the bottom of the sea
> There's a hole in the bottom of the sea
> There's a hole, there's a hole
> There's a hole in the bottom of the sea
> There's a log in the hole in the bottom of the sea
> There's a log in the hole in the bottom of the sea
> There's a hole, there's a hole
> There's a hole in the bottom of the sea
> There's a bump on the log in the hole in the bottom of the sea
> There's a bump on the log in the hole in the bottom of the sea
> There's a hole, there's a hole
> There's a hole in the bottom of the sea

Suddenly Rainer, who wasn't a singer and had walked a few yards ahead on the trail, turned and held up his hands.

> There's a frog on the bump on the log
> In the hole in the bottom of the sea
> There's ….a …..frog ….on ….the …….. bump…

There was another voice that they could barely hear, off in the distance. It grew louder.

> In the hole in the bottom of the sea
> There's a hole, there's a hole
> There's a hole in the bottom of the sea.

And there he was, a little unsteady from his long trek back along the trail, but with a smile that told them what they wanted to know. They ran to meet him. Hugs and high fives ensued.

"What happened?" Greta asked, as things quieted.

"Bucephalus didn't want to go back to school," Simon responded. His voice broke at the end. He looked down and wiped at his tears.

Greta ran up and gave him a hug.

"I'll bet Empress can get him to change his mind," Laurie said, remounting. "Let's go girl." Empress turned and they started back up the trail.

"Why would he do that?" Stefan asked.

"He's angry at me," Simon said.

"Why would your good friend be angry at you?" Mark asked.

"Because I told him I wanted to be here. At Wind Lake. With you guys." Mark walked over to him and they exchanged looks that didn't need words. Then Simon turned to the others. "Thanks for coming out to find me."

"You found us," Greta said.

Simon laughed. "You're right. And boy am I lucky."

They all turned and started back toward the truck. When they'd loaded their stuff and taken their places, Simon looked back toward the trail.

Mark thought for a moment and then, afraid for the worst and wanting to get Simon back to a place where he could help him deal with his loss, said "OK, let's head back. Laurie will be a while and Simon hasn't had any lunch or breakfast."

Luke got behind the wheel, started the engine, turned slowly into the rutted road and headed back.

It wasn't until they had arrived back at the school and were unloading the truck that they heard the sound of horses approaching at a slow canter. Simon ran to meet them. Bucephalus, with a nervous whinny and a nose-to-nose greeting said that he was sorry and glad to be back.

Chapter

54

The
Stardust
Kid

It was the third week in March, a Wednesday, and everyone was looking forward to the big event in only three days. The residents of Wind Lake school had grown even closer than in the months past. It was, after all, a community where young and old shared ideas, chores, produce from their shared labors, and even their homes. But the anticipation of sharing all of that with the world outside had brought them all even closer. What would ordinarily have been differences left on their own had become opportunities for coming together. Some of the faculty had had reservations about putting what had so long been quiet and largely peaceful before the rolling cameras of the media, but seeing the project engage the imaginations of the young, they had, in many cases, relaxed those concerns. Oh, there were a few sceptics and critics, but they kept all but their occasional frowns pretty much to themselves.

It had snowed for the last two days without much promise of letting up and the trails were becoming something of a challenge. Not that there was all that much trail-riding in the winter anyway. Mark had built a simple kind of plow that could be drawn by a team of horses so that at least one trail could be cleared after the snow fell. But this snowfall may be a little more than the plow or the horses could cope with. Still, there were two days left until the visitors came, and if the skies cleared the snow might settle just enough.

Simon and his friends weren't taking any chances, however. They had shoveled the Tagalong Trail that had led to their best discoveries over the past weeks. Not only a fox hollow and a beaver dam, but a copse of rich evergreens upon which the deer banqueted. A bald eagle, nesting along the trail, had fished the pond well into the late fall after which Rainer had provided, nearer the nest, fish and meat waste from the kitchen.

A boy named Ryan who lived up the hill at Wentworth House had befriended an opossum that lived in the woods out behind his house. Reading up on the furry creatures, he learned that they are fond of nuts and berries. Those were easily come by during the summer months and Ryan collected boxes of them. Opossums don't hibernate in the winter. Neither do they store up food. They stay pretty much in their dens but they do have to get out and search for food now and then, and Ryan could be counted on. Originally all this had happened behind Wentworth House, but as plans for the visitors got under way the nuts and berries found their way down to the Tagalong Trail.

Three television stations and three networks had responded affirmatively to Mark's invitation sent the month before. One of the networks was the BBC, urged on by Professor Benson. One of the stations was WHGB in Boston, the home of the Bill Miller Show. Everyone had agreed that Bill Miller should be the organizer and greeter of the event. Simon was particularly excited by the thought of seeing Bill again. Simon, who was no longer shy about being the Stardust Kid, had allowed downloads from YouTube of his time on stage with Bill. Quite a few students looked forward to appearing in Simon's company. In fact, that had been a little bit of a challenge as plans for the event moved ahead. Mark decided that he would ask the visitors to get as many students as would like to be on camera in their shots. In one of several conversations on the phone with Bill Miller, they worked up a few ways of doing that.

It was now Thursday, and as they all sat at breakfast the snow continued to fall. The forecast was for a major storm. That afternoon Mark had calls from two of the television stations saying that because of the bad weather they would not be sending crews for the filming. Friday morning he had a call from one of the networks also canceling their visit. Things didn't look good. After all Simon and his friends had done to prepare. It would be a big mood changer at Wind Lake. He called the BBC and discovered that the crew had arrived in New York and were on their way north. Then he called Bill Miller. He'd be there if he had to ski in, he'd said. Mark thanked him and relaxed.

Tom and Jenna arrived Friday afternoon about two o'clock, and Roger shortly after. Simon had prepared himself, given the snowstorm and Roger's explaining that not all the camera crews were coming, for disappointment. He was more than happy to see them, imagining what they had to drive through. "I've driven through worse," Roger said with a grin that Simon read quickly. Yes, Roger had come to the farm often in the winter months when the snow was pretty deep. Not like this, but close. Jenna explained that the storm was pretty much limited to the western part of Massachusetts, and being that their route was on major highways, it hadn't been all that bad.

"So what was the problem for the TV crews?" Simon asked.

"Probably getting around with their cameras once they were here," Tom suggested.

"Right." Simon looked at Roger in a way that he hoped would say how glad he was to see him. It worked. For the first time ever Roger opened his arms and Simon walked into them. Not a big hug, but enough to close the small remaining space between them.

The BBC crew arrived at about five, and much to his surprise, Professor Benson along with them. Simon showed them around the school and then they joined all the others for the evening meal, Benson and the two cameramen at a table with Mark, Tom, Jenna; Luke at another table with three students; Simon and the five friends who were actually going to walk the trail with him at another. They asked him to tell them more about Bill Miller. He did. About their conversation, the lobster dinner, and walking out onto the stage. There was a good deal of laughter and even more a sense of camaraderie.

It was early to bed and slowly to sleep for those most involved in the next day's events.

The sun rose bright, to everyone's great relief. Roger took an early morning walk with Bill Miller, telling him about his own time as a student at Wind Lake. Bill wanted to know more about Simon's father and his youth. The drive had been plowed the day before and it was warm enough, with thick coats and hats, to walk all the way out to the road. Bill asked if he could speak of Simon's father and his time at the school.

"You should ask Simon," Roger responded. "He has said little of his father these past months and we have followed his example."

"I won't," Bill said. "Leave the past alone. This get-together is all about the future."

"Are you going to introduce him as The Stardust Kid?" Roger asked.

"No," Bill replied with a slight chuckle. "I've never thought the tag was as good as his own name. Simon Seeker? What more could anyone ask for? Seek and ye shall find!" He laughed at his own cliche. "Sorry. But you know what I'm saying."

"I think I do. It's amazing when you thing about it that Reese should have had the name Larkin to play with. He was very pleased with the result. Very pleased." Roger stopped.

Bill took another step, stopped and turned. "He had the right name and the right friend. I wonder where either of them would be today if you hadn't been there all along."

"You're very generous, Bill. I did my best. It wasn't always in a way that pleased Simon, but I tried."

"I'm surprised to hear you say that. Looking at the two of you together last night I would have guessed you were very close."

Roger smiled, realizing that it might be true. Over time. In the weeks, months and years ahead. He looked at his watch. "We'd better head back."

The school gathered outside the dining hall after breakfast. Energy was predictably high as the cameramen set up their equipment. Then, as Bill Miller took the microphone in his hand, everyone quieted. The cameras rolled. Bill held out his arm and Simon walked up beside him, looking first up at his face and then with a serious smile at the cameras. "Ladies and gentlemen! I'd once more like to introduce to you...Simon Seeker."

CPSIA information can be obtained
at www.ICGtesting.com
Printed in the USA
BVHW070814200519
548790BV00010B/276/P